# IN THE CLEAR

CODEX #3

## KATHRYN NOLAN

That's What She Said Publishing, Inc.

His depiction was eerily precise. I wasn't sure if that was a good thing. On the whole, wide swaths of free time didn't excite me, and my hobbies were few and far between. I liked a long, hard run. A captivating book. A good glass of whiskey. A little history and culture sprinkled in. But these were activities for when work was done.

And work was never done.

To Henry, I said, "Sight-see. Visit historical monuments and museums. Eat at expensive restaurants. Perhaps see the opera."

Henry and Delilah watched me, waiting.

"And I wait for emails on my phone, not my laptop," I admitted. "I'm not an amateur."

"No, sir, you are not," Delilah agreed. "Which luxurious hotel are you staying in?"

I nodded at our former librarian and fellow history buff. "The Langham."

Henry brightened. "Perfect pick. You'll be close to all the best things to do as a tourist. You can even get some Sherlock Holmes sight-seeing in."

I kept my face impassive. "Is that so?"

"Absolutely," he continued. "And I can give you a list of the best bookstores in the city. Bring Freya back another stack of paperbacks."

"Please and thank you." Freya grinned. "And I should mention that these Hawaiian shirts I bought for you are *real* lady slayers."

"Am I to be *slaying* women on this trip?"

She spread her arms wide. "What else—or *who else*—are you going to do on vacation?"

I hid a smile while straightening my tie. Freya was going to start sounding like my mother soon. Or even worse, like

Jeanette, my stepmom. Combined, the two maternal figures in my life were like hawks when it came to my dating life, and my lack of romantic entanglements their prey. My last *serious* relationship had been more than five years ago—a woman named Caroline who I'd dated for a year. My *obsession with work* (her words) and *inability to have fun* (also her words) were the death-knell for that relationship.

It hadn't been the first time I'd been accused by girlfriends and lovers of exhibiting a serious dearth of frivolity. And yet, like hobbies and free time, spontaneous fun was never a natural fit for me either. A string of one-night stands had been my only experience with love these past five years —and ever since founding Codex I'd had only one driving motivation in my life.

Well, that wasn't entirely true. Capturing Bernard Allerton no longer felt like a driving motivation but rather something more vengeful.

Maybe I did have a problem with obsession.

"A reminder that while my employees are off dating each other like contestants on a reality show, my *personal* life shall remain personal," I finally said.

"Dry spell, huh?" Freya shot back. She held out her palm for Delilah to high-five it.

"The level of professionalism in this office is disintegrating at a shocking rate." I made a show of pulling up my emails to conceal my amusement. The sudden sight of my messages, and the secret I was keeping from my team, sparked a tendril of guilt in my chest. All of this was compounded by the guilt I felt at leaving them with cases and deadlines while I'd be off—presumably—gallivanting through one of the world's most beautiful cities.

"Uh no," Freya said, snapping her fingers. "Is that your

inbox? It's 5:01 p.m. Which means you're officially on vacation."

"My red-eye's not for five hours," I said, sounding peevish. "What update do you have for me on the contract from the Allegheny Museum?"

"I will be *sharing* all updates in our staff meeting with our working employees," Freya said.

Sam Byrne walked into the office carrying a plastic bag. "Leave him alone, Frey. He's a workaholic in recovery, like me."

"*In recovery* seems a bit bold for a simple, ten-day vacation to London," I said. "Where I'll have full access to my—"

"*Email and phone the entire time,*" Delilah and Freya droned in unison. "Yeah yeah, we get it," Delilah said. "We shall be expressly disobeying those orders for the duration of the ten days."

Sam gave me a sympathetic smile. "It'll be okay, Abe. The first few days will be a struggle, but once your brain lets go of the stress, you'll be able to enjoy it, I promise."

Sam and Freya had just returned from a four-day vacation to Prince Edward Island. Which was one of the reasons why I'd decided to plan this trip. It was true that my last vacation had been taking my mother to Sedona when I was twenty years old.

It was *absolutely* true that I'd been working long hours, catching up on cases and paperwork after Sam and Freya had infiltrated a secret society of book thieves two months ago. The publicity had led more libraries our way, which we were thrilled about. Still I was tired. Tired in a way that I hadn't been for a while, exhaustion snapping at my heels, leaving me feeling unhinged.

Of course, deep down I knew where this *unhinged* feeling sprouted from.

I felt another twinge in my chest and ignored it. I *had* always wanted to spend real time in London—not for the occasional business trip but for leisure. Pleasure. Culture, literature, history, good whiskey, art—London was filled with the things I wanted to enjoy whenever I had free time. It was the right pick for my "rejuvenation."

It just wasn't the entire story.

With a respectful nod to me, Sam sank into the chair next to Freya, his undercover partner. And girlfriend.

When he didn't think I was looking, Sam tugged on the end of her braid. She literally beamed at him. The team had recently deemed me as "going soft" because I'd allowed the four of them to pair off, romantically. Soft had nothing to do with it—I was merely a professional who recognized the loss of skills and expertise my firm would incur if these four brilliant, skilled, and talented detectives left. I didn't relish the idea of starting over when I'd worked so damn hard to build this company from the beginning.

"He's snappy because he's going to miss us," Freya said.

"I wouldn't dare," I promised. "You have my word."

Sam smirked and opened his bag. "I'd like you to know that this was not my idea." Out of the bag he pulled glow sticks and body glitter.

"For raves," Freya said. "London has the best raves."

Henry was trying not to laugh, and Delilah was snorting. Sam's shit-eating grin mirrored Freya's.

"The things I love the most in this world," I said, carefully picking up the body glitter, "are being pressed against strangers in the dark while dance music annihilates my ear drums and everyone is using illegal substances."

"This is your going-away vacation package from your highly competent team of detectives," Freya said. "Enjoy. I know you think of yourself as the Codex *Dad* or whatever—"

"I'm *nine years older than you*, for fuck's sake."

"—but bosses need breaks." Her face, and tone, turned serious. "Especially good bosses, like you. Which, all joking aside, is why I'm so fucking happy you're doing this."

I sighed, shifting in my chair. Her sincerity was kind but unnecessary.

"Burnout is real," Sam added. "You know how affected I was by it two months ago. I think—" He looked around at the team, who were all watching me with very real expressions of tenderness. "I think we were all relieved when you told us you'd booked this trip."

Sam had also been my student at Quantico, and we'd worked together in the FBI's Art Theft unit before I left. His father was the Deputy Director of the FBI, and Sam had been raised in his father's stern image.

After a work scandal, Sam had consulted for Codex on The Empty House case—and had ended up resigning from the FBI and becoming a private detective in the process.

Freya had a lot to do with that life-changing decision. Secretly, I'd been pleased. Freya and Sam had a notorious rivalry as trainees, though beneath their sniping I'd sensed a working partnership that was special. Deep down, I'd also suspected they were in love. I'd certainly never shared that suspicion.

*Soft.*

"You know we care about you Abe," Delilah said. "We care a lot, actually."

Their earnestness and carefree kindness towards me was too much to handle—a beautifully wrapped gift I both didn't deserve and was terrified to open.

"Yes well..." I cleared my throat. "This is good then. I will pack these shirts and *Wed to the Pirate Captain*."

Freya and Delilah did a little cheer.

"Now shoo," I said, waving my hand. "Go work on something that will make us a lot of money." I stared at my laptop as they begrudgingly headed out into our large workspace. The Codex offices were located in an historic Philadelphia carriage house. The first floor was a used bookstore, and we occupied the second.

Sam hung back with a file folder in his hand.

"Updates?" I asked.

"Yes, sir, per your request," he said. His natural tendency toward deference revealed the FBI protocol still ingrained in him. I understood it—even three years after leaving the Bureau, it was hard for me to shake over a decade of hierarchy and power struggles.

"I spoke to my Bureau contact yesterday," Sam said, "and he informed me that resources for continuing to search for Bernard are disappearing, at least in the US. Enthusiasm is flagging."

"Sounds familiar," I said.

He gave a shrug. "Interpol agents have been tracking Bernard's credit card being used in Prague and Germany, so they've sent a team there to do surveillance. The teams in London and Oxford have come up empty-handed. They've started to pull in his colleagues for questioning, but they won't be able to maintain secrecy much longer."

Bernard Allerton had been on the run—and evading the authorities—for eleven months now. Which seemed insignificant to me. I'd suspected the famous, and beloved, librarian was not who he seemed for ten *years*. Thus far the strategy, from what we could piece together, was for the Bureau and Interpol to keep his name from the papers, an attempt to lull him into a false sense of security that would lead to him eventually coming out of hiding. And into a waiting pair of handcuffs. To the rest of the world, Bernard Allerton was simply on a mysterious vacation. A lie that seemed to be holding, for now.

During my long career working in white-collar crime, the most obvious truth I'd learned was that respect and wealth could conceal a bevy of wrongdoing. The wealthy could survive the scrutiny of the law using money as a shield and trust as social currency.

Bernard had all of that in spades: money, respect, trust, and intelligence.

Internally, the man was *the* prime suspect for orchestrating a ring of rare book thefts that had carried on for more than two decades. Bernard had been the head of the McMaster's Library in Oxford, England, and had accumulated a lifetime of academic notoriety and international prestige. He was brilliant, charming, and well-respected by librarians, booksellers, and antiques collectors alike.

All of this had provided the shield he needed to steal some of the rarest manuscripts in the entire world and sell them to private owners for millions and millions of dollars. The net that international authorities had tossed to catch Bernard was fraying to pieces; instead of cinching tighter, it continued to allow the man to slip away.

At Codex, our two largest cases—the infiltration of The Empty House secret society, and the recovery of a rare manuscript by the astronomer Copernicus—had put Bernard Allerton directly in our sights. That, and Henry had been Bernard's assistant for ten years before coming to work at Codex. Henry's suspicions, and months of detailed evidence, had precipitated the man going underground.

*So close, so far.* As Sam handed me the file, those twinges of guilt were replaced with a surge of boiling frustration. It was my usual daily amount, and one of the main reasons why a vacation probably *was* a good idea. With each case we closed, with each book we recovered, with each pawn we toppled in Bernard's pyramid of thieves, I felt us inching closer and closer to his whereabouts.

*So close, so far.*

"What does your contact think of those credit card charges?" I asked, idly flipping through the pages. When I was at the Bureau, I'd been reprimanded several times for obsessing over Bernard. The agency was happy to keep him on a short-list of suspicious people; they were not happy that I used an abundance of work hours diving into research holes and coming up with nothing. Until I pulled Sam to work alongside me for my last year at the Bureau. His enthusiasm for catching Bernard was the only sliver of hope I'd had during my final year.

"For what it's worth, he believes they're a trail of clues worth looking into. Even if they're red herrings, I think their hope is to find out who orchestrated the card usage and press them for info," he replied.

I thumbed through pages of blurred security footage and visual surveillance. Bernard was a master of disguise; he blended in with ease.

"Before this, our last real report of a Bernard sighting was in London," Sam said.

His body language was loose, but his face was grave. Discerning.

"I remember," I said slowly.

He retrieved the folder from my outstretched hand. "Good," he said. "Just want to make sure you're going on vacation, sir." A pause. "Not a cowboy mission."

"I'm no cowboy." I stared intently at Sam despite my eyes

wanting to flick to my email. It was a classic tell, and I wasn't keen to get caught in a lie.

"If one *were* embarking on a one-man mission to capture a known criminal, one *might* want to ask for help," he said quietly.

My heart skipped in my chest. I exhaled, slowed my body's response. Two months ago, I'd had to sit in a car and listen while Sam and Freya were caught in a dangerous hostage situation inside The Empty House auction. Freya had a knife to her throat. Sam had several guns trained on him. When Sam had shot Roy Edwards—the man with the knife—I'd known the truest moment of terror I'd ever experienced in my life. If I'd walked into that room and seen Sam or Freya hurt, or worse, I would have quite happily torn Roy limb from fucking limb. I found it interesting these four kept calling me *soft* when the protectiveness I felt towards them edged close to violence.

Admiring this team was quite different from asking for their help, however. If my father had taught me anything, it was that asking for help got you nowhere. And *needing* help was a weakness I didn't care to explore.

"It's a vacation, Sam," I said firmly. It wasn't *technically* a lie. Tonight, I would dutifully fold those Hawaiian shirts and pack books I wanted to read into a suitcase and set off for a stay in a luxurious hotel with an elegant history.

He tapped the Bernard file, and my fingers clenched into fists automatically. He tracked the movement.

I arched my eyebrow.

With a curt nod, Sam stood. "Yes, sir."

"Thank you for the information," I said.

"Thank you for taking care of yourself," he said. "You taught me the value of that, remember?"

I glanced away, evading the compliment. "Can you close the door on your way out?"

He complied, leaving me alone for the first time in hours.

I turned back to my inbox—staring at the subject line from an anonymous sender that said: *The location of Bernard Allerton.*

Not surprisingly, the location was London.

## 2

## ABE

*London, England*

*I* was taking my mother and step-mom to afternoon tea at the famous Palm Court in The Langham Hotel. Well, virtual tea. It was my first official day in London, and I was seated on an elegant, cream-colored couch sipping black tea from a fine china cup.

My phone was propped up across from me so we could video call. The two women on the screen had never been to London and both dreamed of traveling here. I worked to quiet the pesky voice that suggested a *good son* would have taken them wherever they wanted, whenever they wanted— I was that damn grateful to them.

Work, however, was always in the way.

I raised my cup in a cheer and allowed a small smile when my mothers raised their own, all the way from Miami where they lived in a beach-side condo with three rescue Pomeranians and more friends than I could keep track of.

They were both nearing seventy but had active and vibrant lives, which I was unbearably happy to see. It had been twenty-five years since my mother's car accident that left her with a traumatic brain injury, robbing her of her ability to speak and walk. Over four years, my mother worked day and night with a rehabilitative nurse to regain her strength and abilities—and though recovery was considered a life-long journey, she embraced life with the zeal of a person given a second chance.

And instead of clinging to her anger when my father betrayed us and left, she'd done the opposite. My mother had fallen in love with her rehabilitative nurse—Jeanette. About a year after ending her position as my mother's care-giver, the two began dating. They hadn't been apart a single day since.

Unfortunately, *my* anger toward my father hadn't abated. It crystallized into something hard and immobile in my chest.

"Why are you wearing a suit on your vacation?" my mother asked, peering through the screen.

I smoothed my palm down my tie. "What else does one wear? Leisure is no excuse not to look your best." Jeanette snorted and I flashed her a rare smile. "How are the dogs?"

"They miss you," my mom said. "We miss you. I'm so glad you're taking this time. I really am. But can you sneak in a weekend with us before you head back to the city?"

More guilt, more regret. I thought vacations were supposed to alleviate these feelings, not amplify them. "I can't," I said, watching their faces fall. "Next month, though? Maybe I can take a week, work from your condo if the dogs will allow it."

"Oh they will, Abraham. They *will*," my mother cheered. "We'll clean out one of the guest rooms and turn it into a makeshift office. The glass doors open onto the beach, which would make your employees *extremely* jealous."

"When I'm not inspiring fear in their hearts," I said, "I do like to inspire envy."

"*Inspire* is right," my mother countered. I attempted a scowl. "Freya tells us all the time in our group chat what a great boss you are."

"What group chat?"

"All three of us are watching *Love Island*," Jeanette said. "Which you should watch while you're there. Unwind. Relax a little. Maybe throw on a sweatshirt."

I indicated my attire. "This is my relaxing suit. A man should only wear a sweatshirt while sleeping."

"And have you been sleeping?" my mother asked. I could feel a gentle rebuke, wrapped in nurturing, all the way across the ocean.

"I am trying," I said, which was the truth.

"Please keep trying," she replied. "I hate seeing you like this."

"Like what?" I asked. I hadn't been aware I appeared differently to anyone.

I watched both women exchange a look. "Joyless and frustrated," my mother said.

A dozen standard pithy remarks rose in response. The expression of sincerity reflected on that little screen evoked a tightness in my throat. I wasn't opposed to happiness, nor was I opposed to ease. The instability and chaos that ensued after my mother's accident was only conquered with order, security, and preparation. My work—the pursuit of justice—fulfilled those needs perfectly. Joy was reckless and chasing it low on my list of priorities.

"And yet I'm drinking tea with the two people I love the most in my life," I finally said. "There's a lot of joy to that."

My thoughts pinged to Bernard and the email waiting for me. My fingers tensed on the delicate china. *Frustrated.* Maybe they had a point.

"Of course," my mother agreed. "We're only saying... it wouldn't kill you to let loose a little. Embrace the efforts of your hard work. Maybe bring home a girlfriend."

I worked to loosen my jaw. "Freya and Delilah gifted me Hawaiian shirts for this trip in the effort to *get laid*, as they would say."

The women on the screen shrugged—judgmentally.

"She said it, not us," Jeanette said.

"And I've already reached my limit in talking about this with my family members," I said. "Drink your tea. I'll order some tiny cakes so you can get the full afternoon tea experience."

They *oooohed* when cake arrived and entertained me for a full hour with stories about the dogs and their recent Bingo nights. I was jet-lagged, tired from the plane, and in a city where I knew not a single soul. But this—this virtual tea-time filled with Pomeranian anecdotes—felt like the closest thing to *relaxation* I'd come to in months.

AN HOUR LATER, I was back in my hotel room, setting up multiple screens and laptops on the small mahogany table by the plate-glass doors. Open, they led to a balcony over-looking a bustling London that was darkening beneath a slate-gray sky.

In a few hours, I was attending a lecture called *The Final Problem at Reichenbach Falls and How Sherlock Holmes Refused to Die.*

It was being conducted by Eudora Green, the president

of the Sherlock Society of Civilized Scholars. Bernard was, according to Henry, an absolute fanatic when it came to his devotion to Sherlock Holmes and his creator, Arthur Conan Doyle. Interestingly, Bernard was still listed as the vice president of the Sherlock Society on their website.

*The Problem of Reichenbach Falls...*

I founded Codex because I believed a firm of private detectives could more successfully recover stolen rare books than the Bureau. Museums and libraries hired us to work quickly and quietly—they trusted us to keep the theft out of the press, protecting their reputation and status with their donors in the process. It never boded well when a museum or library had to step forward and announce they'd *lost* a priceless artifact. And yet it was happening all across the industry. While at the FBI, I was hamstrung by red tape and frustrated with the bureaucracy. Yet my Codex agents were recovering stolen books left and right. Often working undercover, my team could manipulate known criminals and gain the trust of potential suspects. We had an impressive close rate and an impressive reputation, made more so by Sam and Freya's infiltration of The Empty House.

The man I'd always believed to be at the top of this pyramid of wide-scale book theft was Bernard.

*Didn't we once meet each other at Reichenbach Falls?*

About a year ago, Freya had started picking up the threads of code words used on the website Under the Rose. Book thieves were inserting coded language into their posts to alert others they had stolen goods for sale or were interested in buying stolen goods. The first one she'd ever uncovered was the phrase "*Didn't we once meet each other at Reichenbach Falls?*"

Every other code word we'd deciphered had roots in Sherlock Holmes.

I was currently staying in The Langham Hotel, where Arthur Conan Doyle had once famously eaten dinner with Oscar Wilde. In the ballroom off the lobby, the Sherlock Society was about to give a talk with an explicit mention of the code word.

Rubbing the back of my neck, I opened my email and clicked on the message that had been burning through my brain. I'd received it three weeks ago, had planned this trip to London a week later. I would call it a happy fluke if ever questioned about it. And deep down, I wasn't entirely sure what I expected would happen here. Only that my need to see Bernard behind bars felt like rocket fuel in my veins, propelling me forward at a rapid pace.

*The location of Bernard Allerton*, said the subject line.

The sender was anonymous, but the tone of the email smacked of an FBI agent's pragmatism. I thought the Deputy Director might be the culprit, except he was much too prideful. Possibly a former colleague from Art Theft had sent it or an old supervisor. Who would think to send it to *me?* Before he'd joined our team, Sam had been my FBI contact. We had a quid pro quo that worked well. I sent him evidence of any criminal acts we stumbled upon. He sent me tips if we were stalled on a case. That contact was gone now—and my leaving had sparked outrage and dismissal from my FBI coworkers. Not a desire to help.

The email was short and direct:

*The Bureau is sitting on detailed surveillance that indicates Bernard Allerton is residing in London. Resources are extremely limited right now. With every picture attached, agents gave chase and attempted to apprehend the man they'd spotted, only to have him elude their efforts. We got word that those Interpol agents are being pulled from the London-Oxford area and sent to Prague instead, leaving the suspect unattended. I'm sending this to you because I believe Bernard will make a move without the daily threat of being caught by the authorities.*

I recognized this feeling—decisions made that often didn't line up with what agents on-the-ground could tell you. Red tape keeping suspects from being apprehended for no damn reason. But it was true that large agencies like the FBI and Interpol were spread thin with limited resources, and so often it deeply impacted the success of these cases.

The pictures and surveillance reports attached were numerous, and I'd spent a number of nights pulling through tedious details and attempting to put together a picture of the man's whereabouts. The Langham Hotel was within a two-mile radius of the most recent sighting.

As was 221B Baker Street, the Sherlock Holmes museum.

They were blurry images, and no guarantee. Which was one of the main reasons why I hadn't told the rest of Codex, because every other clue we'd followed on Bernard's trail had ultimately led to a fucking ghost. Bernard was as brilliant as he was conniving—a dangerous combination when you had untold wealth at your fingertips.

In so many ways, Bernard had profoundly impacted the lives of my team, none more than Henry's. I knew, I *hoped*, the guilt I felt at keeping this secret would fade. Because dragging my team across an ocean on a manhunt with no contract, no money, and no reason behind it was risky, dangerous, and probably a giant waste of time.

As was disappointing them.

I caught a glimpse of my reflection in the mirror above the dresser—the lines around my eyes, the exhaustion etched around my mouth. *Obsession.* This was a giant waste of time and yet here I was.

My phone buzzed with a text from my mother—a

simple, direct message that said, *Enjoy your damn vacation, Abraham.*

I smiled, rubbed a hand down my face. Rolled out my shoulders. I would. I *really* would.

I just needed to attend a lecture on Sherlock Holmes first.

## 3

## SLOANE

*Oxford, England*

"Three weeks into your contract and you've learned what, exactly?" Louisa Davies asked, face pinched and dismissive.

I schooled my features. Crossed one leg over the other and projected as much confidence as I could. What I'd *learned* was Bernard Allerton was a cunning son-of-a-bitch who'd expertly covered his tracks for the past ten months.

What I said to my client was, "I've been undercover as a Sherlock Holmes enthusiast named Devon Atwood, attending all of the meetings and events hosted by the Sherlock Society of Civilized Scholars. Gaining their trust, attempting to find the loose link in whatever circle of people is currently guarding his exact location. It's subtle work. It takes time."

She and I both knew I didn't have much *time* left, necessarily. I forged on, ignoring my rapidly increasing pulse.

"They're a devoted group of literary scholars and academics," I said. "They're insular, community-driven, wealthy. They keep secrets. If Bernard's criminal actions, as well as his location, are known to the Sherlock Society, then it's a secret they're proud to keep to themselves. That's where my cover comes in."

Devon Atwood was a bright and cheerful Sherlock fan, desperate to know every single person in the Society—including their mysterious vice president, Bernard. What I knew—and was reluctant to tell Louisa—was that these past three weeks in London had exposed jack-shit when it came to the man I was going to be paid an extraordinary amount to hunt down.

*Supposed* to be paid. That check would never come if I didn't find him. Which was a damn shame since Louisa was offering five times my standard fee for a successful capture.

The Sherlock Society was a mixture of whimsical fan club and dedicated academic intellectuals. They wore Holmes and Watson costumes and made pilgrimages to sites mentioned in the stories. But they also gave lectures and wrote essays, spoke at symposiums and universities. It was the oldest Sherlock Holmes society in England and had the reputation, and respect, to prove it.

Louisa rubbed her forehead, looking slightly more sympathetic. She was an older white woman, with short red hair and red glasses, and highly respected at Oxford. It had been unsettling to watch her facial expressions around me transform from 'hopeful' to 'concerned'.

"I'm sorry if I'm coming off as a bit cross. I know it's subtle work. I know it's how you succeeded with the Audubon case, which is exactly why I hired you. You can imagine my frustration that eleven months after being made aware of Bernard's crimes we *still* haven't caught him."

Frustration was a feeling I knew intimately. And craving punishment was a feeling I understood even better. I'd been manipulated, used, and lied to for eighteen years by two expert con artists. The lies were like walking around every day with a bandana covering your eyes, obscuring your sight, limiting your senses on purpose.

"I understand," I said firmly. "I expect a break in the case any day now. I'm attending a lecture by Eudora Green, the president of the Society, back in London as soon as I leave your office. We're also meeting tomorrow morning. My instincts are she's close to Bernard."

I couldn't tell how assertive my tone was—Louisa's face remained pinched with worry. And I couldn't really blame her.

Three weeks ago, Louisa Davies had hired me to hunt down Bernard Allerton—a famous librarian who once oversaw the McMaster's Library and their special collection of rare books. He managed their conservation efforts, had unparalleled access to some of the rarest manuscripts in the entire fucking world. Add in his academic prestige, and Bernard's long con was one of the most epic forms of deceit I'd ever seen.

Honestly, my parents would envy it.

Louisa had been Bernard's boss, and since he'd gone missing, she had been impatiently waiting for the authorities to catch the man. When she called me, she explained that it was time the McMaster's Library took matters into their own hands. Apparently, hiring me was the first step in what she hoped would bring about justice. The minute Louisa had finished telling me the story of Bernard's high crimes and misdemeanors, the hunger was there, the urgency was there, sweeping through my veins. I'd flown to London from New York City for my first international case.

Nothing brought me greater joy in this world than to hunt down a man like Bernard—it pissed me the fuck off that he'd lied for twenty years and was currently getting away with it. Contracts like this—clients like this—were the dream for me; they were the sole reason why I started my own private detective firm five years ago.

Recently, I'd helped a library in upstate New York recover a stolen collection of illustrations from John James Audubon's famous folio, *Birds of America*. What I'd assumed would be a minor, run-of-the-mill case had brought me a bit of notoriety in the world of antiquities theft. And Louisa happened to be good friends with that library's Board President, who'd been over-the-moon with my work and happy to recommend me to her colleagues.

Before, my cases had consisted largely of cheating spouses, in-depth background checks, and tedious stake-outs. Good work. *Steady* work. But not the kind of work that made my mind race with exciting possibilities.

Unfortunately, this exciting contract had a deadline and a countdown—only twelve days remained before it was yanked. Hunger only got you so far when going toe-to-toe with a mastermind.

"Bernard's crimes are bigger than this," Louisa said, tapping my contract. "So if you hit the deadline on this contract and you haven't found him, I have no problem hiring the next private detective on my list. Time is of the absolute essence here."

I managed a tiny smile. "I understand. This is a business. It's not about ego. It's about catching a very bad guy."

It was very much about ego for me, though. Ego and money. Argento Enterprises was still young—and had only a single person on staff. Me, which was my absolute prefer-ence. Putting myself through college and clawing my way up through the quicksand of my past had incurred debt and loans and bills that desperately needed to be paid.

The pay—and the prestige—of *this* contract was beyond my wildest fucking dreams. And if, like Louisa had explained, both Interpol and the FBI couldn't catch this guy, I sure as hell would. The feeling of revenge—of catching manipulative thieves in the act—was utterly satisfying. There was a delicious *crunch* to it that fulfilled my deepest cravings.

"Since I'm here, I wanted to ask you a few questions about..." I checked the name one more time. "—your former employee, Dr. Henry Finch? I've been researching Henry and his possibility of being a suspect, given he was Bernard's assistant for ten years. Seems an interesting coincidence that he's now a private detective too."

More than coincidence actually. I'd been pulling through background checks and employment records for any person who'd worked closely with Bernard, and the existence of Henry sent an air-raid siren through my investigative instincts.

The fact that an accomplished rare book librarian had turned PI? It didn't add up. And anything that didn't add up was a goddamn clue. Yesterday, I'd stumbled upon a picture of Henry and Bernard together in the mountain of paperwork Louisa had relinquished to me. It was an award ceremony from years ago. Bernard and Henry were posed together, holding a plaque. Bernard was a white man in his seventies with a distinguished-looking mustache. His eyes betrayed a clever intelligence, his body language depicted frailty.

Next to him stood Henry Finch—a handsome black man in a tailored suit and square-rimmed glasses. I knew he had a doctorate degree in Library Science, had lived across

Europe, and was fluent in four languages. Wouldn't Bernard use an assistant to steal for him *or* cover his tracks? And what would compel such an accomplished academic to throw away his degrees to work at a small detective firm?

"You've been looking into Henry Finch?" she asked.

"Of course," I replied.

Louisa was shaking her head. "It's not what you think. In November of last year, Henry Finch came to me in the middle of the night with a story *many* in this community did not want to believe. He'd become suspicious of Bernard, had been gathering evidence and watching him for more than a month. Henry confronted Bernard, told him he was going to the authorities, ran to me after Bernard threatened to forge his signature on documents that made Henry complicit in his crimes."

*Ah.* Really, Bernard was too obvious. "Henry was his backup fall guy."

"It appears so," she said.

I looked back down at the picture—at the enthusiasm shining through Henry's smile. Did Bernard take advantage of this man's devotion for ten years? The thought was stomach-churning.

"I didn't believe Henry's story at the time," Louisa said. "It's hard to imagine now, but Henry could have been telling me the Easter Bunny existed for how outrageous his story was. I didn't report Bernard. I *did* hire a firm called Codex to recover the stolen book that had precipitated everything."

I cocked my head. "That's the firm Henry works for now."

They were located in Philadelphia, well-known and respected. The owner was a man named Abraham Royal.

"It's how Henry got involved," Louisa explained, with pursed lips. "Abe Royal hired him out from under me."

This Abe sounded like a smart man. "And Henry's officially been cleared of all suspicion?"

"Absolutely he has," Louisa said. "If I'd listened to him, called the authorities sooner..." she trailed off. "Every second counts, and we lost a lot of seconds while I buried my head in the sand."

I sat back, re-crossed my legs. I was in an *every second counts* frame of mind too, since I had only twelve days left to catch this guy and no solid leads. Yet I was hesitant to let the Henry Finch angle go, given how little I had to grasp onto.

"You have to convince yourself the world is fracturing right in front of you," I said. "You're not the first client who didn't want to believe the truth, trust me. Even after producing photographic evidence of affairs, I've had spouses who had hired me refuse to believe me."

Louisa nodded, drummed her fingers on the desk. "Yes, well, here we are. Eleven months later with nothing to show for it."

I hid a wince, re-plastered my smile on. "I know three weeks feels like a long time, but I'm working around the clock. That's why my close rate is at 100%."

I had never—ever—not closed a case in the last five years. I wasn't going to start now.

"Codex is a phenomenal firm," Louisa said, avoiding my statement. "They recovered one of our stolen manuscripts two months ago. They're an investigative force to be reckoned with. Trust me, Henry's not your guy. He's on our side."

I swallowed past the spike of jealousy. "And you didn't want to hire Codex for this?"

Louisa's cheeks pinked, and she seemed slightly embarrassed. Her fingers tugged at her sweater sleeves. "Well... no. I did not. Plus, it's vital to employ fresh eyes and new ideas.

You are my fresh eyes, Sloane. I thought you might see details the rest of us have missed."

"Message received," I said. Noting the time—*every second counts*—I stood, shook Louisa's hand, promised to call her tomorrow. "It'll get done. You don't need to worry. I'm happy to bring you those new ideas."

"I am worried," she replied. "Truly worried. The reputation of this library is at risk, as is the reputation of the antiquities community. We don't appear to be a community of integrity at the moment."

Another tough swallow. Another fake smile. Louisa would hire another firm if I didn't come through. She could even hire *this* other agency. And Henry might not be a lead, but the fact that this Codex firm hired a librarian to work for them was too fucking intriguing to drop it.

"You hired the best, make no mistake," I said. "You won't regret it."

By the time I made it out to her hallway, I had to clench my hands in my skirt to stop them from shaking. Leaning back against the wall, I let out a ragged exhale and a whispered, "*Fuck me.*"

When I'd taken on this contract, there'd been no tremble in my fingers, no anxiety racing in my chest. I'd survived too much, worked too hard, needed this opportunity too badly to feign nervousness. Leaving Louisa's office twenty days ago, I'd felt calm excitement and an eager ambition.

Now, I was struggling to admit the hundreds of threads to Bernard Allerton's life were so complex—and so shrouded in secrecy—I had no concept of where to go or what to do. The Sherlock Society loved him and believed that he was on a long, off-the-grid sabbatical and would return at a later date. In my many, many afternoons spent having tea, Bernard was swooned, fawned, *obsessed* over. I couldn't tell if these people were hiding him in their attics or honestly thought he was a librarian.

As I walked back outside and down the wide steps, I hoped beyond hope the lecture with Eudora tonight would shed light on the direction I should be racing toward.

And after that? I'd need to do more research on Codex.

## 4

## ABE

*I*n the ballroom at The Langham Hotel, long rows of chairs were rapidly filling with chattering Holmes aficionados. In the center, on a stage with a podium, was an older white woman with wire-rimmed glasses and long, gray hair. She wore a deerstalker hat—the same as the notorious detective being discussed this evening.

As I sat in the very last row, I noticed most of the audience wore the same hat. Or were fully dressed as Sherlock Holmes.

"How interesting," I muttered. Crossing one foot across my knee, I settled back in the chair and fought an unusual urge to take a picture of these elaborate costumes and send it to everyone back at Codex. Strange that I almost... missed... the endless clamoring of Freya, Delilah, Henry, and Sam. Barely twenty-four hours had passed, and I couldn't stop thinking of things they would like, jokes they'd find amusing, food they'd enjoy.

I was also irritated that they'd all disobeyed my express orders thus far. I'd received not a single call or email regarding work or our cases.

The sensation of *missing someone* wasn't one I entertained often. Disappointment readily followed in its wake. It was much easier to wall off your heart than risk the painful consequences of letting people in.

The lights dimmed, and the audience hushed their chattering.

"Welcome, everyone," the woman at the podium said in a crisp British accent. "My name is Eudora Green, and I am the president of the Sherlock Society of Civilized Scholars."

The audience hooted softly like owls. Eudora, removing her deerstalker hat, gave a mysterious smile. "For any non-members in the audience, the Sherlock Society is the oldest, and most respected, society of Holmes scholars in the entire world. We're quite a passionate lot, and part of our monthly programming is to conduct discussions on the latest research and theories surrounding Arthur Conan Doyle and his most perfect creations: Sherlock Holmes and Dr. John Watson."

More light clapping, and she demurred, humble. But there was glee behind those wire-rimmed glasses, a preening.

"It's no secret our beloved Doyle felt that Sherlock Holmes had become a sort of albatross 'round his neck. The public demand for Holmes and Watson had reached a fever pitch, although Doyle himself no longer felt inspired to continue their adventures."

Sighs of irritation huffed through the audience. More than 120 years later, Holmes fanatics were still outraged that their beloved detective had been tossed over a cliff. Fictionally.

"In *The Adventure of the Final Problem*, Holmes fights his archenemy, Professor Moriarty, on the cliff at Reichenbach Falls in Switzerland. Watson, rushing to the scene later, famously encounters two sets of footprints to the edge of the cliff. No sets returning. The story ends with Watson presuming Holmes and Moriarty have both perished— Holmes, courageously so, as he had finally defeated a criminal mastermind and quite literally saved the day."

Heads nodded vigorously. Two women next to me puffed on unlit pipes. I scanned the crowd for suspicious behavior—shifty eyes, sudden movements. Another habit from my FBI days I couldn't seem to shake. Another habit former girlfriends had despised.

I tugged at the knot in my tie, fighting a tightness that hadn't been there a second ago. Work was a familiar passion, as comforting as a good book with an ending you've already read. But now I was forty-one years old, on my first vacation in years, and I didn't know how to just... be.

"And yet, as all of us here know, our great and noble Holmes did not die." There was a resounding cheer from the crowd as Eudora continued. "The public mourned the death of the detective so voraciously that Doyle succumbed to the outspoken pressure and resurrected the great Sherlock Holmes. Once again proving the detective to be beyond comparison. In *The Adventures of the Empty House*, Watson is startled when an elderly bookseller approaches him and reveals himself to be none other than Sherlock."

My pulse noticed the mention of *The Empty House*.

"This is not the first time Sherlock Holmes had successfully hidden in plain sight. This was a common theme throughout each story—the most obvious facts were often the most disingenuous. Simplicity is buried within the most complex of human situations. That was the job of Holmes— to hide in plain sight when necessary. And to uncover the facts hidden in plain sight as well. True coincidences rarely exist."

The door behind me creaked open. Every head in the audience swiveled to take in the newcomer. I hesitated, took a moment to gauge their facial reactions to the person interrupting the talk. A few whispers, a flurry of arched eyebrows, some friendly faces waving at the intruder.

When I finally turned in my seat, my gaze landed on the ornate doorway bathed in light. A woman was framed by the glow—a woman with the regal bearing of a queen. She was tall, chin raised, posture proud. Jet-black hair was piled into a bun, high on her head. Large golden earrings dangled from her ears. The deep V of her black jumpsuit revealed tan skin that shimmered. Luminous, midnight eyes that found mine immediately lingered, drew me in, tempted me, *called* to me. My jaw threatened to drop, so I grit my teeth instead. The queen's brow lifted, blood-red lips curving ever-so-slightly.

She knew every goddamn person in this goddamn room was staring at her.

She knew *I* was staring at her.

Openly admiring a stranger wasn't my style. I preferred cool detachment, not the white-hot blaze emanating from her very being. With languid motion, the woman walked toward the only empty seat in the room.

The one right next to me.

"And as I was saying," Eudora began, but whatever words came next faded into a muffled background noise that didn't dare penetrate the experience of watching the queen glide across the room, hips swaying, eyes still locked on mine.

"May I?" the woman asked, pointing at the chair. She had a voice like bonfire smoke, rich and earthy, tinged with ember.

And she was, interestingly, an American.

I nodded, gave her space, watched as she sank down with grace. For a dangerous few moments, we simply stared at each other, barely a foot apart, and the full force of her astonishing beauty engulfed me. She was young, certainly younger than me, long-limbed, and full-lipped, and her hair was rich, black satin.

Her red mouth gave up its teasing curve, became a full smile with white teeth. Her throaty laugh incited a primal urge deep in my body.

Not a queen. This strange woman was too brutally captivating. More like an ancient goddess legions of people would drop to their knees and pray to. A powerful deity who blessed your crops and gave you rain and inspired love and lust for the heartbroken and lonely.

*Or the sleep-deprived workaholics who can no longer have fun.*

The raven-haired goddess was the first to break our stare-down, turning toward Eudora with an enigmatic expression. I flexed my fingers, dragged myself back from the delirious vision I'd been thrust into. Eudora's speech reached me as if through miles of water.

"... It really is breaking news, and we all know how much he'd want us to..."

The older I got, the more tedious I found casual dating to be. The endless pursuit of a sexual partner was exhausting when the work hours were long and my job felt much too important to waste precious free time. Freya had been right about my dry spell. It had been more than a year since I'd indulged in sex, and that event had left me unsatisfied and frustrated. Probably because it'd been a long time since I'd met a woman who inspired *real* lust—wild and uncontrolled. The more tightly I restrained myself, the less I felt like I deserved finding that in another person. Aloofness was my preferred armor. An unfortunate trait I'd inherited from my father.

"... Of course we're coming up with a plan. *Of course*, Robert, let me finish..."

The woman shifted in her seat next to me, and I caught her scent—warm, intoxicating, sunshine through a dense forest, leaves and wildflowers. Why was I sitting here surrounded by deerstalker hats? Why wasn't I taking this woman on a date at an elegant restaurant in this gorgeous fucking city?

"Bernard will be told," Eudora said. I blinked, trance-like. Blinked again, re-focusing on Eudora with real effort. What was she saying? Did she say—

"Bernard Allerton, of all people, would want to know what was happening, yes of course."

I snapped to full attention—although not before noticing that the woman, too, seemed to perk up next to me, a slight lean forward like she'd spotted a rare bird in the sky. Eudora was attempting to quiet an agitated crowd.

"Let me begin again," Eudora said sweetly. "Ten years ago, there was a great debacle when Doyle's last living child died at the glorious age of 100. His son's will did not mandate that the private papers in his possession needed to *stay* within the family. Bernard was our president at that time, and he fought valiantly to gain control of those papers, rightly claiming that the Society had a responsibility to steward his works for both private and public admiration."

Without realizing it, I was leaning forward in my seat.

The woman did as well, upper body tilting more dramatically now.

"We did not win that fight," Eudora said. "And they are now in the care of The British Museum."

I made a mental note of that outcome. Bernard wasn't the kind of man who took losses lightly.

"*However*," she said as the chattering intensified. "Right before coming here, I received a call from James Patrick, the president of the Kensley Auction House in London. Doyle's great-niece has discovered an extremely large collection of her great-uncle's private papers beneath a trap door in her attic—and is moving ahead with auctioning them to a private owner. These are never-before-seen and a complete mystery to Doyle scholars."

There are rare moments during an investigation when a genuine clue drops in your lap as if from the fucking sky. A solid clue, heavy with implication, with edges you can grip.

This felt like that clue.

"The auction will happen one week from today," Eudora said. Hands rose like a college classroom filled with eager students. "*Yes,* I will try and get a message to Bernard. The problem being that his sabbatical is *off-the-grid*, and he isn't really available via the phone or the internet."

*An off-the-grid sabbatical.* I shook my head, impressed at the man's fucking *gall.* And curious to know how or why Eudora Green thought she could contact him, since he was technically in hiding from the authorities.

"Until I can get in touch with him, my decision as acting president is to work with Doyle's niece and convince her to donate those papers to the Society. Obviously, if they end up in the hands of a private collector, we may *never* know what was on them. There could be entire Holmes stories that have never seen the light of day, other mysteries, other villains, other dreams we deserve to appreciate and care for."

"What if they end up at auction?" A man in the front row asked.

Eudora's lips pursed. "I truly do not know. We can see what funding we have in our war chest. I think we all know a treasure of this size will go for millions, which we absolutely do not have. I hate to be pessimistic, but I'd never lie to all of you." A heavy silence hung over the crowd. "This is both the best and worst news."

I scanned the crowd for a third time, noted real distress on their faces. Real distress on Eudora's face. Next to me, the goddess seemed primed for movement, a runner waiting for the gun to fire.

That felt like a clue too.

"I will take questions after we end here if you want to come find me," Eudora said. "If not, the next two days are my shift at 221B Baker Street, giving talks to the tourists. Please come visit. I'll have a pot of tea waiting for all of you."

The maps I'd studied had pin-pointed Bernard's possible sightings within a two-mile radius of *this* hotel and *that* museum on Baker Street. And Eudora happened to be at both of them.

The stranger altered her posture slightly, releasing a wave of body heat that snatched my attention away from Eudora and back to her enchanting scent: sun-drenched branches, the hint of autumn in the air. I wanted to hear her smoky voice say more than *May I*?

So I turned, intending to adhere to the advice screamed at me for the past twenty-four hours and actually *talk* to a woman. Yet the moment I did just that, she vanished. I found her in the crowd immediately, striding with an obvious confidence toward the podium. Toward Eudora. I admired her bare, beautiful neck before I noticed the body language between the two. The woman was being greeted by Society members like a cherished friend. To Eudora, she appeared open, touching the other woman's elbow, smiling with a charm I felt all the way in the back row. Every ounce of light in the room seemed to emanate from her.

I swallowed the beginnings of an impatient sigh—stood instead. There was a bar in the far corner and a glass of whiskey was shouting my name. And as I moved through the crowd in the opposite direction of the raven-haired beauty, I was careful to keep my eye on the interaction between her and Eudora Green. Because *something* didn't feel right—and I was pretty damn sure she'd reacted at the use of Bernard Allerton's name.

And I was pretty damn sure Bernard would want to know about this auction.

As the bartender poured my order, I leaned against the bar and caught the attention of the goddess yet again. For a brief, thrilling second, her lips parted in recognition. I raised my glass from across the room and maintained eye contact as I took my first, burning sip.

What had Eudora said in her speech?

*True coincidences rarely exist.*

## 5

# SLOANE

"*Oh, Devon*, of course. I've heard so much about you," Eudora said. The president of the Sherlock Society of Civilized Scholars looked matronly and projected a naïve, eager innocence from her frumpy sweater to her earrings shaped like cats.

Beyond her sweet smile, I sensed a flash of pointed teeth and a suppressed snarl. The wolf dressed in the grandmother's clothing, perhaps. At the many afternoon teas and cocktail hours I'd had with Society members, it was clear her secret reputation was more canine-like than motherly. They were a social group, and chatty during dinners and lectures, so it was easy to take advantage of their gossipy nature when it came to their thoughts on Eudora.

"A snarling dog off the leash" was one of the descriptors I'd heard. Of course, it was sandwiched passive-aggressively between two compliments, and the person who'd said it blushed furiously afterward and begged me not to repeat.

I'd just watched Eudora mention speaking with Bernard Allerton like he wasn't, in fact, a criminal in *fucking hiding*. Tea with Eudora suddenly seemed even more vital.

"And you as well," I demurred, shaking her hand. "The Sherlock Society has been so welcoming to me on my pilgrimage throughout London. It's been so inspiring. And to think I haven't even gotten a chance to meet the *president* yet."

She touched her hair. "In certain circles, I'm well-known. But I don't consider myself a celebrity. Merely a devoted fan of Doyle and his brilliant creations."

I smiled at her, already mentally sketching her vulnerabilities, the points I could press and poke tomorrow to open the door and see what she *really* knew about Bernard Allerton.

"Well this devoted fan can't wait to see you tomorrow," I said. "Tea at the Sherlock Museum, 10:00 a.m.?"

A flood of people were starting to rush toward her, no doubt as intrigued as I was by the news of the auction and those private papers. Just the kind of thing a criminal mastermind might come out of hiding for.

"Of course, it would be my honor," she said, waving as I backed away. She was swarmed immediately, her posture straightening with every person attempting to speak with her. Eudora had only become president once Bernard had "gone on sabbatical"—which was intriguing as hell. To watch her now, my guess would be she'd been yearning for that position for years.

And I wondered what she knew about where her current vice president might be.

Buoyed by what felt like a tiny victory, I turned back around, toward the bar, and was taken aback by Hot Guy in a Suit, raising a glass of alcohol toward me in a silent cheer.

From the moment I'd stepped into the ballroom, my eyes had been drawn to Hot Guy's like we were two powerful magnets, desperate to snap together. As he leaned against the bar like he owned it, I noticed how tall he was, how broad those shoulders were, his long limbs in a suit clearly tailored to make others envious of his body. Hot Guy watched me walk through the crowd, watched me walk toward him, and I wasn't used to feeling so fucking *fluttery* around a man.

I now had a new understanding of the phrase *devastatingly handsome*. It was a cheesy line, bandied about in romance novels and movies. Definitely not anything I'd ever witnessed before in reality. His face devastated me. My immediate attraction to him ripped through me like a summer storm, all dangerous heat and crackling lightning. The man was white, with a strong, clean jaw, a strong nose. Dark black hair with silver at the temples, a few lines around the eyes making me guess he was a decade older than me, at least. The curve of his lips was downright sinful.

And if I hadn't been so mesmerized by his mysterious presence while we sat together earlier, I wouldn't have observed his physical reaction to the sound of Bernard's name. Which meant Hot Guy could know something—making him even *more* intriguing.

I placed my arm on the bar, leaned in a perfect mimic of his pose. His brow raised at my sudden nearness, one hand gripping a glass of whiskey.

"Hello again," he said. A deep voice. Melodic with a sexy rasp along the edges.

I held up a finger, ordered a vodka martini from the bartender. "Hello," I said. "I pegged you for a whiskey drinker."

My martini appeared in front of me. I stroked the stem with one finger, caught him following the movement.

"And I pegged you for a gin-drinker, not vodka," Hot Guy mused.

I lifted a shoulder. "I'm full of surprises."

The cold liquor burned all the way down. And he watched my mouth while I sipped.

"It's nice to meet another American staying at The Langham," he said.

I wasn't staying at The Langham Hotel. I was staying twenty minutes away at a cheaper motel that better fit my budget. But if this man knew Bernard Allerton, maybe I'd see about getting a room.

"And it's always nice to meet another Sherlock Holmes enthusiast," I replied. I held out my hand for him to shake. "Devon Atwood."

"A man on vacation," he replied. "Happy to meet you."

He shook my hand with pure professionalism—no stray touch or lingering—but the second our palms touched, I felt an electric bolt of desire. From the flaring of his nostrils, I guessed he felt it too.

"*Man on vacation* is an odd name," I mused.

Hot Guy gave me a half-smile but no reply. Instead he sipped his whiskey, swirled the liquid around the glass. "Are you a member of the Sherlock Society?"

"I'm member-adjacent," I said. "Not official. I do attend their meetings and lectures when I'm in London, however."

"Here on business?"

"Of a sort," I said. "So tell me, man-on-vacation. Do you think Doyle should have stuck to his guns and kept Sherlock dead? Or are you a fan of his triumphant resurrection?"

"I'm the minority opinion here, unfortunately," he said. "I think he should have kept him dead."

"Don't say that too loudly in this room." I took a step closer, bringing our bodies mere inches apart. Dropped my voice. "You could get us both killed."

He cracked that half-smile again. "I'm not one to boast,

but I feel confident in my physical prowess against Sherlock fanatics. What's your take?"

I took another long sip of vodka. "Why would you have kept him dead?"

"Why did you evade my question?"

"Because I'm a woman of mystery." I placed my arm on the bar, close enough to feel his body heat. "Would you like to buy me another drink?"

Sharp eyes on mine, he called my order to the bartender without missing a beat.

"Sometimes it's best to say goodbye," he said. "Sherlock Holmes was no longer serving him. Public outcry or not, I think Doyle should have kept him dead. Easier for everyone to move on."

A martini appeared in front of me. I clinked it against Hot Guy's glass. "To moving on."

He studied me over his glass. His fingers were strong. Confident. Was he a source or a suspect?

"I would have kept him dead too," I finally admitted. "Severed ties completely."

When you had the kind of chaotic, ramshackle childhood that I'd had, letting go of dead weight always made the most sense. You couldn't flee in the night unless you packed light.

"So we're in agreement," he said.

"Appears that we are, man-on-vacation." I flashed him a full smile, teeth and all. "Are you used to traveling alone? Or are you not..."

"I'm alone," he said, voice rough around the edges. "And used to it. Preferred, actually. Especially while traveling. There's no better way to truly learn what you want, what you desire, than being on your own."

I agreed again, held my tongue.

"Are you alone?" he asked.

I stepped closer, drawn into his orbit. "I am."

He placed his glass carefully on the bar. "And what do you desire, Devon?"

I ran my tongue along my lower lip, just to gauge his reaction. Felt absurdly pleased at the severe clench of his jaw.

"To find what I came to London for," I said. "I lost something a month ago. I'm currently trying to track it down." It was a partial truth at best.

"What did you lose?"

"That's not for the telling."

"And why not?" he asked. There was no push to his words, only a strangely appealing curiosity.

"Would you be completely honest with a man who won't even tell you his name?"

"Fair point," he said. "Have you had any luck finding what you lost?"

"I'm not sure yet." I slid even closer to this man, this complete *stranger*, heard his breathing hitch. The compulsion to kiss him crept into my thoughts, swept through the stress of this case, the fear of failure. *Devastating.* There'd never been a need for me to seek out a romantic partner in this world. My parents hadn't been a model for love. And marriage itself seemed to combine the very dangerous elements of trusting someone with needing someone.

If you were alone, you could only disappoint yourself.

Sex was a necessity, but I scratched that itch with one-night stands or short-term flings, the less personal the better. Whatever was happening between this stranger and I didn't feel like standard sexual attraction. It felt impulsive and primal.

"How long will you be in London, man-on-vacation?" I asked.

And his steel eyes blazed with a real hunger now. "For nine more days. My employees will fall to pieces if I leave them for any longer."

"And you're staying here at The Langham the whole time?" I asked.

"Yes," he said.

I pressed my body lightly against his surprisingly strong one. Tipped my mouth up so it danced close to his. He went still as a statue, like he was assessing me for risk.

"Maybe my luck is changing," I murmured.

"How so?" His hand landed firmly on the small of my back, fingers spanning across my skin. Those same fingers roamed idly along my spine. A caress between lovers, not strangers. It felt utterly *divine*. And it must have been the vodka and his body and a wayward craving to *keep him*... but I did something I hadn't done since I was sixteen years old.

I dipped my fingers into his jacket pocket and snatched the first thing they brushed against. A business card, by the feel of it. Slipped it into my purse.

"That thing I was looking for? I might have found it," I said. "Which makes me a very lucky woman, indeed."

The animal prowling behind his measured gaze gave me actual goosebumps.

"Who are you really?" he asked softly.

"Devon Atwood. Who are you really?"

"I don't think you are." His expression remained mildly curious. "You see, in my other life, I was trained by the best lie-detectors in the entire world. And while you are very, *very* good, you are also lying to me."

I was momentarily stunned.

A first.

"Spoken by a man who has perpetrated a sin of omission," I countered.

A slight arch to his brow. "I know a thing or two about sin. And that's not what I've done."

Desire twisted in my belly. Those strong fingers flexed—only once—along my spine, drawing me closer. "Do you always try and kiss liars?"

His lips quirked at one end. And then he stepped back, letting me go. I had to steady myself against the bar and prayed he didn't notice. "Don't you worry. You'll know for certain when I actually kiss you."

My hand clenched my stolen treasure—the business card. "And you'll never know for certain if I was lying." I swayed past the sexy stranger, laying a hand gently on his arm. "Good night, man-on-vacation."

I felt his eyes on my hips for the duration of my slow walk out of the ballroom. Was grateful he couldn't see the heat that sent a flush to my cheeks. Instead, I walked as quickly as I could to a back hallway, fishing out the card I'd pickpocketed.

I read the words written there. Felt my brain cells explode in the best way possible.

"*Holy shit*," I whispered, heart hammering in my chest. The card read: *Abraham Royal, Owner*. Beneath that, the name of his company: *Codex*.

Codex.

The renowned private detective firm that Henry Finch, Bernard's former assistant, now worked for.

Abraham Royal.

The man who hired Henry right out from under Louisa.

Now what in the hell was Abe fucking Royal doing in London? And what were the random chances he was simply enjoying a lecture from a woman who claimed to know all about Bernard's location?

I tapped the card against my lips. That man wasn't on a *goddamn vacation*. And maybe, if I played my cards right, he'd lead me right to Bernard.

I strode right to the front desk at The Langham. Revealed my most charming smile. "Hi there," I said. "I was wondering if you had any rooms available?"

6

———

## SLOANE

*E*udora handed me a tiny, china cup with steam rising from the black tea. The gentle matron had reappeared on her features—today she wore an even frumpier sweater with threads loose at the sleeves. Her earrings were book-shaped, and she'd donned a deerstalker hat.

We were sitting at 221B Baker Street—the fictional home of Sherlock Holmes and John Watson and the current Holmes museum where Eudora volunteered twice a week. Sitting in armchairs next to a replica of Holmes's fireplace gave me an out-of-sort feeling I had to suppress.

I was, after all, supposed to be a cheerfully enthusiastic fanatic.

"This is my fifth time here," I said, leaning forward as if sharing a secret. "Does that make me a nerd?"

"Oh, of course not," she said, waving a hand. "I volunteer here twice a week, my dear. And it is, to some, a god-awful tourist trap. And yet..." She trailed off, indicating the red-wallpapered space around us. "I feel happy when I'm here amongst Doyle's ideas and inventions."

49

Sipping my tea, I thought about what I'd done last night after securing a room at The Langham and moving my suitcases and laptops: curled up and re-read *A Study in Scarlet*. When I'd crafted *Devon Atwood* and her Sherlockian obsession, I knew I'd have to read every single novel and short story in order to blend in with the crowd of scholars and fans.

I found myself absurdly drawn into the mysteries—the sense of Victorian London, the intriguing deductions, the aspects of the mystery that never made sense until the very end. It called to the part of me that loved *solving* things. And while I wasn't prone to the stalwart fanaticism I'd witnessed here, I did, kind of, sort of, *get* it. During these weeks of mounting frustration, reading about Sherlock Holmes every night had become a source of comfort.

I did wish I'd had more books during the harshest days of my childhood. It would have felt like a doorway into another world—maybe a world where I was safe or cared for or understood the chaos of our constant movement. Instead, I had to work. *Always*. During the limited schooling I managed to grasp onto in my younger years, I gobbled up books and stories in the classroom like a greedy kid on Christmas morning.

"There is a sense of wonder being here, tourist trap or not," I admitted. "It makes me feel like a child again, excited by the smallest things."

A nod from Eudora. "Over the course of my life, I've been called *batty* more times than I can count. And I am a bit batty. I'm the president of a literary organization, and I have four cats. *Such* a stereotype." She tittered like a bird. "But the Sherlock Society has given me life in this cold and brutal world. This community has sheltered me from storms. Do you know what it's like to connect with other people over a subject so unique?"

No, I did not.

"Absolutely," I lied. "I'm an office assistant back home, in New York City, and it wasn't easy for me to save the vacation time *or* the cash I needed. Yet my soul called me here." I placed a hand above my heart and held her gaze, which softened at my gesture. "And to think I'm now sitting with *the president* of the oldest Sherlock Holmes society in the entire world..."

I trailed off, correctly guessing that Eudora had a tender ego that loved a good stroke.

"You make an old woman quite happy, Devon," she said. "I'm a normal person, like you. A fan who was willing to step into a leadership role when a vacuum appeared."

I tilted my head. "A vacuum?"

"Our current, well *former*, president Bernard Allerton is on a very long sabbatical. He made the tough decision to step down while away, allowing me to step into his role."

Her smile was all wolf—granny was gone.

"You seem better suited to it," I said, adding a wink. "Always nice to see a woman in charge."

"*Always*," she agreed. "I'm very close with Bernard and there are no hard feelings. When he returns—" She coughed a little here. "Excuse me, when he returns, we'll see which leader our members prefer."

I didn't blink. "And when is Bernard coming back?"

Eudora touched her ear. "We shall see, my dear. He's been vague with his return plans."

"Oh," I said, tapping my mug with my fingernail. "Where *is* he, by the way? I know he's a little bit famous around these parts. I was surprised his whereabouts are unknown."

I held my breath, testing the waters, seeing how much she knew and what she was willing to share.

"They're not unknown. They're a *secret*," she said. "Only a chosen few know where he is." Her smile turned smug. I wasn't sure if this was bullshit or not, but *she* believed it. Which made Eudora Green rapidly change from *source* to *suspect*.

"You know where he is, don't you?" I teased.

She mimed a lock at her lips, a key she tossed past her shoulder. I was aware of how tightly I held the china cup— how badly I wanted to throw the tea in her face and demand she tell me where the *fuck* this man was.

"Will you tell him about the Doyle papers being auctioned?" I asked, studying her reaction.

"Yes, I'll get in touch with him," she said. "I'm fully in charge and the key decision-maker regardless of where he is. And between you and me, we won't get those papers. They're not even up for auction yet, and they're basically gone."

I took another sip. "Bernard will be disappointed, sounds like."

"We'll all be," she said quickly. "My job is to lead us through rough waters and smooth sailing alike. That's the job of a leader."

I cranked up my smile—while internally remembering every story I'd heard these weeks about her nasty temper and vengeful spirit. "Do you miss Bernard? I heard the two of you were especially close. Which means you must be special to attract the attention of such a famous man."

Bernard Allerton wasn't famous like a movie star, but he was extremely well-known in the world of academics and librarians, the fields of antiquities and history, and even archaeology. His reputation had a far-reaching impact.

"We've always had a connection," Eudora said.

"Romantic?" I asked with a girlish look.

She giggled—it was jarring. "Not at all. Bernard had one love in his lifetime—she was also an American, like you. That was years ago."

I grabbed onto that lead with both hands and shoved it away for later. Who did Bernard love? And did this woman know where the hell he was?

"No, our connection has always been deeper. I'd say more *intellectual*. We have similar minds." She touched her earrings like a shy schoolgirl.

"I can see why," I said, playing into it. Assessing where to go next—the woman clearly loved Bernard in her own way. Was she protecting him? Or was all of this a fantasy for her?

"Now you haven't told me if you're a Doylean or a Sherlockian?" Eudora asked. "I'm sure the other members have grilled you appropriately."

I'd done my research before coming here. Each member of the Society had a D or an S listed next to their name on the website.

"Doylean," I answered.

"Very good," she said proudly. "Of course, the Society is unique in that we accept members from both schools of thought, and even those who straddle the middle. But..." She leaned across the small space. "I'm a strict Doylean."

"No Great Game for you," I teased.

She rolled her eyes. "That was all Bernard. He was a Sherlockian and a member of the Baker Street Irregulars, you know."

"I did not," I said, which was the truth and only added to my interest in these damn papers. The intensity of Bernard's obsession with Holmes was so deep he believed the characters were real. In my time with the Society I'd learned the community was divided into *Doyleans* and *Sher-lockians*.

A Doylean, like Eudora, worshipped the genius of Arthur Conan Doyle and his stories and characters. A Sher-lockian embarked on *the Great Game*—a form of scholarship that presumed Holmes and Watson were flesh-and-blood human beings. Arthur Conan Doyle was merely their literary agent. *The Baker Street Irregulars* were a tight-knit group of Sherlockians, and the fact that Bernard was one of them intrigued me. Did he truly adhere to their academic ideas? Or were they just a source of rabid literary lovers he could easily sell stolen books to?

"As president, I'm not supposed to take sides. Between us girls..." Eudora lifted a shoulder and smirked.

"I think it's pretty dumb," I said. She laughed, coquettish, and I felt a small sense of satisfaction that I'd read this woman so quickly and so correctly.

Although the original source of these undercover skills —the charm, the easy lies—wasn't something I liked to think too hard about. Immediately, my hand slipped into my pocket and gripped Abe Royal's business card. The advantage this information had given me was thrilling.

The fact that I'd pickpocketed it was not. It wasn't even an old habit—it was an old skill I was forced to do for years, even after I understood the harm it unleashed.

Abe Royal's presence had provoked a chemical, lizard-brain reaction in me, and stealing from his pockets was the result. If I didn't suspect I'd need him over the coming days, I'd steer clear. Because a devastatingly handsome man who made me lose my mind—*literally*—was not the distraction I wanted to deal with as my deadline rapidly approached.

Whatever information he might provide would need to come from a distance.

Eudora peeked at her watch. "I hate to cut this short, but I do have more people coming by today. I'm sure I'll be hearing all about the auction and what their proposed solutions are."

I stood, placed the teacup down next to the fireplace and a replica of Sherlock Holmes's violin. "Thank you for chatting with me. And for answering my nosy questions."

"Anything for another Doylean," she said. "We have to stick together. It's important to cultivate true friends in this world. That's what I've learned from being in the Society. Real friends, friends you can trust, you'd move mountains for."

I fixed a smile on my face. "That's the truest thing I know."

And the biggest lie I'd told all day.

She led me through the small rooms that comprised the museum and out into an even smaller lobby. Already, tourists were starting to stream in dressed in various costumes. Eudora was scanning the room, face brightening at a man standing in the corner.

"My next appointment," she said. "We met last night, and he promised he had information we could use regarding the auction."

"Oh?" I turned, catching myself just in time before my jaw dropped.

Abraham Royal, dapper as ever, stood in a suit with a polite smile directed right at Eudora. Until he saw me, of course. Surprise flared in his expression, followed by a hunger I knew well. Unnecessary distraction or not, that man had appeared in my dreams all night, turning them hot and edgy and painfully erotic. I'd tried all morning to forget those teasing sensations, yet here he was, provoking them again.

"Mr. Fitzpatrick, how nice to see you," Eudora said, blushing a little when he shook her hand. "Do you know Ms. Atwood?"

"We also met last night," I said. "Although I actually didn't catch your name?"

The man on vacation swallowed hard. "Daniel Fitzpatrick."

My mouth curved into a genuine smile. Now what was this private detective doing, meeting with Eudora, using a fake name?

"A pleasure," I said.

He nodded, followed Eudora back into the Victorian-era rooms. And I sank down onto the closest couch to await his return. Last night, after moving into The Langham, I'd done the deepest dive on information about Codex, Abe, and his team. I now knew he was an accomplished, well-respected, former special agent with the FBI. I knew his team was responsible for two extremely high-profile cases in the past few months—including infiltrating an underground antiquities market that resulted in dozens of arrests.

And I knew he'd hired Henry Finch, ten-year assistant to the man I was desperately searching for. The more Abe lied, the more I believed he was here for one reason only.

*Bernard.*

## 7

## ABE

*B*ernard Allerton stared back at me from a black-and-white picture dated fifteen years ago. He didn't have his cane yet, but his posture was meek and timid. Next to him stood Eudora and a man I didn't recognize. The caption read: *Sherlock Society president Bernard Allerton and vice president Eudora Green stand with former president Nicholas Markham outside Adler's Bookshop.*

The picture hung on a wall surrounded by others—tourists at the museum, ribbon-cuttings, re-enactments, costume parties, galas, lectures. It easily spanned fifty years of history through the Sherlock Holmes Museum and other Sherlock-inspired happenings.

Bernard was in many of them.

I'd woken this morning with an overwhelming drive to follow-through on my promise yesterday to visit with Eudora Green at 221B Baker Street. After a night of tossing and turning, tortured by dreams, I knew I'd only rest if I'd tied up these remaining mental threads. It wasn't that I thought Bernard would be sitting at this museum, waiting for capture. But the combination of the auction, the sighting reports, and Eudora's relationship with the man was a compelling enough reason to come here.

And it was only one meeting. One more final piece of a puzzle I'd have to, eventually, let go of solving. After this, I had plans late in the afternoon to visit Parliament and tour the National Gallery followed by a nice dinner out with an even nicer glass of whiskey. *Culture, history, whiskey.* Vacation things for a man on vacation.

As if sensing my guilt from 2,000 miles away, my phone chirped with a text message from Freya. I glanced at the pictures of Bernard, winced. Glanced back down to her text:

*Just a friendly reminder from your team to enjoy the fuck out of your vacation! Sam and I constructed a life-sized cardboard cut-out of you, which we have sitting behind your desk. Every so often we make it say something stern and uncompromising, and we all pretend to be scared.*

I chuckled softly, scrubbing a hand down my face. *Your respect for authority is truly an inspiration,* I typed back.

*Sounds like you miss us,* she wrote.

I didn't reply, casting my eyes toward the door where Eudora would be appearing soon for our appointment. I pictured calling Codex, telling them what few clues I'd spotted since arriving here, imagined their excitement, their thirst for justice that mirrored my own. Deep down, buried beneath the guilt, was the *obsessive* element I hated to acknowledge. The selfish part made me feel like a bastard— if anyone was going to find Bernard, it was going to be me.

And me alone.

Last night I'd given Eudora a name I hadn't used since I was an FBI recruit—*Daniel Fitzpatrick*. At Quantico we'd had rigorous undercover drills, and if I wasn't assigned a name, I chose Daniel whenever I needed something fast.

Today's issue was that I wasn't working a case. I had no

clients, no support, no funding. So I'd flown all the way here and given Eudora Green an undercover name because I was Ahab sensing the presence of the white fucking whale.

I slipped my hands into my pockets, leaning back against the wall. My fingers brushed against the silk material, evoking a memory of what I'd discovered last night. Back in my room, I'd removed my suit jacket and gone to empty the pockets—only to realize my Codex business card, with my name on it, was missing. I had a sly suspicion about the perpetrator. I cursed beneath my breath—even as a smile caught me off-guard. Perhaps the reason I'd dropped a fake name had to do with a raven-haired siren who'd bewitched me completely, a new and not entirely unwelcome sensation.

*Do you always try and kiss liars?*

I didn't, not ever. I did, however, spend a large portion of last evening fantasizing about the curve of her spine beneath my palm, her pliable muscles, her fire-hot skin, the hollow of her collarbone calling to me. I'd watched her seductively swaying hips with the stare of a starved man. My fingers were sore from the way I'd gripped my glass, a futile attempt to temper my response. By the time I'd made it to Eudora, I was off my game, dazzled.

Yet another new sensation.

I was potentially under the spell of a liar and a pick-pocket, so why did she have to be the most beautiful woman I'd ever seen?

"Mr. Fitzpatrick, how nice to see you again." I turned fully at Eudora's voice, caught her outstretched hand and slight blush. "Do you know Ms. Atwood?"

*Goddammit to hell.*

The beautiful liar stood next to Eudora Green looking

as astonishing in the morning hours surrounded by tourists as she had in a grand ballroom framed by golden light.

"We also met last night," Devon said. "Although I didn't catch your name."

The playful tug of her lips made me wonder if she'd read that card—knew my real name.

"Daniel Fitzpatrick," I said, loosening the clench of my jaw.

"A pleasure." Her smoky voice curved around the word *pleasure*, and I was keenly aware that I might have been caught in my own lie. I managed a nod, frustrated. Followed Eudora back into a room designed to look like the apartment Holmes and Watson shared in the stories.

"You've been busy this morning," I said, by way of opening.

Eudora adjusted her wire-rimmed glasses and pressed a strand of hair back into her tight bun. "When you're the president of such a prestigious society, people want to talk with you."

"Especially given the news," I said. "The auction, I mean."

She brightened. "Ms. Atwood and I were just discussing it. She's a fan all the way from America, like you. Except she's been here for an entire month already."

I filed that piece of information away to examine later. Hadn't she told me she was in London because she'd lost something?

"I'm only here for the week, I'm afraid," I said. "I'll barely make the auction."

"It's dreadful news, really," she said. "I tried to put on a brave face for everyone last night, but between you and me, there's no way we'll get those papers."

I straightened my tie, crossing one leg over the other. "Bernard will be disappointed."

"You're a colleague of his?" she asked.

I quickly ran through the options of what could work and went with: "I am. From long ago. More an admirer than a colleague. Obviously not nearly as close to him as you are."

A bit of preening. "We've always been close because of the Society."

I looked around at the paraphernalia—the disguises, the violin, the glasses on the table. "How long have you been a member?"

"Oh, give or take thirty-five years," she answered. "At the time, Nicholas was the president, and Bernard and I were lowly secretaries."

"Nicholas... Markham?" I asked, remembering the man from the pictures.

"Yes," she said. "Nicholas has since died. His grandson, Peter, now owns his bookshop. Adler's. Peter is extremely active in the literary community here in London as well as our Society. He and Bernard are also close, given Bernard essentially watched him grow up."

I faked a smile while mentally tagging the Markham family as potentially interesting. "How lovely. I love a good bookstore. What was the Society like back when you joined?"

Eudora fiddled with her blocky earrings—they were shaped like novels. "Secretive in a good way," she said with a smug sigh. "It was much harder to gain entry. Code words, secret meetings, that kind of thing. We were a Society with more purpose then, not only lectures and conferences."

*Code words.*

"Nicholas was an inspiring president, but things became

even more cloak-and-dagger when Bernard took over. It was a fun time to be a fan, even if the president was a Sher-lockian."

"Proud Doylean myself," I said, raising a finger and pointing it at my chest.

"I wouldn't have doubted otherwise," she assured me.

I'd done my research.

"You enjoy the... cloak-and-dagger elements?" I asked, choosing my words carefully.

"I did," she said. "Although with Bernard gone, it could be a wonderful time to bring back those elements."

I let a second pass, kept my body language loose. "He's been gone for a while it sounds like. On his sabbatical."

A slight casting of her eyes to the left. A tightening around her mouth. "We've missed him, but he's doing well."

My training told me she'd lied.

"I'm guessing you're in contact with Bernard often?" I asked.

"Someone has to be," she said, as if it were a grave sacri-fice. Was she lying about speaking with him? Or lying about his sabbatical?

"Is Bernard taking messages right now?" I asked.

Her head cocked like a bird's. "Why?"

I made a show of glancing once over my shoulder. I was about to swing for the fences. "The reason why I asked to meet with you today is because I need to get a message to your former president."

Her lips parted before she schooled her expression. "And what would it be about?"

*Code words.*

"Didn't we once meet at Reichenbach Falls?" I asked. I had not a single fucking idea if she'd recognize what I was asking.

An awkward silence hung between us. Eudora placed her cup down onto its saucer with a jangling *crack*. "We have."

I nodded, respectful, even as my pulse jumped. "I potentially have special access to what's about to be auctioned. If the Society is interested, I'd be open in sharing more."

There was swinging for the fences—and there was throwing the damn bat as far as you could. I had no idea what possessed me to do this, yet I felt gratified at the flash of greed across her face.

"I'll take it into consideration," she said simply, then stood, indicating the door. "I have more guests to see, as I'm sure you understand." There was a curtness to her tone that hadn't been there a second ago.

"Thank you." I stood, re-buttoned my jacket. Scribbled my cell number down on a slip of paper. "I really would appreciate if you'd pass the message along. You can reach me with this."

Her responding smile was less matronly, more snake-like. "Certainly. And a word of caution, Mr. Fitzpatrick. If a man has gone off the grid, he usually doesn't want to be found."

I paused, momentarily stunned by the warning in her tone. "I see," I finally said. I raised my palms in a submissive gesture. "I'm merely a colleague with something to offer. I'm no threat."

"Good." She indicated the exit behind me. "I suggest you keep it that way."

As I left, a jumble of thoughts raced through my head because I wasn't quite sure what her message meant. For all I knew, she was nothing but hot air, and Bernard was living peacefully in Switzerland right now under an assumed name with zero contact with members of a Sherlock Holmes fan club.

Or possibly I'd successfully gotten a direct message to Bernard Allerton.

A tiny table held loose leaflets, advertising a talk tonight at Mycroft's Pub. *Humphrey Hatcher, Secretary of the Sherlock Society* was listed as the speaker. I picked it up, drawn in, until Eudora's voice sounded directly behind me.

"You're still here?" she asked, a slight knife-edge to her words.

I gave her my warmest smile. "Just interested in this talk tonight, perhaps."

That seemed to win her over a bit. "Everyone loves Humphrey. He's Bernard's oldest friend, actually."

"Excuse me?" I asked before I could stop myself.

"Humphrey," she said clearly. "Bernard's best friend."

"Interesting," I mumbled, surprised that such a greedy, nefarious man could acquire friends—*best* friends. Although my father, at one point, had his fair share of friends he used to invite over for barbecues and drinks. Friends I'd liked actually. Though they no longer came around once he'd walked out the door and left my mother and I to fend for ourselves.

I slipped the piece of paper into my pocket. Tried not to ruminate too much on the last time *I'd* seen a friend.

Eudora slipped out into the main lobby, which was now officially bustling with tourists. And my eyes immediately locked with a sultry siren's—leaning against the far wall with one black-booted foot propped against it. Red lips blossomed into a full smile I was fucking helpless to resist.

"Ms. Atwood," I said evenly. "You're still here?"

Between her fingers, Devon held my Codex business card. "Care to walk me back to my hotel, Daniel?"

## 8

## ABE

*D*evon and I stepped out onto the bustling London street, filled with busy locals walking to work and roaring buses. The sky was heavy with the threat of rain, a crisp nip chilled the air, and for a moment, I caught her eying the storm clouds with fear.

She turned back, nodding towards Regent's Park, a few minutes from our hotel destination. "Shall we?"

I held out my palm. "Before we meander through the gardens, I'll need my stolen property back."

Devon placed the card in the palm of my hand, my real name exposed. "You dropped it."

I shook my head, refused to release her gaze. Today, the goddess wore stilettoed boots that could have doubled as weapons and a black, long-sleeved dress that revealed every sweet and perfect curve to her luscious body. Her satin hair was free, wild around her shoulders, thick and wavy.

"Such an interesting way to explain *pickpocketing*," I chided.

She scrunched up her nose. "Well, you dropped it into your pocket. And I retrieved it."

I slipped the card back where it came from. We were starting to walk, and I hadn't realized it. "Who taught you to do that?"

A flash of emotion behind her eyes before she smiled at me instead. A sexy, feline smile. "Old trick," she explained. "I only do it for men-on-vacation."

I unleashed my own slow grin and felt unbearably pleased at the light flush in her cheeks. "At least now we're even."

"How so?"

I lifted a shoulder. "We're two strangers using fake names while on vacation in London. Some might call it equal footing."

"Ah, so you admit it, *Daniel*," she said. Her smile this time was less edgy, more genuinely amused. There was a corresponding increase of my heart rate. Strange. I'd never thought I'd enjoy walking through a park in London with a woman I fully knew was both a liar and a thief. And yet every conversation I engaged in with this woman felt like sitting down at a chess board with your equal. Every move mimicked. Every thought precipitated.

I laughed softly, shook my head. "I knew it the minute you introduced yourself as Devon."

A sly look from my chess partner but no answer. We were stopped at a red light, waiting our turn. I dropped my mouth lower, toward her ear.

"The name doesn't suit you one bit, Ms. Atwood." I watched goosebumps rise along the side of her neck.

"You're one to talk," she said, teasing. "Why aren't I a 'Devon'?"

"In my experience, Devons are sweet," I said mildly. "They wear sweater sets and run for class president and cheerfully organize every birthday party in the office. Maybe they have one cat named after a character in a Jane Austen novel."

The gorgeous liar stopped in her tracks. To the left stretched the massive greenery of The Regent's Park and the Queen Mary's Rose Gardens. I could hear water, see people and couples stretching out on the green even without the benefit of the sun to bathe in. It was quite effortless to pretend this woman and I truly were two strangers who had a connection while on vacation and were strolling around the tourist attractions together.

I mean, really, we *were* doing that.

And really... I enjoyed it more than I cared to admit.

"I don't strike you as a cheerful organizer of office parties?" One elegant eyebrow raised, mocking me.

"You don't strike me as *sweet*," I repeated. Her bold red lips parted, only further convincing me of this fact. The goddess standing in front of me was bite marks and smoky laughter, clever wit and dark desires. She wasn't fucking sweet, and I'd never liked sweet.

A lift of the shoulder. "Perhaps I own more sweater sets than you're aware of. And while we're on the topic, you're not a Daniel."

"In what way?" The Langham Hotel appeared ahead of us, large and elegant. I was slowing my steps, drawing out my time with this beautiful mystery. Presumably, she knew my name. So why was she teasing it out?

"I haven't known a lot of Daniels who look that hot in a suit."

We'd reached the lobby of The Langham Hotel—and while her words threatened to stop me, literally, in my tracks, she continued walking toward the bank of elevators. I kept pace, barely, and worked to keep my tone even.

She pressed the button for *six*. The doors opened and we stepped inside.

"That was a nice compliment," I said. We were both leaning against our respective walls, tension hanging between us in the wide space.

"Some might even call it sweet," she purred.

I smiled again. I could see her anticipated moves. "What were you doing meeting with Eudora Green?"

Devon paused, dragging out the moment. "I'm here exploring London and every place mentioned by Doyle in his stories. And I'm curious about those Doyle papers. And the only person in the Society I haven't connected with is Bernard Allerton."

The mention of Bernard's name so casually had my pulse racing even faster. Who *was* this woman?

"What do Eudora and Bernard have to do with finding the thing that you lost a month ago?" I asked, referencing our first conversation.

The elevator *binged*. The doors opened. We both stepped onto floor six. Was she following me? And if she came onto me, outside my door, with a giant bed awaiting us inside, would I even *pretend* to resist?

"They have a lot to do with it, actually," she said. "I'm guessing your conversation with Eudora might have been about the same thing."

We were stopped in front of my room—#608. I was back to feeling muddled again—dazzled by the scent of her, confused by her mind games, intrigued by her beauty. She was nothing but a gorgeous, lying, pickpocketing challenge. And god help me if she followed me inside, I'd drop to my knees eagerly. Spend this entire day, and into the next, worshipping every inch of her with my mouth. She could keep the boots on. She could even keep the dress on—I'd only have to slip the fabric of her underwear to one side to give her everything she needed.

"Who are you?" I asked softly—Bernard fan? Bernard hunter? Just a Sherlock Holmes enthusiast from America who likes lying about her name?

"Who are *you*?" Sincerity sparkled in her eyes. "And why is a private detective using a fake name while pretending to be on vacation?"

So she had gone ahead and researched my name, researched Codex. And *god*, why was I growing harder? Since first seeing her last night, my cock had been hard and heavy, body filled with yearning. This cat-and-mouse game was only making it worse because the tension between us was strung tight, and neither was willing to let go.

I refused to make it easy on her. I leaned a shoulder against my hotel room door, nodded at her pretty fingers. "In a past life, I'd arrest you for stealing."

She tossed her gorgeous hair. "Handcuffs and all?"

A vision of slapping cool cuffs around her wrists while I pressed her body to a wall hit me like a truck barreling down the highway. I had to slip my hands into my pockets to hide their incessant clenching. And to prevent them from reaching out, grabbing the back of her neck, and dragging her toward me.

"If that's the kind of thing you like," I finally said—tone grating, raw.

"It's the kind of thing I love," she said, slowly backing down the hallway. "Too bad I don't do that kind of thing with liars."

I swallowed hard, watched her hungrily as she paused in front of the room directly next to mine. #610.

"Are we... neighbors?" I asked, genuinely surprised.

And pleased when she realized the same thing. She huffed out a little laugh. "You've got to be joking."

I shook my head. "This is me."

"Well... this is me," she said slowly. Her sultry demeanor was fading in the face of her real shock.

"There goes the neighborhood, I guess," I said, unlocking my door. Propping it open an inch with the tip of my shoe. "Looks like I'll be seeing you around, Ms. Atwood."

## 9

## SLOANE

*a*be Royal was on the move.

I pressed my ear to my door, heard his open and close, then the elevator doing the same thing. I yanked on my boots, fluffed my hair, and checked my lipstick.

And I set off to follow him.

It had been six hours since our conversation in the hallway—and while I'd intended to stay in his hotel because I'd be closer to a potential source for All Things Bernard, it had *not* been my intention to be his fucking neighbor.

That was, truly, coincidence. A coincidence my sex-starved body had been extremely happy about. During the six hours we'd been apart, every action I undertook inside this room had me imagining Abe doing the same thing. Undressing, showering, crawling onto the wide, soft bed.

More specifically, I'd spent several hours battling the force of this new *handcuffs* fantasy that had appeared ever since the man had threatened to have me arrested for my sticky fingers. There was no denying the allure: bound hands, suddenly submissive, Abe's deep voice at my ear as he informed me of my misdeeds. Bad girl, good girl—I'd be whatever he wanted.

I did deny myself the pleasure of... well, pleasure. Touching myself with only a wall separating me from this sexy stranger could only lead to more trouble when I *only* needed more focus. The excitement I felt at the sound of his door opening was merely because I believed he'd lead me to the next clue about Bernard's whereabouts.

There wasn't—there couldn't be—another reason.

I slipped down the stairs quickly, careful to exit in the alley off the hotel. Pausing, back to the brick, I saw Abe's suit-clad form move past and into a crowd heading toward Cavendish Square.

I followed him.

His stride was deliberate, confident. People stepped aside and made way for him. He didn't appear to be a tourist. He wasn't checking his phone or staring at street signs. It made tailing him simple. He only faced forward.

And I was an old hat at tailing a suspect, even before I was being paid to catch spouses in the act of cheating. Being raised by two con artists meant I was raised to *pay attention*. Every single thing was a tell, a vulnerability, a truth to be manipulated and used to garner trust.

The reverse was also true. Every person my parents became—and over the years I watched them become hundreds of different people—had a fake vulnerability that allowed their mark to trust them. Bernard had nailed his years ago. I'd bet money his frailty was feigned to induce compassion.

One of the many ways my parents used me was to have me follow their potential mark and report back on their *tells*. It felt like spying. It felt like an invasion. And whenever we'd managed to live in a town long enough for me to attend school on a limited basis, I learned fairly quickly that my classmates weren't forced to do the things I did on the weekends.

When I was ten, I made the mistake of asking my parents why kids at school were different than me. I wasn't allowed back to school for a long time.

Abe strolled past green, flowering gardens and busy intersections. If I was tailing this man for a client, my analysis would be that he had a confidence born from a deep-seated sense of self or purpose. He was serious, brilliant, unflappable.

If he was a *mark*, I'm not sure what vulnerability I'd poke at. So far I hadn't found one. But as a private detective, I could only admire him—his ability to blend into the crowd. He was a fucking natural.

He came to a stop in front of a green building I recognized. Mycroft's Pub. Named for Sherlock's brother, it was frequented by members of the Society and used often for informal talks and meetings that I'd attended once or twice. Across the street was a bookstore named Adler's, a few cafes, and quiet-looking office buildings.

Abe checked a slip of paper then stepped inside Mycroft's.

I paused at the windows of the bookstore to check my reflection. Fluffed my hair again. The window opened to a little seating area surrounded by stacks and stacks of old books. Past that were long bookshelves with posters advertising literary events around London. I thought about Bernard Allerton, who'd been trusted by people to *protect* books like the ones I was staring at. I thought about him abusing that trust because he appeared to be—at first glance—a greedy piece of shit.

Anger flooded my veins, sharpening my focus on this

case and the bigger picture it represented. Stealing antique books worth millions of dollars was just a fancier version of my parents' scams, which included fraudulent insurance plans and conning elderly people by pretending to be their grandchildren. It was all just a *trick*—but one that only worked by exploiting people's natural inclination to trust.

A familiar voice came from behind me. "Ms. Atwood, how pleasant to see you again."

My surprised eyes met Abe's smug ones in the reflection of the window. He must have slipped back out of Mycroft's while I was distracted by my thoughts. Although now I was distracted by *Abe*, which didn't help me one bit.

"Don't look too pleased with yourself," I said, turning around to face him. Which was definitely a mistake—his gravitational pull was too strong.

"First you steal from me. Then you're somehow staying in the hotel room next to mine. And *now* I catch you tailing me." There was a surprising hint of mischief in his expression. "There are better ways to get my attention. Better and legal, I might add."

"Where's the fun in that?" With great effort, I took a giant step backwards and nodded towards the pub. "Yet another coincidence. I was heading inside there."

"Yet another lie," he said. "If you followed me all this way, you might as well go in first."

With a smirk, I breezed past him. Picking up a program on a side table, I read: *The Importance of Sherlock in a Mobile-Phone World*. The speaker was Humphrey Hatcher, who was Secretary of the Sherlock Society. Mycroft's Pub was dark and cozy inside with a small stage, a large fireplace, and paintings on the wall. The pub had been transformed for tonight's talk, and instead of its usual assortment of tall tables and bar seating, the room was clear and fully crowded with people. Eudora waved to me from a group of people, and I smiled and waved back.

Abe was peering curiously around the room. It was getting harder and harder not to grab him by the lapels and demand he tell me his real plans. Using a fake name, meeting with Eudora, befriending members of the Society... Had Codex been hired by another library to go after Bernard? Or was this a one-man mission? Because it'd be helpful to know if this sexy, sinfully distracting man was purely fascinating or actually my competition.

Before I could ask him another question, a red-faced, red-haired, burly lumberjack in his seventies came barreling through the crowd.

"Daniel Fitzpatrick," the man boomed. He shook Abe's hand vigorously, practically wrenching his arm off. "I'm Humphrey Hatcher. Eudora told me you know Bernard. A friend of a friend is *my* friend."

Abe let out a startled sound, glancing sideways at me before catching himself. "Well... certainly. Although I can't say I know Bernard that well. More of a colleague, an admirer if you will."

"Bernie's got that skill, I'm afraid," Humphrey said. "He's a charmer."

*Bernie?* And also—*friends?* Abe caught my eye from behind Humphrey's giant form, and I arched a brow in silent reproach. There was confirmation that this man was definitely sniffing around the criminal I was being paid to capture.

"And who is this gorgeous creature?" Humphrey gripped his chest like he was having some kind of attack. "*Please* tell me you're a fan of our venerable detective."

"Devon Atwood," I said, receiving the same vigorous

handshake as Abe. "And I've read *The Hound of the Baskervilles* ten times." Unlike my name, that was not a lie.

"Praise be," Humphrey cheered. "Truly, I've heard much of you Ms. Atwood. You've taken all of these gents in this room to tea, and yet you haven't called me?"

"Well, I haven't met you," I mused, giving him a flirtatious wink.

Abe cleared his throat and stared at the ground.

"I've been traveling. My mistake," Humphrey said. "I'm home this week and available to be enchanted by you."

My answering smile was absolutely genuine. "We'll be in touch."

"Sorry, Daniel, I've completely forgotten you were standing there," Humphrey said to Abe.

"Understood," Abe said dryly. "Were you traveling with Bernard? How long have you known each other?"

Humphrey stepped close. "I've known him since we were ten years old. Went to school together, university, joined the Society together. As we've gotten older, we've stayed in touch through these events. And I drag him to the pub about once a month when he's not too busy changing the world and bringing books to people who need them."

In all of my research, I'd had no idea Bernard had a close friend. It seemed far too pedestrian—and precious—for a man so slyly deceitful.

"How charming," Abe said softly.

"Do you know where Bernard is?" Humphrey asked, swiftly changing the subject. His worried voice carried in the hushed room. Eudora's head snapped up at the words.

"Um... no," Abe stuttered. Clearly as surprised as I was. "I do not know where he is."

"It's not like him," Humphrey said, looking agitated. "We always talk. He sent me one email, months ago, letting me know he'd be on sabbatical and *off the grid*. Eudora assures me he's fine but..."

I almost went to catch Abe's eye before I remembered we were *absolutely* not working together. The urge was there— to tug on my earlobe or flash him a secret code. To get his sense of the situation. Strange, because I'd never, ever worked with a partner before and didn't need one now.

"I'm sorry to hear you're so worried," Abe said.

Humphrey nodded, shrugging it off before checking a giant wristwatch. "Bollocks. Sorry to vent and run, but off I go. Hope I don't bore this enchantress to tears."

With a rather saucy wink, Humphrey left Abe and me fairly surprised.

"So... you read *Hound of the Baskervilles* ten times?" Abe asked, facing me.

"Not a lie actually," I said. "I am a fan."

"When I was in high school, I read *A Study in Scarlett* every night for a week," he said. He was being honest, I could tell.

"You would look handsome holding a pipe," I said.

"So what are you doing taking these *gents* to tea, Ms. Atwood?" he asked, voice light.

"Jealous?"

"Hardly."

"Shall I take you to tea?"

"Now that," he said, "would make Humphrey jealous."

I cracked a big smile before I could help it.

"Truly enchanting," Abe said, so softly I almost missed it. The lights dimmed, and Humphrey took the stage, practically by force. He gripped the podium to hoots and cheers and slightly rowdy clapping.

"Keep it friendly now," Humphrey mock chided. He towered on the stage. It was impossible to picture him being

KATHRYN NOLAN

friends with *Bernie*. Especially since Bernard's characteristics—from what I could tell—so successfully mimicked my parents. 'Friends' were steppingstones, marks to be used to gain entry to whatever dodgy world they were attempting to gain access to. Humphrey didn't have the look of a *steppingstone*. He was solid, happy, and he cared for Bernard. And seemed as confused as Abe at Bernard's whereabouts.

"Like many of us in this room," Humphrey began, "I despise modern technology, and proudly. And nowhere is that more evident than when I am entrenched in Victorian London, following Holmes and Watson to St. Bart's Hospital or the Café Royal. Deduction was the key, listening was the key. Paying bloody *attention*. Our universe is much too clever, much too complicated, for our connections to each other to be arbitrary."

Next to me, Abe shifted an inch closer until our arms brushed. Bathed in darkness, it was harder to resist the primal pull the man evoked in me. He was temptation personified.

"Don't place too much faith in the strange coincidences, the déjà vu, the dreams that bear a startling likeness to our reality. Doyle wanted us to know these things are never, ever random. They are vital, they are connectors, they are the *truth*." With a rather wolfish grin, Humphrey stared right at Abe and me, drifting against each other in the sea of Holmes fanatics. "The people we meet are all part of the universe's plan."

Abe Royal dropped his mouth against my ear. I swallowed a gasp. The feeling was too seductive—the hint of breath, the suggestion of teeth, his raspy voice. "You must be part of the universe's plan, Ms. Atwood."

"Because I happen to be staying in the hotel room right next to yours?" I replied, voice shaky.

"No." He growled softly. "Because, like Doyle, I don't believe in *bloody* coincidences, either. If the queen of lies is going to pick my pockets and follow me around London, there's a reason for it. And I aim to find out why."

I turned my head to gaze up at him. With a slight smirk and a tilt to his brow, his face said *Gotcha*.

Mouse, meet cat.

## 10

### ABE

*H*umphrey Hatcher, Bernard's oldest friend, gave a powerful speech at the podium in front of us. *Bernie's* friend. Was it possible there was someone in Bernard's life that loved him like a friend...and had no idea he was a criminal mastermind? Although I shouldn't have been shocked. Henry had been his colleague and confidant, and the man had concealed his true nature easily.

Next to me, the woman who had been charming the members of the Sherlock Society scooped her long, jet-black hair over her left shoulder, exposing the elegant line of her throat, the arch of her high cheekbones. *These things are never, ever random.*

Her dramatic appearance in my life was *definitely* not random. She was a lying, clever pickpocket who had tailed me from The Langham Hotel to the Sherlock Society building with the skill of a federal agent.

I'd only caught her because *I* was a former federal agent.

*A queen of lies.* A breathtakingly beautiful one. I'd been far too tempted to brush my lips along her temple when I'd whispered in her ear; instead, I'd soothed myself with a deep inhale of her scent. Earthy, rich, mysterious. Before the lights had dimmed, I'd caught the freckles that decorated the bridge of her nose, barely visible against her warm skin.

Uncovering the mystery of Devon Atwood felt like a critical clue, positively screaming in my face. The fact that uncovering her mystery meant getting close to her shouldn't have made my chest feel light rather than its usual daily heaviness.

It shouldn't have made me want to unravel her many secrets while I unraveled every article of clothing from her body. If Sam or Henry were here, I'd ask them to physically shake the stupidity out of me. Actually—I'd have Delilah clock one across my face. Anything to shake me from this siren's song.

The applause at the end of Humphrey's speech brought me back into the space, the deerstalker hats, the pipes, the cheerful conversations around me.

"Shots?" Devon said.

"Excuse me?" I asked, sure I misheard her.

"I'm walking to the bar," she said, pointing to the back. "And I'm going to order shots. For the two of us."

Without waiting for my response, she swayed confidently over to the bartender, and I followed her like a heartsick sailor. *Enjoy your fucking vacation.* Something told me Freya and Delilah would do shots of vodka if they vacationed together. It was what people did for fun, right? A few weeks ago, the Codex team had spent a Sunday drinking beer at a brewery near our offices. Freya had threatened to kidnap and drag me to join them. But I'd declined, a hundred times, even though my only plan was to work.

The next day, as Freya showed me pictures of the four of them on her phone, I'd felt that odd *tugging* sensation in my chest again. A retroactive yearning to have been there, laughing, enjoying the sunshine because wasn't that what life was about? Freya had accused me of having *fomo* which I still refused to learn the true definition of.

The day of my mother's car accident was the day my entire life imploded. From then on, too many people had relied on me to ever truly relax—the teams of federal agents I used to lead, the team at Codex, my mother and Jeanette. Fun was a luxury I was happy to deny myself. And being a strong, professional leader was important to me. Bringing donuts into the office to celebrate closing cases was one thing; drinking beer in the sunshine felt indulgent and decidedly *un*professional.

Although that tendency to remain separate also brought me a large amount of fear. My father had never contacted my mother and I again, so I would never know the full story of why he left the day after his wife was in a terrible car accident. In my mind, it was easy to imagine my aloof father flipping a switch from *on* to *off*. *On* meant he loved his family, was dedicated to providing for them. *Off* meant he could walk out with nary a care in the world.

*On, off.*

The bartender—who bore a handlebar mustache and a checkered vest—poured, sent two shot glasses coasting across the bar. Devon caught them easily, pressing one into my hand.

"The last time I did *this*," I said, indicating the glass. "I was a senior in college." Guessing the gap in our ages, I added, "So twenty years ago."

A lift of her chin. "An older man. I like it."

I stared at her—the longer I drowned in those midnight eyes, the less any of my hang-ups mattered. The less *anything* mattered.

"When did you leave college?" I asked.

"Six years ago."

*For fuck's sake*, I'd spent the past two days lusting after a woman who was fourteen years younger than me.

"Don't worry," she said, probably noting the wariness in my expression, "I have an old soul."

"And why is that?"

She shook her head, snagging her lower lip with her front teeth. "Not yet. Shots first, truth after. Unless you think I'm only capable of telling lies."

"I think it's more likely you'll make off with my wallet," I drawled.

Her eyes flashed with humor. "The *truth* is you were actually impressed with my skills." She clinked our glasses together. "Truth? Or lie?"

I held the glass to my lips. Thought about how unbearably aroused I'd been that night, when I realized the most beautiful woman I'd ever fucking seen had bested me.

I took the shot. "Truth."

And goddamn the liquor felt good going down. All around us rose the chattering excitement of the audience; music was piped in over speakers. It was a happy crowd, an academic crowd. Yet the woman in front of me dominated every sense, demanded I pay attention to her and no one else.

So I shed my jacket, unhooked my cuff-links. Slowly rolled up my sleeves. Devon arched a haughty brow. I indicated her still-full shot glass, thought about a burning question I'd had since we'd stepped into the elevator together.

"You booked a room at The Langham Hotel only after I told you I was staying there."

She picked up the glass, drawing the moment out. "Is that so?"

"I *assumed* you were staying there the night we met," I

said. "You never confirmed it. And yet the next day you're suddenly my neighbor."

She raised the glass to her lips. Playful. Then she knocked it back smoothly.

"Truth." She grinned when she saw my face. "Don't get cocky."

"I would never," I said evenly.

She hooked the tip of her boot into the rung of my barstool and pulled herself directly into my space. Our mouths, our lips, were barely a foot apart. A wall of her body heat hit me, sending even more blood south. If the goddess looked down, she'd absolutely see the outline of my erection.

"Your name is Abraham Royal, and you're a private detective."

My heart stuttered, stopped, re-started at twice its regular beats. It was the sound of my real name falling from her lips, the delicious curve on every syllable. She'd stolen my business card—I *knew* she knew who I was. But this admission felt like honesty.

"Truth," I said, voice rough at the end.

A strand of unruly black hair fell across her face. With sure fingers, I brushed it back behind her ear, cupped the back of her neck. Pure, rampant lust exploded across her face. I was grateful for it, grateful I wasn't the only one chained to this erotic wildness.

"You're not a Sherlock Holmes tourist," I said. "Are you?"

She leaned even closer. "No."

My hand tightened on the back of her neck. Her lips tipped into a half-smile. "Two more shots please," she said over her shoulder. I was tempted to slide my hand beneath her dress, see what other truths might spill free.

She turned her face, watched the drinks being poured,

the glasses placed neatly in front of us by the bartender. The sudden glimpse of fear in her gaze shocked me. Slowly, Devon curled herself into my body, the pose as familiar as a girlfriend's.

"I'm going to tell you something bizarre, and you're going to need to act natural," she whispered. I stilled—but then smoothed my palm down the curtain of her hair, tugging her closer.

"Sounds like a plan," I whispered back.

"I'm pretty fucking sure the bartender slipped something into our shots just now."

I fought back the very human urge to turn and see for myself. "Is our friend still there?"

She faked a giggle, and I held her tighter—simply two people flirting, hugging, enjoying a romantic evening. "Yep," she said.

"Why on earth would we be targeted by a random bartender?"

My detective brain rattled through the usual crimes against tourists—mugging, stealing their credit cards, petty theft. *Coincidence*, I wanted to say—except Devon and I were both, potentially, skulking around a secret that was much larger than petty theft. In my arms, she was rigid, muscles primed. I was still turned in the opposite direction, facing the door we'd come through. Humphrey caught my eye in the crowd and gave a funny little dance. Such a prosaic scene surrounding us as Devon attempted to assess if we were about to be poisoned.

She flinched suddenly—no, not flinched. Devon cursed and *fled* from my arms before I could stop her.

"Wait—" I whispered, frantic. No bartender, no other workers tending the liquor. Only a door that said *Employees Only* now swinging back and forth from the force of Devon pushing through it. Humphrey shoved through the crowd, concern on his jovial face, as I attempted to roll down my sleeves and throw on my jacket with feigned ease. My heart was a veritable jackhammer as I scanned the bar, scooping up a small glass bottle rolling on its side. It was in my hand and hidden in my pocket just before Humphrey arrived.

Devon wasn't the only one with fast fingers.

"All right, lad?" Humphrey asked, staring at the back door. "Where'd the enchantress go?"

I huffed out a laugh. "Sprinted off. Saw a friend, I guess."

He nodded as if this made sense and slapped a meaty paw on my shoulder. "Chin up. I'm sure she leaves a lot of men looking as devastated as you do right now."

## 11

## SLOANE

*T*he bartender's sleight of hand would have impressed the hell out of my parents.

If I hadn't seen his fingers at *just* the right second, I would have missed it. The bartender with the handlebar mustache tipped a tiny glass of clear liquid into my shot glass and Abe's. One minute earlier, I'd been hazy with longing, thrilled by the electricity sparking between Abe and me. Every caress of his fingers, every truth he shared, only ignited my body's need for him.

It had dulled my senses to a fact I'd learned was always true—danger was ever-present. Peril always strikes the second you let your guard down. Curled against Abe's suit-clad chest, I was all fury, synapses firing as I put together what it might mean: another private detective was in London, searching for Bernard, surrounded by Bernard's closest and most trusted colleagues.

And a random bartender slips something into our drinks.

The moment I'd landed on my conclusion, the

bartender had tossed his towel and was escaping through the *Employees Only* door.

I ran after him without a thought to asking for help from the man I'd been revealing secrets to. Beneath that drive to chase down my biggest clue since starting this case was an urge to punch the shit out of a person who'd tried to harm Abe. I didn't have time to over-analyze these new protective feelings.

I sprinted down a long hallway and kicked open a back door.

The man I surprised in the alley wasn't the bartender. He *was* enormous, tall, and powerfully strong. And the second he saw me, he attacked.

The smirk on Big Guy's face only ratcheted up my fury. His left arm swung forward in a slow, sloppy punch.

Before he could connect, I slammed my palm directly into his nose.

"Jesus, *fuck you*," he snarled, tilting forward slightly. One hand protected his bloody nose, the other tried to lash at me again.

I ducked and grabbed his shirt, using gravity to propel my pointed heel into his groin. He yelped, dropped to his knees, and I dashed around him to check for the bartender at the end of the alley, on the street.

"Goddammit," I whispered. Where *was* he?

I felt his fingers tangled in my hair, yanking me backward. Big Guy returning with a vengeance.

I grabbed his hand, pain spiking across my scalp, and spun fast. My elbow cracked across his face as I *kicked kicked kicked* as fast as I could.

He let go, wailed again, but fear had hold of me now, wrapping around my throat and restricting my air. The rage on his face as he came at me a third time conveyed the reality that he was huge and angry and I was all by myself in a dark alley.

I opened my mouth to scream for help when a sharply dressed figure stepped between me and Big Guy.

Abe Royal. Who, while leaner, was as tall as Big Guy— and apparently much faster. Abe punched the attacker so hard he dropped to the ground immediately. I was bent over at the waist, panting, staring at my rescuer in disbelief.

Abe, to his credit, only shook out his fingers and nodded once at me. "Ms. Atwood."

"Thanks for the save," I said, catching my breath.

He surveyed the body on the ground. "I only did the last bit. You were magnificent with him."

My cheeks warmed at the unexpected compliment. "I've had training."

"I can see that." He studied me with concern.

I shook out my limbs, dispersing the adrenaline. Enjoyed the sense of safety his presence gave me, which I'd never yearned for before. This, this *having my back* thing was nice.

"How's your scalp?" he asked. I touched it, winced.

"Tender but fine." I held out my elbow, which also seemed to have survived. Kicked my boots out for his perusal. "These did the trick."

"I'm grateful for their existence." Abe looked both ways, past me toward the street. "Any sign of our friend?"

I shook my head. "And I don't know who in the hell this asshole—"

At my words, the asshole in question hauled himself upright and ran toward the street.

"Mother*fucker*," I said and bolted after him. We needed to know details. We needed to know why we'd been targeted. I needed to know how this related to Bernard.

A vice-like grip around my arm kept me in place. Abe.

"What are you doing?" I said, tugging at his hold. "We need to go *after* him."

Abe shook his head. "Chasing down goons only ends well with a calculated plan and effective weapons. Maybe some backup. Of which you have none."

"That's my lead," I hissed.

Understanding flooded his features. "Talk now, chase down goons later."

"Chase down goons now, talk later," I argued.

He tugged me close, until our faces were inches apart. "No more secrets. No more *fucking* lies. You and I are talking. Now."

He released me like a gentleman, stepping back and waving his hand toward the pub across the street. While his body language was loose, his tone indicated there'd be no more quarrel.

Deep down, I knew he was right—running after that guy was reckless and stupid. But one of the reasons I worked alone was instances like this. I didn't want to ask permission to do what my gut instinct demanded.

I was nothing if not an opportunist though, so if one clue was currently running down a London street, then the handsome-as-sin clue standing right in front of me would be the next best choice.

"I'm not a tourist. And you're not a man on vacation," I said shortly. "So I'm not going into that pub unless you give me information I can use."

Abe raised his palms, looking pissed, frustrated, and aroused all at once. "I'm not giving you information unless you tell me who you are."

"Deal," I finally said. I extended my hand, and he shook it, squeezing tight. Flames of desire licked along my skin where we touched, so instantaneous it robbed me of breath and burned through my rational thought.

One tug from Abe, and I'd fall into him; one tug from me, and he'd fall against me.

A muscle ticked in his jaw; my lips parted on a shaky breath.

"Deal," he said.

## 12

# SLOANE

*A*be and I ducked into a tiny pub right next to Adler's —a barely lit, cozy space with few patrons, which perfectly suited our need for a covert conversation. As I found a small table in a secluded corner, he walked to the bar and returned with a single whiskey, a bowl of ice, and two clean towels.

The whiskey sat untouched between us. Unlike before, during our game of vodka shots, I knew I needed to stay as clear-headed as possible to maintain my sure footing around this man. It was far too easy to cede control of rationality while staring at his devastatingly handsome face.

"For your elbow," he said, pushing the bowl of ice toward me with a single finger. "It'll bruise tomorrow. That goon had a face like a brick fucking wall."

I stared down at the bowl, then back at Abe. Perhaps sensing my hesitation, he picked up two cubes of ice and wrapped them in the towel. Handed the bundle over to me. Cool relief spread through my body the second I placed it on my skin.

He was right. It was already bruising.

"Thanks," I said a little awkwardly. My brain struggled to process this gesture of kindness. Had my unconventional parents ever gotten me ice when I skinned my knees?

Abe examined his knuckles, which were bleeding. "It's been a few years since my hand-to-hand combat skills were used outside a boxing gym."

"I meant what I said back there." I nodded at my elbow. "The save was appreciated."

"Where did you learn to fight?" he asked.

It wouldn't help to lie at this point. The week after I'd escaped from my parents, I enrolled in my first self-defense class. It wasn't that I was physically afraid of my parents. I was, however, physically afraid of the people they'd defrauded. And once I started getting paid to take pictures of furious spouses, well... it was smart.

"I have about six years of self-defense training, including Krav Maga and mixed martial arts. A little boxing too."

"Why did you start?" he asked.

"Safety."

His eyes narrowed. "From what?"

"My family." His face registered the slightest jolt. That was too much truth, even for our game. "Anyway," I said quickly. "You should put ice on those too."

He did as he was told, resting his knuckles in the bowl. The other hand reached into his pocket and removed a small glass bottle with a dropper on the end. "Thank you for interrupting our poisoning mid-act. Is this what you saw the bartender use?"

Surprised, eager, I dropped the ice and grabbed the bottle. Scrawled on the side were the words *gamma-hydroxybutyric acid*.

"GHB," he said, face impassive but fingers flexing.

"The date rape drug?" I said, shocked. "Do you think that guy in the alley was supposed to mug us?"

"Did he go for your wallet though?" Abe asked.

I shook my head, mind racing as I ran through the possibilities.

"Although, to be fair, I believe you scared him off."

I grinned. "He thought fighting me would be easy."

"Nothing about you is easy," he said quietly. "In smaller amounts, if we'd taken those shots, the GHB would have made us groggy. Easier to attack."

"But why?" I asked.

He was shaking his head. "I think the *why* might be uncovered when you tell me who the hell you really are and why you're lying all over the goddamn place."

I hesitated, suddenly unsure now that I was facing admitting who I was and potentially threatening my chances of capturing Bernard on my own. My deadline hovered between us—*eleven days left*. All this time here, and real, juicy leads hadn't started appearing until Abe Royal had landed in London. Actually saying the words *I need your help* to another person went against every fiber of my being. I didn't need help. What I needed was information, money, and opportunity.

I looked at Abe, pictured myself receiving that check from Louisa and all the professional goodwill that could come of it. This man had *information*. And if I played my cards right, it could lead me to that money and opportunity.

Reaching into my purse, I removed my private investigator's license and my own business card. Laid them on the table. He placed his license right next to mine. I picked his up, studied his official documents.

"Nice to meet you Abe Royal of Codex," I said.

"Not new information for you though, is it?" he countered.

I stayed silent, watched his whole-body reaction to reading my own license. Fingers tight, brow furrowed. "You're a private detective?"

His voice scraped across every nerve ending. "Sure am," I replied.

"*Sloane Argento.*" Each syllable out of his mouth was curved, slow. Savored.

In my seventeen years living with them, I'd worn any number of names—until answering to a name not my own was as comfortable as an old, favorite sweater. Being Devon Atwood had felt absolutely fine, normal even. When I'd finally left my parents, I'd kept my birth name. My real one. And even though my first name was chosen by my mother and my last was all I knew of my father's Italian heritage, it still felt like *mine*.

"Argento Enterprises?" He held up my business card. "This is you?"

"It's my firm in Brooklyn," I said. "I opened it the year after I graduated from NYU."

Abe placed both hands on the table. "It's nice to formally meet you, Sloane Argento. It appears I am vindicated in my assessment that you are not, in fact, a Devon."

"And you're no Daniel."

"So why are you masquerading as a Sherlock Holmes enthusiast and taking members of the Society to tea?" he asked.

I tilted my head, stalling. Tapped my nails on the table. "I've been hired by the McMaster's Library to find Bernard Allerton."

The sentence plummeted between us like an anvil. Abe's

jaw tightened to the point of breaking, irritation carved into his face. "Louisa Davies hired you?"

"Officially, she's my client," I said. "I know she almost hired you eleven months ago, when Bernard went on the run and you met Dr. Henry Finch for the first time."

"That I did." His tone was brittle. "I thought she was making a mistake. Still believe she made a mistake."

I lifted a shoulder. "I agree with you. Louisa is frustrated with Interpol and the Bureau and thinks they're not doing enough to find him. She thought a PI could find him more quickly, and she's willing to pay a lot of fucking money for it."

"Color me surprised," he drawled. "Yet *you* got the contract. Not me."

"I've done my research on you, Mr. Royal," I said. "Codex hasn't been sitting idle."

He was silent for a moment, turning the whiskey glass around on the table. "We've been busy, yes."

"Louisa contacted me after the Audubon case I solved three months ago," I explained. "For The Murphy Library in New York."

Abe looked pleasantly surprised. "That was you?"

"Sure was."

He cleared his throat, slid his arms back down his side. "My team talked about that case nonstop. We were impressed."

I fought a smile at the thought of Abe Royal being impressed with me months ago, before we'd known each other, before all of this, before everything.

"Your cover, the Society, the dinners with people...?"

"Research," I said. "Trying to meet sources that can lead me to where he's hiding."

"And you think he's in London?" he asked.

"Don't you?"

"Believe me, if I knew where that man was, I wouldn't be sitting here," he replied, sardonic. The hunger to catch this criminal was so fucking *obvious*—it was his body language, his face, the curl of his lip. From the moment I'd said *Bernard,* he was mere seconds away from snapping.

"Why did you come to London if you don't think he's here?"

"I'm here on vacation." He shrugged.

I leaned across the table, felt that dangerous chemistry stretched taut between us. Abe's throat worked as his eyes trailed down my throat, my collarbone, my breasts.

"I've been given access to his office and all of his papers," I said. Then watched him almost flip the table over.

"His what?" His tone was sharp enough to cut.

I sat back, crossed my arms. "All of Bernard's papers, his entire office at the McMaster's Library, are available for me. There's interesting stuff in there."

Abe's assurance that he was here for leisure was pissing me off. He'd promised me information, yet he kept avoiding his true motivations. He was practically vibrating across from me.

"How nice for you," he finally said, each word grating through his clenched teeth.

"That afternoon, before we met at Eudora's talk, I'd been with Louisa, asking her questions about Henry," I said. "She told me all about you, about Codex, how Henry left his job to go work for you."

Abe's inflection held a fair amount of warning. "Henry Finch is innocent and was cleared of *all* suspicions. If he hadn't been, I wouldn't have hired him."

"I don't doubt it," I said. "Seems like he was a private detective in the making."

"And an ethical and brilliant man," he said.

My chest tightened at the devotion in his voice—my lonely soul recognized a similar one in Abraham Royal. He appeared to be fiercely independent. But a *tiny* part of me felt jealous that he had a... a *team*. A team he clearly admired.

I leaned in, dropped my voice. "You've been hot on Bernard's heels for months now. It's why you're here, in London, using a fake name and meeting with Bernard's closest friends and colleagues. If you're my competition, I want to know who I'm racing against. And if you're not, and you have pertinent information I could use, I'd gladly take it, per our deal."

He picked up the glass of whiskey and took a long, slow sip. His steel gaze remained on my face the entire time until I felt heat in my cheeks. "I abhor loose ends. When I arrived in London and learned about Bernard's role in the Society, I followed my instincts to that lecture. The auction of the Doyle papers intrigued me, so I used an undercover name." He set the glass down. "It was a mistake. A minor detour in my vacation plans. That's the truth, as much as it pains me to admit it. My team could tell you that *leisure* isn't my strong suit."

"I don't believe it was a mistake *or* a minor detour," I shot back.

"Believe what you will, Ms. Argento. I'm not your competition. And you can follow me, tail me, steal from me, stay in the hotel room next to me... I won't break. Although I'm glad to finally understand why you wouldn't leave me alone."

It might have been my imagination, but Abe seemed briefly hurt. Which caused a corresponding sensation in my *own* body. I just didn't think it right, in this moment of tense truth-telling, to grab him by the face and admit my all-consuming lust had a fair amount to do with my actions too. This yearning I had to be around him was equal parts exhilarating and baffling. The sheer urgency of this case hovered between us—my timeline, my contract, the stakes, everything. I'd already bared my name and a handful of other secrets. He didn't need to know about his erotic presence in my dreams or my many, many fantasies.

"I was seeking your sources," I said. "And I'd like the record to show that you're full of shit."

His chuckle was humorless. "That might be true, but you are free to pursue Bernard Allerton at your leisure. I am a private detective, not a vigilante. If I had a case, a contract, a client, this would be different. The *books* that are stolen are, above all else, my investigative priority. Taking down Bernard is one piece of a system that's gone rotten. My interest is in the whole system, not just one man."

My lip curled with a swift anger that shocked me. "Bernard *is* the system. He's a psychopath who deserves to be in prison."

A softness entered his gaze. A pause. Then, "We don't disagree."

Abe twisted the glass back and forth, ice hitting the side. "Bernard Allerton is no longer my purview. So you can be happy catching that psychopath."

"Do you have information that could help me?" I asked, feeling like a buzzard, picking for scraps. Yet the smallest detail could make the difference for me.

"I surely do not," he said mildly. "You don't have a team at your firm that could help you?"

"It's only me. Always has been." *And always would be.* "Why?"

He plucked at his cufflinks. "Seems like you were maybe asking to partner up and go after Bernard together."

I took the glass of whiskey from his fingers. Placed my mouth directly where his had just been and took a satisfying sip. "I've never worked with a partner before. Don't worry, that wasn't my motivation here, Abraham."

A sense of loss was already lodging itself in my sternum. I pressed my palm there, attempting to sooth the newness of feeling so raw. Every single second of my time spent with Abe these past thirty-six hours had been like diving through uncharted waters. A tiny voice in my head whispered *you're going to miss him.*

"Okay then," he said. "Now that we've fought off an attacker together and I've learned your true identity, we can go about our business separately. I've got plans the next few days to enjoy all the rich culture that London has to offer. I doubt we'll see each other again, except coming and going at The Langham."

This was what I wanted—to clear the air between us, uncover his real purpose, and get back to the hunt. So I wasn't sure why my emotions felt so out of *control* as we reached the natural end of our... whatever this was. *What was it?*

I pointed at the vial that had held GHB meant for both of us. "What would you like to do about our imminent brush with illegal drugs?"

He reached across the table, stole his whiskey glass from my fingers. Took another generous sip. "Tourists get drugged and mugged all of the time. It's natural to read into things when you're in the thick of an active investigation. We were two loud Americans getting intoxicated. We were a target for a crime of opportunity."

"Would Bernard know what you looked like, Abe?" I asked.

*There*. Another flicker of curiosity—more than that. A tangible passion. He was desperate and denying himself. "Why would he know that?"

I lifted a shoulder. "You currently employ the man who sent him underground. I'd know what you looked like."

He tapped the glass. "We were targeted for a crime of opportunity. I'd drop it."

*That* didn't match what my instincts were telling me at all, but if Abe Royal was going to be this stubborn and prideful, we'd reached the end of the road.

I stood, pocketing my things and tossing some cash down onto the table. "Consider it dropped," I said. I took the little vial with me though. "Have fun on your vacation."

His entire body flexed and tensed, as if he was bound to his chair by invisible rope. With a curt nod, he said, "I shall see you around. Neighbor."

I yearned for a pithy response and came up empty, feeling flipped upside down by the surge of anger, frustration, need, lust coursing through my veins.

And hurt. That was there too, buried beneath the other, more vocal, emotions. Since graduating from NYU, there hadn't been much effort made on my part to meet people or make friends beyond the occasional one-night stand or brief fling. My love life centered around anonymity—I preferred my partners to know as little about me, or my past, as possible. And in college, attempting to make those friendly connections was like trying to learn a brand-new language not a single person had ever taken the time to teach me.

On the occasions that I attended a campus party or a study group or a dining hall rendezvous, their experiences and memories were bizarre to me—the little coded ways they spoke to each other, their teasing and affection. I believed this social comfort came from people who grew up with siblings or friends, who went on field trips or had back-yard birthday parties. More often than not, I'd leave feeling embarrassed or at the very least confused. At the end of the day, I found it easier to not try at all.

So I opted for turning on my heel and striding out of that pub without a clever goodbye for Abe Royal. And as I walked down the street, heading back to The Langham Hotel, I recognized the familiar feelings of embarrassment and confusion, of longing for something I didn't under-stand. Maybe, just maybe, I *had* been trying to partner with Abe on this case.

Those were deceiving thoughts. I was better off alone anyway.

## 13

### ABE

The lights in the Royal Opera House dimmed. The luxurious red-and-gold curtain opened on the stage, revealing the symphony orchestra and their instruments. The conductor bowed to the audience and turned to her musicians, who held themselves still, awaiting instruction. The long note of silence echoed in the hushed room—perhaps the most beautiful room I had ever seen. The domed ceiling sparkled with golden designs that mimicked a Renaissance classic.

The opening strings of Bach's *Concerto for 2 Violins in D Minor* sang throughout the grandiose room, growing louder as the rest of the instruments joined in.

I closed my eyes, let the rich sound wash over me, stirring feelings I'd rather not explore. This moment in time was true leisure, true pleasure—a *true* vacation.

Every note from the violin loosened the hard coil in my chest that contained my anger toward my father's betrayal.

Every note soothed the remnants of work stress, calmed the edges of my anxieties about cases and close rates and worrying that my team would get hurt while undercover.

Every note made me feel more like a man, less like a workaholic that generated outputs. Surrounded by London's elite, seated in a building known for its opulence, it wasn't easy for me to turn off the part of my brain desperately seeking criminals. Yet in the face of such gorgeous music, couldn't I *enjoy* myself for a change?

The final note held, sustained, captivated every person in the audience. As they cheered and clapped, I shook my head and smiled to myself. *Music, culture, history*. Maybe it made me odd, but a reminder that I actually had hobbies now and again was a good thing. They were easily forgotten in the sheer intensity of my thirst for justice.

The crowd quieted, and the next song began. To my right, a young woman with jet-black hair walked down the narrow aisle and sat. I smiled once more, wider this time, already preparing to feign surprise that Devon—*Sloane* —was tailing me again.

It had been two days since she'd sauntered out of that pub without a goodbye. I'm sure it wasn't possible to miss someone you barely knew. Yet during those days, I'd felt slightly lop-sided and disappointed at every tourist location I visited only to find myself... alone.

Every minute of that strange evening had been a combination of thrilling, frustrating, illuminating—and sexually arousing. After pocketing the tiny vial of GHB, I'd rushed around the front of the pub and heard sounds of a fight from the alley. It was Sloane, fighting off a giant attacker with a set of skills that rivaled my own. The very first puzzle piece began slotting into place then. And by the time I was picking up her private investigator's license, it finally all made sense. A charming personality, a fake name, sly motivations, and a palm-strike straight from a Bureau textbook.

She was a detective. And not just any. Sloane had the job

I'd desperately wanted eleven months ago, the job stolen from me because Louisa had opted to bring in the formal authorities. It was hard to fault her decision. Bernard *was* a criminal mastermind and technically should have been handled accordingly.

Except *goddamn* if my pride hadn't taken notice that Louisa was now, potentially, regretting her decision. Not enough to re-hire me, no. She had sought out a bright, young, talented detective who could absolutely do the job asked of her. Including what I would have done if I'd suspected another detective was on my same trail—follow him until he gave up a clue.

I shifted in my seat and tried to catch Sloane's eye in the row far ahead. That curtain of black hair shone in the golden light and obscured her face. She had displayed her secrets for me, and I'd purposefully refrained from sharing *all* of my information. The email, the start of all of this, was private, and it would stay that way.

*Even if you should tell your team about it?*

I coughed, cleared my throat. Closed my eyes to focus on the music again, the slide and pluck of every note from the cello.

Maybe... maybe I should have cautioned Sloane that the Kensley auction of Doyle's private papers was the incident that had really captured my attention. Maybe I should have shared the code words or my old reports. *Maybe* I should have added that Eudora Green appeared shifty and morally gray to me, and if there was anyone to watch, it'd be her. Maybe—

I gripped the arm rests and manually forced my mind to listen to every fucking musical note. Sloane had resources, time, and access to the intimate documents of Bernard's life. She had made it clear that if I couldn't disclose any details for her, there was no reason to continue our cat-and-mouse. Whatever attraction she might have felt toward me was clearly not the priority. Her priority was to catch Bernard using everything she had. I *absolutely* could not fault her for putting her client, and her contract, first.

And I *absolutely* wanted her to be following me now for a better, more personal reason.

The tone of the music shifted, turned slow and elegant. A melodic tease for the senses. I sank back into that space of leisure granted me by every note. I'd been correct in my intuition that the goddess wasn't a Devon. *Sloane* fit her like a glove; *Sloane* was a better descriptor of her earthy sex-appeal and sultry allure. And Sloane hadn't vanished from my thoughts after coming clean and revealing all of her mysteries. Instead, she had taken up permanent residence in my hourly sexual fantasies and tormented my every dream.

All night long, she had taunted me, crawling up my body with her hair wild around her face, trailing the silky ends across my stomach. Over and over I palmed breasts cupped in pink lace, ran my tongue along the column of her throat as she moaned. The last image I remembered was her lithe body—pinned beneath mine—as we rocked against each other in a furious, uncontrolled rhythm. I woke with my face buried in my pillow, grinding my hips into the mattress in a vivid interpretation of what I had been doing to her in my dream.

What happened next didn't spring from any semblance of real, rational thought—more biological need. I rolled onto my back, took my cock in hand, let myself fall back into the fantasy. Except this time it was no dream, and I had full command. Which was my preference, anyway. My fingers worked, stroking up and down, while I entwined my fingers with Sloane's in the ornate, metal headboard. Her legs wrapped high around my waist as I fucked her in a sweaty, panting, demanding rhythm. The fantasy could be called romantic if loud, bruising, animalistic sex was a person's idea of romance. It certainly was mine. The Sloane I fucked in my fantasy felt the same way—her orgasmic euphoria had my hips thrusting off the mattress and come spilling down my fingers. I hadn't been quiet either, and I prayed to every god I knew that she hadn't heard me through our shared wall.

The lights in the Royal Opera House slowly brightened, filling the room with a warm, glittering glow. Intermission had begun. I immediately searched for Sloane and caught a glimpse of black hair moving toward the lobby. Straightening my tie and re-buttoning my suit jacket, I walked confidently into the large room, filled with elegantly dressed patrons sipping from glasses of champagne. I located the goddess, moved past groups of people, reached out and touched her wrist.

"I'll remind you again, Ms. Argento, you can knock on my door if you want my attention. You don't need to keep up this charade of following me everywhere." I paused, waited for her to turn around.

And when she did, it was decidedly *not* the gorgeous private detective. This woman's mouth dropped, hand flying to her chest. "I'm sorry, what?"

"My apologies," I said quickly. "I thought you were a friend."

I walked back into the red-and-gold room before embarrassment could get the best of me. Embarrassment and disappointment, which was numbing the former effects of all that glorious, leisurely music.

My phone buzzed with a text from Delilah—a picture of

my desk with Sam sitting behind it doing an extremely dramatic *glower* I was sure was meant to be an impersonation of me. Freya and Henry were pretending to cower, hands above their heads, while Delilah grinned goofily right at the camera. *Things are getting weird without you, Abe,* she'd written. *Don't worry, Sam was happy to step into your role of Office Dad/Dictator. Freya and Henry were scared yet obedient.*

Another buzz. Another text—this one from Sam. *We had been drinking, sir.*

I scrubbed a hand down my face, smiling at their antics. I started and stopped a dozen different replies before landing on: *Happy to hear I've been replaced by someone with such a talent for Dictator-ing. Will be shopping for your souvenirs tomorrow. Send requests please and keep it PG.*

I withheld the rest, even though everything that had happened to me in the last days would have shocked them to their core. *Would Bernard know what you looked like?*

Every feeling of guilt rose to the surface yet again. Until the magic of the symphony, I'd felt inklings of this the past two days and had restrained it as best I could, distracted myself with sight-seeing and fine whiskey. I'd been in the field of criminal justice for far too long. I knew when the facts presented to you, the story you *told* yourself, no longer made sense. It happened all the time at the Bureau; for whatever reason, an agent would latch onto a potential suspect even as their viability unraveled in the most obvious ways. The story no longer matched the facts.

And these were the hard facts: in four days, a priceless collection of Doyle's papers would be auctioned off at London's premier auction house. Years ago, Bernard had desperately wanted to own Doyle's papers, and they were taken from him, publicly. Louisa had dispatched a private detective to track down her former employee. The moment I met with one of Bernard's closest colleagues, Eudora, and gave her the *Reichenbach Falls* code word, Sloane and I were almost drugged and attacked in an alley.

There was another problematic detail I hadn't mentioned to Sloane at that pub. I couldn't trust what I'd seen because the alley had been dark, and my recollection was hazy. But the man, the attacker, was giant and broad and had a military-style haircut. Plenty of men fit that description. As did the Dresden guards, the rich-and-shady security company used by the famous heiress Victoria Whitney, Bernard, *and* The Empty House.

On stage, the musicians began filing back into their seats. The lights flicked once, twice.

And I seriously considered stepping out of the Royal Opera House and calling my team.

We'd followed hunches before—most notably Delilah, who correctly guessed that Victoria had stolen a priceless artifact from The Franklin Museum. That had been pure intuition, and I'd been happy to trust her bloodhound instincts. All four of them would be here in an instant.

Distracted, I leaned forward in my seat, elbows on my knees. The musicians were picking up bows and arranging string instruments. The conductor walked out to applause and the remaining patrons sat back in their seats.

*Would* Bernard Allerton know what I looked like?

I swiped my thumb across my phone, pictured flying my team out here only to have us lose Bernard for the fourth fucking time. I winced inwardly, remembering how cheerfully Sloane had called my bluff. *You are full of shit.* This woman barely knew me, yet she could sense my desperation for vengeance regardless of how forcefully I denied it.

My father had been like this, even before he'd walked out the door that fateful night. He was vindictive and imperious, always needing to get what he wanted regardless of the harm it caused in the process.

The not-Sloane woman sat down in her seat. I caught her giving me a strange look. I settled back, let out an exhale as the cello released a note of sweet melancholy.

I deserved this vacation. I deserved this time. Louisa had moved on and hired Sloane Argento, who would probably be the person to *actually* capture Bernard. Whatever dreams I'd entertained of being *the one* needed to be let go of once and for all.

## 14

## SLOANE

*F*orty-eight hours after leaving Abe in that tiny pub, and I was back in it. I was on day two of a long and boring stakeout. And the skies above threatened thunderstorms. I had a troubling and total fear of thunder—a bone-deep, primal reaction that led me to shake and panic. London had been rainy and dreary, but I'd avoided a thunderstorm so far.

I swallowed around a lump of nerves and nursed my martini.

The long and boring stakeout had started yesterday afternoon. In the morning I'd woken energized and focused. And whatever strong feelings of longing or lust I might have felt for my hotel-room-neighbor I mentally crushed with my stiletto-heeled boot.

I had nine days left, a fact Louisa made sure to remind me of when I called to check in with her that morning. The auction of Arthur Conan Doyle's private papers was in four days. Abe had offered little in usable information, and so I went back to my first juicy clue: the bartender.

If my instincts were correct, the bartender and the Big

Guy who had attacked us were working together. Find one, find the other, find out who was paying them to scare and threaten two private detectives searching for Bernard Allerton. So now I sat at the window, watching Mycroft's Pub across the street and hoping I didn't look too obvious.

The amount of money I'd be paid if—*when*—I caught Bernard played on a loop in my brain. Money, opportunity, freedom. Recovering those prints from *Birds of America* for The Murphy Library had been the crucial entrance into this world. And catching Bernard was *the* ticket to bigger clients, better jobs, and a chance to be free from any financial burdens holding me back. As disappointed as I'd been after leaving Abe that night, I'd reminded myself that this meant if I discovered a straight shot at Bernard, I'd be the one to take it.

There was a rumble in the distance that could have been a train. I took a fortifying sip of vodka, enjoyed the burn in my chest. The bookstore, Adler's, was lit full of patrons tonight. I'd watched from the side window as they came and went in the past two hours, and now a small circle was set up with people on chairs. A bearded white man, maybe mid-thirties, was leading a discussion and pointing to a book at the same time.

A door opened in the back of the pub and my eyes darted to the sound. Seemed like regulars, laughing with each other, cheering about a sporting event. I watched them as covertly as possible, drinking my martini. They appeared harmless. Yesterday I'd camped out here, ordering drinks and meals every few hours, and no one had noticed or at least hadn't cared. Today, it was more obvious I was sitting here, by myself—not talking to a single soul. I'd come undercover as Devon, carrying Sherlock Holmes mysteries and prepared to give a story to any Society members that could spot me here, somewhat out in the open. *Just resting my feet after a few frantic days of sight-seeing!*

No one had bothered me, yet. For every second I observed Mycroft's for movement, I kept one ear trained on my surroundings. I was no stranger to the shady underbelly that existed in the brightest of places.

My first case, when I was barely twenty-three years old, was a simple cheating spouse. I'd been given a presumed location by a scorned wife and found myself in a run-down motel parking lot awaiting this woman's husband and his mistress.

I'd barely concealed myself as the pair made their way past parked cars and toward room #6. My entire childhood was spent engaged in illegal con tricks with my parents, where every day was cloaked in a malicious secrecy. But being a PI was legal, and I was performing a contractual service, all of which numbed my senses to fear. In the broad daylight, surrounded by a busy street and a handful of strip-malls and photographing a middle-aged man, I felt not a hint of threat.

The cheating couple was on top of me a second later, their violence born from the terror of getting caught. The husband ripped the camera right from my hands and smashed it to the ground. The mistress was a force to be reckoned with, and I'd only escaped her clutches by using the self-defense moves I'd been practicing at night. Later, back at my apartment, I realized how extremely lucky I'd gotten. I didn't believe in nine lives. Just this one.

I didn't make a mistake like that ever again. And if I wasn't going to have the extra safety of a partner—Abe— then I couldn't afford to lose focus.

Another rumble in the distance. I twisted in my seat, bringing my ear closer to the windowpane. Definitely a big

truck. I released a breath, pressing a loose strand of hair back into my high bun. If there was a storm tonight, would I go to Abe? Knock on his door and beg him to... what? Take care of a practical stranger who had stolen from him and followed him around like a weirdo?

Besides, I'd never told *anyone* about the night my parents had left me alone in a motel even dingier than the one where a cheating spouse had tried to beat me up. I had been seven, and my parents were working a long con on a rich couple in the area, attempting to gain access to their circle of wealthy friends so they could commit identity fraud. My parents loved this kind of manipulate-cheat-dash lifestyle. We were staying in a midwestern city in Tornado Alley. My parents had left the TV on for me, tuned to the weather channel, and they hadn't returned until the early morning. All night, the scariest thunderstorm I'd ever seen thrashed the tiny motel, rattling the windows. Water leaked in from the bathroom window, and the electricity went out. Right before, the newscaster had been talking about dark, greenish skies and potential hail.

Signs of an impending tornado. And my parents didn't return until breakfast the next morning. I only recalled the starkest, iciest terror I'd ever known. Alone, at seven, convinced a tornado was going to destroy the motel and kill me.

The door at the back of the pub slammed closed, and the sound made me jump. I winced, cursed. Thinking about my parents never did any good except to fracture my focus. As if to prove a point, at that exact moment the goddamn bartender stepped out of Mycroft's Pub.

With Big Guy.

They were on the move, and so was I. Leaving my half-empty glass, I yanked a hat down onto my head, low over

my face, and slipped out of the bar, careful to not let the swinging door make a sound. Their body language was casual yet attuned to their surroundings. No conversation, simply heads down and on the move. I'd worn all black for the occasion—it was both my usual attire and worked well for sudden, covert stakeouts. I kept to the shadows, body pressed to each building, ducking into every alley I could as I kept my eye on them. Big Guy was still big; the bartender still looked like a Brooklyn hipster.

Neither of them noticed me. I hoped. About a quarter of a mile down the road they stopped. The buildings were mostly non-descript offices and stores. Nothing stood out. They slipped into a side alley to speak and I crept down a long wall to get close. I searched for fire escapes or open windows to sneak into. Their conversation was completely muffled by the sounds of London at night—cars, horns, more trucks rumbling. Glancing once behind my shoulder, I slipped out a pocket mirror, angled it towards them. Body language still casual, as in non-threatening. But Big Guy appeared upset, and the bartender appeared neutral.

A little closer. Then a little more. A group of loud locals walked past me—I acted quickly and pretended to be texting on my phone. They were noisy and obscured the secret conversation. *Right* near them was a little hedgerow of bushes about ten feet from where they were speaking. Before I could doubt my choice, I leapt, ducked behind the bushes, crouched low. A gust of wind muted their conversation. I pushed my ear directly to the bush, looking like an extreme nature enthusiast.

*"He wasn't fucking happy..."*

I inhaled sharply. Tightened my fingers in the branches.

*"Whose fault is that, hey?"*

If they were talking about Bernard, was he pissed about

the other night? Technically, Abe and I had foiled their plan. We hadn't been drugged, and we'd beaten back our attacker. Maybe what this meant was—

"*Devon Atwood!*"

I was so focused on the conversation I didn't recognize my own undercover name for a moment. Whoever had *yelled* it had a voice that boomed like an explosion even down a busy street at dinner time.

"*What on earth are you doing in the bushes?*"

I turned, swallowed a gasp at the sight of Humphrey fucking Hatcher lumbering toward me with a giant grin and an expression of total delight. I couldn't have been happier, except I was hiding in the bushes to eavesdrop on a conversation between two men who had conspired to drug and attack me. Instead I froze, crouched in the bushes, staring at Humphrey with my jaw dropped open.

*Think Sloane. Think.*

I stood up, tore off my hat, dislodging leaves from my hair and on my clothing. Dislodged my earrings and cast a wary glance behind me.

Caught the bartender *and* Big Guy glaring at me. I wasn't sure if they'd recognized my name. They sure as shit seemed to recognize my face. I blinked, and they vanished. The mistake of this moment, of getting caught, hit me like a punch to the gut. But I didn't have a second to fret before coming toe-to-toe with Bernard Allerton's closest friend.

"Humphrey," I exclaimed, holding out my hand for his aggressively friendly shake. He seemed genuinely happy to see me. "What a lovely surprise."

"What's an enchantress doing hiding in the bushes?" he bellowed.

I held my earring. "Fell right off, if you can believe it. I was lucky to find it in the dark."

"Lucky indeed," he agreed. "Although I have a feeling you have a lot of luck in your life, Ms. Atwood."

"I've been very fortunate," I said, lying through my teeth. Attempting to redirect the course of my mission. Yet again, I'd lost my fucking lead. Yet again, another had appeared in front of me, and I didn't take this kind of opportunity lightly. "What are you doing skulking about? Don't you have some place to be on a rainy Wednesday night?"

"I do actually," he said, tucking his fingers beneath his suspenders. "I'm off to Mycroft's for a drink with Reginald." His eyes grew wide. "And *you* shall join me. I will not take no for an answer."

I laughed—and it was a real laugh. Until my mind caught up. "I was just coming from that way. Weren't you only there two days ago giving a talk?"

Humphrey leaned in. "I know. It's a bloody tourist trap, though I do love it. Used to be Bernie's favorite pub for lamb stew."

"Bernard's?" My smile became fixed.

"The one and only," he beamed.

I pulled a final leaf from my hair. "Well then, sounds like I have a date with you and whoever Reginald is. I'm assuming he's a gentleman, like yourself?"

"An absolute gentleman, and I should know." Humphrey waggled his eyebrows. "He's my husband."

"I have a million questions for him," I replied. "Shall we?"

He held his arm out, and I hooked my hand through his. I wasn't sure what to do with, well, the all-consuming, tangible presence of Humphrey Hatcher. He was like a sharply dressed British Kool-Aid man, and I was helpless to resist his natural charm. Was this what it was like to have uncles and brothers and family friends? People who made you laugh and feel better after a hard day?

"You could call your Mr. Fitzpatrick," Humphrey suggested as we walked.

"What?" I asked, confused for a moment.

"The handsome devil you left looking lonely at this pub the other night," he said.

Oh, *Abe*.

"Maybe," I said, trying to dodge the question. "Or maybe it should be you, me, and your husband."

"Are you having a lovers' quarrel?" he asked.

Again I was briefly confused. He meant lovers' quarrel between me and *Abe*? I did have several quarrels with him, namely that he wouldn't provide the help I needed. And the act of asking for that help had stripped several layers off my soul, leaving me tender in a way I hated.

My other dispute was less with him and more with my own libido—which couldn't stop filling my mind with endless sexual fantasies about the man. And dreams too. Sexy, erotic, vivid dreams of slick, naked bodies and entwined fingers and Abe's full lips, gasping my name.

"Devon?"

I blinked, flushed. "I'm quite fine to spend the evening without Mr. Fitzpatrick."

The look Humphrey gave me was cunning in a friendly way. "I've been in your position, Ms. Atwood. Love is a rocky path, and partners must navigate the pitfalls together if they hope to succeed. There is no stronger pairing than a couple that faces life's challenges head on and declares, for all to hear, that they are an unstoppable force of valiant passion!"

I huffed out another surprised laugh. "Well... Reginald must be a happy man."

He barked a laugh. "We've faced our own rocky paths,

believe me. Perhaps you and Daniel need to face things together."

I shook my head, smiled. Caught the glow of Mycroft's Pub ahead and hoped no one in there had spotted me spying on them from across the street for two straight days.

And *really* hoped the bartender and Big Guy weren't planning on returning.

Luckily, Humphrey appeared loose and chatty and happy, and maybe this was the kind of night where I uncovered the *real* dirt on Bernard's location. Regardless of what he claimed, a close friend could ultimately reveal the man's hiding place.

"Thank you for the relationship advice. And for the invite," I said.

He clutched his chest. "Like Mr. Fitzpatrick, we are all mere mortals, beholden to your siren song."

He pulled the door open, and I stepped inside. "I promise to keep the singing to a minimum."

Although I'd use whatever tricks I had in my arsenal to uncover the truth.

## 15

### ABE

*N*ot a single star shone in the London sky by the time I left the Royal Opera House. Rain was coming, the clouds were heavy, but that didn't stop the mood of the people around me from dipping into liveliness. It wasn't far back to The Langham, so I opted to walk, turning up the collar of my coat to protect against the chill. Groups of people spilled from pubs as others walked their dogs, chatted on their phones, sat on city benches, smoked cigarettes, and hailed taxis. Couples held hands. Friends walked toward restaurants with purpose and ease. Maybe they never felt the weight of the world on their shoulders. Maybe they did and had managed to come out the other side, to balance. Like my mother, who'd laid to rest her anger toward my father and happily started a new life—one that suited her much, much better.

The thought of my empty, quiet hotel room sent a twinge through my chest I hated to admit was loneliness. I might have passed on invitations to brewery tours and movie nights with my team, but I hadn't realized until now how much their daily presence shaped my sense of real connection. Every morning when I stepped into the office, I was surrounded by people who *cared* about justice, cared about the world. Cared about me, even.

They were more than my colleagues, and more than friends. I wasn't sure what that made them, exactly. The issue being that the longer I felt this way, the more I was going to end up needing them. The more I'd have to let them *in*, past fortress-high walls I'd been happy to build.

And that wasn't the future I'd seen for myself. That future felt messy, prone to emotion and vulnerability. A cocktail of things I avoided the most. I endured the first year after my mother's accident—the time at hospitals, the grueling doctor's appointments, the sleepless nights—by calling my father every single day to beg him to return. My mother's spirit was resilient, but nothing could prepare a sixteen-year old boy for what it would be like to care for a woman who had temporarily lost her ability to express herself, to stand on her own, to balance, to access her memories.

The morning of the accident we'd had a long and entirely pointless conversation about my history teacher, who my mother secretly believed was a spy for the CIA. She'd made me laugh as she spun a completely untrue story about my shy, mild-mannered teacher. And then she kissed the top of my head and rushed out the door to the grocery store.

By dinner time that night, my mother had survived a horrifying car accident and lay in a coma, which ultimately lasted for three days. And it would be three months before I would be able to hold her hand and help her walk again.

My father wasn't entirely gone. I was young, and my own memories of this time were hazy, but he must have legally taken care of things for my mother, signed documents and papers, handled insurance. A lot of household bills still fell on my shoulders, but our giant mortgage was paid. His financial presence lingered, made it possible for his selfish act to still keep us clothed and sheltered. But that wasn't what I was seeking when I desperately dialed him every night.

I was seeking an explanation. I would have believed even the wildest story if it meant my own father cared about me.

Every call went unanswered. Every day was harder than the one before. Messy, emotional, vulnerable, I felt as exposed as a raw nerve and hated every second. Brick by brick by brick, it was that easy to wall off my vulnerable heart. My mother, and then Jeanette, would always have access to it. But by the time I was eighteen and earning a criminal justice degree at one of the most prestigious Ivy League institutions in the country, I had a new plan and a new purpose.

My phone rang, and I answered it without checking the number, hoping it was a member of my team calling from Philadelphia. The voice that rang out, instead, was Humphrey Hatcher.

"Mr. Fitzpatrick!" Humphrey yelled through the phone.

I looked around me, sure he must be here in person. "Humphrey?" I asked.

"Eudora gave me your phone number," Humphrey said. "So apologies for invading your privacy and the like. My husband and I are having the nicest drink at Mycroft's Pub, and we'd love for you to stop by and enjoy yourself."

*Jesus.* Even the best friends of criminal masterminds were trying to get me to *loosen up.* "Uh... you know, I'm coming from the symphony and already on my way back to the hotel."

"Nonsense! Take a cab. We'll see you in a few minutes. I will not accept no for an answer and *will* hunt you down, lad."

I had to acknowledge the man's innate charm. Had to acknowledge the tiny sparks in my brain lighting up at Humphrey's access to Bernard Allerton as a person, not only an idea, a thought, a shadow in the night I was endlessly searching for. Perhaps he would offer a usable clue about Bernard's location.

Perhaps after this drink I would... go to Sloane's room and give that information to her. A gift, albeit a small one, but one that would help her see I wasn't just a useless bastard who refused to help her.

"I like expensive whiskey," I told Humphrey. "I expect you to be buying, sir."

"And I have absolutely no self-control when it comes to my finances," he bellowed back. "A perfect pairing!"

I hung up and hailed a cab, shoving my hands in my pockets. Why did I feel so *light-hearted* thinking about sharing a drink with Bernard's *best friend*? The man was the definition of frivolity, and my last serious girlfriend, Caroline, would have never believed I'd do something so spontaneous. She'd seen me at my unfortunate worst, at the height of my burn-out and frustration with the FBI, when I wasn't sure yet what the answer was to my angry questions —*why do we keep losing priceless artifacts? Why are these thieves still out-smarting us? Why does everything take so fucking long?* The answer, ultimately, was founding Codex. Until then, I only knew that I was frustrated, closed off, distracted. So much of that had disappeared in the last four years, and my mother loved reminding me this would be a *fine* time to begin dating seriously again. *Don't you want a girlfriend who can celebrate the good changes in your life? Don't you want to finally make me and Jeanette grand-mothers?*

The cab dropped me off at Mycroft's Pub, and it was a challenge to repress the memories of Sloane and me at that bar before things had turned dangerous. Her body, her smile, her flirtatious teasing and smoky laughter. Inside, the bar was cozy and filled with people on this rainy night. I spotted Humphrey and a smaller man chatting at the bar. He waved to me with an intense excitement. I merely nodded, removed my coat, and turned toward the roaring fireplace. Over the mantle hung a sign with cursive writing. I must have missed it the other night—because this sign flashed at me like a warning and a clue, all at once.

*Didn't we once meet at Reichenbach Falls?*

My blood chilled, goosebumps springing across my skin.

"How... interesting," I murmured.

An ember-tinged voice to my right said, "How so?"

I turned, saw my goddess for the first time in two days and felt the strongest urge to sink to my knees in front of her, press my face to her skin in adoration.

"Ms... Atwood," I said, remembering our cover. "What a surprise."

Her raven hair was in a high bun, leaving the curve of her throat exposed, her high cheekbones bare. She was dressed in all-black, as usual—ripped black jeans, stiletto boots, a sweater that hung off her smooth shoulder. Blood-red lips.

I took a step into her orbit and placed my jacket across a bar stool. "What on earth is going on here?"

Sloane waved to Humphrey with a big smile. "Humphrey believes you and I are having a *lovers' quarrel.* His words." Her midnight eyes were sparkling with intrigue and intelligence. A truly dangerous combination on a woman so beautiful. "He invited me here for drinks tonight, and he must have called you when he was outside."

"The man has a certain charm," I said. "What are we arguing about?"

"Apparently the way I ran out of the talk here and left you *looking lonely*," she said.

"Yes, it was quite rude of you to leave me and run to an alley to fight a man twice your size," I said, mouth tipping up. Every nerve ending in my body roared with a primal joy at seeing her again. I had no idea if I wanted a romantic partner right now. I did, however, want this woman in my bed, preferably underneath me.

Aware of Humphrey watching us, and using it to my selfish advantage, I dipped my head and pressed my lips softly to Sloane's cheek. Her hair brushed my forehead, and my lips dipped down to her ear. Her body, this close, overwhelmed my senses.

"You've stayed safe?" I said quietly.

"I have." I saw her swallow, saw the goosebumps along the side of her neck.

"Good," I said. Stepped back but stayed close. "Shall we inform him that our disagreement is finished?"

"Is it though?" she asked—and I heard the genuine meaning behind her words. The way she'd walked away two nights ago after I refused to admit to the real reason behind my trip to London betrayed all I needed to know about her frustration with me.

Humphrey was already walking back with a whiskey in hand, and I contemplated an escape plan. I shouldn't have come. I shouldn't have invaded what was clearly Sloane's work, especially if she was holding a grudge.

"That depends," I replied. "Does it bother you that I'm here?"

Her eyes searched mine as she bit her bottom lip. Finally, she echoed, "That depends."

I smirked. "A stalemate, I see."

She took a drink from her martini. "Humphrey said the only way for two people to have a healthy romantic relationship is if we, and this is a quote, *join together to become an unstoppable force of valiant passion*. End quote."

A smile spread across my face. I didn't even attempt to suppress it. "Sounds like love advice for Viking warriors."

Sloane returned my smile, and hers was free of any barriers. No silky teasing, no sultry flirting—it was wide, toothy, quick, and bright. "You do have the look of a Norse god about you. A very dapper Norse god."

Up high, in the walls around my heart, a brick loosened. Tumbled. Emotion flashed across her face so sincere I wondered if she too had a wall around her heart. Which only made me want to test my ability to knock it down.

"So Humphrey believes we are..." I trailed off.

She finally broke eye contact, following Humphrey's movements through the bar and back toward us. "A romantic item."

"Being a romantic item with someone is not my expertise, I'm afraid," I admitted.

"I'm also in the fucking dark when it comes to romance." Another smile, this one even more alluring. Inviting, even. When Humphrey reached us a second later, I was glad for the whiskey. At least I could place my hand there and hold the glass tightly, instead of cupping Sloane's face and kissing her.

"Good lad," Humphrey said. "I could see your valiant passion all the way from the bar. It helps not to fight. Life is too gorgeous and much too short. For example, have you met my handsome husband, Reginald?"

Humphrey finally stepped aside to reveal a short black man with wire-rimmed glasses who seemed besotted with the giant, red-haired lumberjack hugging him around the shoulders. He too appeared to be in his seventies, like Humphrey, and was dressed in an academic-looking tweed jacket and a bowtie.

"It's Reggie," the man said, shaking my hand and Sloane's. "I apologize, my husband is ridiculous."

Sloane, for her part, appeared genuinely delighted at the pair. "How long have you been together?"

"Forty years," Reggie said. "And every one of them spent with Humphrey has been a miracle. Even though he is a bit of a loudmouth. A loudmouth I love."

It was said without teasing, and the brief look they exchanged reminded me of my mother's wedding to Jeanette, the adoration there went deeper than attraction or affection. It was real partnership, in all its forms. Which seemed to be more than the sum of bringing two lives together in equal fashion but agreeing to shoulder the burdens, share the pain, hold more of the weight when your partner couldn't.

"We met at a meeting of the Sherlock Society, and the rest was history," Humphrey said, giving Reggie another squeeze. Now drink," Humphrey raised his pint glass. "We've got a long night ahead of us."

Glancing at Sloane, I prepared to make my exit. "This has been lovely to meet you, Reggie, but my hotel room awaits."

I thought Sloane looked disappointed before schooling her expression into one of charming nonchalance.

"Nonsense," Humphrey said. "If you're both here, I *know* you'll want to hear stories of Bernard when he was a boy."

Sloane and I both went rigid. I chanced a look her way; she subtly arched her brow.

"Stay," he continued. "You know Ms. Atwood wants you to."

*Ms. Atwood* blushed slightly yet remained silent. Staying, engaging with Humphrey who, while charming, was technically her *source*, meant helping her. Even though it was obvious her views on asking for help mirrored my own.

Staying, engaging with Humphrey, meant admitting I wasn't, technically, *entirely* on vacation. I turned fully toward Sloane, hiding my face from Humphrey and Reggie as much as I could. Since we weren't actually work partners, we had no built-in code-words or facial expressions to communicate with each other in short-hand.

"Perhaps we've reached a... stalemate in our quarrel," I said slowly, watching her closely for signs of distrust.

She tapped her fingers on her glass, bit her lip. "I guess... a night of leisure, alone, doesn't really suit you."

The ends of my mouth quirked up. "I guess a night of being on your own doesn't suit you?"

Fifty—fifty. Or, at least, our best attempt at it. Turning, I raised my glass in appreciation of the tiny victory. "Bring on the stories about Bernard."

## 16

### ABE

With a jubilant cheer, Humphrey dragged another barstool over for me. I leaned against it, one leg outstretched, and tried not to notice when Sloane's knee pressed against my thigh.

"That was nice of Eudora to give you my phone number," I said.

"Eudora can be nice occasionally," Humphrey said.

"Be civil," Reggie chided.

"I *am* civil," Humphrey said. He leaned in close. "I'm sure you've heard the stories about our current president's temper."

"A few members have shared their less-than-kind memories," Sloane said with a secret smile. "Although she has been sweet to me."

"She is sweet," Reggie said. "If she likes you and you don't get in the way of her perfect vision. If you do..."

"They'll find your body under her floorboards," Humphrey said.

"Has she always wanted to be president of the Sherlock Society?" I asked.

Humphrey shrugged his massive shoulders. "She made it known to us all that she was gunning for Bernie's position long before his sabbatical. We had a president, before Bernie, named Nicholas."

"Markham?" I said, remembering what Eudora had told me about their former president and his bookstore, Adler's. Which was directly across the street from where we sat.

"The one and only, god rest his soul," Humphrey said. "He's since passed, ten years now, but Eudora and Bernie revered the man. Back in his early days of leadership, the Society was more secretive, more exclusive. It should be a club open to anyone who loves the genius of our country's greatest writer, not a secret society."

Eudora had insinuated something similar, right before I'd said the code words inscribed above the fireplace across the room. Which was interesting as hell given that Bernard was responsible for The Empty House—the secret society that Freya and Sam had infiltrated just eight weeks ago. Bernard was, of course, conspicuously absent during the festivities. My agents had discovered a group of eleven individuals that met every year at the Antiquarian Book Festival in Philadelphia, where they conducted an underground, black-market auction filled with stolen antiques valued at millions of dollars. It was a massive case, and the Bureau was still putting all the pieces together, but Bernard Allerton appeared to be at the center of it all. He provided the stolen books to auction off, he provided the guests that could keep a secret and had an abundance of wealth, he received the money paid for his stolen items. He was the buyer, the seller, the one who ultimately profited while others went to prison.

Learning that he admired a man who wanted to make the Sherlock Society even more exclusive made absolute sense to me.

"I agree," Sloane said. "Strange that Bernard felt that way given his career was about democratizing our access to the written word."

I slipped my hand down my side, hiding it from Humphrey and Reggie's view. It allowed me to tap my finger against her wrist—which I did now.

Humphrey took a hearty sip. "Humans can't be placed into neat and tidy categories, as we know. And as passionate a librarian as that man is, his devotion to the Sherlock Society is—"

"—fanatical," Reggie said.

I was beginning to like Reggie.

"Passionate." Humphrey grinned. "Which is why I've been trying to get him a message about these damn papers being auctioned off."

I felt a *tap*. Sloane. I took it as a cue. "He hasn't communicated with you once since he left for his sabbatical, right? I'd think he'd respond to papers that we all know he would do anything to have."

Humphrey rubbed a hand through his bushy red beard. "Trust and believe poor Reginald has heard me say that a dozen times for every month he's been off the grid. He's done it before. It's longer this time. Feels more dramatic, if I can be quite frank. I've talked to every single person in my life about this. Every member of the Society. I've called Eudora countless times, called the McMaster's Library. The story's the same."

Interesting that Humphrey used the word *story*. I too was surprised that the lie being propagated about Bernard's whereabouts had stayed bullet-proof for so long. Interpol and the Bureau couldn't possibly keep it under wraps forever. And if Bernard was announced, publicly, to be a wanted man, would he flee, out in the open, easy to capture?

Or only dig himself further underground?

"Where does he go in the city to hide out?" Sloane asked. "Not to belittle your friendship. Perhaps he's just in need of a little isolation right here in London."

Humphrey was shaking his head vigorously. "Reggie and I have spent a lot of time at Bernie's other houses. Greece, Switzerland, Paris... his vacation homes are *much* more beautiful than his flat here in London, even if it did cost him a pretty penny."

The reminder that Bernard could have fled to Switzerland—the perfect place to hide if you were a wanted man, internationally—had me hiding a wince. I caught Sloane covering hers just in time.

"You're a good friend to be worried," she said. "It sounds like he's a real man of mystery. He's dipped out on you before, correct?"

"Ah," Humphrey said, waving a hand. "The man disappears often. I've gone a full year without speaking to him. He's extremely focused on his travels to acquire the rarest of books. Bernie does not permit distractions."

*Even from his best friend*? I wanted to ask, except Sloane and I needed to appear friendly toward Bernard, not combative.

I took a long, deliberate drink. Thought about how quickly I'd positioned Sloane and me as partners, working together, when no such thing was happening. We didn't *need* to appear to be doing anything right now—I was merely here while she got information from her source. Perhaps my newly paired-off employees were finally rubbing off on my behavior.

"He hides it well, but Bernard has a sensitive heart," Humphrey continued. "All the pressure of running that library, being a spokesperson, speaking across the world. It's a dream come true and also far too much stress for any one man to take. Plus, he's always working with new people, interns or museum employees, or traveling to book shows or up late on a conservation project."

I felt not an ounce of sympathy for this portrait of an overworked-and-underpaid Bernard. I knew those "interns" to be hired thieves he worked with; the museum employees were all part of his pyramid of criminals; the book shows, the conservation projects—often excuses he used as he dealt rare books like drugs and profited like a king.

Sloane leaned forward, elbows on her knees, and placed her chin in her palm. "What do you guys think is in those private papers after all?"

"Everything Eudora Green has ever wanted," Reggie said.

Humphrey *harrumphed* into his beer. "Everything *Bernie* has ever wanted."

I tapped Sloane. She said, "And what is that, exactly?"

Humphrey looked at his husband, who smiled dreamily before speaking. "Arthur Conan Doyle was the greatest literary genius our country, and I'd say the world, has ever known. He's been studied and profiled and written about for decades, and scholars like those in the Society can *never* read enough. But..." Reggie paused. "There comes a time where one reaches a limit of what can truly be known of a man who's been dead for ninety years."

"I've not seen them, *no one* has seen them," Humphrey added. "They could be notes he wrote about birds he saw out the window for all we know. None of us bloody care. These papers mean we have a new limit. These papers *expand* the limit. For the first time in ages, we have something new to learn about the man, and the characters, we worship so much."

KATHRYN NOLAN

Even I was sitting forward, drawn into the implications of what he was saying. Sloane tapped me. "Bernard..." I stopped, pretended to think for a second. "Bernard would be trying his hardest for the Society to own those papers as part of their collection, correct?"

"With what funds though?" Reggie said. "Even with our best efforts, we can't compete with the collectors of the world who have millions at their disposal. We are mere scholars."

Bernard wasn't a mere scholar though.

Bernard had access to millions of dollars.

Bernard had access to a network of highly trained thieves who could easily pull off a theft of this magnitude. They'd been helping him pull off stunts like this for twenty years now.

I imagined laying out this story for Freya, Sam, Delilah, and Henry. I imagined them yelling at me, in their own special ways, to *pay attention.*

"Did Bernard ever get over losing the first batch of private papers?" Sloane asked, immediately on the same wavelength. "Eudora mentioned it at the talk, the one at The Langham."

Humphrey laughed, a little joylessly. "No. Because I've known him longer than anyone, I can tell you the man's a god-awful sore loser and a cheat at that. I had to take him here every night for a week and ply him with fine liquor to get him to smile again."

"That was very nice of you to do," Sloane said, laying her hand on his arm. Humphrey touched it, held it, stared at us with real vulnerability.

"Thank you," he said. "Current members of my marriage disagree."

I snorted, nodded at Reggie. "What's the disagreement

134

here? Unless there are other members in this sacred union I'm unaware of?"

"Just one," Reggie said dryly. "I adore Bernard. We all do. But I tell Humphrey all the time that the man uses him."

Humphrey's pale face blushed—he seemed as innocent as a schoolboy. I couldn't, for the life of me, parse Humphrey's moral code. Good or evil? Thief or innocent?

"Some people in this world are more difficult to love than others," he said. "Do they not still deserve to be loved?"

Sloane let go of Humphrey's hand, sat back. Slid her hands down her thighs, but not before I caught her fingers trembling.

"Tell me how you met," I said. "Knowing him for sixty years is an incredibly long time."

He brightened. "Bernie and I grew up in Canterbury and went to school together there. My grandparents raised me, and I was a wily and rambunctious thing, always prowling the streets looking for trouble. Bernie was the same, although we often got into *less* trouble once we had each other."

"Is Humphrey still rambunctious?" Sloane asked Reggie.

"Only where it counts, love," Reggie said. Her laughter rang out like a bell, and I was completely enchanted by it. Did everything she do have a kind of magical spell attached to it?

Humphrey leaned in close. "Bernard once orchestrated a street-wide game of hide and seek. All the kids he could wrangle, sent us off running into the woods and behind cars and every nook and cranny we could imagine. A large field ran the length of our street, and we couldn't help but head there as Bernie yelled out the numbers. He gave us a full minute, which set us off laughing. And *then* the lad couldn't even *find* us."

My eyes narrowed. "Why not?"

He paused, preparing to deliver a punchline. "The bastard slipped into every single one of our houses and stole our toys."

Sloane laughed—this time, it sounded forced. "How very devious for a child." I could feel her body's reaction next to mine; that blood-in-the-water response so closely mirrored my own.

"How did you find out?" I asked, feigning lightness.

"Well, he did a crap job of hiding them." Humphrey chuckled. "And after about twenty minutes, we went lurking back across the field in search of him, unsure of what had happened. When we found him in his room, he was surrounded by toys like a little *king*."

This boyhood image didn't resonate with youthful innocence for me. It resonated with the sense of *ownership* that Bernard Allerton must have been born with.

"Were you angry?" Sloane asked.

"Of course. Although also we were damn well impressed. He did give them back to us, although I always told him it made him a right bastard from such a young age."

I raised a brow his way—he anticipated my next question. "He was eleven."

"You don't say," I muttered.

Humphrey sighed, clinking his glass against mine and Sloane's. "Here's to Bernard. He does always get what he wants."

## 17

# SLOANE

*a*n hour later, Abe and I had to place Humphrey and Reggie in a cab. Together, they were adorably drunk. As the cab had prepared to drive off, Humphrey had called back, "Thank you for a magical evening, enchantress. Have fun bewitching Mr. Fitzpatrick. Remember, *valiant!*"

Abe and I waved them off—looking, I was sure of it, like a couple. The more drinks they enjoyed, the sloppier their stories became. And while Bernard was in quite a few of them, no other relevant information was revealed, other than the confirmed fact that the man was a self-centered asshole.

The Kensley auction in four days had become my primary investigative focus, given what Humphrey had revealed in there. If Bernard was going to make *any* moves while in hiding, it would be to steal those private papers for himself. I just needed to figure out how I was going to handle a giant auction with tons of guests and multiple exits and entrances.

A drop of rain landed on my head. The drop turned into a sprinkle immediately, and I shivered, hoping these rain clouds stayed thunder-free. A second later, a large umbrella opened over my head courtesy of Abe.

"Oh, thank you," I said, surprised again at these tiny gestures of thoughtfulness. "I didn't bring one."

"My pleasure," he said smoothly. "Shall we walk back to our hotel? It should be less than a mile if you don't mind sharing this enclosed space with me."

I cast a glance his way. It wasn't that I was nervous. It was that I craved being in Abe Royal's space the same way I craved water, food, and air. From the first moment I saw him in that ballroom, being around him had felt like a necessity. Suddenly faced with his presence again, I realized how much I'd ached these past forty-eight hours, ached the way you do with fever.

"The closer I am to you, the easier it is to steal from your pockets," I mused.

He laughed softly, a dangerous sound that raised the hair on the back of neck. "I am a willing victim this evening, Sloane."

We headed down the street, the sides of our bodies brushing together, and I almost stumbled at the use of my real name and the words *willing victim*. We were about to walk, together, to our neighboring rooms. Together. Where we'd go sleep... separately.

I shivered again, but not from cold. Abe had walked into that pub this evening looking too handsome, too dashing, too refined. His tuxedo was tailored perfectly, exposing the long lines of his body, the poetry of his broad shoulders, the elegance of his clean-shaven jaw. He'd been at the symphony, and really, the man *was* a fucking symphony: no note wasted, no scale imperfect, no crescendo too loud.

Although the second his eyes had landed on mine, they flared with a lust so raw that heat pulsed between my legs.

And those lips on my cheek spoke of the sinful devil in him, the man so confident he simply took what he wanted.

*Take me*, I wanted to beg.

"Thank you for allowing me to stay this evening," Abe said. "I hope I didn't ruin your operation."

"Humphrey wanted to talk with the both of us," I replied. "You helped him share what I needed. You asked the right questions."

"As did you," he said.

"So, thank *you*." I swallowed hard, saw him do the same. Given our last conversation, when we'd both refused to budge, this *tiny* allowance felt like a major milestone. Certainly, the experience I'd had with Abe was bizarre as hell, given that I'd never had a work partner before or ever worked with a team. I was distractingly attracted to Abe. I also felt *safe* around him. Protected, even though I'd always been able to hold my own, physically and intellectually. Our on-the-fly *tap* messaging caused a giddiness in my stomach. We were two minds, working as one, playing off each other's ideas. I felt connected to him. I felt *entwined*.

I wasn't sure if it was a smart idea to feel professionally *entwined* with a man who made me literally faint with lust.

We crossed a busy intersection, the rain falling harder against the umbrella. Abe looked both ways, laying his palm at the small of my back to guide me forward. More heat flared there.

"You did extremely well back there, Sloane," he said. "In fact, you're a natural. If you were coming through the FBI's training academy right now and I was your instructor, you'd be the one I watched for excellence. I didn't do anything back there you couldn't have done on your own." He paused. "I'm sure I'm not the first person to comment on your remarkable charisma."

I avoided making eye contact, even though I appreciated everything he'd said. He was right. I was often told I was charming and alluring. But that was because I was the biological byproduct of two professional grifters. *Charm* was our bread and butter, and while undercover I could slip into those roles without hesitation.

Technically, I was using my powers for good now. Only a former con artist could catch other con artists so easily. Being a private detective was my way of enforcing my own moral code.

But having those attributes commented on made me uncomfortable. It was the reminder I didn't need that my genes and upbringing predisposed me to be an excellent liar.

"Do you think we convinced Humphrey that we are valiant in our passion?" I asked, dodging the compliment.

"If I'm a *dapper Norse god*, as you say, you are definitely a Norse warrior princess." A smile tugged at the sides of his mouth. "The kind that devours the hearts of feckless men for breakfast."

I hummed a little, hiding my own smile. "They do say it's the most important meal of the day."

The Langham Hotel was ahead. Our hotel. My heart rate sped up again, and I felt a corresponding flutter low in my belly.

"Speaking of being remarkable, you weren't so bad yourself tonight." Receiving compliments made me feel vulnerable. Giving them even more so. Each word was foreign on my tongue, and I wasn't sure I'd nailed the delivery.

Abe turned, caught my gaze, and held it. "Thank you."

*We make a great team.* Those words—even more unfamiliar—tried to force their way out. I managed to restrain them. I didn't trust that yet.

"You can't turn it off, can you?" I asked.

His jaw tightened. "Turn off what?"

"This job."

His light expression became a grimace. "Codex has been under an enormous amount of pressure since Henry joined our team back in February. And *as* my team likes to remind me, I've taken not a single damn day off during that time. I need this time to let go, sort myself out."

There was a long pause. "Yes. I can't fucking turn it off. The world spins forward, and people take vacations, and I can never seem to stop myself from caring about what's happening in the shadows."

"Same here," I said. "I struggle with that. I pretty much work every weekend and every night."

"No leisure for you, either?" he asked.

"Not as much as I probably should have." We shared a quick look—absent of rampant sexual lust, it was more emotional.

"You're a true lone wolf, Abe Royal," I said.

"Am I?"

"Tell me I'm wrong," I said, flashing him my own mischievous smile. Every single thing about him screamed *workaholic army of one*.

"You're not wrong," he finally said—softly. "I find it challenging to reach out to people."

"What's it like for a lone wolf to have a team?" I asked, genuinely curious.

"They are extraordinary," he said. "The four of them, they're... a group. A team within a team. I'm their boss and therefore separate. As close as they are to each other, I'm merely a bystander. As the ones in charge often are."

I smelled bullshit but didn't push. I did say, "They must like you enough to want you to enjoy a vacation."

"Or they'd rather be rid of me," he said, except there was affection in his tone.

We walked through the opulent lobby toward the gold-plated, antique-looking elevator doors. Abe pressed the button for number six, then leaned against the wall.

"My mother and my step-mother have been begging me to watch this show called *Love Island* while I'm on vacation. So that's one thing I could do with my free time."

The elevator doors slid open, and we stepped inside. Immediately we both chose opposite walls to stand firmly against, leaving the entire small space between us. Abe shook out his wet umbrella and raised his eyes to mine.

"Do you know what it is?" I asked.

He shook his head. "Enlighten me."

I swallowed, nervous. "It's a British reality show where a bunch of sexy singles are filmed on an island, and they have to date each other to stay on the show. It's basically a non-stop fuck fest."

"Non-stop fuck fest." He said each word slowly. "That's one way to spend my time here."

"Watching the show?" I clarified. I was hot, my cheeks were hot, this elevator was a million goddamn degrees.

He didn't reply. He did hit the emergency stop button. We came to a grinding halt, suspended in the air. I raised my eyebrows at his arrogance, but he only shrugged.

"We're having a conversation," he said and didn't move. "What's your deadline on this case?"

I blinked, surprised at the shift. "Nine more days to capture Bernard or I lose the contract."

He nodded, face empathetic. "I'm familiar with this kind of pressure. It's a lot to manage if you're only one person."

I lifted a shoulder. "I guess I'm used to it, being on my

own." I cocked my head. "Do you find having a team of people helps you manage the pressure?"

"Makes it harder," he said. "I manage the pressure for all of them."

"Because they ask that of you?"

"Because I *should*," he said firmly.

I gave him my most charming smile, until he returned it.

"What?" he asked.

"You love your team," I said.

"I do?"

"The lone wolf loves his staff. It's not a bad thing," I replied.

"I have acquired some fondness for them."

I snorted. "You talk about them like they're a litter of kittens you found in your backyard."

"In many ways, that is exactly what they are." His tone was sardonic.

My smile widened. "You forget I've done my research, Mr. Royal. Aren't all of your employees engaged to one another?"

Abe looked away. "No, not *all* to each other. Henry and Delilah are engaged. Sam and Freya live together, are together. Romantically."

"And on a team that small, that intimate, the fact that you've willingly allowed two couples to work for you shows a real trust in them. A trust in their ethics and integrity. *That* doesn't come from a simple fondness." I kept my voice light, an attempt at teasing the dashing and unflappable man in front of me. I had to work to soften the jealous edge to my words.

"Are you suggesting I turn in my *lone wolf* membership ID card?" he asked, playful.

"Maybe." I crossed my arms over my chest. "Mostly, I'm

suggesting you're no bystander in the lives of these people. You might even have a heart beneath that stoic facade."

Abe unbuttoned his jacket, made a show of looking down at his chest. "Here?"

"I'm afraid so."

"Shouldn't I fear you'll devour it for breakfast?"

The force of my attraction to him walloped me across the face. Stunned, I succumbed to weakness and took three steps toward him. Pressed the tip of my finger to the spot where his heart resided. The echo of its rhythm pulsed in the hollow of his throat.

"You're not the first man to fear me, Mr. Royal."

His answering grin was truly beguiling. "I'm quite positive of that, Ms. Argento."

He gripped my finger where it rested. "Those were interesting revelations we received at the pub tonight about our friend Bernard."

"Sure were."

Abe's grip moved to my wrist, turning my hand open. He examined my palm like he planned to divine my future. "I'm sure all of those details about Bernard dovetail nicely with everything else you've uncovered as you've been tracking him."

"Certainly," I said evenly. "But I'm not sure why I'd share that information with a private detective insisting he's not here tracking the same man. Insisting he's on vacation."

His nostrils flared. He *wanted* in. It was written all over his handsome face. "You're right. I don't want it. And since you clearly work alone..."

"And since you're on vacation..."

"We're back at square one," he said dryly.

I reached forward, hit the elevator button. The machine started again, gears grinding, taking us to the sixth floor. We stared at each other for the entire thirty seconds it took to reach our floor, his grip on my wrist never loosening. When the doors finally creaked open, I wasn't sure what was going to happen next. If we *weren't* competing for the same prize, then couldn't I allow this man into my bed for one night?

As I stepped up to my door, and he stepped to his, I saw his hand on his doorknob. He dragged one finger down the panel, head down, body language suddenly full of shy hesitancy. Was Abe like me in every way? Beneath his steadfast independence, was there a core of loneliness?

He turned, stared right at me, slightly bashful and a little bit too real. I was already unsure if I could truly open myself up to the instant attraction between the two of us. That look on his face convinced me I couldn't give in. Nine fucking days to achieve the case of my dreams, and the very last thing I could allow was a distraction that would devastate me. Because this man was hotter than sin, brilliant, ambitious, a challenge to my talent in every goddamn way.

One taste of Abe Royal, and I'd never kick the habit. He didn't have the makings of an anonymous fuck. And I wasn't made to do anything but.

"Having trouble?" His voice was velvet, low, tempting. "You can't seem to open your door."

"Oh, my key card won't..." I trailed off because he was walking toward me, panther-like, stunning me into silence. He plucked the card from my fingers with an irritating confidence. My back brushed against his chest. His lips landed in my hair. One large hand pressed against the door, turning this banal act into something erotic. Seductive.

"Do you prefer being alone in all aspects of your life?" he asked. With a firm stroke, the key card *beeped*. My door opened an inch. Abe gripped the handle, holding it still. Holding me in.

"It's my natural state," I said, turning my head slightly. I could feel his breath on my cheek. "I'm guessing you don't let any women into that stone-cold heart of yours."

A raspy chuckle. "Access is denied to most everyone, yes."

"What about a woman that devours men's hearts for breakfast?" I asked, voice barely a whisper.

"Allowances could be made for a woman like that." He brushed a few wayward strands of hair from the nape of my neck, baring me completely.

I felt his mouth there. A kiss. Almost a bite. A low rumble rose from his chest.

Another kiss, this one on the side of my neck.

One more, lower still.

My eyes closed, soaking in this seduction. Savoring it. "Abraham," I said, voice a plea.

"Yes, Sloane?"

I steeled my spine and accessed the very dregs of my willpower. Turned my head to the side, and still avoided eye contact. I couldn't—*couldn't*—look him in the eye right now. "I think you and I are smart enough to know the kind of devastation that sex between the two of us could leave in its wake. Complicating devastation. Not an easy night between strangers."

Oh *god,* every word of that physically hurt. The casual sexual experiences I had rarely involved more than our first names and a frank discussion of birth control and testing. I'd basically told this man I was *too attracted to him* to fuck him for fun.

"I am smart enough to know that," he said. "I am smart enough to feel the same way actually." He kissed my throat one more time, a searing burn. "And because you were so honest with me, I'll tell you that I'm also stupid enough to still want this, Sloane."

"You're not a stupid man, though," I said.

His mouth dragged to my ear, and I whimpered. "Generally, I am known for my brilliance, yes. But you're the first woman who's ever robbed me of my senses."

He stepped back, stepped away, and I almost begged again, begged for more, wept at the loss of his masculine strength, and his hard chest, and the confident grip of his fingers.

I finally did catch his eye. There was that shy vulnerability again. My throat was dry, body trembling. "I feel pretty senseless around you too, Abe."

A smile, a sad smile from him. "I know what's needed to win a case like the one you have. I know what's needed *from* you. The focus, the time, the stress. Please forgive my—" He waved a hand at my door. "—reckless actions. I know you can't afford distractions right now."

I opened my mouth to tell him his apology was so unnecessary it was laughable. He unlocked his own door, held it open as he stared at me one last time. "Don't doubt yourself, Ms. Argento. If anyone can succeed in that man's capture, it's you. I'd wish you luck, but I don't believe you need any."

## 18

### ABE

*What about a woman that devours men's hearts for breakfast?* Sloane purred, slipping first one bra strap, then the other, down the curve of her shoulder.

*Allowances could be made for a woman like that*, I said, although it was more guttural growl than words. I was naked on my bed, fingers wrapped around my cock, the sole witness to Sloane's strip tease.

*You want me to devour you?* She stared at my length, tongue darting out to wet her lips.

*Christ, get up here*, I begged. She only shook her head, endlessly coy, knowing it drove me up the goddamn wall. Fingers hooked into the fabric, she dropped her bra to the ground. Began teasing at the sheer material of her panties.

*Should I keep going?* I was so close, so close to seeing everything.

*Yes*, I demanded. I was going to come. *Yes.* I was going to—

The ringing *crack* against my hotel door startled me awake from the hottest sex dream of my life. Gasping, naked, cock aching, I stumbled out of my bed. Glared at the clock, which read 2:15 a.m.

Only silence filled the room.

"*Shit*," I sighed, relieved. I sank back onto the bed, scrubbing a hand down my face. The dream—*that dream*—had been so real I could still taste my desperation, could still feel my skin, hot for her touch. I'd fucking *pleaded* for her touch, which I'd never, not once, done for a woman.

Instinctively I placed my palm to the wall behind me, the one I shared with Sloane. It slowed my heart to a manageable rhythm.

Another sharp crack shattered the stillness. A third and another. And the unmistakable sound of a doorknob being rattled and jarred—an attempt at a break-in.

But it wasn't my door. It was Sloane's.

Not once in my life had I ever run *toward* a person, yet this woman I barely knew was the one I felt compelled to protect in this moment. Yanking on my briefs, I grabbed my phone, ran to the door and pulled it open. Sloane was already there, eyes wide with fear and hair a tangled mess around her face.

"Abe," she said. "Oh my god, are you—"

I hauled her into the presumed safety of my hotel room and glanced both ways, caught a blur of movement at the far end of the hallway that could have been anything. Including whoever had just been here, trying to scare us.

Stepping back inside, I slammed the door. Locked it. Sloane had her palm to her forehead, chest rising and falling rapidly. Clutched in her hand was a note.

Beneath my feet was another note. I scooped it up, distracted, then bent to catch her eye. "What happened? Are you okay?"

I sat her on my bed, sank down in front of her to check

for injuries. She wasn't hurt—physically. She was, however, trembling.

"Did you get this?" she asked. I grabbed the note, held up mine to compare. It was a picture of the two of us sitting next to each other at Mycroft's Pub earlier this evening. The picture was slightly blurred, clearly taken from a secret vantage point. Sloane is laughing at Humphrey.

I'm staring at Sloane with a look of unfiltered devotion.

For a split second, my mortification outweighed my fear —I didn't need an outsider's perspective showing me how badly I wanted this woman. Or how badly my pride had been damaged when she turned down my advances just a few hours earlier. She was right—*she was right*—that sex between us could be complicating and distracting at a time when she needed clarity and focus. Because *look* at this picture—this picture had nothing to do with overwhelming lust and everything to do with an instant attraction so strong I literally didn't know what it meant. I was staring at her like she was my goddamn wife walking down the aisle towards me on our goddamn wedding day. I didn't even *recognize* the look on my face.

Sloane reached out, wrapped her fingers around my wrist. "Abe."

"Who took this?"

She shook her head. Swallowed. "There's a note."

I flipped the pictures over. In identical spots, in identical handwriting, was written: *Get the hell out of London and go home. Next time will be worse.*

"We just received a threat," she said softly. "In our hotel rooms. Which means whoever did this *followed* us from that pub to this hotel. Could be paying someone who works here to find out which rooms we're staying in."

"And followed us to the pub in the first place," I added. "Unless Humphrey…"

Her forehead creased. "I can't… my gut doesn't like him for this kind of maliciousness."

I stroked my finger across lettering. "I agree," I admitted. "I'm calling the front desk to report to security first."

I stood up, dialed. Paced the room to dispel the adrenaline. Sloane let out a long breath, pushed the mess of hair from her face. And looked down at my cock, which was still half-hard from my dream. And growing harder beneath her gaze. Just as the receptionist answered, I realized that I was half-naked, in black briefs, walking around for Sloane's perusal.

"The Langham Hotel front desk. How may I be of service, Mr. Royal?"

My mouth had gone dry. Sloane, slightly flushed, turned away, stood, and wandered toward my desk and luggage.

"Hello? Mr. Royal?"

"Yes, hello," I said. "I need to speak with hotel security. Can you send them to room #608 please? The woman staying in #610 and I received threatening letters at our doors at the same time. And in #610, it seemed like the person also tried to break in."

The reaction from the receptionist was one of shock. I was sure The Langham wasn't a hotel where *threats* to their patrons occurred often. She promised to send security as soon as she could as well as a complimentary pot of tea.

As I hung up, Sloane turned around, fingers near my laptop. Displayed on my screen were articles about Bernard, a few documents, and case notes I found myself turning to the past two days. Scratching an itch that made me feel both vindicated and guilty at the same time.

"Security will be here in a second," I said, grabbing a

pair of sweatpants from the ground and tugging them on. "But we need to be vigilant. If someone's giving out our information, we can't be sure who to trust here."

"Smart idea," she said. "Also we should both be much less naked."

Which was when I finally realized she was wearing a white sleep shirt that barely skimmed her thighs. Every swaying movement bared the curve of her ass. Her legs were strong, toned. The polish on her toes was a mysterious purple.

"Yes," I said.

"Would you mind waiting outside my room while I put on real clothes?" she asked.

"Of course," I said. We left my room, and she opened hers—an odd echo of our moment earlier this evening when I'd kissed her neck and asked to come inside.

My cock hardened again, and I gritted my teeth. Sloane went to step inside her room, but I grabbed her wrist. "Wait. We should... check first."

Blasting the room with light, we checked her bathroom, beneath her bed, inside the closet. Convinced she was safe, I waited with my back turned in the doorframe.

"Are you okay?" I asked.

A snapping sound of elastic and shuffling. Then, "I thought a man was trying to get into my room."

My fingers tightened painfully on the wood of the doorframe. "I think a man was. Or at least wanted you to feel fear."

More muffling, the sounds of water being turned off and on. "I hate... admitting... when I'm afraid."

I turned my head to the side and kept my eyes lowered. "Fear is our most important sense."

"Or weakest sense," she countered. "And you can turn around now."

I did, slowly. Her hair was now in a side-braid, and she wore black leggings beneath her sleep shirt. Toes were still bare, face still scrubbed of makeup. Face still effortlessly, startlingly beautiful. My desire for her nearly incapacitated me.

"Fear keeps us alive," I said, voice rough. "Fear is our survival instinct. I've known plenty of agents and trainees and PIs in my lifetime who didn't trust their fear. Didn't develop a relationship with their fear. And once that sense is deadened, you're much more likely to take risks, be reckless, put your life on the line when you shouldn't."

She stayed silent. Her body was tensing, flexing.

"You're the furthest thing from weak," I said.

Sloane nodded and looked behind me where two hotel security guards were approaching. We spent the next ten minutes relaying what happened to the guards, who were more distressed than we were.

"Do you keep security footage of who enters and exits?" Sloane asked.

The guards exchanged a look. "We can take a peek at it for you. They'd have to have used another guest's room key to access the elevators or the stairwell doors, though."

"Could a member of your staff have given out this information?" I asked.

The guards exchanged another long look, both grimacing. "We've both worked here for years. I'd like to believe our staff wouldn't do that, but we do have hundreds of employees, some recently hired."

"Just let us know what you find," I said.

"And you'll be fine for the rest of the night?" the guard asked.

"As long as no more terrifying men try to bust down my door," Sloane said with a sardonic lift to her chin.

"Of course, ma'am, we'll keep an eye on it," the guards promised.

The second they left, she turned to me, tugging on her braid. She held up the picture, tapped the message written on it.

"You and I both know who sent this," she said. I rubbed the back of my neck, leaning against the wall. Acceptance was settling over me, washing away the fear of being attacked in the middle of the night.

"Bernard Allerton," I said, the name heavy in the room.

But Sloane was smiling—sly, almost excited. "If he's handing out threats, my guess is he's scared."

And before I could stop myself, I returned her smile. "My guess is this means we're hot on his trail."

Her brow arched. "*We?*"

I placed the pictures together, side by side. They were the exact same, down to the handwriting. "We both got these threats. At the very least, we should talk."

She sat on the end of her bed cross-legged, watching me carefully, like I was a rare butterfly about to float off for good. Silent. I wondered if it was obvious I was fighting my own internal battle, right in front of her. Behind her, I noticed she'd taken over every single flat surface in the room for various laptops, screens, files, and whiteboards. It was like a mobile PI's office—the only thing missing was a corkboard with pictures of Bernard and red string connecting the dots.

Frozen on her laptop screen was a black-and-white picture of Bernard at an awards ceremony. Next to him, looking young and fresh-faced, was Henry.

My chest actually hurt, looking at this picture and

knowing the future that awaited Henry—how deeply betrayed he'd feel, how scared, how utterly taken aback when the crimes hidden within his vocation were fully exposed to him.

If Bernard merely pretended to value libraries and antique books, Henry was the complete opposite. He was so devoted to the preservation of literature it was ingrained in his very soul.

I knew what I had to do now.

"You were right to be pissed at me the other night," I said slowly. Sloane only tilted her head. Still silent. "I did withhold information that could help you find Bernard. Or at least narrow the search down to a two-mile radius. Potentially. And I saw you looking at my Codex files in my room."

Now she was reacting, her whole body going taut. "You have a lot of extra years of information-gathering that I don't have. Won't have, given my deadline."

"Ten years, actually."

Her lips parted. "You've been tracking Bernard for *ten years*?"

I didn't answer right away, because if I didn't jump now, I wasn't going to. "I'll let you in. Let you have access to everything. Fill in the missing pieces you can't."

"The catch?"

An hour earlier, I'd been dreaming of this woman stripping for me. A woman who was technically my firm's competition and more than a decade younger than me. A woman who'd enchanted me from the very first second I'd laid eyes on her—and who would remain a distracting, dazzling temptation for as long as she was in my presence.

This was potentially the worst idea I'd ever had.

"When we capture Bernard, I want to be the one to fucking do it."

## 19

### ABE

*O*ur complimentary tea arrived. It sat untouched as Sloane and I squared off again in her hotel room. I was still seated in the chair by the dresser—barefoot, in sweatpants and a worn Quantico sweatshirt.

She faced me in her chair, elbows on her knees. Serious, focused, enthralled. Her posture was without her usual sultry teasing. Instead she appeared solely interested in catching the same man I was.

My cock noticed, of course. My cock responded to her sultry teasing as much as it was responding to her investigative interests.

"Explain what you mean when you say you want to 'be the one to do it,'" she said. "Because I'm not ditching my contract for your vendetta."

"The contract is yours. In fact, any money you get from Louisa for catching Bernard would be yours too. I only want to be in the room, whatever room it is, when he's found."

Her eyes searched mine, concerned. "I have an objection to not paying you if we partner on this."

"Why?" I asked.

"It's..." She rubbed her palms together. "It feels manipulative. Like I'm using you to get what I want. I don't want you to feel like I conned you into this."

There was an emotional emphasis on the words "conned you into this." I frowned. "You wouldn't be. Besides, it's not like Codex is here. You're not sub-contracting with a firm of detectives. I'm just a civilian who desperately wants Bernard to be punished for his crimes."

She sat back, assessed me further, like I was a file of open case notes she wasn't quite sure about yet. "If we go after Bernard together, you won't fly your team out here?"

"No." I spoke firmly through the guilt. "My agents are working cases right now with critical deadlines. And I can't risk flying them all the way to London when we have no legal right to be here, no contract, no client."

Henry and Delilah had disobeyed my express orders the night they recovered the missing Copernicus from Victoria Whitney's mansion. Freya and Sam broke into an historic academic building in Philadelphia without telling me. We had all kept things from each other in the past—this would now be one of them.

"Only the two of us *is* complicated enough," Sloane said. "And if our target is the auction, that's only three days away."

I was soothed by her logic.

"As long as I still get the credit, and as long as I'm standing right beside you, I'm comfortable with you being in the room."

I swallowed, felt my pride's response at sharing the moment with Sloane. "What... what can you offer me if we partner together?"

She bit her lip, rubbed her palms together again, but slowly this time. She was thinking. "I know you want to get into his office."

"Yes," I said. "Very badly."

"Louisa gave me access to whatever private papers Interpol hasn't taken. His books, his notes. Plus, I have three weeks of goodwill generated by my cover as Devon Atwood. The Society likes me, feels like they know me. Could tell me secrets, if we wanted them."

I *felt* how greedy I was for any scrap of information I could get.

"This is personal for you," she said.

"As personal as this job can be, yes," I said. "And what you are offering is extremely valuable to me."

She stroked her braid. "What made you suspect Bernard ten years ago? From what I can tell, the man never caught the eye of the authorities, either here *or* in the States. Why were you so obsessed with him?"

"When I was with the Bureau, my specialty was white-collar crime," I said. "My job was to know who held the most power in our country and who was using their power for evil instead of good. The Enrons and the Bernie Madoffs of the world were my focus, and I learned quickly that the more power you have, the easier it is for you to hide your sins."

My father had been a hedge fund manager—a world of tremendous wealth and privilege I now recognized as a great place to engage in all kinds of lies and treachery. When I would ask him what he did all day, he rattled off any number of golf course outings and lunches at country clubs and drinks at exclusive restaurants. Exclusive, secretive, elite —the perfect hiding places for the uber-wealthy who wanted to bend the law to their liking.

"Eventually I was moved to the FBI's new Art Theft division," I continued. "And I grew obsessed with learning all about the auction houses, the art galleries, the black markets, the forgers. Then I started looking into librarians."

Sloane leaned in, braid falling over her shoulder. "Like Bernard."

"Specifically Bernard." I looked again at the picture on her laptop—the fawning admirers in the crowd behind him. "Most librarians aren't famous the way he was. He always came across so confident, and his access was so vast. At the FBI, we knew that his private collection was extraordinary."

She arched her brow. "Well that's a sea of red fucking flags."

I smirked, amused. "That's exactly how I saw it. My supervisors were fine to keep him on a short list of suspicious collectors, but I was told, time and time again, my *obsession* with Bernard was disruptive."

She looked past me and at the wall of documents she'd taped up. Scanning it, she said, "Based on my research, he was never charged with anything, right?"

"He was a person of interest. I doubt it would come up on a search since he was cleared."

"What was it?" she asked. Her eagerness, her attentiveness, was everything I'd been missing these past days without my team. The call-and-response of working with other smart detectives was apparently something I'd grown quite fond of without realizing it.

The complication being that the more I got to see this side of Sloane, the more I wanted to lock her door, order in room-service, and not leave until we'd fucked for three days straight.

"When Sam worked for me at Art Theft, he was investigating a large-scale theft of antique maps stolen from a museum in Baltimore. Eventually the maps were traced all the way to Bernard's private collection here in London."

She walked over to her desk. "How the hell did I not know this?"

"Bernard presented Interpol with documents of authentication. Forged documents, although he claimed he couldn't possibly have known they were forged."

"No shit."

"So the *seller* was arrested, and Bernard used his experience to speak publicly about rare book theft and the ways his community could be more vigilant."

She chewed on her lip, clearly still thinking. Looked at me with a mysterious expression. "Bernard conned the hell out of Interpol. The best con men play the most convincing victims. It's a real smart way to assess the vulnerabilities of your next grift. I'm sure Bernard learned *a lot* about the blind spots in the justice system."

It took me a second to hide how impressed I was at that analysis. "Well... yes. Actually, that's a damn good point."

A *tiny* bit of the tease flitted to life, curving her lips as she said, "Well... I'm a damn good detective, Mr. Royal."

We held each other's gaze for much too long, the electric sexual chemistry between us burning up, burning bright, burning every inch of my skin. Every time I thought we'd doused it, there it was—an ember blazing to wildfire.

"That's my story," I finally managed. "Ten years' worth of my own research is what I could bring you. That and the cases Codex has worked recently that I believe implicate Bernard and his possible movements."

Sloane studied me, foot tapping—the only sign of her discomfort. I knew little about this beguiling goddess, but she had made it clear she was used to working alone. Preferred it. And yet as much as she kept claiming she could see through my thinly veiled vacation, I saw through her thinly veiled attempts at seeking my help the other night.

She didn't *want* to want help, which I found highly relatable.

"Show me the piece of missing information," she said.

I let out a heavy exhale. Walked toward her laptop. "May I?"

"Have at it."

I leaned forward, logged into my Codex email. Her scent, her body heat, invaded my senses. When I turned my face, hers was right there, mere inches away.

I saw her delicate throat work, her eyes on my lips. "I'll let you read the email and the reports attached."

Then I backed away slowly before I could give in to sweet temptation and kiss her. Instead, I busied my hands with pouring a cup of tea, water still steaming. Behind me, I heard her clicking, writing things down, muttering beneath her breath. A slew of curse words.

"You have FBI surveillance reports that triangulate Bernard's position between this fucking hotel and 221B Baker Street?" Her words were part tense edge, part hungry excitement.

"Yes," I said.

"Also in this radius are Mycroft's Pub, Adler's Bookshop and Kensley's, where the Doyle papers will be auctioned off," Sloane said. She scrubbed her hands down her face, re-examined her wall of notes. Looked at me, looked back at the email on her screen.

"Is that enough information for you?" I asked.

Her lips quirked. "You know it is. And I think you know what it's like when everything about a case that made no fucking sense suddenly starts speaking to you in a language you understand."

I softened my tone. "I do. It's a lot to process."

"You're a lot to process, to be honest," she said. Hushed,

like she hadn't meant it. She walked toward me until our legs almost touched. She was tall enough that I had to look up at her slightly.

"You're Ahab," she said, pointing at my chest.

"In what way?" I asked, careful to hide my astonishment. I'd been thinking of myself as Ahab since I'd arrived here.

Propping her hands on her hips, she said, "Bernard is your white whale. You came all the way here to London for a fake vacation because you want to take this asshole down all by yourself."

I sensed how tenuous this partnership was, how tenuous her trust was. She was right—there was nothing I wouldn't do to get him. "It is a real vacation," I said slowly. "I hoped I might *stumble upon* Bernard while here. I'm not a vigilante."

"No," she conceded. "But don't lie and tell me catching him by yourself isn't a point of pride for you. That's why you've kept this from your team."

Sloane was a huntress in the wilderness, bow raised, arrow aimed straight at my heart. The woman cut through my bullshit easily and without remorse.

I weighed my options, considered going after the man myself after all. Leaving The Langham, staking out that auction, waiting for Bernard to show up and steal it. I could do it; it was available to me.

Except hadn't that always been my father's weakness? *Off, on.* He was there, until he wasn't. And god help me I couldn't stop wanting to *be there* for Sloane Argento.

"That is a fairly accurate portrayal of my motivations," I said. "Well done."

Her expression turned sympathetic. "I'm only pointing out the obvious. If we do this, Abe, we're doing it together. Every step of the way. We just gave each other too much usable information not to. I need to know you're okay with your personal man-hunt becoming a two-person show." She looked like she wanted to say more but at the last second shook her head. "Are you? Okay with it?"

"I will become okay with it," I said through clenched teeth. "I promise."

She dropped her voice. "There's no shame in the way you feel. I chose this vocation because I wanted to spend my life punishing people that deserve it. Landing this case was already a huge deal for me. If I succeed, it blows the doors right open. I understand the tunnel vision aspect of working this job."

This woman was fourteen years my junior, had her entire career ahead of her. And goddamn if I didn't respect the motivation burning in her gaze. The hungry kind, the reckless kind. The *do-anything-to-win* kind.

It was the only kind of motivation I respected.

"You'll succeed," I said. I held out my hand for her to shake. "Partners?"

She waited a full three seconds before clasping my hand, squeezing with determination. With only a few inches between us—and a king-size bed behind us—lust surged at the point of every finger brushing against my skin. Her chest was rising and falling, lips parted, pupils dilated. If she glanced down, she'd discover the outline of my cock against my sweatpants. Shaking hands was a bad idea, touching was a bad idea, sharing a wall was the *worst* idea.

Sloane let go first, surprising me when she pulled open her mini-fridge and removed two tiny bottles of vodka.

"Are we celebrating?" I asked. I couldn't decipher the look on her face.

She handed me the tiny shot bottle and leaned back against her dresser. Six feet away from me. "I've been thinking about tonight, what happened to us. *If* we were followed back to our hotel from the pub, then we were tailed for at least twenty minutes. Tailed and photographed without our knowledge."

"What's your point?" I asked.

She crossed one ankle over the other. "I don't have formal training. But I know when I've caught surveillance. I'm guessing a former federal agent does too."

"They could be very skilled," I said. "Wouldn't be the first time two people were surprised when they weren't expecting it."

"*That's* my point," she said. She took the shot of vodka with ease, slamming the plastic bottle down. "I was distracted on our walk home tonight because I was thinking about fucking you. That's my truth. I *wasn't* concerned for our safety one bit. When, given what happened to us two days ago, we both should be aware at all times."

I blew out an irritated breath. Leaned forward with my elbows on my knees. Tried, unsuccessfully, to not experience a wave of desire at the thought of Sloane wanting me so badly.

"You may be right, Ms. Argento." I twirled my own bottle between my fingers.

"Were you distracted by me?" she asked.

I allowed myself a deliberate perusal of her body—allowed myself to enjoy a moment I'd have to deny until we saw this thing through to the end.

Then I knocked back the tiny bottle of vodka and grimaced through the burn. "I was very distracted by you. So much so that I came on to you if you recall."

"Devastation," she said softly, looking as tender-eyed and vulnerable as I'd ever seen her. Which, unfortunately, only heightened my longing. She clinked our empty bottles together. "We're going to stay focused. We're going to tell each other the truth. We are *not* going to fuck each other. And we're going to be the ones who catch Bernard fucking Allerton."

I tossed our bottles in the trash, clapped my hands together. "Right again, Ms. Argento."

## 20

# SLOANE

*A*t 10:30 the next morning, my new partner and I boarded the London underground to Oxford—which would include a transfer to another train and at least an hour of sitting next to Abe Royal in a compressed space with nothing to do except look at each other.

From the tightness around his mouth—and the clenching of his jaw—I guessed Abe felt the same tension as the doors of the train closed and we set off on our journey to the McMaster's Library.

I was taking him to Bernard Allerton's office.

We were seated directly next to each other—and every time I turned my head, I caught him watching me. "Do you have something on your mind?"

A quirk of his lips. "Did you enjoy your morning of devouring the hearts of foolish men for breakfast?"

I tapped my chin, pretended to think. "Knew I forgot to eat."

He chuckled softly, briefly touching the knot of his perfectly straight tie. Yet again, he rocked a perfectly tailored suit that made me want to straddle him in the middle of this packed train. Last night, after we'd shaken hands on the idea of being partners, I'd sent him packing for his room with strict instructions not to come back unless we received another creepy threat. Because I couldn't —*fucking could not*—take one more tempting second of that man sitting so close to my bed. In sweatpants and bare feet and a worn sweatshirt pushed past his muscular forearms. It was disarming to say the least to see Abe Royal both sleepy-eyed and protective.

It was disarming, to say the least, to recognize how quickly I'd run to him after receiving the note. My first instinct was to protect the stranger in the room next to me, in direct contradiction to the parental advice my parents had ensured I understood from a young age.

*Always save yourself.*

Con blown? Save yourself.

Identity uncovered? Save yourself.

The few times cops literally chased us from towns I had to beg my parents in the heat of the moment to take me too. I was only a child, for fuck's sake. It wasn't like I could hot wire a car and squeal on out of there. Which we'd actually done a half-dozen times before I turned sixteen.

I'd sat up in bed for another hour after he left, pulling through the notes I'd gathered over the past month, the pieces beginning to fit with the added information Abe was providing me. That email put a pin on Bernard's location in the middle of London, eliminating my fears that the man had high-tailed it across Europe, never to be found. At least by me. These reports were everything.

Feeling safe with Abe by my side was another issue entirely. I'd felt it the second he'd walked into the pub last night. Felt it the moment he opened his hotel room door.

Felt it when we shook hands—that sense of *we* instead of just me.

He smiled at me again, and my heart exploded with happiness. I pressed a hand to my chest. Wondered when I'd started to resemble a teen girl going to prom with her crush.

"How long have you had your own firm?" Abe asked, rocking gently against me with the rhythm of the train.

I gave him a curious look. He shrugged. "We have an hour. You might as well entertain me."

I snorted. "Five years. I got my license when I turned twenty. Picked up odd PI jobs until I graduated to help pay the bills."

"That Audubon case you worked really put you on the map," he said. "At least in a world like ours."

"Fucking birds, man," I said. His smile widened—the muscles of his face brightening in a way I hadn't seen before. "If you think Sherlock Holmes fans are obsessed, you should try going deep undercover as a bird watcher."

He turned fully toward me. "You went that deep?"

I nodded, tapped my knee. "The Murphy Library in upstate New York has strong ties with this rabid bird-watching group called The Painted Buntings. Picture retired bird-watchers who love to enjoy birds in their natural habitat while also being blood-thirsty and petty."

"Like a Eudora," Abe mused.

"Yes," I said. "Exactly like a Eudora. They were all Eudoras, basically. So this library is well-known because it owns ten illustrated prints from *Birds of America*."

I was new to rare books at the time I'd been hired. I later learned that John James Audubon's full, four-volume guide to birds was one of the rarest in the world and worth millions of dollars. Which boggled my mind.

"Let me guess. Their security systems are shit," Abe said dryly.

"They weren't great," I conceded. "In between conservation cycles, they'd loan the illustrations to The Painted Buntings for their annual fundraiser. The ticket price included time with the pages, examining them from behind protective glass, taking pictures. Six weeks before the event, the prints were stolen from the library."

The theatrical tears coming from The Painted Buntings when they were informed of the theft had been what made me suspect them in the first place. Too over the top, no nuance. It had the feel of performance, not real emotion.

"I infiltrated the bird watchers," I whispered dramatically.

"What was your cover?" he asked, matching my tone.

I beamed a cheery, mega-watt smile his way—gave his hand an enthusiastic shake. "Samantha Jenkins, event planning intern, amateur bird watcher."

"Always a pleasure to meet one of your many characters," Abe said smoothly. "So that's how you got into their meetings?"

"The bird meetings *and* the fundraising meetings," I said. "I spent weeks learning everything there was to know about birds and silent auctions. Then sat back and watched for mistakes. I'd never met a group of people as gossipy and conniving. And *horny*."

His brow raised imperceptibly. "You don't say."

"These bird-lovers were breaking hearts left and right," I said. "It wasn't hard to take in the feuds, the old arguments, the ancient history people couldn't let go of. Which is what led me to Mrs. Maeve Hawthorne. She was sleeping with *three* other birdwatchers and described herself as John Audubon's number one fan. When she had me over for tea, she'd framed reproductions of his prints and hung them on every wall and available space in her home. And she'd seduced two of her bird-loving lovers to take the *actual* illustrations."

"Let me guess—" Abe smirked. "She wasn't even worried nor felt guilty."

"I swear to god the woman was a sociopath dressed in a Laura Ashley sweater-set. But she shouldn't have left me alone in her house while she went outside to accost the mailman. Five minutes was all I needed to slip into her basement and find the makeshift storage unit she'd created to make sure the artwork remained undamaged."

"Sneaky, Ms. Argento," he said in a tone that caressed like a lover's.

"People should lock their basements if they don't want undercover private investigators to find their loot."

"Remind me to keep an eye on you the first time you're in my house."

The idea of *Abe's house* had an atom bomb effect in my brain, shattering my concept of this intense attraction from something unexpected and sexy to real and even long-term.

"When would I be in your house?" I asked, lips pursed.

He swallowed hard. "Time will tell, I guess."

I stole one more heated glance at Abe before turning back, toward the other passengers, hurtling toward Oxford. "So, uh," I said, clearing my throat. "When Maeve came down the stairs and found me, I asked her why she had stolen illustrations worth two million dollars in her basement. She said, '*Oh, those? How on earth did they get here?*'"

"Sounds like an heiress I know," he said, smiling slightly. "It's the amazing thing about working undercover, earning their trust. There's a certain kind of criminal that will lead you right to the smoking gun."

Our train pulled into its stop, and we made the crowded journey across the platform and toward the library. Even a few streets away, the gorgeous greens of Oxford's gardens were visible, only slightly muted beneath the cloudy sky.

Next to me, Abe slipped his hands into his pockets. "You know, it does say quite a bit about your talent and skill that Louisa hired you."

"She might be regretting her decision at this point," I said grimly.

"I've had to talk quite a few clients off the ledge before," he said. "It never gets easier, and I only ever feel more like shit."

I laughed. "Inspirational."

He cast me a sideways glance. "No lying to each other, right?"

That look of his made me almost trip on the sidewalk. "Right."

"I won't ever tell you it gets easier when it, in fact, does not."

We hit the long stone path leading to one of the most well-respected libraries in the world. Bernard's library.

"The day Louisa officially hired me," I said. "She told me I had a 'fire in my eyes' that she found seriously lacking whenever Interpol agents came to update her on their progress."

"Yes, you do lack the dead eyes of bureaucratic drones," Abe said.

"You're still pissed though," I said.

"About what?" He was staring at the magnificent, historic building with an impassive expression, but the flare of his nostrils and rigid posture betrayed his true feelings.

"That she hired me and not you."

He looked down at the ground, toeing along the stone. "Vanity, thy name is Abraham Royal."

I nudged my shoulder deliberately against his. "I know why it could be hard for you to come back here. You thought you'd snagged the biggest case of your career, only to have it taken away and given to the authorities you've come to despise."

"Maybe I don't have enough fire," he drawled.

I remembered his conviction when he spoke about his ten-year hunt for Bernard, his passion for justice, the hunger there that mirrored my own.

And I remembered the sinful feeling of his lips on my throat.

"You seem to have more than enough fire to me," I said with full honesty.

Then I led us both up the winding stone path, back to where it all began.

## 21

## ABE

"*L*et's head straight to Bernard's office in the library," Sloane said. "I have keys."

My fingers curled into fists. I hadn't been inside the McMaster's Library since last November, when I'd dropped literally everything and flown out here after receiving Louisa's call. Bernard hadn't disappeared from my thoughts, but the cases Codex had been working at that point were opportunistic and disconnected from each other. There didn't seem to be anything tying the abundance of rare book theft to a larger purpose—or a larger person.

Until the night I met Henry, looking shell-shocked and guilt-ridden, and he handed me a file of evidence he swore implicated his famous boss of a crime he couldn't believe was possible.

Now, I was walking with Sloane toward Bernard's *office*. What would it be like to view the elements of Bernard's life that were banal and pedestrian?

We walked past the reception area—to the left was the small study room where I'd found Henry, holed up and guilt-ridden. And to the right...

To the right was a veritable cathedral of knowledge. Narrow skylights caught the dreary gray daylight and transformed it into something glittering and incandescent. The center of the room was filled with table after long table, where students bowed their heads over books next to softly lit lamps. Curved around them were dozens of mahogany bookshelves filled with books and towering almost as high as the vaulted ceiling.

"Incredible, isn't it?" Sloane whispered next to me.

I nodded, throat tight. I didn't often get to remember the emotional aspect of founding Codex. We received cases, my agents tracked down the books, we received payment, we celebrated with donuts and tacos. It was a satisfying and fulfilling cycle. This 300-year-old library was a testament to the gravity of Bernard's many abuses, the callousness with which he viewed this vital part of our cultural history.

"Last time I was here, I didn't get to see this," I said.

She walked in front of me, crooking her finger. "Wait till we get to the best part."

I followed her swaying hips down a long row of books to the bottom of a wrought-iron spiral staircase. We climbed it to a loft area. The floor was carpeted, quiet. A few tables up here were occupied by stressed-looking students. And in the middle stood a medieval-looking door. Next to it, an engraved plaque: *Dr. Bernard Allerton, Director.*

Beneath it was a typed note from Louisa: *Dr. Allerton is currently on sabbatical and not receiving student emails or requests. Thank you for your patience during this time.*

There were students all around us, so I held my tongue at the word *sabbatical.*

With a sly grin, Sloane opened his office door and pulled me inside. When she flipped on the lights, yellow police tape marred the luxurious-looking office like an ugly scar. I could see remnants of my former profession—empty evidence bags, taped-off cabinets, dust stains from items clearly removed. Still, the essence of who Bernard *pretended* to be was there: overstuffed green chairs perfect for meeting or reading, large shelves filled with books and displaying his many academic accomplishments, framed degrees and pictures with famous thinkers, academics, and philosophers.

On the edge of the floor lamp hung a deerstalker cap, like Holmes. The shelf immediately next to it held slim volumes of every Sherlock story by Arthur Conan Doyle. On his desk was a pair of glasses, opened books, high-lighters, a coffee mug. I bent down by the space where I assumed his computer had been before being confiscated. Dull and fading was a sticky note: *Bernard, I received a strange request about the Mary Shelley retrospective. Can we discuss when you have a free moment? -Henry*

I shook my head. Sloane touched the note, looked at me. "Your Henry, right?"

"My Henry," I said softly. "It's more difficult than I thought it would be, seeing the reminders that Bernard's actions have hurt real people in my life. People I—" I stopped, cutting off the foreign words *care about.* "People that are currently in my employ."

Her sharp gaze let me know she didn't miss my verbal stumble.

I cleared off a small space on Bernard's massive desk to perch. It was disheveled, unorganized, and I wasn't sure if that had been the work of the agents or the man's general state of being. Sloane settled into a massive recliner. "I believe Bernard is hiding within the two-mile radius mapped in that report you received."

"I agree."

"And I think our best shot is to assume *someone* is going to make a grab for those Doyle papers being auctioned off on Friday at Kensley's."

I removed my jacket and laid it across a nearby chair. "There's no way Bernard actually makes a play for it obviously. But if we can gain access to that auction, examine the papers and the exits, we could catch a crime before it happens, use leverage to get the thief to unburden his soul and tell us Bernard's location."

She ran a hand through her hair. It tumbled back down in silky waves. "The *worst* case scenario is we catch a crime in the act and the authorities get called in. That's still a way to cinch the net tighter around Bernard."

I stared at that sticky note again, Henry's bold handwriting. The stakes had never felt higher. "Agree."

"So our potentially involved characters are Eudora," Sloane started.

"I also think we should look at the director at the Kensley Auction, James Patrick," I added. "He alerted Eudora to the sale and would be the closest to the actual item on auction night. And Peter Markham should be on that list, the grandson of Nicholas and owner of Adler's. He's apparently close with Bernard and enthusiastic."

"A dangerous combo here," she said. "What about... Humphrey and Reggie?"

I considered it. "We shouldn't discount Bernard's best friends. He could be staying with them for all we know, and Humphrey is a classically trained actor."

Sadness flashed across her face. "For what it's worth, my gut says they're innocent."

"Mine too," I promised. "He is, at the very least, a gold mine. He's given us a lot of good information and insight already."

"True. All of these people are also potential hiding spots as well, if he's actually in London." She stood to pace the narrow burgundy carpet that ran down the hardwood floor. "According to Louisa, Bernard's emails are being monitored as well as voicemails. His apartment is less than a mile from here and is currently under surveillance. Credit card activity is being monitored." She stopped, tapped her fingers against the shelf of Sherlock books. "I've torn through this office more times than I can count, but I thought you could provide vital information here that I wouldn't have known was important. Interpol took everything of value, of course..."

"They don't get everything though," I said. "And some things only feel pertinent if you have the background to understand its relevance."

I was already starting to inch toward a pile of papers on Bernard's desk, needing to see the evidence of his years of misdeeds out in the open, the thefts and the crimes hidden within meeting notes and conservation records.

"Wait," Sloane said, cocking her head. "Codex. The past eleven months. I need to know the rest of the missing pieces."

Blowing out a breath, I stood. Wandered to a wall of framed degrees and pictures—Bernard in magazines, at galas, teaching in classrooms, working with Henry and other staff.

Turning, I leaned against the wall and crossed one ankle over the other. "It all began with a code word," I said, launching into a summary of Codex's recent cases and the way I came to meet Henry Finch in that tiny room. The evidence he shared, the stolen works and carved-up pages, the books from their collections reportedly sent to other museums, never to arrive. The interns, the tours, the loans never approved—all pieces of Bernard's system of moving rare books to private sellers through his work at the library. I told her about the code words, their use, and the way they'd unlocked doors for my agents at various levels of Bernard's pyramid.

"*Didn't we once meet at Reichenbach Falls?*" Sloane repeated, brow furrowed. "That was on a sign above the fireplace at Mycroft's Pub."

"I know," I said. "I noticed the same thing. Bernard clearly uses elements of his own life throughout his criminal empire. Also, I tried the code with Eudora when I met with her."

"And?" She was leaning forward.

"She recognized it immediately." I lifted a shoulder. "Given she's one of our suspicious people, it doesn't surprise me in the least that she's worked closely with the man since the day she joined the Society and she's also involved in either buying or selling stolen books. It wouldn't surprise me if every member of the Society had some *small* hand in it."

"It honestly wouldn't surprise me if they didn't think what they were doing was that bad," Sloane continued. "It seems like the community is tight-knit enough to see this as part of what they do."

"I believe that to be undeniably true," I said. "But it does put another check in the Eudora column." I leaned back against the wall. "Do you know who Victoria Whitney is?"

Sloane shook her head. "Who is she?"

"Philadelphia's wealthiest heiress with an antiquities collection that rivals Bernard's."

I filled her in on Bernard's *lady love*, their whirlwind romance in different European cities, her role in the theft of Copernicus's *On the Revolutions of Heavenly Spheres*. "And not only that, she was in possession of other antiques that Bernard had stolen for her," I added. "Their romantic relationship ended a decade ago, according to Henry. But he appears to have been her main contact any time she wanted a book for her collection. And when she was brought in for the theft, she didn't give Bernard up."

"Wait," she said, "Bernard Allerton was in... *love?* Eudora mentioned that he'd had an American girlfriend."

I pondered this for a moment. "I'm not sure the man can love, at least not the way other people can. I believe he probably felt real affection for her, though. I always thought Victoria might be his vulnerability in the end."

She was biting her lip and shaking her head. "A man like that is unable to love. I think his vulnerability is his greed."

A wide range of emotions moved across her face, and I struggled to interpret what they meant. Struggled to admit I *wanted* to see beyond her sultry, confident mask to the vulnerable woman beneath. I was pretty sure her past wasn't filled with sunshine and fucking rainbows. Maybe because I recognized an emotional skittishness that mirrored my own.

I tapped the cane that Bernard gripped in some of the pictures on the wall. "Bernard had this cane and a hunch in his back for years. You can see it in all of the recent photos. But Henry told me that the night he confronted Bernard, he stood on his own without the cane. Had a lower voice even, plus a straight posture."

She huffed out a breath. "I know this game. A disguise that plays on people's sympathies. We would never suspect our elderly grandfather of trying to steal our shit. It allows con artists to hide in plain sight."

"Because the human mind loves to make up excuses when we don't want to admit what's right in front of us," I said.

Oddly enough, Caroline had said something similar the night we'd broken up. She had reminded me, quite pointedly, that while I *checked off* her list of desirable qualities in a romantic partner, there was nothing else there. I was a well-dressed package complete with ambition, drive, intelligence, and a rising career with the FBI.

What I *wasn't* was in love.

*Off, on. Off, on.*

Sloane brushed past me in a quick, back-and-forth pace through Bernard's office. She was talking quietly to herself.

"Are you getting ideas?" I asked.

"Everything's coming together, you know?" she said. "I'm happy we're... I mean it's nice to, like... have this."

"What?"

She shrugged. "A partner to bounce ideas off of."

"Don't get used to it," I said. "You're back to being a lone wolf after this, remember?"

I'd meant it to be light and playful. I caught the hurt in her eyes before she clapped her hands together. "Are we going through Bernard's office or are you just going to stand there?" Now she gave me a flirtatious smile, a silly tap of her foot as she crossed her arms like the world's sexiest drill sergeant.

"Partners for twelve hours, and you're already issuing demands?"

"I'm very demanding," she purred. "Now get to work, Royal." She clapped her hands again, and I retaliated by undoing my cuff links and slowly rolling my shirtsleeves to my elbows. She sashayed past me and yanked open a filing cabinet full of papers. "I'll take this one. You take the desk."

"Yes, ma'am," I said. And we got to work. As partners. In Bernard Allerton's office, surrounded by a lifetime of lies and deceit and inventive manipulations. I'd always assumed

I wanted to punish that man more than anything else in my life—more, even, than I wanted to see my father punished for abandoning us.

Yet that need was quickly outpaced by another, more pressing need. The need to watch Sloane as she quietly sank to the ground, surrounded by files, the curtain of her black hair obscuring half of her face. The need to lean forward on my knees, wrap my arm around her waist, and yank her beneath my body; the need to fuck her on this office floor with one hand pressed to her mouth to keep her quiet in this historic library.

The need to ask her more, listen more, learn more. The desire to unravel a mystery as captivating as the ones I'd been chasing my entire life. The mystery of the woman who had bewitched me from the second I'd laid eyes on her.

Which was a shame, since I had plans to revert to being a lone wolf after this as well.

## 22

## SLOANE

*T*wo hours later, and it was like a small tornado had torn through Bernard's elegant academic offices. Abe was standing by one of the bookshelves, pulling open pages and searching for hidden notes. He was slightly disheveled: tie off, top two buttons of his collared shirt open, sleeves rolled up. I had ink running down my fingers and smeared along my arms and had kicked my boots off ages ago.

We'd worked in a quiet, comforting silence, in between moments of finding potential clues and dissecting them. It was invigorating and helpful and far too fucking pleasant. What I needed from this partnership was to use Abe's connections and skills to find Bernard. What I *didn't* need was any kind of proof that needing someone could add anything else to my quality of life or state of happiness.

Happiness in life wasn't my goal anyway—success was.

I'd been tearing through old planners, taking notes on who Bernard often met with, any patterns that might illuminate where the hell he was. Henry Finch was all over this calendar as was Victoria, who Bernard noted as *Lady Love*.

Meals with Humphrey. Flights to Istanbul, Prague, Tokyo. Train tickets to Paris, Edinburgh. Staff meetings, galas, ceremonies celebrating libraries and academic research. A weekly meeting at an apothecary with "E," which I marked on a sticky for further questioning.

"Abe?" I said, breaking a long, productive silence.

He *hmmm*-ed, distracted, before putting down a book and looking at me.

I held up the planner, waved my hand around the office. "Do you think Bernard cared about any of this? The libraries, the conservation, the fundraising. I mean *truly* cared?"

Abe rubbed the back of his neck, winced a little. "Henry thinks he does. We've talked about this a lot at Codex. The complicated tapestry of Bernard's moral code. Even with all that Henry's seen, and all that he knows, he firmly believes his former mentor exists easily between the world of well-respected scholarship and shadowy underworld. *Exists*, as in believes both are necessary."

I tapped the calendar, stared at the picture of him standing with Victoria. "If that's true, it goes back to that story Humphrey told us. About Bernard taking their things. Because he could. He adheres to a different set of rules than the rest of the world."

"The man clearly believes in the power of libraries *and* clearly believes in the power of money and greed," he said.

I shifted around the pile of planners, tucking my feet beneath me. "I met with dozens of Sherlock Society members before you arrived. Attended their luncheons, their meetings, took them out for drinks. They were all eager to talk about Bernard when I asked."

"Anything in particular stand out?"

"I couldn't pull together a clear picture of Bernard's

motivations at all," I replied honestly. "And the more I met with people the murkier my understanding of him became. He..." I paused, gathered my thoughts. "He manipulated every single one of them. Maybe not for nefarious purposes, but they all spoke about his charisma. When he spoke to you, you were the only one in the room. He remembered little details, he brought gifts, he noticed things about you that others never did."

Those meetings had always made me squirm. Because Bernard's techniques were classic con man tricks. I knew them, my parents knew them. And as a detective, I still used them to gain trust.

"I once led a team of agents that arrested and charged a powerful CEO who was responsible for a pyramid scheme that stole millions of dollars from people in this small town in Connecticut. This was about six years ago. And he was so charismatic I used to send in three agents at a time during interviews. Because he'd charm the first two so easily they'd come to me claiming his innocence. And they weren't new agents fresh from Quantico. These were stalwart men and women who delighted in locking up men like that. He was just too good." Abe was looking away, almost dreamy—like he was holding back.

"Good memory?" I asked, chasing the source of that dreaminess.

"Professionally, yes, actually. At the time, I was pretty frustrated with my work at the Bureau, but that case was one I'll never forget. And one I'll always be proud of. Because that CEO was a goddamn sociopath who destroyed people's lives. Putting him behind bars had a real effect on the scales of justice." He slid his steel eyes toward me. "I had a girlfriend at the time who didn't see it that way unfortunately. Although I admit that case dominated my every waking thought. Not much time to tend to our relationship."

There was a bizarre feeling in my belly at the thought of Abe in a relationship. "When did the two of you break up?" I asked.

"About five years ago. She's married now and has a baby. Which makes me happy. I felt guilt for a long time knowing she spent a year of her life with a man who wouldn't give her what she needed."

I brushed a few strands of hair behind my ear, tilted my head. "Have you ever dated anyone that distracted you from work?"

Abe stared at me. "No. Not yet. Although my mother and Jeanette beg me to find her so they can finally become grandparents."

"Your moms sound like smart ladies," I said. "You must be Philadelphia's most eligible bachelor. There are a lot of women who would kill to date a man who cared so deeply about righting the wrongs of the world." *While looking that hot in a suit.*

He didn't respond to my observation. Instead, he countered with, "And how many hearts are you breaking in New York City right now? Ten? Twenty?"

I laughed, surprised. "Not a heartbreaker," I said. "That would imply I stayed around long enough for them to learn the language of my heart."

His throat worked behind his collar. "Has anyone learned that language?"

"Not yet."

To avoid bursting into flames, I re-focused on that picture of Bernard and Victoria. Thought about vulnerabilities, the soft spots and weaknesses of a con artist. For my parents, my best guess was their marriage was one of criminal conve-

KATHRYN NOLAN

nience, a distorted partnership that bound them together
through years of lies and thievery. I stood up, tugged at the
deerstalker hat hanging from the end of the floor lamp.

"I take back what I said about vulnerabilities. It's not
only greed."

"It's Sherlock Holmes and Arthur Conan Doyle," Abe
said softly. "Bernard's one emotional obsession."

"The private papers from Doyle that he lost the *first* time
they were made available was also the first time he'd ever
been denied. Been told *no* and had it mean something," I
continued.

He nodded along, then scrubbed his hands down his
face. It'd been a long two hours, and I could feel my scratchy
eyes and aching back. "Everything here, all of these books,
have something to do with Sherlock Holmes or Doyle. It's
like a kind of shrine."

He grabbed the last book on the shelf and opened it.

A photo fell.

He snatched it up as it hit the ground. "Sloane."

I was there in an instant. And there was a fluttering in
my belly caused by Abe's firmly speaking my name. Not
*Devon* or *Ms. Atwood* or *Ms. Argento* or any other teasing
moniker. Abe flipped the picture around and tapped it with
his fingers. "That's Bernard. And *these* are the members of
The Empty House that Sam and Freya got arrested."

I took the picture, looked at Abe. "I only know about
The Empty House from the articles written about the case
in the newspaper."

He pointed to a white man with an Indiana Jones-style
hat on. "That is Dr. Bradley Ward, the head of The Empty
House and formerly a well-known academic and professor."
He indicated an elegant-looking white couple. "Thomas and

Cora Alexander, also in the secret society and close with Ward. We believe Bernard had the Alexanders steal a first edition of *Don Quixote* from Ward. And we believe Bernard also had them steal the George Sand love letters that Sam and Freya ultimately recovered. Thomas and Cora admitted to my agents on multiple occasions that Bernard was stirring the pot, potentially destabilizing the group without concern for anyone other than himself."

"That matches his personality," I said grimly. "Were the Alexanders the thieves themselves? Or did they use someone?"

Abe grimaced slightly. "We think they used a librarian intern named Jim Dahl. Dahl was working at The Franklin Museum in Philadelphia for six months prior to them receiving the Sand letters. He stole them and forged additional copies to sell. He was never caught, so we can't be sure, but our guess was always that he was the thief used to steal from Dr. Ward too."

"He's still on the run?" I asked.

"No sign of him," he answered. "I'm sure he's one thief of many that Bernard has used throughout the years." He flipped the photo over, frowned. "Apparently this picture was taken during an annual trip to Reichenbach Falls in Switzerland."

"Interesting," I drawled. "Look there's our friend Eudora." She was dressed in a poncho and rain hat, smiling beatifically. Hard to place this innocent-looking cat lady as the same lady Humphrey said would bury your body beneath her floorboards if you crossed her.

With narrowed eyes, Abe brought the picture closer. "Well you don't say. That is our favorite president. I wasn't aware Eudora Green was an official member of The Empty

House. Maybe this wasn't specifically a trip for the secret society but a trip for the Sherlock Society."

I squinted at two men off to the side, slightly blurred. One man held the hand of a little boy. "Then who are they, and whose kid is that?"

He shook his head. Examined the scrawled notation on the back again. "Peter, Nick, and James."

I pulled out my phone, typed in *James Patrick, Kensley Auction House*. The first picture returned was the man in that photo, just aged by twenty years.

"So, this young boy must be Peter; the older man, his grandfather Nick. The bookstore owners."

"The Sherlock Society. Adler's. Kensley," I added. "That's our net, our radius. *Those* are our suspects."

He held the picture close, squinting. "Can you find a current picture of Peter Markham?"

"I think I saw him the other night," I mentioned. "Leading a discussion at Adler's. This is him." I found a picture on their website. He was a younger white man with red hair and a beard. Abe stared at it for a long time.

"What is it?" I asked.

"Something about his face is jogging my memory, and I don't know why," he said. "Which is infuriating."

"Like you recognize him?"

He rubbed his brow. "Yes. I'm just not sure how. He's a London bookstore owner, and unless he's committed a crime in the States, I'd have no reason to recognize him. Right?"

I shrugged. "You and I both know our field is built upon a system of hunches. Don't discount it. Maybe let it sit for a while."

"True," he said. "Hopefully you won't be offended when I take this picture, by the way."

"I saw nothing," I winked. Stalked back to the pile of calendars I'd been sifting through.

"Speaking of hunches, one of Bernard's weekly appointments is bugging me," I said, scooping down to flip one open. Abe followed, looking over my shoulder. His breath sailed along the curve of my neck, igniting more fluttery feelings. More longing.

"This one," I said, steeling my voice. "Every Wednesday night last year it says 7:00, *Midnight Apothecary with E.* I'm thinking Eudora, right? Illegal or not, they would have had plenty of Sherlock Society business to talk about given their roles in the organization."

"Likely it's her," he said. "And tonight is Wednesday oddly enough. Do you think she still keeps her appointment?"

"With Bernard?" I asked, disbelieving.

"That would be extremely risky, and that man is anything but," he said. "If *anything*, Eudora might still go there, and we could happen upon her. Use it as an excuse to work her for info."

I tapped my phone against my mouth, thinking. Liking this plan. "I had a rather boozy brunch with Gertrude, the office secretary for the Sherlock Society. She liked me."

"Who wouldn't?" Abe said.

I winked at him. "Let me follow a feeling."

I called Gertrude's number in my phone, remembered that she adored chocolate and biscuits.

"Sherlock Society for Civilized Scholars," came Gertrude's bouncy English accent.

"Gertrude?" I said, tentative. "It's Devon Atwood."

"Oh *Devon*, what a nice surprise, love," she gushed. "I was thinking about you last week actually. We must do lunch again before you head back to America."

"I'd love it," I swore. "Can I bribe you with biscuits for top-secret information?"

A sweet, tittering laugh came through the phone. I placed her on speaker, looked away from Abe's face before I got too distracted. "You know me too well! Ask away, bribe away."

I bit my lip. "It's Eudora."

"What about her, love?" An edge to her tone that hadn't been there before.

"You're going to think I'm an airhead, but she and I made plans tonight, and now I can't get a hold of her, and I can't remember where we're meeting. She didn't mention anything to you, did she?" I made the mistake of catching Abe's slow grin at my acting. Took a step back.

"For tonight? No that can't be right," Gertrude said. "Every Wednesday night she's at Midnight Apothecary, blocked off. She never goes anywhere else."

Abe's grin transformed into an intense focus.

"I see," I replied. "Well, I must have gotten the dates wrong. I'm sure we're meeting tomorrow night instead. Since I'm in town, is Midnight Apothecary a place I should visit?"

"Oh, it's *darling*," she said. "Cutest little cocktail bar. Right near the old auction house. Kensley's. You know it, love?"

This time, Abe and I couldn't help but lock eyes. "Oh, I know it," I said. "Thanks again for the tip. I'll bring you biscuits this week."

When I hung up, Abe was already starting to put Bernard's office slightly back together. "If we want to get back to London and to that cocktail bar, we should get going." He stopped, looked back over at me. "Nicely done, by the way. If she's no longer meeting with Bernard every week, I want to know who a book thief is meeting, weekly, right next to the auction house we're staking out."

I exhaled, proud of myself. Invigorated that another person was here to catch me in the act. That *never* happened.

A quick thirty minutes later, and I was shutting the office door firmly and re-locking it. We both let out deep breaths. I pulled my hair into a ponytail while Abe stretched his neck, brushed a few wrinkles from his jacket.

"To cocktail hour?" I asked softly.

"Making demands and taking me on a date," he whispered. "Partnership with you sure is strange."

"Girls like me do enjoy dates that involve watching potential suspects from behind bushes."

He stared at my mouth for so long I worried he'd kiss me right here, in the middle of the fucking library. Instead he growled, "Let's go."

I was helpless not to follow his broad back, his refined and elegant profile. Down the spiral staircase, we were back in the ethereal library. The same students were still in the same seats, same positions. Different books. The room was filled with the devotional scratch of pencils, the clicking of keyboards, the sound of books being shelved by various librarians.

A dark-haired girl wearing a black sweater sat in a far corner by herself. She looked like me, so much so that I stopped walking. Stared. Felt transported back to those four years in college when I was constantly alone. The girl didn't appear sad, but the look on her face didn't convey happiness. I'd floated in that same gray area, accepting my goals were to make enough money to pay for classes then graduate and make enough money to pay my bills. I worked nonstop, very aware that any fuck-up with my grades or behavior could lose me the scholarship I relied on.

Those connections—with friends or boyfriends—never excited me anyway. My background was a tightly guarded secret, and that meant *no one* got in.

Abe touched my wrist with a look of genuine concern.

"Are you okay?" he whispered. The pressure of his fingers was comforting.

"Of course," I replied. "Let's go make our train."

He didn't let go immediately. And when he did, he seemed disappointed in me.

I knew why. I had lied to him.

And not lying to each other was one of our rules.

## 23

## ABE

*a*t 6:00 p.m. on the dot, I smoothed a stray hair back into place. Brushed one piece of lint from my cuff. Shut my extremely organized suitcase.

I was ready for a night of cocktails with Sloane.

I was *ready* for a night of surveillance on a potential suspect that was probably part of a web of international book thieves.

My laptop *pinged* with two emails bearing Codex addresses. One from Freya with a bunch of pop culture memes attached I refused to understand. One from Delilah, with a quick summary on *The Black Stallion* case: *I wouldn't normally do this, since you're on vacation, but the Thornhills win again! Book was retrieved, in mint condition, from the museum's secretary who thought she could make extra cash. She shouldn't have admitted all those secrets to her favorite married couple. And because I know you'll ask, our fee has already been paid by the client.*

I blew out a relieved breath. *Nice work*, I wrote back. *"Never trust a married couple" has been my life's motto since day one. And, because I know you'll ask, yes, I am enjoying my vacation.*

I was getting better and better at the outright lies now. Although, as Sloane and I strategized on the train-ride back to London, I couldn't stop hearing the voices of my team in my head. Not my usual guilt over wanting to capture Bernard all by myself. I could hear them chatting logistics, devising plans and maps, getting ready to strike a big target.

Because, if this was starting to come together the way I thought, Sloane and I would have a *lot* to do the night of the auction. Having four other skilled private detectives as backup would be extremely helpful.

Another ping, dislodging my train of thought. It was from Sam. *I'm sorry for the number of memes Freya is sending, sir. She misses you. We all miss you.*

I caught my own reflection in the mirror and didn't appreciate the affectionate yearning on my face. So I closed my laptop, slid my suitcase neatly inside my closet. There wasn't an article of clothing out of place, no socks on the floor or towels across the bed. Old habits die hard, and during the years of my mother's rehabilitation, I did most of the cleaning and tidying in our house when my relatives couldn't pitch in. A time of such life-changing chaos didn't need the added mess of a dirty house.

Past girlfriends, Caroline included, had teased me about my immaculate house, my perfectly organized drawers, my bookshelves organized by color.

I touched the wall Sloane and I shared. Out of respect, I'd truly restrained my thoughts about my new work part-ner. Because I knew she was 'getting ready'. I knew that meant she was peeling away her clothing, stepping naked into a steaming shower, washing her hair, drying her skin—

*Sloane wouldn't be neat, and she wouldn't be organized, and I wouldn't give a good goddamn. I'd take her against this very wall and let her scream until she was hoarse, let her wreck my clothing, wreck this dresser, wreck this bed. Wreck me.*

I knocked my fist against the wall to stop the wild train of my thoughts. This was why I couldn't open the lock on those fantasies.

"Abe, is everything okay?"

The muffled sound of Sloane's voice startled me. I realized I was banging on her wall one day after we'd had men threatening us.

"So sorry," I called back. "I'm heading to the lobby."

"I'll be down in five," she replied.

All the way down the elevator, standing in the lush and ornate lobby, I attempted to curtail those images, those dreams, those visions that had haunted me since arriving. If Sloane wanted to tease me about fortress-high walls guarding my heart—and she wasn't wrong—I needed to raise them higher to guard against the threat of her enigmatic charm.

Tightening my cuff links once more, I glanced up as the golden elevator doors slid open. Sloane walked out with the posture of a supermodel on a high-fashion runway—hair dark and untamed, dress dark and short, spike-heeled leather boots that climbed mid-thigh. The lobby quieted, patrons watching open-mouthed as she strutted right towards me. I knew, in that moment, what it would feel like to be Sloane's, to be the man she was *always* walking toward. Her partner not only on this case but romantically.

I'd be a lucky bastard indeed.

Now, as she came toward me with an eyebrow cocked, I tapped into the deepest well of restraint I had and managed to remain impassive by the skin of my teeth.

"Ms. Argento," I said mildly.

"Mr. Royal. Shall I call us a taxi?"

"One's already waiting," I said, placing my palm low on her back. We walked through the doors, and I allowed myself the luxury of *feeling* like a couple, the honor it would be to escort this brilliant woman to a night of cocktails and whatever the hell else she wanted.

Once inside the cab, I put as much space between us as I could. Even then, her sultry presence dominated every square inch. I watched her profile in the moonlight, the shape of her mouth, the glittering diamonds dangling from her ears.

"Are we going to talk about how you lied to me back at the McMaster's Library?" I asked, keeping my tone friendly, warm. I wasn't trying to incite her skittishness. I *was* trying to see inside that enigmatic head of hers.

"Classic cab ride conversation," she countered.

I lifted a shoulder. Waited. I'd avoided pushing on the train ride back, but this small space felt like a more intimate place for secret sharing.

Sloane's fingers twisted in her lap—which I'd never seen her do before. I reached across, stilled them. She stared at me with her chin raised. "It wasn't about the case."

"I know," I said. "I trust you."

"I saw this student and she reminded me of... me, I guess. My time at NYU was paid for by a full scholarship I could *not* lose. I never felt as young as the other eighteen-year-olds. I felt old, full of responsibility, and every interaction made me feel confused. I didn't get it, didn't get their lives. They seemed silly." She looked out the window for a full minute before she continued. "I was pretty much alone always. Lonely, I guess."

"You were lonely?" It was so hard to envision this strong, confident woman as a lonely creature without friends.

"I mean, everyone's lonely, right?"

"I don't believe everyone's lonely, no," I said.

She turned to me, clearly startled. "Oh, well. It was just a memory. And it doesn't matter anymore. Work is more important."

Was this what my team members saw in me? Was this what my mother and Jeanette feared? Sloane was so much younger than me, yet her life was so similar to mine. Work, focus, ambition, and drive.

When was the last time she'd had fun? When was the last time *I'd* had fucking fun?

"My father left my mother and me when I was sixteen," I said, needing to even the scales between us. "My mother was in a catastrophic car accident that left her with a traumatic brain injury. She required four years of intensive rehabilitation. My father decided he couldn't be inconvenienced by such a massive change of plans, and so he walked right out the door of our giant house in the Main Line and never returned."

Compassion flooded her features. "Do you want me to find him? Abe, you know I could. That's my job."

The protectiveness in her tone, the protectiveness for me, had me reaching for her hands again. It was the farthest thing from professional. I held them, stroked my thumb along the side of her wrist.

"Thank you," I said, and meant it. "Technically, I could find him now. I don't think he's truly hiding, more avoiding. He's not my real father, and I don't need him in my life." The words sounded neutral. The hollow feeling in my gut revealed the truth. Because now *I'd* lied.

She studied me as the cab raced down the street, and I knew she could see through my bullshit, as always. But she let it go. "It makes sense now. Your mother, what happened. You're a protector. You don't sleep until everyone sleeps."

"Is there another option?" I asked.

Her fingers flexed against mine. "Some people, like Bernard, steal everything when you sleep."

I chuckled, shook my head. "That is true. I told you because... well, I get it. I saw a lot of my classmates toss their academic opportunities down the drain when I felt lucky I'd made it, given everything that had happened."

Sloane was looking down, at our entwined fingers. With my other hand, I pinched her chin, turned her toward me. "For what it's worth, I would have studied with you at NYU."

Sloane actually laughed. "Oooh, boy. I would *not* have known what to do with you."

"With my what?"

She looked me up and down suggestively. "All of *that.*"

"I beg to differ," I said, voice soft. "I'm positive I wouldn't have known what to do with *you.*"

Against all of my better judgment, I swiped my thumb across her lower lip. Defiance dueled with openness in her pretty eyes. I ultimately let her go, settling back in my corner with only the best of intentions moving forward.

"How did you spot my lie?" she asked. "At the library. And the first night we met."

I smiled slightly. "This was always a favorite class at Quantico. Lie detecting. Being able to tell if your suspect was being honest. Did you ever take classes on it or receive training?"

"I have a little experience," she said, voice light, but her spine had gone rigid. "Not formal."

The night we met came back to me easily. "You over-complimented me. Touched me. Brought me into a private world. Probably told me at least *one* truth, or a half-truth, which made the lie more believable." I lifted my brow. "And you too, Ms. Argento, have a micro-expression when you lie." I pointed to the left-side of my head. "You look here."

There was nothing subtle about her expression now. She was *charmed* by this information.

"I'm not saying I've *never* been caught," she said, "It's just few and far between."

"Why do you look like you're enjoying this?" She was warm, flirtatious, provoking a smile to spread across my face.

"I don't know," she admitted. Which was the truth, I could tell. "Maybe I've always been searching for the man who'd catch me in my lies."

We pulled up to a slow stop in front of Midnight Apothecary—a roof-top bar that shimmered on top of a hotel. We exited, and I pulled my jacket tight, re-buttoned it. Right down the street, I could see bold white lettering that read *Kensley Auction House.*

I took Sloane by the wrist and halted her brisk movement.

She turned, face still smiling, bright with energy. "What's wrong?"

"Who taught you to lie?" I asked. Beneath that sultry facade beat the heart of a vulnerable loner, hungry for justice. And dammit if I didn't want to get to know *that* woman better. A lot better.

Sloane sized me up fully—then immediately dropped the act. She brushed a strand of hair from her face, hunched her shoulders—a first for her.

I felt like a bastard. "You don't have to—"

"My parents," she said, interrupting me. "My parents taught me how to lie. It was how I was raised. I had a very unconventional upbringing." Her shoulders moved back again, equilibrium achieved. "That's why I'm good at it. That's why I'm good at going undercover. It's all one big lie."

My hand curled into a fist by my side. "Sounds like your parents were assholes."

Her smile was bitter. "That's the goddamn truth."

## 24

## SLOANE

$\mathcal{W}$e were at our location, with Eudora's weekly appointment starting in fifteen minutes. Abe and I didn't have time to say anything else while lingering publicly in front of this bar. But I did hook my pinkie finger through his and apply the lightest pressure. He looked stunned, in a good way.

"The rules we made can be helpful," I said. He pressed back with his finger.

As we walked up the curving staircase to the bar, every single part of me was shaking. Which was neither smart nor safe for the situation we were about to enter.

I stopped us as we reached the open space—a large, wide patio filled with trees, flowering vines, potted plants, and a plethora of twinkling fairy lights. Chairs were arranged around firepits, and waiters served cocktails that appeared to be fragrant and magical. As we approached the hostess, I knew we'd need a table that concealed our presence. I felt like our covers still held with Eudora—but depending on who she was meeting, her perspective of us could rapidly change.

After speaking with the friendly hostess, we were led to the far right corner where a small, cozy couch was entirely surrounded with bushes and trees. A firepit blazed in the center. I stood where the couch was, getting an idea of how much of the venue we could see. There was a perfect circle of missing branches—like a porthole in a ship—that would let us watch every damn table.

"This is wonderful, thank you," I said, giving a little clap.

The hostess smiled brightly. "All October we're hosting campfires." She pointed at the blaze. "I'll bring you two some marshmallows."

"And a whiskey for me," Abe asked.

"Dirty vodka martini," I added.

I perched on the couch, holding my hands to the warm flames. Nodded at the porthole. "Check out this view."

Abe stared at the branches, the surrounding high trees, the privacy. "If she comes in the same way we did, we'll see her first and won't be caught off-guard." He studied the minuscule couch. With a hard swallow, he unbuttoned his jacket and sat. We were shoulder-to-shoulder, thigh-to-thigh. If I swung my leg up, I'd be straddling him.

"So now we wait," he said. "See who she meets. Depending on who it is, perhaps Devon Atwood and Daniel Fitzpatrick can intercept her, press her for auction info."

"I think that's a grand plan," I agreed. "And I have to say, I've sat through a lot of boring stakeouts. This isn't a bad one for sitting for a couple hours."

He leaned back against the couch, arm up, crossed his ankle over his knee. This position of relaxed leisure was even more tempting. Our hostess arrived with our drinks and a tiny plate of marshmallows with two sticks for roasting.

"Thank you," I said.

She gave us a nod and left us to our own devices. Abe set his drink on the table, untouched. "For cover, not for drinking," he said.

"Good call," I murmured. The elephant in the room, at least for me, was being joined to Abe's side in a romantic bar, surrounded by secluded trees in front of a roaring fire.

It was not a situation where I needed any extra *looseness*. But I did like seeing him spike a marshmallow on a stick. He handed it to me, looking uncharacteristically boyish in the crackling firelight.

I allowed it to roast, watched the flames dance and lick across the sweet surface. When I pulled the marshmallow free, blowing on my fingers, he flashed me a serene smile that curled my toes.

"Why did you choose criminal justice to pursue?" he asked. "It can be a lonely and frustrating career, especially without a team working alongside you."

My eyes found his over the fire; I worked as hard as I could to maintain contact. Not because I didn't want him to think I was lying. I wasn't. The truth was just as hard to say with a straight face. "My lying parents didn't have a strong moral code, to say the least. They would steal an apple from a kindergartner's hand if they wanted to and they didn't think they'd get caught. After I—" *fled in the night* "—graduated from high school and didn't see them anymore, it felt like my responsibility to punish people like that. To balance the scales of justice, no matter how small. My first criminal justice class felt like..." I pressed my fingertips to my sternum, then stretched my arm out straight. "I felt like a hook had been lodged in my chest and I was being yanked forward. In a really, really good way."

"You found your calling," Abe said simply.

"I did," I said. "I wanted to be a private detective because

I wanted to work for myself, work on my own. But I'm slowly learning that taking pictures of employees who are stealing from the company is only so gratifying. *This*, taking down something bigger than me, feels like the hook in my sternum is on fucking steroids."

Fewer than four weeks had passed since the first day I'd walked through that dazzling library on my way to meeting Louisa for the first time. This afternoon I'd felt differently towards those books, those students, the value of such a place to our world. I wasn't a person who had a cultured upbringing, who discussed literature or history or under-stood classical philosophy. But the vitality of rare manu-scripts in what they offered the world was becoming clearer and clearer to me. And the absolute *destruction* Bernard's crimes had caused was becoming a cause closer and closer to my heart.

"I understand this feeling well," Abe said. He removed a Codex business card from his pocket, holding it by his fingers for me to see. "Why did you take this? I don't doubt at all what you told me. I don't know what happened to you in the past, Sloane. My guess is your lying parents had something to do with your ability to steal without getting caught. It feels like your past. Not your present. Definitely not your future."

My lips parted on a surprised inhale.

Sweet, sexy, *take-no-bullshit* man. No wonder he was so tempting.

"You reacted to Bernard's name," I said. "When I was sitting next to you, I caught you respond."

He swallowed hard. "I caught you respond as well."

We'd been evenly matched from day one, Abe and I.

"At that stage in the case I was desperate to follow *any* lead, no matter how small. It was a spontaneous decision, a dumb one, but I wanted to know who you were. Figured checking your pocket was a good start for a small scrap of identifying information. At that point, you weren't revealing your name to me, remember?"

Emotion flickered across his face, fraught and a little wild. "I remember."

That *still* wasn't the full answer. The full answer was my body's raw, primal response to Abe. He knew too—was merely waiting for me to reveal the core truth I was hesitant to fully address.

"Growing up, the only way I ever received attention from my parents was by stealing. My instincts, I think, were to steal from you and get your attention. I liked you, Abe."

The words had spilled out without any editing or uncertainty. My face burned like the fire, and I distracted myself by licking the warm sugar from the tips of my finger.

"Your plan worked," he said, voice low. "You had my attention, Sloane. Have kept my attention, actually. Even when I should be focused elsewhere."

I actually gulped beneath the erotic intensity of Abraham Royal studying me like a gourmet dessert he couldn't wait to savor.

"I am... sorry if it upset you," I managed. Whispered. "Truly, I am. That was the first time I'd done that since I was a teenager."

He was watching my lips. Staring at my fingers. Staring at the marshmallow, dripping into my palm. I licked more sugar from my thumb, sighed a little with happiness. It *was* good. Campfire marshmallows were a brand-new experience for me.

"Why didn't you give me your real name?" I asked, nudging his knee with mine.

KATHRYN NOLAN

"I stand by that *man on vacation* is my legal name." Lips quirked, dry tone, Abe Royal was flirting with me.

"Don't you dare try to get out of the hot seat." I pointed my marshmallow stick right at his heart. "Truth for truth. You know the drill."

He lifted a shoulder. "Honestly? I'm not quite sure. I've never done that before. I've picked up women, enjoyed sex with strangers where we only exchange first names and pertinent health information. But never once have I given *no name* on purpose."

I mirrored his earlier action, waiting for the truth to appear.

"I do need a vacation." He sighed. "And I really, truly have not had fun in an awfully long time. You were..." He paused, ran his tongue along his lower lip. "You were the most captivating woman I had ever seen, Sloane. Not being an obsessed workaholic for one night—not being Abraham Royal—was suddenly a very alluring option for me."

This time, I handed him a marshmallow. He took it, popped it into his mouth with sparkling eyes. I laughed. "Talk about *alluring*."

He swallowed. "Did that answer your question?"

I nodded, bit my lip. "There's a real thrill in being another person for a night. Flirting with a stranger at a bar for no reason other than the pleasure of it."

"Does breaking the rules give you a thrill?" He was still staring at my mouth.

"Not usually," I said, heart beating fast at his nearness, the scrape in his voice. "Only if I see the action as a means to a greater end. There isn't much I wouldn't do, for example, to bring down a person as evil as Bernard. Even if that means bending the rules a little."

"We do that too," he said. Swallowed hard. "At Codex."

"Do you like bending the rules?" I asked, transfixed.

Abe slipped his own thumb between his lips—just the tip—sucking sticky sweetness from the end. Desire was a drumbeat between my legs. If I touched myself now, I knew I'd be wet.

"I am usually well-known for my integrity," he admitted. "And my stoicism. Chaos, spontaneity, fun..." He paused. "These things aren't in my repertoire. Makes integrity and conforming to the rules a lot easier."

"Should fun become part of your repertoire?"

His thumb swiped across his bottom lip. "I never thought so before," he whispered. "Perhaps I need to open myself up to being convinced."

He wrapped his fingers delicately around my wrist. Just held it there. Tightly. "I've enjoyed *bending* the rules for Codex more than I've ever actually admitted. To anyone."

"What would convince you to break a rule now?" I was fucking spellbound. Abe brought my hand toward his face. Turned it left and right. My index finger was still covered in sugar.

He stared at me, arched one brow. I knew what he was searching for—any signs of unease.

I had none. So I pushed my finger against his lips, granting permission.

He took the digit into his mouth.

My breath caught; my sex clenched. I felt his tongue, the light scrape of his teeth. In slow, dreamy motion, he dipped his mouth to my palm, tasted the sugar there. Kissed it. Kissed right below it. Kissed the pulse point at my wrist. Slid my thumb between his lips.

Bit down. He appeared savage in the most intoxicating way. I was burning up with lust and frozen in place—enraptured, entranced. He kissed my wrist again, an inch lower. Lingered, exploring me, inhaling me.

"Abe," I said, voice a velvet plea.

"Ask me again," he demanded.

"What would convince you to break a rule now?"

He scraped his teeth across my skin. And pinned me in place with a gaze full of dangerous things. "You, Sloane."

## 25

## SLOANE

*Y*ou, *Sloane.*

Every remaining rational, logical thought in my brain fled at the speed of light. The fire crackled next to us, surrounded by green, leafy privacy, enveloping us in electric heat and seductive darkness.

Abe's lips continued their journey up the inside of my forearm, the crease of my elbow. His other hand slid around my waist, palm big, firm, confident. Held me close to him, so close my leg rose, curved against his body.

"When we... when we first met," I whispered. "You told me I'd know when you were about to kiss me." He scraped his teeth across the ball of my shoulder. I shuddered, skin buzzing.

"I'm about to kiss you, Sloane," he said, the words rough, hot, vibrating with need. His mouth moved across my collarbone—each kiss sure. Hard. Singular. My hand flattened against his firm belly, slid up the planes of his chest. The other gripped the hair at the back of his neck.

And my leg rose higher. Higher still. His fingers left my waist, slipped confidently along the curve of my thighs.

"I knew you were a rule breaker," I panted.

Abe's mouth was on the front of my throat. I tipped my head all the way back, ends of my hair brushing the couch.

"Only for you," he said. And since we weren't meant to lie to each other, the brazen truth in his words had me holding him closer, a gasp slipping from my lips. "Because I didn't know breaking the rules would feel like this."

I clung to him now. His right hand was moving beneath my skirt, and his fingers caressed my ass, squeezing. But his left hand gripped my face hard, holding me still, fingers in my hair. Possessive as hell.

"What does it feel like?" I asked. His mouth had arrived fully at my ear, and desire detonated inside of me. Abe was tilting me back—back—back, pressing me onto the cushions of the couch. In this bar. Surrounded by people. Were we tailing someone? Did we have a case? Did I have a single need in the world besides the delicious sensation of his strong body on top of mine?

"I am utterly bewitched by you," he whispered. "Spellbound. Charmed. Whatever you've done to me, this *electricity* I can't shake, don't *want* to shake, I'm addicted to it now. There's no other explanation for why I can't keep my hands off you. Can't stop thinking about you. For fuck's *sake*, you've been in my dreams every goddamn night."

He punctuated his dirty words with a brutal bite to my earlobe. A kiss at the corner of my jaw. More along my jaw. My cheek. My own mouth was wide open, waiting, desperate for his kiss. Instead of diving in, like I so desperately needed, he pressed our foreheads together. Our shared breathing came in short, hard pants.

"Why?" he demanded. "You've turned me into an animal when I've only ever been a man. *How?*"

*Devastation.*

I'd known it. Known it from the very second I'd first caught his eye. His lips hadn't even touched mine yet, and I was already ruined for all other men, all other kisses. I tipped my lips up, seeking, but he kept us apart. Abe pinched my chin. Lifted my gaze to meet his. I knew what he wanted from me. We were no longer doing shots of vodka, but we were still playing *truth* or *lie*.

Abe wanted my next truth.

"You're the first man to ever catch my dishonesty," I said. His nostrils flared. "The first man to ever catch me tailing him. The first—" I swallowed hard, scared to reveal the final one. "The first man to ever make me feel so out of control. And trust me when I tell you I don't *let* myself lose control. Ever."

He blew an angry breath through his nose. "Then why is this happening to us?"

"Because we're the same," I said. "Don't you see it?"

Slowly, so slowly, he dipped his mouth toward mine. Not like we were in the middle of a bar. Like we were lying on his bed, with hours of pleasure ahead of us. When our lips met, a bolt of ecstasy shot right through my core, brought actual tears to my eyes. Not tears of grief or sadness—I didn't cry—but a sensation more primal than that, a consequence of consuming lust, finally freed. Abe kissed me. Sweet at first, only a brushing of our lips, like he was again testing for hesitation.

I had not an ounce of it.

His mouth grew shockingly strong, firm, confident, like every other part of him. My hands slid through his hair, and my tongue slipped between his lips. I deepened our first kiss, opening for him like a bouquet of flowers. And with a possessive groan, he released the final latch on his restraint and devoured me.

I was more than happy to be his for the taking.

## 26

### ABE

*We're the same. Don't you see it?*

For the millionth time since meeting her, Sloane Argento had bested me. Cutting through my best defenses and scaling my walls with ease. Maybe my fortress-high walls were there for a reason. Maybe Sloane was the woman meant to climb them—her and only her.

Besides the overpowering desire, the fraught lust, the total *pleasure* of finally kissing her was a deeper emotion. Deeper, troubling, and absolutely complicating.

My heart.

The organ in question thrashed wildly against my ribcage—so untidy, so chaotic. The exact opposite of what I thought I'd wanted for my life. Yet what I wanted was the raven-haired goddess writhing beneath me right now as our lips bruised each other.

I'd been right—Sloane was all flashing teeth and long, sultry kisses, her body equal parts lush and dangerous, softly voluptuous and ridged with strength. She was a goddamn bombshell, and for some reason, she was as drawn to me as I was to her. My fingers teased along the curve of her round ass, gripping her hip beneath her tantalizingly short dress. My lips moved back to her neck, needing to taste her skin. I breathed in the scent of her hair, wrapped the strands of it around my other hand, pinned her down so I could more easily savor her.

Although *ravish* was a more accurate description of what I was doing to her right now. I licked her collarbone, tongued the swell of her breasts, pushing up from her dress. Took the side of her neck between my teeth, bit her like a fucking vampire. She responded by gripping my cock and giving it a delicious drag of her fingers.

"*Sloane.*" Was that my voice—ragged and rough? She crashed her mouth against mine again, palmed my cock, whimpered with pleasure as I growled and lost my mind.

She bit my bottom lip, tugged it. I sat up, brought her with me, my hands moving up her spine to grip big fistfuls of her untamed hair. She held my face, kept our mouths an inch apart. Her gorgeous legs were straddling my waist. I could feel the heat of her pussy through my pants, knew she'd feel so sweet, taste so sweet.

Actually, *sweet* wasn't the word. *Intoxicating.* I was drunk out of my goddamn mind on Sloane, who was staring at me with absolute vulnerability. How was *that* possible? But there she was—open for me, still an ancient, warrior goddess but a humble one, a seeking one.

My heart noticed. Responded. *God, no*, my subconscious yelled. This wasn't supposed to happen. *She* wasn't supposed to be staring at me like this, emotions out of control and messy and needing me. I didn't do *need*. I didn't do *yearning*.

So why couldn't I stop staring at her like we were lovers reuniting after years apart?

"Abe?" she whispered. "What just happened to us?" Her

thumb traced my lip. I kissed it. She dipped her head back down, kissed me, lingering, breathing me in. My hands moved over her body, tugging her closer, fisting in her hair again.

*What just happened to us?* The fuck if I knew. I only knew a desire so compelling I didn't care if we were wrapped around each other in the middle of a fucking bar, in the middle of a fucking case, waiting for Eudora to—

*In the middle of a bar, in the middle of a case.*

My body froze, my hands froze, my eyes flew open—and Sloane sensed my shift in focus.

"Shit, we can't be—"

"*Oh my god.*" Our server screeched to a halt by our table, so surprised by what she saw that she dropped her tray of drinks. In a second, glasses were tumbling to the ground, glass shattering, the hostess exclaiming.

"It's okay, it's okay," Sloane said quickly, launching off my lap and dropping to the floor. She grabbed the woman's hand.

"We'll clean this up. It's our fault," she said.

"I'm so sorry, I didn't, um, I mean, we can't have you—" She flushed, visibly shaken. I felt like an ass. I made a mental note to leave the largest tip possible for her before we left tonight. A tip and a written apology.

"We're so sorry," I said, placing the tray back in her hand as Sloane scooped up ice. "It's our fault. Things got out of hand. It won't happen again."

"It's a romantic place," the server said. "You're certainly not the first couple or, rather, group of people I've caught snogging each other's brains out."

Sloane and I both sputtered a little, shook our heads. Avoided eye contact completely.

"Can I bring you replacements for your drinks?" she asked.

"Please," Sloane and I said in unison. Although I still wouldn't be touching a drop of it. Everything about this situation *and* my instincts had already been compromised by that kiss.

As if sensing my thoughts, Sloane stared up at me from her position on the ground, holding tumblers and napkins. Her lips were parted, chest still heaving slightly. The server scurried away, and I reached out, squeezed Sloane's shoulder. She covered my hand with hers, and we both took one, long, steadying breath together.

As if realizing what we'd done, we both let go and avoided eye contact again. How many times was I going to keep turning to this woman during any time of emotional distress?

I glanced at my watch. 7:25. Cursed beneath my breath. Had we missed Eudora, our one strong lead? Missed her because we'd broken the most important rule we had?

And *I'd* been the one to initiate.

I clenched my fists for a moment but kept helping Sloane clean. She was distracted, staring through the leafy branches.

"Abe," she said sharply.

I was there in a second. She moved, pushed my head where hers had been. I was able to line my sight right at the break in the branches—and see Eudora Green drinking a glass of red wine with Peter Markham, the grandson of Nicholas and current owner of Adler's. My brain made a last-ditch effort at recognizing Peter's face before giving up. Finally seeing him in person was making me doubt the memory of seeing him before.

Sloane's cheek was next to mine as we watched them

both, how out of place they looked surrounded by hipster couples and botanical cocktails. Sloane grabbed my hand—less romantic and more investigative.

"There's the bookstore owner," she whispered.

"Yes," I said slowly. "Maybe they're meeting about the auction?"

We watched for another second. "Have we visited the bookstore yet?"

"Not yet, although I did peek inside." She shifted, gently moved a leaf out of her line of sight. "Look at her body language. She's pissed or worried or both."

"A nervous Eudora with the grandson of the former Society president," I murmured, trying to tie the two threads together.

Peter Markham was speaking emphatically. Eudora was shaking her head. Trees and bushes were in the way of hearing them or reading their lips accurately.

"This used to be her weekly meeting with Bernard," Sloane murmured.

"Maybe Eudora *does* know where he is," I said. "The little minx."

Eudora took a piece of paper passed to her by the bookstore owner. Slipped it into the front pocket of her long skirt.

"What are you doing now?"

Sloane and I peered up from where we were crouched on the floor, surrounded by glass and ice cubes. The server seemed even more concerned than last time, although she was holding a much smaller tray now.

"Funny story," Sloane said. "Some of the glass went into the bushes so we were trying to find it." Sloane stood, held out a palm with glass and drink straws in it. The server looked about to call us on our bullshit.

As did Eudora Green, who appeared behind her with an

especially feline smile. Not domesticated. More panther-like. Peter's wary expression was easier to read.

"Funny story," Eudora said. "Because I just caught these two spying on us." Her scary smile became a very angry scowl that raised the hair on the back of my neck.

Had Eudora uncovered the real identities of Devon Atwood and Daniel Fitzpatrick?

I didn't risk making eye contact with Sloane—attempted instead to rise from the floor and tidy myself with as little fanfare as possible. Next to me, Sloane did the same—her posture and smile held even more of a silent deadly cat feel than Eudora's. Despite the mounting tension, I felt a real thrill at having this woman, my partner, next to me. I had not a doubt in my mind she'd fight tooth and nail. And win.

"*Spying* seems like a strong word. We were merely excited to see our favorite president while out on the town enjoying a cocktail," I said mildly. I straightened my immaculate tie as the server looked between the four of us.

"Sure, yeah," she said. "I'm going to go now." The woman turned on her heel and left.

"Truly, it's lovely to bump into you here, Eudora," Sloane said. Her hair still fell in elegant waves down her back. No sign of the havoc my hands had wreaked to her curls. "And I'm not sure we've officially met. Devon Atwood. This is my friend, Daniel."

I had my eye on Peter, whose rangy energy was distressing to say the least. He took a step back and refused to shake her hand.

Something was wrong.

"A very odd coincidence to meet here of all places, don't you think?" Eudora asked. "Especially since Gertrude passed your message along. We most certainly did not make plans, although that was a brilliant way to learn my location this evening."

Sloane didn't blink. "*Gertrude*, the old bat! I was asking her to help me *arrange* plans for the future. A dinner or maybe drinks at a nice restaurant. Why would I be spying on you?"

"Maybe because you two aren't Holmes-loving Americans but rather private detectives sticking your noses where they do not belong?" Eudora's teeth were pointed as knives when she flashed them at us.

This time, Sloane and I held eye contact long enough to allow a brief connection to pass through. Which was, essentially, *we're fucked, time to go.*

"I wish," Sloane said breezily. "I'm an office assistant at a big insurance firm, as you know."

"And I'm a lawyer, *unfortunately*," I said. "I guess I've always wished I was a detective."

"Funny that I'm so coincidentally bumping into the two of you, given what I've just learned," Eudora said. "Peter had an eye-witness view to the two of you assaulting a man in an alley, which doesn't seem like the kind of thing an *office assistant* and *lawyer* would engage in, does it?"

The snarling dog was out. I could see it now, what Sloane had said people's descriptions of the *real* Eudora could be.

Sloane held up a solitary finger. "First, have you ever coordinated a staff meeting for forty-five people in an HR department, Eudora? Things get ugly. I'm no stranger to threatening people with violence. Especially when we're going to serve cake."

I repressed a smile.

"And secondly," I added. "Devon and I were enjoying a

nice drink at the bar before the bartender tried to roofie us and then have someone attack us in that same alley."

"I don't know what your great game is," Eudora hissed. "But the Sherlock Society doesn't need two ignorant Americans stomping about and ruining our club. If you're going to start drama where there is none, you should get the *hell* out of this city."

They were almost the exact same words that had been scrawled on the threats left beneath our doors at The Langham Hotel.

"If you know what's best, if you know what's *smart*, you'll fly home back to your office jobs and legal degrees." Her tone dripped with sarcasm.

"Ms. Atwood and I aren't finished with our vacation." I rocked back easily on my heels, half-tempted to whistle. "So we'll be staying. Won't we?"

I turned to Sloane, who was now holding her martini glass with exquisite precision. Her expression telegraphed a message I couldn't decipher—but it *felt* like I needed to be paying attention to whatever plan she had brewing behind those eyes. Eyes that moments earlier had been staring into my soul like she was trying to memorize it.

"We will be staying, of course," Sloane said, cheerful. "Should we get drinks again soon, Eudora? I enjoyed the time we spent together."

For a moment, Eudora faltered. Then she steeled her spine. "No," she replied. "If I see the two of you again at a Sherlock Society event, I will call the authorities."

Sloane and I exchanged a glance. "Very well, then," I said. "I'll be prepared to greet the authorities at the next event. Devon, shall we?"

Her smile curved, pretty like a diamond and just as sharp. "We shall."

Sloane splashed her entire martini into Eudora's face.

Eudora shrieked, Peter cursed, and Sloane was moving through it all like an Olympic swimmer gliding through water.

I was powerless not to follow, reaching her in time for her to grip my wrist and move us through Midnight Apothecary. Guests were openly staring, the entire restaurant hushed as we moved around tables and made our way through the back door. Sloane flew down the spiral staircase, and I was fast on her heels. The street in front of us was silent, but there was a large, wooded park running next to the bar. The road across from that rushed with cars. Most importantly, *taxis*.

We didn't even have to discuss the plan, although I had questions, so many questions: about the martini, Eudora, the bookstore owner, our cover. But I was tethered to my adrenaline, starting to run around the building with Sloane. If our cover *was* blown, and Eudora was responsible for the threats against us, I wasn't comfortable with sticking around with nary a soul around.

"If we go this way," Sloane panted, running. "We can make it to the next street—"

She hit a wall of a man.

Hit him hard enough to send her flying backwards, arms outstretched, scream muted at the last minute.

I dropped to one knee, caught her before she could hit the ground. The urge to protect her from any harm wrapped around my throat.

"You okay?" I whispered against her hair.

"Yeah," she gasped. "Yeah, I'm fine." I stood, lifting her easily. I kept my fingers wrapped around her wrist. The man's shirt said *Dresden Security*, and his muscular figure wasn't nearly as scary as the look on his face. I scanned him for weapons—a knife, maybe, in his front pocket.

"Can I help you, sir?" My tone was light. "You seem to have taken out my companion. That's not very nice."

"You didn't get our message, did you?" His voice was thick. American.

"You left us a voicemail?" Sloane asked. The man's nostrils flared in response. "Or like a text? My text messages are out of control right now."

"We were told not to harm anyone," the Dresden guard said. "Which is why you got a *note* instead of much worse."

"GHB seems much *worse* than a note, frankly," I countered.

The man glowered. "You are to leave London immediately."

Sloane and I looked at each other. Shrugged. "I think not," she said. "Thank you for the suggestion."

She took off running, reading my mind.

Except the second she darted around the mountain man, another guard stepped from the shadows and tackled her to the ground.

She screamed.

My heart jerked like it was being torn clear of my body. Before I could make a move, the first guard punched me right in the fucking jaw.

## 27

# SLOANE

*I* didn't see the blur of movement to my right.

Not until it was tackling me to the ground.

My attacker was built like a linebacker, but I'd trained well for this exact scenario. Distantly, I was aware the other guard had clocked Abe, sending him down. Fury lanced through me, white-hot and vengeful. I'd taken these classes to defend myself—from the past, from my present, from anything terrifying that might be in my future. I'd only ever considered my own personal safety to be the goal.

Now, I barely registered the linebacker landing on top of me. If the other guard hurt Abe, I was going to rip him limb from limb.

The linebacker was still on top of me, wearing a smirk I didn't fucking appreciate. With my arms outstretched, I was able to scramble in my purse for my pepper spray. I turned my head, squeezed my eyes shut and nailed him right in the face, holding my breath to keep from breathing it in.

When he rolled off me with a snarl, I punched him right in the dick.

My lungs expanded, grateful for air, making me dizzy.

The linebacker was yelping as I started to stand, watching Abe executing a complicated-looking series of Krav Maga defenses in his suit, with hardly a hair out of place. His expression was dangerous, revealing the FBI agent who'd trained for twenty years for situations just like that. The guard made another big lunge for Abe, who ducked easily then kicked the man in the side of the knee and slammed his palm into his throat. The guard fell back, gasping for air. Abe was staring right at me.

"Hey," I panted. "Are you o—"

"*Sloane, look out*," he yelled.

The linebacker backhanded me across the face. The force of it smacked me to the ground like a high-speed train. Stars catapulted across my vision, a searing heat cracking across my face. Abe was sprinting toward me, and the guard was already standing over me, eyes streaming from the pepper spray.

So I kicked my leg straight up and caught him square in the groin again.

He collapsed.

"And... down he goes," Abe said approvingly. He had me against his body in a second. He gripped my face with unbelievably tender fingers, examining the spot where I was hurt.

"It's just a scratch," I said, smiling a little. I touched the bruised skin around his jaw, and he winced slightly. The thought of Abe's pain was unbearable.

"You?" I asked, struggling to keep my tone breezy.

"I've survived much worse, believe me," he said.

The linebacker groaned, tried to sit up groggily. Abe punched him in the nose. Shook out his fingers with a quiet grunt. "Man's got a face like a bank safe."

The back door of the Midnight Apothecary opened, and

Eudora and the bartender stepped out, spotting us. Eudora shrieked again.

Abe and I turned as one and raced toward the headlights on the other side of the park. I was wearing a short dress and high heels, and the twisting roots and trees kept trying to drag me down.

And my face fucking hurt.

A crashing behind us sounded a lot like the guards. Commotion, yelling, Eudora's voice echoing through the night. A root caught around the tip of my boot, and I went crashing into the undergrowth.

"*Shit,*" I cursed, hitting hard and back on my feet a second later. Abe gripped my arm, turned behind him, then back at me.

"You won't like this," he said.

"What?" I gasped, bent over at the waist.

I was deposited on his shoulder like a sack of potatoes. "We're close to the street, and I think this might be the fastest way," he said apologetically.

I looked out, saw my linebacker muscling towards us with pure fury radiating from his brick-like shoulders.

"Run," I said, too scared to think of my pride and the fact that I was having to be *carried* like the fainting maiden I wasn't. But Abe was strong, his body moving through the woods and toward the street like a track and field star. We lost the guards, reached the road, and my arm was already waving in the air to hail a cab before my boots hit the concrete.

"You're the only man I've ever let carry me," I said, grinning when a black cab squealed up to us.

Abe passed a hand through his hair and opened the cab door like a gentleman. "Your chariot."

With a smirk, I jumped inside and pulled him in after me. "Langham Hotel, please," I said to the driver.

"And I feel it important to note I feel grateful you allowed that to happen," Abe said. "I promise it was more out of concern for you breaking your ankle than a belief that you can't handle your own. We only have to ask Goon #2 how his face and groin are doing."

I huffed out a short laugh, let my head fall back against the car seat. Gazed at Abe, who bore a similarly surprised expression. "So I think our cover's been blown, what do you think?"

He rubbed his mouth. "Yes, I believe you may be right." Reaching forward, he plucked a small twig from my hair, a leaf from behind my ear. I tugged at the knot around his tie, centering it.

Beneath the adrenaline and the sharp bite of fear, my body remembered what we'd been doing right before this evening had taken a more dangerous turn. I had not an ounce of shame about what I'd been prepared to do to Abe in that bar—couldn't find an iota of regret for wanting to fuck him on the couch. It would have been all too easy to free his hard cock, shove my underwear to the side, and ride him until pleasure overtook us both.

In the cab, he cupped my face with both hands again, long fingers sliding against my scalp. I leaned my cheek against his palm for one final second. Being touched by this man just felt so *good*. I was literally helpless to resist him. And I wasn't a woman who was generally *helpless*.

He leaned in, wrapped his arms around me, and kissed my forehead for a perfect few seconds. "I was terrified you had been hurt, Sloane," he whispered. "I'm not used to the way it affects me."

I basked in this display of raw, human tenderness. My

body seemed to crave this even more than our passionate make-out back at the bar. Words froze in my throat, refusing to be spoken aloud. I did wrap my arms around his neck and held on tight, giving Abe Royal a long hug. After a full minute, I pressed my lips to his cheek, once, twice, three times. His fingers flexed along my spine, keeping me close.

This chemical attraction between us had almost cost us catching Eudora in the act of meeting Peter Markham. And it had *definitely* contributed to every single misstep right after, including being surprised by the guards. Our devastation was leading to dangerous distraction. So with monumental effort, and labored movements, I eventually untangled myself and reached into my purse, revealing the *real* reason why I'd tossed my drink in Eudora's face.

"Sticky fingers strike again," I said, holding out the piece of paper in the gold wash of streetlights filtering in through the windows.

"What is that?" Abe asked.

"It's whatever note Eudora placed in her pocket from Peter," I said. "We may have gotten a bit too distracted—"

His mouth twitched.

"—but this might be a helpful piece of the puzzle."

He took it, then proceeded to stare at me like I was a miracle. "How?"

"I watched her place the note in her pocket. I splashed the vodka into her face and used the momentary confusion to snatch it right up." I turned my index and middle finger into a pair of scissors, pinching them together. "It only took a second."

He opened it, peeling back the pages. In big black ink, there were a few scrawled lines. *JP is a yes. Irene says we're a go.*

"I don't know what the hell any of that means," I said

slowly. "Except doesn't this handwriting look familiar to you?"

I reached into my purse and pulled out the threat we'd both gotten. I'd kept it in there for this kind of moment. Side-by-side, it was obvious they were a match.

"I'll be damned," Abe drawled. "Either Peter Markham wrote that threat or is taking messages for the person who did."

When we pulled up to The Langham Hotel, two fire-fighters were walking out of the lobby and back to a truck with flashing lights. Groups of people stood huddled in corners, and I saw hotel staff rushing around with blankets and bottles of water.

"Interesting," I said slowly, glancing at Abe. We paid, exited the cab quickly, only to be immediately rushed by two important-looking staff members.

"Ms. Argento," the one man said. "Mr. Royal, we're so glad you're here. We weren't sure—"

"What happened?" Abe said sharply.

The man escorted us into the lobby, past groups of people—and gasped when he saw our faces. "Dear god, are you alright?"

"One hell of a baby shower, trust me," I said. "Now what's wrong? Something with our rooms?"

"I'm so sorry to tell you two small fires began in your hotel rooms about an hour ago," he said. Alarm bells exploded in my brain. Abe was gripping my wrist. "No one was hurt, the fires didn't spread, and the brigade got here quickly enough, thank heavens. Seems like faulty wiring with one of the lamps in your room, Mr. Royal. The spark caught and spread to Ms. Argento's room, unfortunately. The sprinklers went off, and while they did their job, I can't speak for the state of your laptops and other items."

Abe's fingers tightened on my skin. I knew his mind must be racing at a sheer gallop as quickly as mine.

"The police will investigate, of course, and in the meantime, we've been gathering your items and getting you new rooms, and *obviously* the Hotel will pay for everything, and I mean *everything*. We will spare no expense, and please know we feel positively dreadful about all of this."

"Especially since we were also threatened just last night," Abe said. "I would find it hard to believe these two situations are separate or random."

My fingers were flexing open and closed, adrenaline starting to shiver up my spine again. I didn't yearn for these threats, yet each one was another clue, another lead, another tie to Bernard's anger at our existence. Regardless of whatever this manager *or* the police believed, Abe and I knew this was no coincidence.

"Of course," the manager said, looking seconds away from fainting. "Both our security and the police are conferring as we speak and will be by shortly to take statements."

"Can we see our things first?" Abe asked. "Privately?"

We were ushered into a small side room by a group of apologetic staff—but Abe was having none of it. "Sloane and I need to look through our things without interruption."

The manager nodded and said, "I'm so sorry, I didn't realize you... knew each other?"

"Yes, we do," Abe said curtly and slammed the door in his face. Exhaled long and slow before finally turning around and making eye contact.

"Before we evaluate what happened, I need to tell you something," he said. "The guy, the *guys,* who attacked us were wearing shirts that identified them as *Dresden Security*."

I cocked my head. "Why do I know that name?"

"I'm sure you've come across them in your travels as an investigator," he said. "They're a private security firm favored by the extremely wealthy and the extremely criminal, often overlapping. They're trigger-happy and more than willing to do their worst if a client asks. They have been used by Victoria Whitney, Dr. Ward—"

"—and let me guess, Bernard," I interjected.

His nod was grim. "That night, with the bartender, I think our attacker was Dresden."

I ran my hand through my hair, stared at our wet and watery clothing. "And I bet those same guards did this, don't you think?"

"Absolutely," he murmured, coming to stand next to me and staring at all of our water-damaged items. He picked up his laptop, which was as drenched as both of mine. My files had curled in on themselves and were soggy to the touch. All of the pictures splattered and ruined. I tried to turn my laptop on—a fruitless endeavor that had me sighing with real frustration.

"Goddammit." My head dropped to the wet machine, fingers clenching in a soaked dress. I could care less about clothing, but my research, the evidence, *my computers* were essentially my entire business, my entire life. Abe's hand landed on the top of my head, stroking lightly.

"This is a very real fucking message," he said. "People could have been hurt. Or worse. This isn't a lame attempt at mugging us to make us feel unsafe. If we don't listen, I don't think their next threat will be one we'll be *able* to ignore."

I looked up at him from my squat. His fingers sifted across my forehead. "Bernard is scared."

"Very much so."

"So we can't leave now."

He gave me a half-smile. "Glad to know I'm not the only foolish one in this partnership."

"No, sir, you are not," I said. A very *un*-Abe-like fabric caught my eye. "Is that a Hawaiian shirt?"

His hand left my head. He rubbed it once down his face. "A going-away gift from my team. They thought these shirts might lead to romance."

"You'd never wear this," I teased.

"I swear it," he replied.

"You packed it anyway?"

The slightest blush lit his cheeks. "It was their gift to me. Of course I would bring it."

The way this man restrained his emotions incited a tender ache in my chest. "How about that romance?"

His eyes dropped to my mouth. Our kiss. *That kiss.* "Romance has found me on this trip. Unexpected, to say the least."

Now I was blushing. And blushing hotter when my fingers uncovered a soggy book beneath the shirts. "*Wed to the Pirate Captain*?" I read.

"Another gift," he grunted.

I peeled open a page, aimed a discerning smile at the man standing over me. "You intrigue me, Abe Royal."

"The feeling's mutual."

He held eye contact, and I finally realized I was kneeling. In front of Abe. Whose expression was equal parts lust and a growing affection.

"I don't mean to bring us back to—" he started.

"Of course," I said, startled. "Of course, we, uh... we need to talk to the police."

I stood up, righting myself, re-orienting my body away from his.

"We need to inventory the damage," he said. "And I'm

going to suggest when the manager comes back that we share whatever room he has available to us."

"Uh, what?"

His face softened. "Twice now we've been directly threatened in our rooms. They've followed us here, lit our rooms on fire, delivered missives beneath our doors. We need to stick together for safety, and we need them to list us under aliases. Eudora doesn't believe our undercover names anymore, but I have no idea if, or how, she'd be able to discover our legal names. Either way, I want neither of them listed on the hotel's guest register. Especially if there's someone working here we can't trust."

"Abe."

The man in question swallowed, looking uncomfortable. "Yes, Sloane?"

"We almost lost a source because we couldn't keep our hands off each other in a public restaurant. How the hell will we abide by our *no fucking* rule when staying in the same room, in the same bed?" My breathing was already rapid at the thought of it—from anticipation, from worry, from sheer arousal.

"We'll make sure they have a trundle bed," he said, a distinct roughness in his voice.

"Two people can fuck in a trundle bed."

"Sloane." Even rougher.

"We're just... Abe, I think we're in the most danger because we're the closest to our target. I want to be safe. I want to stay with you, I do. Our rule has to stay." I paused, scraped the bottom of the barrel for my last shred of willpower. "Right?"

"Right," he said. "Yes, absolutely. The auction is in seventy-two hours. We're not animals."

No, we weren't. But we'd been prepared to fuck like two

people with no common sense or rational thought, and if that didn't make me an animal, I didn't know what did.

"Exactly," I managed.

"Unless my being in a room with you is too unpleasant or uncomfortable, then obviously we can—"

"—no, I want to," I interjected. "I guess... I guess the thought of being in a room alone right now is even scarier. We need... we need to be able to strategize and stay focused."

"Focused," Abe repeated.

"On the case."

"Of course," he replied.

We stared at each other for far too long, chests rising and falling. I fully understood the danger we were embarking upon. Except not being in constant eyesight after everything that had happened felt *more* dangerous.

A dance of painful emotion rippled across his normally stoic face. "Listen, I believe I need to—"

There was a knock on the door, stopping whatever he had been about to say. He shook his head, opened it to reveal police officers and hotel security, here to take our statements and talk about our safety moving forward.

I passed my hand across my laptop, devastated at the loss of my investigative tools. Invigorated at the thought that we were *close* to Bernard.

And terrified to admit I'd be more comfortable taking on a team of Dresden guards by myself than sharing a hotel room with Abe fucking Royal.

## 28

## ABE

*T*wo exhausting hours later, and we were finally relocated to room #486—which had two regular beds *and* a trundle bed, eliminating the temptation we *didn't* need to sleep together.

A hotel security guard would keep watch over our room, just in case. The police officers had taken our statements, heard about our threats, promised to get back to us in a few days with their reports and progress. None of it mattered. I would most likely be flying back to Philadelphia at that point, regardless of what happened. But having extra protection couldn't hurt.

Our clothing was still soaked and being laundered by the hotel, who'd dropped off pajamas and sweats for us from their gift shop. Every electronic item I'd left in that room was ruined, every note, every folder. Yet, as I watched Sloane peer outside the hotel window at the newly stormy weather, I understood none of those things were as important as keeping her safe. I would have pushed for the two of us to stay together regardless of our intense attraction—would have pushed to protect her. If I were here with Codex, I would have demanded all five of us stay in the same room and barricaded the door from intruders. Freya would most likely have turned it into a slumber party with snacks and alcohol and horror movies.

I would have spent the night awake, watching over them as they slept.

*Off, on.*

Were these actions really the actions of someone like my father? An aloof asshole beholden to his most selfish desires? Or was I more than that? Because, staring at Sloane sitting gingerly on the bed, I knew *walking out* was the furthest thing from my mind. The image of Sloane being tackled to the ground as she screamed was going to haunt me for the rest of my life.

I tossed my jacket on the bed and rolled up my sleeves, tearing at my tie. Grabbed the first-aid kit the hotel left for us and ice from the machine in the hallway. Then I got down on my knees in front of Sloane, who kept staring at the rain outside like she feared it would bite her. When she dragged her gaze to mine, registered the ice and the bandages, up went those walls again. But her external discomfort was possibly from the "unconventional child-hood" she'd mentioned and been unable to say more about. I got the very strong impression she hadn't been cared for. Ever.

"Can I take a look at your ankle?" I asked.

"Okay," she said.

I slowly unzipped her thigh-high boots, freeing her feet. Bare, smooth legs. Bare, pretty feet. Even with all that we'd done at that bar, this act alone felt overwhelmingly intimate.

I looked at her ankle, which luckily wasn't swollen.

When I touched it, she didn't wince. Happy with that news, I placed a bandage across a nasty scratch on her thigh, checked her knuckles and fingers for signs of injury.

"These will be sore tomorrow," I said.

She touched my own split-open knuckles. "So will these."

I lifted a shoulder. "I'm more concerned with this gorgeous jaw of yours." A purple bruise shaded the skin, and I grimaced in sympathy—which only caused my own bruised jaw to ripple with pain.

"We're a hot mess." She smiled.

"All part of the job when you're chasing a criminal mastermind." I held out the ice. "May I touch you there?"

Cheeks pink, she said, "Yes."

I gripped the non-bruised side of her face. Tilted it gently.

I held the ice to her skin, caressed the bruise. "It's okay if being cared for is a brand-new feeling for you."

Her eyes slid toward mine, relief there. "It's extremely new," she said.

I wasn't used to seeing her so reserved, so quiet. I cleared my throat. "I was my mother's caregiver after her car accident, after my father left. This stuff comes easy to me now. We spent a lot of time in hospitals and at medical appointments. I spent a lot of time bandaging her up when she banged into things."

Sloane kept looking at me, so I kept talking. "Her traumatic brain injury left her in a coma for three days, and when she woke up, it took about four years for her to recover from the after-effects. Three months for her to stand on her own and walk again, but her balance was impacted for a long time. Thus the bandaging."

I gave a wry smile, wrapped ice in a towel and laid it across Sloane's fingers. "Her speech fully returned about eleven months after, with a lot of hard work on her part. And her rehabilitative nurse, Jeanette. And after school, and in between when I worked, my mother and I did things like this. Or flashcards, or memory exercises, or muscle strengthening."

"How long did you care for her?" she asked.

"Two years," I said. "Then I started my undergraduate at Penn. I considered deferring for a year, but my mother had Jeanette, and I was able to come home every weekend. We made it work, although it was hard. Harder than I ever thought it would be."

"Where is your mom now?" she asked.

I grinned. "Well, she married Jeanette."

Sloane laughed—a bright, happy sound. A surprised sound. "Well good for her."

"That's what I say." I tilted her head from left to right, searching for more injuries. "They live in Miami in a retirement village for vibrant seniors. Brain injury is a lifelong journey to healing, and even twenty-five years later, there are things that happen to her because of it. She's a little more forgetful. She struggles in big groups of people or loud parties. Some of her memories never came back. Yet she's rebuilt her life from the ashes, found love and joy. She's a real inspiration."

"And your dad?"

"Just a ghost," I said softly. "A non-entity in my life."

She placed her non-injured hand on my chest, right over my heart. "Told you it was in there."

I grabbed it, squeezed it, then touched her face one last time, this time for the very selfish reason of *just because*. Sloane picked up another ice cube from the tray and held it to the bruise on my own jaw. The shock of it sent a hiss through my teeth.

"Sorry," she said quickly, removing the ice. I gripped her hand, brought it back.

"Just a shock," I said. "It feels good. It helps."

"I'm not very good at caring for... anything," she said. "I don't even think my parents gave me BAND-AIDs when I fell as a kid."

I had about a million questions about her parents, but I sensed the gravity of each bite of information she gave up, respected that space.

Outside our room, the London skies poured with heavy rain. Sloane tracked the sound.

"You're doing great," I said. "This is the second time we've iced each other. I'm starting to sense a pattern."

A tiny smirk returned to her face and I was goddamned grateful to see it. "That's right. The *first* time we fought off a man together. We didn't touch each other."

"A lot has changed," I said, burying untold emotion and yearning within that one simple phrase. The sensations of tonight came back to me with a painful need—Sloane's lips, her kiss, her skin, her hair. This small room, these shared beds, our few dry things mingling together on the counters and dressers. "I broke our rule tonight. I'm sorry."

I was still on my knees in front of her, too captivated to move. As she stared at me, lips parted, I backed away. Stood up. Moved six feet away from her beauty.

"I kissed you back," she said. "You don't have to apologize. We were caught in a moment."

"Trust is our main rule though," I said. "Kissing you betrays our trust. The trust that I'll respect you, respect what this case means to you."

"Honesty is part of those rules," she countered, ever the

challenge. "The honest truth is that I'm happy I know what it's like to be kissed by you, Abraham. If you'd gone home, back to Codex, and I'd never known, I would have always regretted it."

I wanted this woman so badly it was actually painful. My bruise was a paltry expression of it.

"My attraction to you is all-consuming, Sloane." I watched her jolt on the bed, respond to words I'd never thought or spoken aloud. Ever. "I couldn't not know what your lips tasted like."

"And what was that?" she asked, smiling a little.

"Marshmallow." I unleashed a real, full smile—didn't hide it or rein it in, like I usually did. "There's my honesty."

Immediately her shoulders softened, eyes softened.

"We'll need more rules, though" I said. "I'll take this trundle."

"Abe, the bed next to me is—" she started.

I shook my head. "I cannot sleep in a bed near you, Sloane."

Lust carved ragged edges into the words, and I saw the way they affected her—the tangible arousal writ across her face.

"Okay," she whispered. "No touching. No sleeping together. No kissing."

"At least I'll be able to see you steal my things if we're staying in the same room together," I managed, trying to be light.

She grinned, looking shy. "And I'll finally get to see what a man like you does on vacation." Sloane bit her lip. "Partners, still?"

"Partners," I promised. There was more to discuss now, more than this electric chemistry. We'd been interrupted before I could tell Sloane the conclusion that had smacked me upside the head the moment my brain had a second to process everything that had happened tonight: the attack, the fire, the threats, the destruction of our things. The giant auction, the many suspects, the vastness of London.

*I needed Codex.*

I needed my team. I needed four brilliant minds to shoulder this burden and *help me*. What good was a vigilante manhunt against Bernard Allerton if I failed because I didn't—wouldn't—do what was right and necessary? Because I clearly wasn't my ghost of a father. I'd run to Sloane in the middle of the night, protected her. Had turned to her when I was vulnerable, felt the pain of her pain. I wanted to do right by my team—overly protect them and ensure their safety at all costs. I wanted to do right by Sloane—keep her close, guard her from any dangers lurking in the corners. I could only *be* like my father if I remained bound to my pride and blind to my own vulnerabilities. It had taken a raven-haired bombshell with a skill set that rivaled my own to bring me to my knees *and* my senses.

"Since we're still partners," I said, "I need to talk to you about something important."

She was instantly wary. "Okay."

I slipped my hands into my pockets, fully knowing now what we needed to do. I wasn't sure how Sloane was going to take it. Her thirst for revenge was as real as mine. But her walls and her fear and her resistance to working with a team were also very real. Technically this was her client, her career, her contract to win or lose.

"This case, this work we're doing, has gone from zero to sixty in a matter of hours. As talented as the two of us are together, as partners, I'm worried the auction will be overwhelming, and we'll miss our one shot to catch a thief in the act. I always *believed* that Bernard was here in London. Now I'm as sure as ever."

"Which means?" she asked.

I couldn't decipher her tone. I forged ahead. "Which means I think it's time I call Codex."

# 29

## SLOANE

*R*ain thrashed against the hotel window, and every time I blinked, I *swore* I saw lightning. Tonight, this night of sharing a room with Abe, was not a good time to have a full-on panic attack because of a little thunder. Especially since the two of us were squaring off like caged lions, attuned to each other's bodies, every small movement, every indication of vulnerability. Except, instead of the threat of physical attack, we were waiting to pounce on each other like sex-starved teenagers.

Which was how I ended up sitting against the head-board of the bed, blankets pulled around me, while Abe remained tall and impassive by the dresser.

Telling me he was going to call Codex.

"You want them... here?" I asked, surprised. A little shocked.

A little *jealous* although I loathed admitting it.

He looked to the side for a second. "You were extraordinarily accurate when you questioned my ability to *pair up* to capture a man who has always been my equivalent of the white whale. I've spent these past few days wrestling with that attitude, with this antiquated idea that Bernard was mine, and mine alone, to bring to justice. He has deeply impacted the lives of all four members of my team. Especially Henry. At first, I was genuinely concerned that if I told them why I was here, it would only get their hopes up. Only disappoint them when I—" He paused, toed the ground. "When I failed again."

When Abe caught my eye, the fire there took my breath away. "But here's the thing. I think we're going to fucking catch him."

I squirmed beneath the intensity, turned on and excited all at once. "I agree we've got him in our sights. Do we have the time, though? Can they get here? Won't it only draw more attention to ourselves?"

These were pathetic questions disguised to hide the jealous reaction bubbling inside my stomach. It had taken a lot out of me to be honest with the man standing in this room. And a close-knit team like Codex was already giving me bad-college-memories; all those secret languages and hidden social cues I struggled to interpret. Being naturally charming was one thing. Being able to make friends was another.

"It's early evening for them right now," he said. "They could easily be here by tomorrow, giving us time to prep and get them up to speed. We have, at least, four active suspects we want to be watching on Thursday. We haven't even seen the auction space yet to assess entrances and exits, or weak points in their security system. And if you and I stake out the auction, who's watching the other properties where we suspect Bernard might be hiding?"

Abe was so very right, and I was so very uncomfortable. I'd known this man barely five days, and already I wanted to snatch him to my chest and keep him as *mine*. Which was an issue regardless because this man was going home to Philadelphia either way, and then where would we be?

He dipped his head, caught my eye. "So what does my partner think about that?"

*Honesty, Sloane.* Hadn't we just openly declared our attraction to each other? Hadn't I already exposed more of my secret, inner self to him than I had to *anyone else*?

"Your partner doesn't like teams," I said slowly, although I did smile. "Lone wolf, and all that. You'll have a chemistry with them, you'll work together great. It's hard for me to jump in and work with people I don't know. It makes me feel nervous, I guess."

"If it's hard for you to work with people you don't know, what would you call *this*?" he said, pointing between the two of us. "Because, most assuredly, we did not know each other when we started working together."

I opened my mouth and found I had no argument. What *would* I call this? A fever dream? A waking fantasy? Or a glimpse into a life that was finally possible for me? A life filled with real human connection and even, against all odds, friendship?

"This," I said, mirroring his action. "Is a first for me."

"I think you underestimate the value you'd bring to a team like Codex. But this is your case and your client. Ultimately, it's your decision, Sloane."

I wiggled on the bed, getting comfortable with being uncomfortable. "Call them. *Of course* call them, especially if they can help us catch this asshole. We both know this case is bigger now than *my client* or a payout. If our instincts are right about the auction, we'll have one shot. So we better bring our best."

I knew that now. Every hour, every day that passed working alongside Abe exposed Bernard's crimes as a universal injustice we had a duty to correct. "Besides," I added. "If I was your team, I'd be pissed as fuck if you caught Bernard without me."

He winced. "To be perfectly honest, I'm worried they'll still be pissed. I didn't tell them about the email, and I lied about my true motivations for coming here."

I looked at him, dashing and disheveled in equal measure. "I bet you underestimate your qualities as a leader. They'll forgive you. And they'll follow you here."

"Hardly," he drawled. He was tapping his phone against his leg, clearly on edge.

"Call your damn team, Abe." I grinned.

"I wouldn't suggest it if I didn't think they'd help," he said. "I would hate for you to think I doubt the two of us in anyway. Because trust me when I say that is not the case at all."

A pleasant heat spread from the tips of my toes to the top of my head—less sexual, more affectionate. Appreciative. Which only intensified my hesitation to mix up this sweet, heady chemistry between us by adding four more people at the last minute.

Except I was twenty-seven years old, in London, working a case even *Interpol* couldn't solve with a man that challenged and pushed me in the best possible ways. Trusting another person, especially a man, had never been in my top priorities. Yet here I was putting my life and career in Abe's extremely capable hands. *Trust* was now something I could reach out and grab on to, cling to, clutch to my chest and keep safe. Surely I could do the same with four people who trusted him the way that I did. And as Abe sat on the edge of the bed and dialed a number on his phone, I knew the success of this case depended on my doing just that.

Abe placed his phone on the bed, hit the speaker button.

Kept his eyes trained on mine when a deep voice said, "Hello?"

"Henry, it's Abe." He ran a hand through his hair, exhaled. I gave him a nod and a smile. There was a lot of noise in the background of the call, a shuffling.

"How are you, sir? How's vacation treating you?"

"Well," Abe said, "I guess that's why I'm calling you. I don't even quite know where to begin, to be perfectly frank. I, uh... I need your help, Henry."

"You need my help?" Henry asked.

There were sounds of a scuffle, voices. Then a bright and cheery voice came on the line. "Abe?"

"Freya?" Abe's brow creased. Softly, like an afterthought, the sound of a robotic intercom voice echoed from the phone. *Now boarding American Airlines flight 5703.*

"Wait, where are you?"

"Hilarious story, boss," she said. "We're at the airport. All four of us. The cardboard cut-out we'd made of you wasn't the same, so we figured we'd surprise you in London."

"*I'm sorry, what now?*" Abe's voice was shocked, surprised.

The phone must have changed hands—Henry, back on the line. "Sir, what Freya is trying to say is that you happened to have hired four of the most brilliant investigative minds this world has ever known. Forty-eight hours after you left on vacation, we started to suspect why you were really there, obviously. For a human lie detector, your lying ability is total shit. All due respect, of course."

I covered my mouth with my hand—a laugh trying to force its way out.

"Respect noted," Abe said, looking *almost* flustered. "And what exactly did you realize?"

"That you're there for *him,*" Henry said. And even I could

feel the emotion rippling through the phone from across the Atlantic Ocean. "And we're not going to let you do this alone. We're a team, remember?"

Abe glanced back at me. "And who taught you this?"

"You, sir."

Abe swallowed hard, nostrils flared. He stood, breaking our eye contact, and paced across the room with his phone. "So am I to believe all four of you are at the airport right now?"

"Our flight leaves in a few hours, bound for Heathrow Airport," Henry said. "We should be arriving at The Langham Hotel around breakfast time. Figured you could catch us up to speed over tea and scones. Oh, and we closed *The Black Stallion* case and put a pin in the others. It'll be a little chaotic, but if you need the four of us in London for a couple weeks, we've all committed to it."

More scuffling. Freya again. "Next time, hire shittier private detectives, and we won't *detect* your lies. Also, London in October is literally the worst time to go, and Sam told us two months ago there were reported Bernard sightings there. Frankly, I'm offended you didn't think we'd put it together."

Abe had a small, secret smile on his face. He still held the phone out so I could hear but was now standing at the glass doors, overlooking the city. Without his knowing, I admired Abe Royal on the phone with his team and admired the awed respect and admiration evident in the voices of Henry and Freya. Gentle teasing, teamwork, a mutual regard for one another. Codex would fly to the ends of the earth to support this man—a feeling I understood since I felt extremely compelled to do the same.

"Abe," Henry said quietly. "You know we're happy to do it. We'll be there. I'm guessing its big if you're calling?"

"Yes," Abe said, voice tight. "An auction. Two nights from now. New private papers from the estate of Arthur Conan Doyle coming up for auction, and the Sherlock Society wants them."

There was a heavy pause on the other line. "I'm also guessing you know how big of a deal that would be to Bernard."

"I wouldn't have made the call if I didn't think this might be it." Abe's voice was low, urgent. I could see the tension in the way he held his body. Through the speakers I could hear a muffled boarding call. "We'll need to work fast as soon as you land."

"We?" Henry asked.

"One of the many things I'll need to update you on is a private detective named Sloane Argento. She and I met here. She's been hired by your former boss, Louisa Davies, to do exactly what we're about to do."

"*Louisa?* You have to be joking," Henry said.

"I am not," Abe said. "Lots to tell you. Go board the plane, sleep as much as you can, and call me when you're all in the lobby."

"Absolutely," Henry said, sounding a little shell-shocked. "I'll tell the team. We'll be there soon."

Abe was staring right at me. "Thank you. For coming to help."

My chest was filling with light and buoyant air. I was *proud* of him. Another dangerous element to add into the mix.

"And thank you for asking," Henry said.

The moment Abe hung up the phone, exhaustion crashed over me like a tidal wave. I broke into a massive yawn I couldn't have stopped if I tried. Although as soon as Abe looked at me, I steeled my spine and kept my chin raised.

"They're no litter of kittens you found in your backyard, Mr. Royal," I said.

He chuckled softly. "No. They are not. They are extraordinary."

My chest pinched at the emotion in his words—what would it be like to have coworkers like Abe and Henry and Freya? What would it be like to go to work with people who were proud of you? That you were proud of?

"It's so obvious to me, the way they feel about you," I said, a little tentative. "And it's so obvious the way they call you on your epic amounts of bullshit."

He put the phone down, leaned back against the window with a playful smirk. Tie tugged off, first two buttons open on his shirt, exposing a patch of skin I wanted to see more of. The man just *embodied* sex.

"I'm starting to believe I'm the kind of man who needs to be called on his bullshit," he said. "You seem to enjoy it."

Abe was flirting with me, and I was pretty sure he didn't even realize it. And I literally couldn't flirt back without wrapping my fingers through his belt loops and tugging him down on top of me.

"Tomorrow will be interesting." I shrugged, sidestepping those urges.

"They'll love you," he said. "And you'll love them. Just in case you have any doubt."

"I'll do anything to catch Bernard," I said firmly.

With a nod, he pushed himself off the wall and rearranged himself back into impassive, serious observer. He must have sensed my raising walls—it was sheer survival mode at this point. Abe Royal was standing *over my bed* in a room we were going to *sleep* together in. My head literally spun with sexual fantasies, and between that, the adrenaline, my various cuts and bruises, and the nerves at meeting Codex, I was a hot goddamn mess.

"You and I need to sleep before the chaos of tomorrow," he said. "What do you need? Water? Food?"

"Just this bed and the lights off." I bit my lip and watched him prowl back and forth, grabbing the clothing that the hotel had given us from their gift shop.

"I can facilitate that," he replied. "I'll shower and flick the lights off, okay?"

I smiled until he was assured of my comfort. I'm sure he pegged my silence as a symptom of exhaustion when I was actually tongue-tied with wanting him.

He turned off the lights, slipped into the bathroom. A second later, I heard the water come on, and I quickly tossed my dress, threw my hair into a hasty braid and yanked on a gift-shop shirt easily three times my size. Beneath the covers, I tried to sink into the pillowy escape of sleep.

Instead, I could only think about Abe sliding his shirt off his shoulders. Could only think about his bare chest, his back, his naked body slipping beneath the steam. His hands, slicking back his wet hair. Would he think of me while in there? Think of me and touch himself? Stroke his cock beneath the arc of water and stifle his moans?

A flash of what I *hoped* wasn't lightning streaked across the room, smashing my fantasy to pieces. I pulled the blanket all the way to my chin and tried to get comfortable, tried to mute my fear. Tried to strengthen my willpower to resist Abe Royal in all of his glory.

If only he'd stayed Hot Guy in a Suit—a hot, quick, anonymous fuck I'd take home as a souvenir from my first trip to London. Instead he was a tender, brilliant, funny, respected leader who had the magical ability to beckon my secrets from the most private corners of my mind. And was easily the world's *best kisser*. But forty-eight hours was all that existed between us and a crucial break in the biggest case of our lives. If it was only sex between the two of us—only raw, physical attraction—surely we could resist each other until then?

## 30

## ABE

*T*he scream that tore through the hotel room ripped me from sleep. I gasped, fumbled for the lamp next to the trundle bed. Outside, London was being lashed by a powerful thunderstorm, rattling the windows with ominous rumbles amidst a torrential downpour.

And Sloane was sitting upright, hair disheveled, looking like she'd seen a ghost. I was up and onto the bed with her before a single rational thought could stop me.

"What happened? What is it?" I said quickly, reaching for her face.

She was panting, terrified. "It's nothing. Nothing. I'm so sorry. I, uh…"

I'd never seen Sloane Argento look so *unsure*, and it fucking terrified me. Sensing her discomfort, I slowly flipped on the lights in the room until everything was ablaze. No more shadows. By the time I was done, Sloane was sitting up fully, hair pulled over her shoulder, a large shirt stretched past her knees. And from the steel of her spine, she was already trying to convince me she was fine when it was clear she wasn't.

"You what?" I asked softly. I didn't sit back on the bed. I wouldn't, unless she asked me. I ran my hand through my hair, dislodging any remaining mental cobwebs. The clock on the nightstand said 2:30 a.m.

Her shoulders slumped a little. "I'm afraid of thunder."

"Thunder?" I asked. I wasn't sure if I'd heard her.

She lifted a shoulder, attempting to be casual. "Thunderstorms. I've... always been... afraid of them."

I'd watched this woman get tackled by a man five times her size and dismantle him with ease.

"Don't make fun of me?" she asked. Her fingers clenched in the sheets.

"I would never," I said with as much sincerity as I had.

There was a whack of thunder so loud the lights in the room flickered. She flinched like she'd been slapped across the face. My own fingers curled tightly with the repressed need to *go to her*.

"May I... sit with you?" I asked softly, fully expecting her to say *no*.

Avoiding eye contact, she said, "Can you?"

I was there before she'd even finished in the affirmative. With pillows piled behind me, I settled near her trembling form. When our eyes locked, I reached out and entwined our fingers. Her eyes fluttered closed.

"Thank you," she said. "I feel embarrassed."

"Don't," I said. "Don't ever feel embarrassed for what you fear. I'm here. I'll be here."

Even entwined, her fingers were shaking. I was out of my mind with fear *for* her. "Tell me what I can do, Sloane, please."

Inch by slow inch, she slid across the bed. I opened my arms, and she curved into my side. The fit was perfect and utterly divine.

I laid one hand on her head, scratched her scalp. The other reached around and pulled her close. "Does this help?"

"It does," she whispered. "Thank you."

Thunder shook the room violently. I held her tight through each roll of sound, her body shaking as violently as the storm outside. The thought of Dresden security guards torching our rooms with flames to send a message made me furious. And yet, for a single second, I was grateful. Because it placed me here, for Sloane. When she needed me. My palm stroked firmly into the strands of her hair. "Like this?"

She nodded, clung to me. Any second and I guessed the storm would land right over us, if it hadn't already.

"Can you distract me?" she asked—a request that, knowing her, was probably excruciating to make. "Tell me more about your mom? Something happy?"

I stroked her hair again. "Sure," I said. "Let's see... well, I was the officiant that married my mother and Jeanette on their wedding day."

Her muscles relaxed an iota. "That's adorable, and I'm listening."

My lips nuzzled the crown of her head. "They got married on the beach in Miami, about four years ago—although they've been together for more than two decades. I was ordained online, and they requested I wear a Hawaiian shirt and shorts."

Sloane's laughter was muffled against my chest. "Abe Royal wore a *leisure shirt*? And you just told me you would *never*."

"I did, and I never will again," I said. "It was a special occasion. And I would do anything to make those two happy. It was lovely, truly lovely. They were ecstatic throughout the whole ceremony. When I first met Jeanette, I was a pretty anxious and worried teenager. She swooped in, cared for my mother, helped *me* be a better caregiver. I was so glad the day they told me they'd fallen in love. Jeanette's heart is four times the size of a regular person's."

"Did you cry?" she asked.

My hand paused in its motion. "Yes," I said. "I rarely do, but I did that day. My mother is an inspiration. She survived an accident and the betrayal of her spouse with a cheerful and resilient spirit. Allowed herself to fall in love again without fear, to open her heart..."

I stopped. Buried my nose in Sloane's hair and sought comfort in the feel of silk against my skin.

"Did you love your dad, Abe?" Her voice was tiny.

"I loved him most in the world," I whispered. "He was my hero, until, of course, the day he wasn't. And my heart loved him for many years longer than it should have, given what he did to us."

She was quiet, fingers twisted in my sweatshirt. "It's easy to barricade your heart after its been broken. That's always been my preference."

*We're the same, don't you see?*

"We are partners in barricades, Ms. Argento," I said softly. "That day on the beach, watching my mother grab this second chance at life with abundant zeal, I felt this hope, this hope that we can overcome monumental loss and find the person that transforms our weaknesses into strengths, our flaws into interesting imperfections. Jeanette has done that for my mother, and vice versa."

She stroked the collar of my sweatshirt, almost absent-mindedly. "I'm sure they're very proud of you."

"They most certainly are. Although they'd prefer me to be married—yesterday, if possible. They have also kindly requested that I provide them with grandchildren." The clock declared it was approaching 3:00 a.m., the witching hour. No wonder I felt so verbose. It felt like Sloane and I were the only two people in the city of London right now.

"I can see you being a dad." Her voice was barely above a whisper.

"You can?"

Her head nodded against my chest. "Yes. A good dad, too."

My fingers traced patterns through her hair, sifting, caressing. "I've never thought about it. Doesn't feel like a life that's available for me." She was silent for a moment, so I asked, "Do you want to be a mother?"

Her entire body went rigid again. I tightened my hold on her and didn't push.

"I don't feel like that's a life available to me," she echoed. There was such longing in her voice I briefly forgot how to breathe.

"Have you found a girlfriend like that yet?" she asked. "Someone who turns your weaknesses into strengths?"

I thought about this woman curled against my side. Sloane's mysterious charm had literally stunned me the night we met. Her skill and talent and sense of justice mirrored my own in a way that was tantalizing and terrifying in equal measure. And combining all of that with *this* —this softer, more vulnerable woman buried behind her own barricades, well...

What was I to do except want her with a desire I'd never known possible?

"No," I said. "Whether I've *met* a woman like that is another story."

Her fingers left my collar, grazed the un-bruised side of my jaw. I felt that seeking touch radiate throughout my body. "What would you do if you met that woman?"

"I'm not sure," I said quietly. "Perhaps steal her business card to keep her attention."

Her gentle laughter against my chest set my heart ablaze. A moment later, the storm moved over us, thunder growing more subdued.

I felt the relief infuse in her limbs, felt her muscles begin to relax. After a long few minutes, Sloane unfurled herself from my embrace. She wore a giant shirt, legs bare, braid messy.

She was so fucking *pretty.*

Her legs stayed close to mine, but she kept our upper bodies apart, which was a good thing. "When I was seven, my parents left me alone, overnight, in this motel during a thunderstorm. We were staying in the Midwest, and all night the weather channel was reporting a possible tornado touch down. Green skies, hail. The electricity went out, and rainwater came in through the shitty bathroom window. I was little, and all alone, so I spent the night terrified a tornado was going to suck me right up. That I was going to die."

I watched her closely, grateful to receive this story and already pissed her family had left her there. "Where the hell were your parents, Sloane?"

"They were out, I guess," she said, distracted. Until she caught my eye as lightning flashed. She let out a long, steadying exhale. "My parents are con artists. Grifters. I was a con artist too, until I escaped when I was seventeen with the help of my high school teacher, Mrs. Oliver."

It was a challenge to neutralize my expression. The full truth of her unconventional childhood didn't surprise me as much as it devastated me. Yet the puzzle pieces tumbling together made sense: her lack of community, her real loneliness, her stalwart independence, her charm.

"Did your parents use you for certain cons?" I asked.

"Yeah," she said, voice soft. She was quiet again. I sat there, our legs entwined, and let her sit with her past. "Wasn't until high school that I realized not all children had to help their parents earn a living the way that we did. By lying, by cheating. I literally did not know that we were strange or that my home life was so unconventional."

"How much school did they let you have?" I asked.

She tilted her head, braid tumbling to the side. "Limited. I'd go in three-month-long stretches in whatever town or city we were stuck in. Then I would try and teach myself when we were on the run. My junior and senior years were my first consistent schooling, but I was still behind my other classmates."

I had so many questions. Instead, I sat quietly. Waited. Eventually she said, "It's why I'm a good pickpocket. Children have small and nimble fingers."

Fury built in my veins like the clouds outside. I stifled it, again. We would have time for her to tell me the types of criminal acts her parents had forced her to endure. Tonight was about thunder and lightning and the sudden violence of storms.

"What happened when your parents came back that next morning after they left you?" I asked.

"I don't know," she said. "They probably just told me to shut—"

Every muscle in my body stretched taut. "They told you to what?"

"To stop talking," she amended. "Kids have nimble fingers, but at the end of the day, my parents weren't interested in any of the other aspects of me being their daughter."

Another head tilt, staring at the rain outside. Watching for the next lightning strike.

"My existence was absolutely, 100% a mistake and an accident. I just think they discovered quickly how much more sympathy, how much less suspicion, we have of parents with children. And we *never* suspect children of wrongdoing. So." She shrugged. "Sloane Argento is the name I was given when I was born, but I've also had many, many others, *been* many, many others."

"And Mrs. Oliver, your teacher?" I asked. "How did she get you out?"

A genuine smile lit her face. "Mrs. Oliver—Debra—helped me a lot my junior year, saw potential in me when I was used to pretty much being ignored. By my senior year, I knew I couldn't keep doing what my parents were asking of me but had no viable options to leave. I'm sure my parents have biological family *somewhere*. I've never met them, though."

No friends, no family, no parents. Her skittishness towards meeting Codex made more sense now—the fact that this woman felt like she could open up to *me*, a near stranger, was evidence that this secret of hers was a true gift and I'd need to receive it wisely.

"I told Debra my story, and she took me in that last year. Helped me report my parents to the police. They're technically considered *on the run*, but I've heard nothing about their whereabouts in ten years. I don't really care, to be honest. I don't consider them to be *parents* so much as two criminals that dragged me around." She peered out the window one last time. The rain was slowing, gentle against the windowpane. Almost soothing now. "Debra was the one who helped me get my GED, get that full ride to NYU. She changed my life."

"And where is she?" I asked.

Another smile. "She and her husband and their three dogs moved out to Colorado a few years back. We call each other once a week. I guess..." A pause. "I guess she's my family. Actually, Humphrey reminds me of her. They're both so *sure* of their place in this world. You're the only other person I've ever told, besides Debra."

"And I won't tell a soul," I said, voice firm.

"I know," she said. "Besides, if you did, I'd track you down. I am a private investigator, after all."

"I enjoy being tracked by you, as you recall," I said.

Her smile was just for me this time and just as dazzling. I was more than tempted to keep asking her questions, keep peeling back the intricate layers of that captivating life of hers. But she and I had bared too much of our souls already lately. And if Sloane *was* like me, she probably felt out of sorts and exhausted. I didn't want to push her, push *us*, into vulnerability so deep, and so uncharted, we couldn't find our way out.

There was another flash of lightning, another threatening roll of thunder. She closed her eyes. "Must be coming back."

"We'll keep the lights on," I promised. "And I'll stay up with you." I grabbed the remote from the side table, flipped the television on. "I've heard *Love Island* is basically streamed twenty-four hours a day in London."

The screen winked on and revealed a trio of couples running down a beach. She let out a laugh, looking delighted.

"You're not tired?" She was getting comfortable back against the headboard.

"Not at all," I said lightly. I sat near her without touching.

The lightning flashed rapidly. Just as thunder struck, I said, "Should we take bets on who's going to make it?"

Her wince at the sound this time was smaller, briefer. Replaced by a sexy grin. "Detective versus detective," she mused. "I bet our investigative skills and ability to read body language should help."

"Surely two people with advanced understanding of human nature can guess who's going to make passionate love to each other," I said mildly. She snorted, head falling to her knees.

"Surely," she agreed. She turned her head. I could barely make out her face beneath a curtain of hair. "Thank you, Abe."

Her gratitude wasn't necessary. And the more Sloane revealed her secrets, her fears, her sweetness, the faster I was falling for her.

Which was—*surely*—going to be a problem.

## 31

## SLOANE

*I* woke a few hours later—disoriented, unsure of the time. Hazy morning light filtered in through the curtains, and the alarm clock read 7:18 a.m.

And Abe Royal was asleep on top of me.

I had nodded off eventually after our third episode of *Love Island*. As the storm ebbed away, he kept me laughing with his dry humor. We didn't speak again about my parents or his father, my past or his. He kept things light and distracting, reading my needs perfectly.

For which I was unbearably grateful.

My body, my muscles, even my heart felt tender. Last night had been a true unburdening, and it was actually *painful*. Every time I'd laugh at a joke, I'd catch him watching me with a cautious, but obvious, affection. A friendly affection that respected my boundaries.

It appeared he had *also* read my boundaries and needs as we slept. Deep down, I wanted this man with a blinding lust, and my subconscious had made sure we found each other. Abe's head rested on my breasts, my arms holding him there tightly. My bare legs hooked around his waist.

His hand had slipped beneath my white sleep shirt, palm hot on the bare skin of my ribcage. His long fingers were splayed there, *barely* brushing the sides of my breasts. Every time he exhaled, his breath caressed my nipples, already hardening through my shirt. And against my hip I could feel his cock, hard and heavy.

*No fucking no fucking no fucking*, I chanted. My fingers caressed his hair. His fingers caressed my bare skin. What had he said last night? *My attraction to you is all-consuming.*

His back muscles flexed beneath my wandering hands. His head moved slightly, breath hot on my collarbone.

*No fucking no fuck—*

"Sloane." The man's voice in the morning grated like boulders. It literally *dripped* with sex.

"Abraham."

"It appears we've broken our rule," he said. "*Again.*"

My thigh moved higher around his hips. His palm skated down my ribcage, exploring.

"We can't be trusted in our sleep," I said, smiling against his hair. If this was wrong, and we'd declared it to be wrong, why did it feel so deliciously good? We were melded to each other in what was essentially a sleepy weekend cuddle. And my body was on fucking *fire*.

"I'm sorry," he rasped. He turned his face, dragged his open, hot mouth along my skin.

"Please don't be," I gasped. His fingers traced the swell of my breast. Tentative. I wanted more. Harder. Rougher. I wanted *dirty* from Abe Royal. "I'm probably at fault here."

"Why is that?" His nose caressed my throat. I actually whimpered.

"Based on our positions, I'd say I captured you." I tightened my hold on his body to prove my point.

His laugh was low, sleepy. "Is that so?"

"*I* broke the rule." I traced the shell of his ear with my finger, and he shivered.

"I'm fairly certain I was a willing participant." He cupped my breast inside my shirt, rolling my nipple beneath his palm. My entire body arched clear off the bed with a breathless, grateful moan. He responded with a frustrated-sounding growl against my neck. "Why did we have this goddamn rule again?"

"I don't know," I panted. I gripped his hair. Gave it a hard tug. His open-mouthed kiss became a bite at my throat. His ragged groan became snarl-like. "I can't remember why we made it."

"Distractions." Abe's tongue lapped at the mark he'd left. Then he bit me again. "We can't be distracted right now, Sloane." His thumb circled lazily around my nipple. My eyes fluttered closed.

"Uh huh," I sighed. His mouth moved lower, hovered over my shirt-clad breasts. He nudged his nose against my nipple. Sucked it right into his mouth.

Through my fucking shirt.

I didn't even recognize the sound that clawed its way from deep in my body.

"And this... *this* is a distraction." My legs rode higher on his hips. He settled his body more firmly onto mine, face against my breasts. One hand was still palming, kneading, my breasts beneath my shirt. The other was languidly stroking up and down my thigh, teasing it higher until he could hook it over his shoulder. He increased his suction, sending hot, electric jolts to my core. "And *this* will only lead to devastation."

"A distracting devastation," he murmured. "Remind me why fucking you is going to devastate me again, Sloane?"

I couldn't *fucking* remember. I couldn't— "Because if our fucking is anything like our kissing, there's no going back, is there?"

He stilled completely. I gripped his face with both hands, needing to anchor myself to him through this once-in-a-lifetime feeling I'd never experienced before.

"No," Abe said. "There's no going back." He kissed my palm. "The problem being, *not* fucking you is now the distraction. I'm not sure I could focus on this case right now if it was a matter of life and goddamn death."

I traced his bottom lip with my thumb. He nipped it with his teeth. Beneath his hips, my legs began to shake—a sure-fire sign of impending orgasm for me. My hips rolled, mindless. He noticed, his eyes burning into mine. His lip curled back into a snarl, and his composure was *this close* to snapping. I'd craved this from the moment I'd seen him, restrained as hell in that tailored suit.

"If we hadn't been interrupted at that bar," I said, "I would have gotten on my knees right there and—"

"*Sloane, don't.*" His hand landed over my mouth. Hips pinning me harder. "I'll lose my damn mind if you say it."

I arched my brow, defiant. I snatched his hand from my mouth, wrenched my hips up, had Abe Royal on his back a moment later.

As his look of surprise turned wolfish, I pressed his hands into the mattress and lowered my sex onto his erection, straining at his sweatpants. "Sucked your cock." I whispered the words against his mouth. But when he reared up to capture my lips, I kept us separate. Just like that night, before our kiss, when Abe made absolutely sure I was prepared for what happened next.

"Do to me what you will," I said. "Fuck me until we can't

stand and I've forgotten my name, your name, the date, and where the hell we are." I dropped my mouth to his again. "Ravage me, Mr. Royal."

## 32

# SLOANE

*I* released Abe's wrists, preparing to be ravaged. Like our first kiss, he held my face tenderly, fingers sifting through the strands of my hair draping around us.

"We're doing this, together," he whispered. "No matter what."

My answer was a slow, sincere smile that I saw reflected on his face. "Partners."

He kissed me with an aching reverence. An adoring morning kiss, a lingering feeling, spreading a soft desire through every nerve ending in my body. When he finally pulled back, I was absolutely breathless. He wrapped my hair around his fist and tugged. Not gently. I hissed, every muscle going taut with anticipation.

"Sloane."

"Mr. Royal."

Another sharp tug. I moaned.

"I am *past* my ability to fuck sweet. Regardless of the *sweet* ways I feel about you." I sighed, smiled, arched a little as his fingers kept pulling. "So if you want me to ravage your body, I am more than willing. But only if you're —"

"Yes," I said. "Please. Yes. *Please.*"

He sat all the way up and crashed our lips together. We were voracious, starved—it was a kiss without mercy, a kiss without barriers. My mouth was consumed. I could only receive the full force of his skillful lips. And they were *skillful.*

Abe was a man whose competence met no insurmountable barrier. He was, quite simply, the best. Holding my face still and kissing me, kissing me, *kissing me*, and *oh god it was too good.* Every moan from my lips made Abe *wild.*

He tore my shirt clear from my body, leaving me barebreasted and in nothing but a scrap of underwear. He pressed his face against my skin and uttered a low string of curses that gave me goosebumps. I was on my back a second later, arms over my head, as he stood and removed the shirt he'd slept in. He was broad-shouldered with strong, muscled arms and a defined chest with gray chest-hair mixed in with the black. He flicked a crooked grin at me when he caught me staring. I retaliated by slipping free of my underwear and tossing it at his face.

Then spread my legs wide.

He growled and threw my underwear clear across the room. Dropped his face to my belly and ran his tongue to the space between my breasts. He bit my skin, sucked it between his teeth, rolled my nipples into tight, aching peaks. I cried out, wept, begged as he sucked and sucked, leaving me boneless with need. The sounds Abe made against my breast were the sounds of a man pushed to the breaking point. Only the teasing descent of his fingers down my body tethered me to earth—fingers that landed firmly on my clit.

He placed his forehead on mine and let out a shuddering, grateful breath. "Look," he said, voice strained. Gripping his shoulders, I looked down. Saw his strong, skilled hand between my legs. Watched his index finger circle my clit once. Slowly. "I've been dreaming about your pussy, Sloane."

Oh, god.

"Every fucking night," he whispered. He began working my clit faster, more firmly. Perfect. *Perfect*. "And wouldn't you know, touching you, feeling your slick skin, how hot you are here, is more beautiful than my wildest fucking dreams."

I wanted to watch his fingers on my clit forever. And when he dropped his mouth to my ear and slipped his finger inside me, I cried out his name.

"You're going to stay on this bed and keep these legs wide," he growled. "And I'm going to eat your pussy until you beg me to stop. Do you understand, Ms. Argento?"

"Yes yes yes," I said, wrenching a raspy laugh from Abe when I gave his head a little shove downward. He responded by pinning my hands down as he fell before me.

"Spread them wider," he commanded. I complied. Eager. He took several long, hungry perusals of my naked body, splayed out before him. "I have no idea what I did to deserve this." He dropped his face to my cunt, inhaled. Released my hands so he could grip my ass and yank me harder against his face. "To deserve a woman so gorgeous my world stopped the second I saw you."

"Abe," I whispered. Overwhelmed.

He licked my pussy, *really* licked it. Shot me a look that threatened my very existence as a cool, independent loner. The look made me want to toss everything to the wind, leap into his arms, and beg him to marry me.

"I am going to taste every inch of you, Sloane." My legs

started to shake in anticipation. He grunted, shoved my knees down hard. I wound all my fingers into his hair and forced his tongue against my eager skin.

"Are you calling the shots now?" The look on his face wasn't angry. Not at all. I rolled my hips, rolled my clit against his mouth, and he rewarded me with a nice, long suck. Two fingers slipped back inside me, stretching, teasing, curling against my inner walls. I smiled—big, bright, happy—and let out a satisfied "*thank you*" that had him chuckling against me.

"I'll let you get away with telling me what to do," he said. "Because you're cute as hell, and if it's not extremely obvious, I'd do anything you asked of me." He curled his fingers just right. An electric current went through me. He kept his fingers moving, working my pussy, as he prowled up my body, forcing my head back into the bed. His other hand gripped my face, thumb on my pulse-point. "But if I'm going to fuck you into sweet forgetting, you're going to let me devour you." He licked my bottom lip lightly. Caught it between his teeth—the pinch of pain was everything. "Are we clear?"

My response was to lean in. Nip his jaw. Drag a sexy, crooked grin from him. "Clear," I purred. I lay back down like a good girl.

And I was devoured.

## 33

## ABE

*Intoxicated.*
I was drunk on Sloane.

Naked, glowing skin; full, rounded breasts and her soft belly; strong thighs, pretty feet, bare neck, hair in strands of midnight chaos. The goddess was curvy and feminine, dangerously edged; the enchantress was an erotic dream, a glimpse of sexual paradise I wasn't sure a man like me deserved. Now she was splayed out for me, a feast fit for a king, every naked inch of her available for me to obsess over.

And it felt like an obsession. Her fingers landed back in my hair; my mouth landed back on her clit, licking her in long, decadent strokes that had her body rolling and writhing on the bed. I buried my tongue inside of her, tasted honey, tasted heat, tasted sweat and salt and everything good in this world. Her legs tightened around my ears as my palms slid up her hips, her belly, cupped her breasts greedily. They spilled past my hands, voluptuous, gorgeous—I pinched her nipples harder than I intended, but her response was a raspy moan I'd be jerking off to the memory of for years to come.

I pinched them again—increased the pressure of my tongue on her clit—and she pulled on my hair. Gasped out a breathy, "Yes, *Abe, oh god*," as her feet kicked my back. She was writhing, wild beneath me, and I was starving for every moan, every sigh, every indication her body offered up that was evidence of her sexual pleasure.

Beneath my mouth, her pussy was wet and hot, open and eager, her clit responsive against my tongue. I watched her face as I fluttered my tongue quickly, watched the glide of her body, the curve of her ribs, the tightening of her pink nipples. Between my own legs, my cock was heavy, rock-hard—already I was sweating from the effort it took not to grind myself to orgasm against this goddamn bed.

My tongue dove between her folds, dipped deep into her center. Sloane's cries grew louder, more out of control. I gripped her hips and yanked her higher, giving me greater access to tongue-fuck her as deep as I could. The look of euphoria on her face tattooed itself on my soul—once, twice, three times, a hundred times. I was going to wrench orgasm after orgasm from this siren, bring her so much fucking pleasure she'd forget this case, forget her past, forget her loneliness and her disappointments.

Ecstasy was all that mattered, and I was more than willing to stay here on my knees until she demanded otherwise. I was dimly aware of the sounds I was making against her pussy, of my fingers bruising her hips. Time and reality held not a scrap of meaning to me. I replaced my tongue with my fingers—one, two. I worked a third finger into her tight cunt, and her hands slapped my shoulders, pulled my hair. I allowed myself thirty seconds to lift my head and watch her, to press my face to her soft, supple thighs and bite her skin, marking her.

"I am going to fuck you into goddamn oblivion," I growled. "But not before you come on my mouth."

Sloane sat up on her elbows, chest flushed, fucking my hand. I reached forward, gripped her neck, and yanked her face against mine. She kissed me so hard I couldn't breathe, didn't *need* to breathe. Her fingers scratched at my chest as I finger-fucked her faster. Faster. Her kisses grew ragged, whimper-filled.

"It never feels like this, Abe," she whispered. "Abe, *Abe*, it never, I've never, what if I can't?"

I kissed her throat as she tilted her head all the way back, the ends of her hair brushing the bed. "Can't what, beautiful?" I murmured. "Can't come?"

"No," she wailed. "No, I'm so... god, I'm so... it's too much..."

I dipped my head. Sucked her nipple between my lips. She shrieked, starting to tighten, tighten, *clench* around my hand.

"Can't let go for you," she panted.

My tongue dragged back up her throat. My mouth landed back on her lips. I kissed away her fears, kissed away her nerves, kissed Sloane until she understood I knew *exactly* how she felt. My fingers were slick with her arousal, she was so close. So close. I gripped the back of her neck and forced her to look at me.

"I am not going anywhere," I promised. Relief flooded her features. I waited until trust returned to her eyes before placing my palm in the middle of her chest and forcing her back down to the bed. I concentrated all my energy on licking her clit with skill and dedication as I kept half my hand fucking her, sliding against her G-spot, opening her to pleasure, to sensation, to *me*.

Her legs wrapped around my head; her hands stayed attached to my shoulders. Her hips thrust up, up, up against my tongue until I gave her the pressure that she needed.

Her orgasm was a beautiful free-fall of total elation. Her hips shot straight up, and I held her still, cradled the lower half of her body and sucked her clit hard, and then soft, until her screams became cries and her cries became moans. Until she could only whisper *Abe, Abe, Abe.*

I couldn't wait a second longer.

I stood, removed my remaining clothing until I was completely naked in front of her for the first time. She climbed my body, throwing her arms around my neck as I dipped, scooped her up, legs around my waist.

When we kissed, I tasted like the most secret and alluring parts of her; when we kissed, I shared those parts with her, sliding our tongues together. The second she pulled back, breathing hard, I scraped my teeth at her jaw.

"Sloane," I said, voice rough. "What will make you comfortable? I have condoms, in my suitcase. I have —"

"When was the last time you were tested?" she asked.

"After the last woman I had sex with a year ago. I haven't been with anyone since," I admitted. Holding a hot, pliable, warm woman against my body threw my cold and lonely nights into stark relief. Only I hadn't felt lonely. Alone, sure, but not *lonely*. Sloane was the missing piece, tumbling into my life and making me yearn for a future I'd never once considered.

"It's the same for me," she said. "I have an IUD. I'm clean."

My chest heaved at the thought of fucking her without a

single barrier between us. Her mouth hovered over mine, hands gripping my face as my arms held her close.

"Please, Abe," she begged. "Yes, please, *now*. I need you."

I didn't need to be begged twice by the most beautiful woman in the world. I hoisted her higher on my waist and walked us back into the dresser, depositing her on the end. I shoved bags and clothing to the ground. Knocked down a lamp that clattered loudly, the light going out. My hips hit the dresser, ramming it against the wall, as I dragged her knees high along my body.

One hand spanned the wall, my other hand gripping her waist. I watched as she wrapped her gorgeous fingers around my cock. Held my gaze with her sultry one as she jerked me slowly. Too slowly. My snarl sent heat to her cheeks, sent her teeth sinking into my chest. She stopped teasing. Pressed our mouths together in a breathless kiss. Placed the head of my cock to her entrance.

I fucked into her with a single, confident thrust and experienced my second dose of true, mind-altering intoxication.

"I'm still here," I whispered against her lips. She felt *so fucking good*. "And I'm not going anywhere." I slid all the way out, slammed back in.

"Oh my god, *don't you dare fucking stop*," Sloane cried— which sent the final semblance of my restraint hurtling into the atmosphere. She clung to my neck as I gripped her hips and plunged recklessly into her pussy, thrusting in a steady rhythm that was no less brutal.

She was on me like a wild cat, all teeth and nails, as she called my name out. I stopped being aware of anything other than the sight of my cock sliding into her pussy, the sounds we made, how slick and hot she felt, how tightly she squeezed me. It was far too easy to spin her around, so we faced the mirror over the dresser together. I gathered her heavy hair between my fingers and tugged until my lips could land at her ear. Our eyes, in the mirror, met, burned with fever, burned with the understanding that it was all different now. Like she had predicted—*there was no going back.*

I fucked her from behind, against the dresser, kept my mouth at her ear and our eyes locked.

"The next time you want to be ravaged, Sloane, you say the word," I growled. "If you want to be fucked until you can't stand, I'm more than happy to oblige. Because whatever spell you've cast over me, I'm still yours, and I'm still here, and making you come just became my new fucking hobby."

I buried my face in the nape of her neck, kissed her there, the crook of her shoulder, the space between her shoulder blades, worshiped all the vulnerability she hid back here. Sloane, for her part, met me thrust for thrust with a look of total bliss on her face. My lips stayed on her neck, my groans of pleasure growing more ragged, out of my control. With a sharp bite on her throat, I pushed her down, increased the speed of my motions, noted I'd probably have to pay the hotel for damage to the wall. All I could see was her ass, shaking with my thrusts. The magnificent curve of her spine and the feel of her hair in my fingers. Her face, a mask of pure ecstasy, her irresistible smile, the way "*please, Abe, please, Abe*" had become a mantra, spilling from her mouth.

*Please, Abe.* She didn't need to say please, she didn't need to say *thank you*, she didn't even need to ask. I'd give her this freely, with nothing expected in return.

Her cunt gripped, *gripped*, fluttered, clenched. I swiped a palm along her spine, used my other hand to massage her clit. She needed only one rough flick before her orgasm sprang free and she cried out. I dropped my face to hers, let my own orgasm free, let myself experience the full-body high of sex with Sloane, coming with Sloane, fucking Sloane against a goddamn hotel room dresser.

I buried my face in the side of her neck, catching my breath over a long few minutes. When Sloane Argento kissed my cheek with a satisfied smile, I recognized this as the natural conclusion to our electrifying connection—even if it was mere days ago.

Maybe this woman's entrance into my life wasn't coincidence at all, but something much, much more romantic. And that felt like the most dangerous risk of all.

## 34

## SLOANE

*A*be wrapped me in a warm blanket as I sat back against the headboard and watched him make us our first coffee of the day. The sun was brightening, it was now closer to 9:00 a.m., and we didn't have much time to avoid the reality of our rapidly ticking clock.

Codex would be arriving any second.

He pressed a small mug of coffee into my hands—wearing nothing but sweatpants, feet bare, hair untidy. Messy, adorable, with a hint of morning stubble.

*Devastating.*

With concern, he touched my bruise. "Did I make it worse?"

"You made it better," I promised. I pulled my hair to one side and displayed the string of hickeys he'd left there—a surprise discovery I'd spotted in the bathroom mirror.

"Christ, I'm a brute," he muttered.

"The bruise on my jaw doesn't hurt one bit. And these bruises hurt in the way that I like."

His throat worked. He kept his steel-gray eyes on mine as he sipped his own coffee. "You are magnificent, Sloane."

*I'm still here. And I'm not going anywhere.*

During the course of Abe and I fucking each other senseless on a hotel-room dresser, I'd been delighted to learn his extensive vocabulary included a litany of filthy words. Made filthier by that growly sex-voice of his. Pleasure roughened the edges of his refined presence, made him dominant and greedy, skilled and possessive.

The man had delivered on his promise to *fuck me into sweet forgetting.* Like his intelligence, his integrity, his competence—he also wielded his cock with an elegant skill.

Although, elegant or not, he'd also shoved me down, face first, and fucked me from behind with a righteous fury. His skill had given me two earth-shattering, life-changing orgasms. And one perfect, golden memory: *I'm still here.*

Throughout my life, I'd learned change was the only constant; I'd either accept that fact or burn. Which was why I rarely complained about my upbringing—complaining meant I was out of control instead of embracing the change, no matter how scary it was. At seventeen, my reality had been terrifying, so I took off sprinting toward my future— changed my identity, changed where I lived, hid, fled, reappeared someplace new. Still, Abe shone a light on the tenderest parts of my soul; all the cobwebs, the old nightmares, the fears that plagued me. Those fears had led me to *choose* to be alone, even if it meant I was also lonely. Because my greatest fear was to be abandoned.

*I'm still here. And I'm not going anywhere.* Giving in to the temptation of Abe Royal was only going to devastate me if, ultimately, he left.

I reached forward and held his hand. "Thank you. For everything that you said. For listening to me. Last night, this morning, when we had sex. I can tell you more about myself, about my parents; it will just take time."

"I've got time," he said.

"Well, we don't have *that* much time," I said—hesitant but aiming for light. Fun. "Beyond the auction tomorrow night, don't you leave for home soon?"

"I do," he said—tone heavy. He didn't look away from me. A new and surprising shyness gripped me, made me unsure of what to ask for next from this man who had so easily given me everything a few moments ago.

"So I guess we broke our main rule in a pretty big way," he said.

"We sure did." A wild vortex of erotic memories passed between us. I could see him getting hard again, the outline clear in his sweatpants.

He chuckled softly. "Not how I expected this morning to go. Figured our morning would be us watching *Love Island* and placing bets."

I hummed a little. His hand left mine, cupped my cheek. I turned my head and kissed his palm. "I preferred my morning of being ravaged, thank you."

A grin slid up his face. "We can't go back, can we?"

No, we couldn't. This sexual dam had been broken and we were swept away on the current now. "I believe you said you'd be more than happy to oblige my dirtiest desires. *Fucked until I can't stand* being one of those promises."

He tilted his head, assessing me with a steady expression. "I'll put a stop to it immediately if it makes you uncomfortable in any way."

I set my coffee down. Let my blanket fall away, revealing my naked body, tangled hair, marked skin. On my hands and knees, I crawled toward him. Captured his mouth with mine. The kiss was instantly frantic. My tongue met his, our lips danced together, a tease that became a bruise that became a brutal, hungry, snarling clashing. Abe had my hair gripped in his hands, and I stroked the head of his cock.

My cell phone ringing was the only thing that stopped our frenetic, sexual energy. Panting, I pulled back. Smiled at him with swollen lips. He was fucking insatiable, and I loved it.

"Are you going to get that?" he asked, voice tight.

"I am," I whispered, kissing his cheek. "And I think we have to admit we *definitely* aren't able to go back, Mr. Royal."

He gave me a crooked smile. "Happy to oblige, as I said."

I reached past him for my phone and enjoyed the delicious drag of his hands through my hair. Unclear future or not, I planned to revel in these sexy moments, taste them fully, memorize this heady feeling. These memories would provide a warm spark on a lonely night.

I huffed out a surprised breath when I saw who was calling. "Humphrey." I showed Abe the screen. His brow arched.

I answered with a cheerful, "Humphrey Hatcher, is that you?"

Abe pulled me back down onto his lap while I set the phone to speaker.

"A hearty good morning to the *enchantress!*" Humphrey boomed. His roaring laugh brought a smile to my face. And even Abe looked mildly delighted. "It's been years since we've last seen each other. Perhaps, even, a millennium. We must rectify this situation immediately."

"I believe it's been forty-eight hours," I replied. Abe kissed the ball of my shoulder with a thoughtful expression. "But we would love to see you, of course."

"And who is *we*?"

Abe pressed another kiss to my neck, and I giggled. My hand flew to my mouth. Abe's expression was smug. The man barely knew me, and yet it was probably pretty obvious I wasn't much of a giggler.

"Daniel Fitzpatrick is *we*," I said.

"Valiant at last! Reggie and I are pleased to hear it. What do you say to accompanying my husband and me to a fancy little party? Our friend James whipped up a last-minute party at the auction house tonight to celebrate the arrival of Doyle's private papers. They'll be bid upon tomorrow evening, and all of London is clamoring to see them early. There will be alcohol!"

I turned on Abe's lap until we could make eye contact. "James... Patrick? The man who runs the auction house?"

"The one and only," Humphrey said. "It's open to the public, and you know the Society will be out in full force, possibly dressed as the esteemed detective. Which reminds me, I shall bring you hats."

*Yes*, Abe was mouthing. I tapped my lip, nodding in agreement. This event was a fucking *windfall*. Not only would we see our favorite Sherlock Society suspects, but we'd be able to scope out the entire venue, investigate all of its entrances and exits, its security weaknesses.

"We're in," I said. "What time should we meet you?"

"Eight, and it's a date," Humphrey said. There was grumbling in the background, and it sounded like Reggie and Humphrey whisper-arguing. "Listen. I'm going to come clean and tell the two of you what's been going on. I cannot abide secrets."

"And what's that?" I asked, voice tight.

"It's Eudora again."

Eudora had the power now. She'd attempted to blow our cover last night. "What's going on with our favorite president?"

Abe glanced at the clock, muttered something. He stood and began gathering his clothes, a sexy body in sexy motion.

"She's focused all of her earthly ire on the pair of *you*," he said. Abe was sliding a crisp white button-down over his shoulders. He paused, mid-motion, at Humphrey's words.

"Well, no shit," I said. How far had our covers been blown?

"*No shit*. You slay me. And, to be abundantly clear, any person that angers the head dragon is a friend of mine. Do you remember how you insulted her sensitive ego?"

Abe shook his head at me while his fingers moved over buttons. "I met her for tea earlier this week. And Daniel and I bumped into her at this cocktail bar last night. Midnight Apothecary."

"Bernie's favorite bar," Humphrey boomed. "Do not fret. Her temper exists on the world's shortest hair trigger. As well as her grudges. They've been known to take a second to form and a lifetime to endure. I wouldn't worry. However, I didn't want you receiving any strange looks tonight and not understand why. Especially you, Ms. Atwood. The Society has been charmed to death by your visit to our fair shores."

"Always happy to hear it," I said. "And thank you for both the invitation *and* the warning."

"I won't have you stay home when you could be enjoying a night out on the town with an elite literary circle," he said. "Reggie and I will see you at the auction. Make sure you put your Mr. Fitzpatrick in his most dapper evening attire."

When I hung up the phone, Abe was already tightening his cufflinks and slipping on pants.

He nodded again at me while grabbing a suit jacket. I watched him smooth down his hair in the mirror. "I see you're already heeding Humphrey's request to look dapper."

He caught my eyes in the mirror. "Codex will be here

shortly. They expect a certain debonair look from their leader."

I tossed my hair in an ineffectual attempt at hiding my nerves. "So. We've got a date tonight, and Eudora Green is starting shit."

I finally climbed out of bed and pulled Abe's faded Quantico sweatshirt over my head, inhaling the scent of aged whiskey and mahogany. Came to sit on top of the very same dresser I'd recently been ravaged upon. Next to me, Abe was buttoning the final two buttons of his shirt.

"Somehow, Eudora's been tipped off that you and I are private detectives," he said. "I'd love for that to be Bernard, but how or why they've connected those dots I have no idea. At the very least, it's obvious she thinks we're investigating something we shouldn't."

"She didn't tell Humphrey, or the Society, her full suspicions though," I said, biting the tip of my thumb. "Telling people to avoid us but not that we're liars."

He peered at me. "Perhaps she's actually protecting the person who suspects us."

My stomach hollowed out with a burst of excitement. "Then we're getting closer to Bernard. We have to be."

"That we are," he said. His face changed when he lifted his hand from his suit pocket—and held a small note between his fingers. The note I'd stolen from Eudora. In the intense activity of the fire and moving rooms, its existence had slipped my mind.

"Remember this?"

I snatched it from his fingers. "*JP is a yes. Irene says we are a go.*" I tilted my head, a light bulb flicking on in my brain. "James Patrick?"

"The man we're going to see tonight?" Abe asked— elation curving around each word.

"You're goddamn right we are," I replied. Slammed the note on the dresser and drummed my fingers on it. "It would be a curious thing indeed if the man responsible for auctioning off these papers was going to have a hand in getting them stolen."

"Wouldn't be the first time," he said. "We've worked a few cases tying thefts back to auction houses. I can't parse who 'Irene' is or what she's giving a go. If we have a fancy party tonight, good thing our team arrives in twenty minutes. We need to get Codex up to speed on everything, plan for tonight, and pin down the best strategy for being Humphrey's guests while avoiding Eudora, and any Dresden guards, as best we can."

He looped a tie around his neck with practiced motions. I hooked my finger into his belt loop and dragged him in front of me, joining my legs around his waist.

"Let me," I said, starting to tie his tie. Abe Royal went still as a statue. When I finally allowed myself to peer up at him, the naked affection in his face stilled my fingers.

"This is very domestic," he said softly.

"I'll be nagging you to organize our basement in no time," I said. He leaned in, kissed my forehead. I resumed my motions yet glued my eyes to his. A sense of peace infused my very being—one I'd never felt before.

"I hope you like being grilled by a team of highly trained professionals," he said.

"I know a thing or two about withstanding pressure," I smirked. "I'll be okay."

"They'll ask if we're..." He paused. My fingers paused too.

"What?" I knew what. I just couldn't discern his feelings yet, or my own.

"They will tease us endlessly about our romantic situation. And our obvious gap in ages."

"*Obvious*?" I grinned.

"What's a decade, after all?" he said softly.

"Ah," I said. "How would you describe this situation, Mr. Royal?"

A smile tugged at his lips. "You go first."

I gave his tie a well-timed yank and his smile grew devilish. "We are enjoying each other's company right now."

"I agree," he said, palms smoothing along my thighs. We proceeded to both wait each other out—see who might break and crack open the well of deeper emotions. But Abe was silent, which silenced me.

*If* he left me—or *when* he left me?

"Sounds like we're on the same page," I said. More of a suggestion than a statement. He responded by taking my hand and holding it to the center of his body.

"It won't be only the two of us anymore, working this case," Abe said. "So I wanted to talk to you before Codex arrived, while its just you and me."

I swallowed hard, noted the twisting sensation in my belly. "Go for it."

"I've been thinking a lot about what you told me last night. You are not your parents, Sloane." He stared at our hands, joined together. "And you were only a child."

My throat was unbearably dry as I exhaled, raggedly. Surprised. "I didn't... I didn't escape from them until I was *seventeen*. Teenagers can make decisions about what's right and wrong."

His grip on my wrist tightened. "Sloane."

I felt the urge to hunch, to curl inward, to hide. "What?"

He dipped his head until he captured my gaze. "Teenagers are children still. Especially if your parents indoctrinate you, force you, demand you help them in order for you to receive... what? What did they give you in return for helping them do jobs?"

"Certainly not love," I said quickly. Regretted it. He didn't press. "They fed me. Most times. We had places we stayed. Apartments, motels, that kind of thing. They let me go to school."

"Usually children receive those things because they are children."

I looked away. Fiddled with the tie I'd just straightened. "I worry."

Those two words were like shoving a boulder out of the way using only my pinkie fingers.

"About what?" he asked.

"I want to live on the right side of the law. I want to punish people like my parents. Protect other people from criminals, thieves, bad guys. People that manipulate. Like Bernard." I chewed on my lip, shifted on the dresser. "I still worry. Because the reason I'm good at being a detective is because I was raised to lie. I was raised to be charming. I was raised to seek out weaknesses and exploit them. I can slip into any undercover identity in seconds, without hesitation. It feels wrong to use evil skills for good. It makes me feel like I'm stepping too close to the edge. One toe over the line..."

Abe studied me. "How often are you tempted to toe over that line?"

I searched my memories for the last time I'd defied the law. Came up... empty.

"Ah," he said. "Maybe you're good. Maybe you've *always* been good."

"You think so?" I was trying to be funny, but the words came out eager, needy. I went to look away, and he trapped my chin, tilted me back.

"I know so," he said. "Honesty, remember?"

I nodded, conceding his point, feeling flushed with a newfound feeling. Conversation done, at least in his mind, he started to walk away. I snagged his tie. Tugged him back between my legs.

"May I help you?" he asked, tone playful.

I replied with a kiss more sweet than smoldering. "You are not your father."

His face hardened. "Excuse me?"

I matched his hard expression, unafraid. "Lone wolf or not, you are not him. It's okay to still be angry with him. It's also okay to let it go. It's okay to find that hope your mother felt, to want someone in your life. It doesn't make you weak. The opposite, in fact."

He softened—he kissed my forehead again, breathing me in. When he stepped back, the expression on his face was one of a man seeing the golden hues of a sunset for the very first time. "You are not at all what I expected."

My voice was shaky when I finally answered. "And that heart of yours is bigger than you think."

A line appeared between his brows. "It's hard for me to crack open this fortress. There's not a lot of room in there for others."

There wasn't time for us to continue this conversation—wasn't time for us to pin down the unruly chaos of this instant attraction. Abe's phone chimed with an incoming message that he read immediately. Whatever he saw put a genuine smile on his face, which stole the breath from my lungs.

"They're here and waiting in the café," he said.

I jumped down from the dresser, did a mini twirl. "And this look is okay, right?"

His hungry perusal of my bare legs only intensified the

butterflies in my stomach. "The image of you in my sweat-shirt will feature in many fantasies to come."

I gripped the bathroom doorframe to keep from swooning. "Give me... um, give me five minutes, and I'll be ready."

Those five minutes became ten when I realized my shirt was on backwards and I applied mascara to my right eye—twice. The butterflies in my stomach roared, my fingers shook, my breath was unsteady.

Codex was here.

We had less than two days to pull everything off.

Every opportunity I had *ever* craved relied upon tomorrow night's success.

And all I truly wanted in that moment was for Abe to make room in his heart.

For me.

35

---

## ABE

There were several moments in my life I would always remember.

The day my mother was able to say *Abraham* again.

The feel of the keys in my hand when I opened the Codex offices for the first time.

The second I first locked eyes with Sloane.

And the sight of Henry, Delilah, Freya, and Sam— looking jet-lagged and slightly bedraggled—standing in a café in London. Those slightly bedraggled expressions transformed into brilliant smiles as Sloane and I stepped inside the bustling space.

I immediately slipped my hands inside my pockets to hide their traitorous shaking. Gave my team a short nod. "Lovely to see all of you."

With an exasperated eye roll, Freya launched herself at me, arms wrapped around my own stiff ones. Delilah was next, joining Freya—although her hug was softer and a little more understanding.

"Well, *cheerio, guv'na*," Freya said. "We're here to save the day. Don't worry, no thanks necessary."

290

"I'd never even consider it," I said—although I worked my arms free and finally hugged them back quickly. Sam clapped me on the shoulder, and Henry shook my hand—warmly and with a real smile as he adjusted his glasses.

"It's good to be back here," Henry said. "I've missed London."

"Enjoying the raves, sir?" Sam smirked.

"Oh, every night," I said.

"We see you're not dressed in your vacation attire." Delilah frowned, tapping her chin. "Would have thought those Hawaiian shirts would have done wonders here in rainy London for your much-needed time away."

"Oh, are we calling Abe on his bullshit already?" Freya clapped her hands together. "I've got some good ones locked and loaded, trust and believe."

With my own smirk, I turned to the woman standing next to me, who I was sure appeared as her usual calm and confident self to this group of detectives. Only I sensed her hesitant nervousness. Only I understood her feeling of being a social misfit who never quite fit in—that was a struggle I knew intimately. A struggle I knew and respected.

"Before I am skewered, please introduce yourselves to the sixth member of our team here in London. Sloane Argento, a PI from Brooklyn currently working to find Bernard with the McMaster's Library."

I was positive that Henry had already informed them of this on the plane. But, still, the very real looks of surprise, then intrigue, then mutual admiration that flowed across their faces reminded me of just how emotional—just how vital—this case was for us all.

They took turns shaking Sloane's hand.

"Dr. Henry Finch, former special collections librarian."

"Delilah Barrett, former police detective."

"Freya Evandale, proud Quantico drop-out."

"Sam Byrne, former special agent."

Sloane shook their hands, maintained strong eye contact. And unleashed the wide, charming smile that was her trademark. Every member of my team melted toward her like flowers to the sun.

"It's nice to finally meet all of you," she said. "I own my own investigative firm in Brooklyn, and I'm being paid by Henry's old boss to catch Bernard. And I'm truly looking forward to calling Abe on his epic bullshit with the rest of you." She cast her eyes at me. "*Skewer*, if you will."

"Well, I'll be damned," Freya drawled, propping her hands on her hips. "Now how did you meet our Office Dad again?"

"It is a *mathematical impossibility* for me to be your *dad*," I interrupted.

Sloane's smile only grew, her shoulders relaxing. "I picked his pockets, tailed him across the city, and accidentally booked a hotel room right next door to his."

Four heads swiveled toward me as one. Four sets of eyebrows shot right up.

"Seems like those Hawaiian shirts did the trick, huh?" Freya shrugged.

"No comment," I said.

Delilah flagged down a passing server. "Any chance you can send a bottle of wine to our table? And yes, we know it's breakfast time."

## 36

## ABE

*O*nce seated, our table was piled with an odd assortment of tea, wine, and scones with jam. Beneath the table, Sloane's leg was pressed to mine in a silent show of support I appreciated more than I could say.

Across the table, the familiar sounds of teasing and messy affection among my team dragged forth a feeling I couldn't deny was *yearning*. I'd gone and missed them, even though it had been barely a week since I'd seen them last. And now they'd gone ahead and flown across the world to fight my fight before I had even, technically, *asked*.

Again, their devotion reminded me of that beautifully wrapped gift—only this time, I wanted to work on my ability to open it. Enjoy it. Not be afraid to receive their loyalty and affection. I wasn't a betting man, but I'd place my money on this new openness being Sloane's doing.

"So forty-eight hours is all it took, huh?" I asked, spinning my teacup between my fingers.

Delilah smiled at me above her wine glass. "It was the night we pulled an all-nighter to close *The Black Stallion* case. There was way too much alcohol and coffee involved and combined."

Henry grimaced. "Worst hangover of my life, actually."

"It had kind of been our office inside joke," Freya continued. "The only time Abe would ever dare to go on an actual vacation was only if he could catch Bernard Allerton while doing it."

Next to me, Sloane made a kind of *hmmmmm* sound. Hiding a smile, I placed my palm on her knee and squeezed.

"And as much as we *all* support you in breaking your workaholic habits," Sam said. "You're not the kind of guy who would enjoy ten days of leisure."

"You're a *hunt a man to the ends of the earth* kind of guy," Freya continued. "Which is why we adore the shit out of you, of course."

"And here I thought I was being slick," I said mildly.

Henry glanced at Sam. "That night, all of us punch-drunk and up late, Sam got an email from his contact at the FBI." Henry dropped his voice immediately. "The email contradicted what had been sent earlier and now listed London as one of the highly likely places where Bernard could be. And it's only been nine weeks since The Empty House case, and I, for one, feel like we're closer to catching him than ever."

Henry leaned across the table—the look on his face so open, so trusting, it only made me feel like more of a bastard for keeping things from them. "You might not remember this, but the night that Delilah and I recovered the Copernicus from Victoria's house, you told me that you often needed to hear your own advice when it came to Bernard. As our boss, you repeatedly reminded us that getting the damn book back was all that mattered."

"That I could be unnecessarily prideful in my thirst for

revenge," I added—because I did remember that conversation and how conflicted I'd felt at my righteous anger. Worried it would obscure the focus of Codex, which was always rescuing the book over capturing the thief.

Four sets of heads nodded with knowing looks. "Call it a bloodhound instinct," Delilah said. "But it didn't take much to get us from *there* to sitting right *here*. The worst that would happen is we found you relaxing by the pool, and we spent a few fun days with you in the city."

"It's hard for me to ask for help," I said.

"Yeah we know," all four replied in unison.

"I'm loving this by the way," Sloane added.

I brought my hands together on the table, looked each one of my team members in the eye.

"When I was deciding where to go, I received an anonymous email from an agent at the FBI with information they felt confirmed, without a doubt, Bernard's location here. And not just here but within a two-mile radius of The Langham Hotel and the Sherlock Holmes museum. Surveillance reports attached to the message checked out. Those other reports Sam had received about his credit card use I believe to be a red herring."

There was an explosion of *what*s and *are you serious* and *what the fuck*s. Delilah crossed her arms, looking rightfully irritated. "And why the hell didn't you tell us? Seems pretty crucial, Abe."

I chanced a glance at Henry, who seemed genuinely hurt. "I am truly, *truly* sorry for keeping this from you. What I've done, my actions, none of that reflects the kind of leader I pride myself on being. I've always valued integrity above all else. In that, I failed you."

Now Sloane's hand rested on my knee. Before I could

doubt the gesture, I dropped my own hand beneath the table and curled my fingers through hers.

"It's challenging for me to admit how personal catching Bernard feels to me; it's challenging for me to admit I've always wanted to be the *one man* to do it where everyone else had failed. It would be the ultimate *fuck you* to the Bureau and to everyone that doubted private detectives could be as successful." I swallowed past the urge to stop. "I had no money, no warrant, no client, no jurisdiction. I was comfortable risking myself. Much less so risking all of you."

I set my eyes on each one of them, didn't shy away from the mixture of loyalty and anger I saw there. "Unlike my previous statements, I do feel more than a mild affection for all of you. Tomorrow, nothing could happen. We could take a massive swing and miss again. The thought of asking all of you to have hope one more time..."

I trailed off—smacking hard against my limits of emotional vulnerability. Between my night, and morning, with Sloane and this hard conversation, my body felt like a marathon runner's at mile twenty-three.

"It's hard to risk the ones you care about the most," Freya said softly.

Nodding, throat tight, I managed, "It's no excuse. Please, forgive me."

"I think we can make that happen," Sam said. "By lording it over you for months and accepting your apology gifts." He flashed me a shit-eating grin. "Sir."

"Of course," I promised. "A genuine bounty of donuts awaits."

I was still focused on Henry, who had yet to say a word. Now, he was shaking his head, a tiny smile on his face. "I can't say I haven't had those same dreams. I get it, I do. But we're doing this together, Abe. Like we were always supposed to."

I let out a big exhale of relief. Placed my hand on Henry's wrist, who clapped his on mine with a look of understanding I wasn't sure I deserved yet. He was right, though—Henry and I had inadvertently started this journey together, sitting in that claustrophobic room at the McMaster's Library. We would get him—together.

"Sloane and I have a lot to catch you up on. We've had an interesting few days, to say the least. We believe Bernard will be making a move on a collection of Arthur Conan Doyle's private papers tomorrow night. We'll need every idea, every strategy, and all the help we can get. And tonight, we were invited to a fancy auction party held at the very same place where we believe the move is going to take place."

A familiar feeling settled between all of us at this tiny café table—electric and exciting, thrilling and wild. Reunited, a team again, with only our biggest case yet ahead of us.

I would never again doubt that I needed them in my life.

With a sly grin, Delilah said, "Let's get the damn book back."

## 37

## SLOANE

*A*be scrubbed a hand down his face—looking momentarily tired—before straightening. Crossing his arms, he nodded at the four private detectives assembled in front of him in our hotel room. "Plan. One more time. Go."

Delilah tapped her pen across a notebook, pointed to the large white paper on the wall. Codex had packed light and smart—most of the items in their suitcases were designed to create a mobile office, which was good since everything Abe and I had brought was either soaking wet or totally destroyed.

"Eight is the start of the auction. Sloane and Abe will be there accompanying Humphrey and Reggie with their undercover personas, Devon and Daniel," she said. Delilah grabbed Freya's shoulder. "It's a public event, so Freya and Sam will be attending with a cover as two Sherlock-loving tourists from America here for the spectacle of it all."

"Freya and I are putting the finishing touches on our cover now," Sam said. "We'll have everything memorized by the time we show up. And we'll be pulling together a disguise as best we can. We're stepping into an audience with people who could recognize us as Codex agents, given some of the people in attendance might be opportunistic book thieves."

"Good," Abe said. "Disguises should be a requirement. Give nothing away, listen as best you can. My and Sloane's covers have already been blown, so the night will be a tense one. If anyone else at this event recognizes me as a private detective, or any of you, we need to agree ahead of time on our exit plan."

"Yes, sir," Sam said.

"And we have promised to be cheese farmers from Vermont who run weekly classes of goat yoga," Freya said soberly. "Winifred and Winston are our names."

I grinned at Freya's joke, and she flashed me a cartoonish wink. We'd been sitting in this room for close to seven hours now, with the exception of stopping to eat. And I was slowly learning that I *liked* them. Henry was this bright light of intelligence; his adoration for literature was an extra glue tying this team together. Delilah was calm, assured—and behind those eyes was a sharp intellect well-matched with her partner and fiancé.

Freya was playful and silly, and her big, messy heart was evident in her sisterly affection for everyone. And Sam, her boyfriend, was her perfect counterpart in every way. Smart, serious, competent. And clearly obsessed with her.

I was still jealous of their fondness and teasing spirit, but Abe's obvious trust in me seemed to unlock an instant confidence from them. Those age-old feelings of being kept out —of not understanding—were the source of the jealousy. Seeing groups of friends like this at NYU, or out in the city when I was working, always incited a yearning in my chest. But now, sitting here, being myself and working toward a common goal, there didn't appear to be anything else I needed to do except enjoy their company.

"Pleasure to meet you, Winnie and Winston," I said. "Daniel and I would love to take goat yoga one of these days. Bucket list, and all that."

"I can't imagine *the* Abe Royal would abide something as chaotic as a goat," Sam said. I cast a look Abe's way—noted his effortless posture, his gentle charisma, the utter ease of being the one, the center, the leader. These seven hours of non-stop strategizing had flowed around him like he was a boulder in a river. No wonder they flew all this fucking way to help.

"Goats are not my friend," Abe said, idly touching his cufflinks. "Now keep going."

Smirking, Delilah looked down at her notes. "The four of you at the auction will be targeting entrances, exits, weak points. Observing, as Abe said, and keeping a close eye on Eudora Green, James Patrick, and various terrifying security guards. *I'll* be in the parking lot, taking pictures of the space, noting who's coming and going and any back entrances we should be aware of." Delilah pinned Abe and me with a serious look. "Given that your cover *is* blown, at least for Eudora and Peter, you should stay with Humphrey. No more fighting."

"Del will handle the fighting," Henry said proudly. "And I'll be here, keeping an eye on things and gathering any extra evidence for the real auction tomorrow."

In a tag-team effort, Abe and I had filled them in on every last detail, starting with my weeks of working the Sherlock Society and the items we'd discovered in Bernard's office. We covered Eudora, Humphrey, the fire, the attempted mugging, the attack at the cocktail bar, the notes, the code words. Throughout it all, the four detectives listened, asked thoughtful questions, compiled ideas and bounced off each other with a practiced skill.

I was fucking astonished. Not once had I ever had the purpose of a high-functioning team demonstrated to me the way I had on this day.

During those hours, we'd learned right away that Henry could still be recognized everywhere in this city. During his time working with Bernard, he'd met Eudora, met Humphrey, attended a handful of lectures at the Society from time to time. So he was our silent sixth partner, working behind the scenes.

"Keep pulling through the files Sloane brought from Bernard's office," Abe said. "And if you can start mapping out where we'll be tomorrow night, that would help. The auction is our hot spot, but Adler's, Mycroft's Pub, and 221B Baker Street are still places of interest."

Henry was nodding along while taking notes. The reflection of a laptop screen appeared on his glasses. I could see him scrolling through websites. "Anyone else get a good look at the picture of Peter Markham? The bookstore seller? I never met him in person, just heard a lot about his grandfather. And Bernard and Humphrey loved going to Adler's."

"What about him specifically?" Abe asked.

Henry touched his glasses, squinting at the screen. "He looks familiar, but I can't place him."

The rest of the team gathered around the librarian. Freya and Delilah shook their heads as Sam leaned closer. "Yeah. I see what you mean. He looks familiar to me. No fucking clue how or why we'd recognize him though. Maybe you met him before when you lived out here and don't remember."

"Abe thought he looked familiar too," I said. "Have you had any revelations about it?"

"No," Abe said thoughtfully. "I was ready to write it off as nothing, but if the two of you feel the same way, then I'm less likely to think it's a fluke. Peter is already suspicious because of his ties to Bernard and whatever he's been doing with Eudora."

Delilah tapped her pen against her keyboard. "Peter and his bookstore are seeming more suspicious by the second. Henry, if you went in disguise, and made it quick, could you do a walk-by of Adler's?"

"Absolutely," Henry said. "And I'll make it fast, just enough to get a sense of anything that could jog my memory —of him *or* the bookstore. I'll raid Abe and Sam's suitcases and cover myself as much as I can."

Delilah pressed her hand to his cheek. "My handsome secret agent."

Henry kissed her palm, smiled. I was slowly getting used to the fact that the Codex team was comprised of two extremely happy couples unafraid to display their happiness. It was an odd thing for me, seeing couples working together in a way that was positive. Joyful. For all of Abe's grumbling about PDA, his quiet contentment around these four was palpable.

Abe rubbed his face one last time before exhaling loudly. He clapped his hands together once and examined the slowly drooping bodies of his team. We had just under an hour to go. "You all appear tired."

"Why would you say that, boss?" Freya yawned dramatically, head in Sam's lap. The brawny ex-FBI agent scratched her hair with a love-struck expression.

Abe flashed me an extremely sexy grin. "Shall I get my illustrious team takeout, you think?"

"It's only fair, given your history of lies and deceit." I shrugged.

The team's scattered laughter warmed my cheeks. "Picking his pockets *and* unafraid to call him on his shit," Delilah said, approvingly. "Welcome to the team, Sloane."

My cheeks grew hotter. When I caught Abe's admiring look, I went up in flames. "Just happy to be here," I grinned. "I bring a lot of skills to the table, mainly my ability to fluster your boss."

There was another round of laughter, and Freya stood to clap. I laughed too, caught Abe still smiling at me like we shared the best secret.

Abe backed out of the room and raised his palms. "Giving a man a fake name, stealing from him, then following him across all of London would fluster even the most stoic of individuals." But when the rest of the team was turned around, Abe gave me a wink that melted my insides. "Twenty minutes until we eat," he called back, before closing the door.

"So can a conversation get *other* people in a room pregnant?" Freya asked.

My hand flew to my mouth, surprised. I was suddenly very aware I was alone with Codex without Abe as a buffer. Instantly, all four of them sat up, spines straight, filled with energy. "Wait, weren't you all jet-lagged a second ago?"

Delilah waved her hand. "That was a ruse to get Abe out of the room. Now tell us everything." She had one arm draped loosely across Henry's shoulder, and his hand squeezed her thigh.

"And technically we can't drink because we're about to go on a case, so imagine I'm opening a bottle of red wine right now," Freya added.

"Or, given you are a stranger and don't owe us any details about your personal life, you can choose to continue preparing for a case," Sam said, sardonic.

Freya elbowed his side. "Way to spoil the party, Byrne."

I flashed him a grateful smile and pulled one knee up, tossed my hair. "What do you want to know?"

The four of them had already thoroughly enjoyed our cat-and-mouse story: meeting at the lecture, his business card, our neighboring rooms, each lying to one another about our names. And I'd sensed them wanting to probe more about the nature of our relationship—and I *hadn't* missed the comical looks on their faces when Abe had said, simply, that we were sharing a hotel room for safety purposes.

"So where's home for you, Sloane?" Delilah asked, her blue eyes kind.

I hesitated. Home never felt like *home*. "Brooklyn. I have a home office there where I can work with clients."

"Do you have a team you work with?" Henry asked. "Or is it only you?"

"Only me."

"Who makes your office memes and brings donuts on Fridays?" Freya asked.

"Um... I do?" I said, unsure. My workdays featured neither of those things.

Henry leaned forward. "If you don't mind me asking, how did Louisa connect with you?"

"Do you guys remember the stolen Audubon illustrations a few months ago?" I said.

Delilah grinned. "Yeah, and it was the obsessive bird watchers who had stolen it. The four of us couldn't *stop* talking about it."

"That's the one," I replied. "That was my case. My first real case working in antiquities theft. Louisa went to school with the Board President of The Murphy Library, so when she was calling around, seeking contacts, my name came up."

"No shit," Sam said. "You closed that case on your own?"

"Sure did," I said.

"That's fucking impressive," he said. The other three detectives were nodding, approving.

"And how old are you?" Freya asked.

"*Frey.*" Delilah laughed.

"It's okay." I smiled. "I'm twenty-seven."

Another round of nodding heads and low whistles. "Damn," Freya said. "Five years younger than me and significantly more badass."

"Well, I'm amazed with your slate of closed cases these past months," I said, still smiling.

Delilah tucked a strand of hair behind her ear, looked at her fiancé. "Do you think Louisa considered hiring us though? I mean, she almost hired Abe when all of this first happened."

Henry peered at me. "Sloane's talked to her more recently than I have. What's your gut sense about her right now?"

It was beyond strange having Dr. Henry Finch seated on my hotel bed, given not five days ago I thought he might be an actual suspect in this case. I remembered Abe's firm insistence to me that he was innocent; I remembered the emotions on his face as he gazed at old pictures of Bernard and Henry together. At the time, I couldn't pin them down, but I now knew those emotions as *protective.* From the little I'd seen of this highly educated academic, he was too good for this world. I'd always hated the word *gullible* because that placed the blame on the mark whose only fault had been being trusting and open-minded. And how could you blame a person for those endearing qualities?

Over time, I was learning most children weren't raised like I was—to view other human beings as many means to many ends.

The man in front of me was the kind of person my parents would have targeted. And thinking about Bernard taking advantage of him for ten *fucking* years was infuriating.

"The truth?" I said, and Henry nodded. "She's well aware that your firm is a force to be reckoned with. In fact, if *I* don't catch Bernard by my contract's deadline, she promised to fire me and hire someone else."

Freya wrinkled her nose. "Ouch."

"She seemed embarrassed," I said to Henry. "Embarrassed and feeling guilty. As much as she might have considered hiring Codex, I don't believe she wants to confront you. Or Abe."

Delilah squeezed Henry's hand. "Henry was right all along, too."

Henry sighed, squeezed back. "I'm one piece of this story though. Abe... I can't even tell you his reaction the night we first met, the night I handed him the first real evidence painting Bernard as a criminal rather than a librarian. He's not always open with the tough stuff, but it's basically his vendetta."

"Agree," Sam said. "The year I worked with him at Art Theft, it was all he cared about. But goddamn, I thought he was *right* to care. The red flags were there; we just needed someone like Henry to set the process in motion."

"You mean send him into hiding," Henry said grimly.

"Almost every con artist goes into hiding at some point. You didn't make Bernard do anything he wasn't already planning on doing," I said. "He may be in hiding, but we're about to find his ass and send him to prison. That couldn't happen if he was still operating his con and avoiding punishment."

"What that babe said," Freya cheered.

"We are going to find his ass," Sam mused.

Henry was watching me expectantly. "I have a lot of experience working with con artists," I said, surprised at how tense my throat felt, how much I wanted to shield Henry from feeling badly about things out of his control. "Your actions were the first domino needed to get you all *here*."

"To get *us* here," Freya added. "You're a part of this story now too, Sloane."

"Oh," I said, biting my lip. I caught Delilah watching the nervous gesture, so I straightened my spine and went for *sultry* over shy. "Happy to help and to fluster Abe when needed."

Four identical smiles beamed at me. I took a precious second to sink into their goodwill and acceptance. This felt *nice*.

"So are we talking about how our boss has a big fucking crush on you?" Freya asked.

I huffed out a shocked breath. "We are... enjoying spending time with each other."

"In a shared hotel room," Delilah said slowly. "For safety purposes."

I crossed my legs, attempted nonchalance. "After the fire, sharing a room did feel safer. But things between us have progressed. Romantically."

Freya and Delilah were shaking their heads slowly. Even Sam had a pleasant look on his face.

"I can't fucking believe it," Freya said. "If you thought *taking a vacation* was out of character for Abe Royal, what-

ever you two are doing is basically in the next stratosphere.
You are definitely a first."

I wished my heart didn't dance in my chest at the
thought of being a first *anything* for Abe. But there it went,
twirling around, refusing to behave. I awaited their collective judgment, unsure. Except all four of them seemed
*happy.* Freya wrapped her arms around me in a tight hug.
Eyes wide, I stared back at Sam over her shoulder.

"She's always been excitable." He smirked.

When was the last time I'd received a hug from
another woman? A woman who could, possibly, be my
friend?

"You can also hug me back," Freya whispered. I was at
least six inches taller than her, and I had no idea how to
arrange my limbs, but eventually I hugged her back.

"What's happening?" I asked.

"Byrne and I have known Abe for a long, long time," she
said. "We can tell you that the guy doesn't *do* romantic
*anything.*"

"According to your boss, he doesn't make a lot of room in
that cold heart of his," I said, brow arched.

Delilah snorted. "If only he could see *his* face every time
he looks at you. If there's a key to that man's heart, you've
got it."

"No pressure or anything," Henry said cheerfully. I burst
out laughing—surprised, relieved, unsure of what entirely
was happening. Key or not, team or not, I *did* have a self-
sufficient life to get back to in Brooklyn after this. My apartment wasn't a home. Yet up until now I hadn't been
searching for more than a place to lay my head while
staying afloat.

I potentially had a key to Abe's heart I shouldn't want.
And a foot-loose and fancy-free heart of my own I was now

unable to control. This situation's potential for devastation was growing by the second.

The door to the hotel room swung open, and all five of us froze like kids caught misbehaving. Abe Royal appeared with bags of food and a suspicious expression.

"Were you all engaging in light-hearted frivolity?" Abe asked.

"Does doing body-shots off of Byrne's six-pack count as frivolity?" Freya asked.

"Evandale," Sam growled—but one wink from his girlfriend, and the former FBI agent melted like butter.

"Gossiping about your supervisor does count," Abe said mildly. "As would body shots, if we're being technical about it."

"We would *never* talk about you, sir," Henry said soberly.

Eyes narrowed, he placed the food down gingerly. Avoided looking at me as he pulled items from bags and drinks from containers. "Eat," he said, smile wry. "Grab coffee and water, nap if you need. We've got less than forty minutes before the four of us need to be at the auction house."

There was a burst of energy in the room, a comfort to prepping and eating together, even in the middle of another country. When Delilah walked past me, she laid her hand on my arm.

"I'm really happy you're here," she said.

"Me too," I said. And meant it. "I'm not sure I could have even attempted it without a team."

"I get the feeling you're the kind of woman who can pretty much do anything if you put your mind to it," she said. "Which is my kind of woman, by the way."

She wasn't wrong—I'd done far worse and much harder in my life than what we were about to do during the next two days. But I'd done it alone, which was a different kind of hard.

The next forty minutes were a frantic blur of eating and dressing while Codex teased each other and chatted about the case. By the time the four of them were done and ready to meet us in the lobby, the silence in my and Abe's room was weird.

Abe and I made eye contact—alone—for the first time since they'd arrived that morning. We let out twin sighs of relief, exchanged dual, flirtatious smiles. The hotel had returned our previously soggy clothing, freshly dry-cleaned and pressed. Abe's navy suit was hot enough to be outlawed in fifty states—as was the slow and lingering way he was studying me.

"You look like a Grecian goddess in that dress," he said in a rough voice. "One that's up to no good."

I blew him a kiss. "Naughty Athena?"

"Exactly."

I caressed my dress. It was a pearl satin, floor-length and high-necked. My hair was swept to the side in a low bun. Desire hung, tangible, between us.

"After you, partner," he said, holding the door open.

Just past him, one foot out the door, I turned to say *thank you*. Instead Abe grabbed me by the elbow and yanked me against his body. A second later, his lips were on mine, his fingers diving into my hair. I lost myself in this stolen kiss, let him consume my mouth, taste me, dive our tongues together while pressing every single inch of his body to mine. With a moan, I shoved him back against the wall, let him drag my leg high around his waist, palm splaying across my ass with a possessiveness I loved. Then he was rocking his cock between my legs. Once, twice, three times, and there I went, shaking already. Our mouths separated, I gasped in air, my sex clenched, needing to be filled, stretched, *fucked* by Abe.

He grabbed the back of my neck firmly, thumb tracing my jaw to land on my chin. Tilted it until our eyes were locked together. "I've been waiting to kiss you all goddamn day."

"It was worth the wait." I tried to catch his mouth again. He dodged me, kept my chin lifted.

"My team likes you," he said.

My mouth curved. "I like them." I let out a shaky breath. "I like seeing you with them."

"Is that so?" His thumb caressed my lip. "Do you want to know what *flustered* me today, Ms. Argento?"

"What?" I whispered.

"Remembering how it felt to fuck you on the dresser," he said.

I didn't need reminding. My memory flooded with every aching, delicious sensation—every moan and pant, every rough word and dirty bruise. And just when I thought Abe might kiss me again, he let go. Resumed his position at the door with his palm outspread, looking goddamn immaculate.

"After you, still," he said, with a dangerous smile. "Unless you're too flustered."

## 38

## ABE

*I* stepped out of our cab and beheld Kensley's Auction House fully for the very first time. It was internationally renowned, and there tended to be one in every cosmopolitan city in the world. The London location was a four-story white building with gold-and-purple lights and international flags blowing in the slight breeze. A large, excited-looking crowd had already gathered, many in deer-stalker hats and carrying pipes. A vintage marquee lighted by bright, white bulbs proclaimed *Sherlock Holmes Lives!* in black letters.

I turned, hand extended, and helped Sloane step gracefully from the cab in her flowing dress. We'd managed to restrict our conversation to tonight's event during the short ride through town. The restriction didn't apply to my fantasies, which included getting on my knees in that cab and burying my tongue between her thighs. The day had been a riot of emotions, many of them challenging for me to navigate, but one thing I knew for certain was the pride I experienced watching Sloane interact with my team. I'd sensed her initial hesitancy thawing away, and whatever conversation had happened while I'd picked up our dinner had shifted attitudes—for her and for them. I just wasn't sure what it all *meant*. And I had not a goddamn clue what Sloane and I were to do two days from now, when our separate lives would almost assuredly slip back into place.

"Thank you, Daniel." She smiled, scanning the crowd in front of the building. I looked and found no indication of Dresden, although auction security guards would surely be present inside. "Any sign of our favorite friend?"

"I'm sure we'd hear him first," I said. We had asked Henry, multiple times, what his sense had been about Bernard's supposed best friend. Henry had been as unsure as we were, though he'd admitted to always being charmed by the man.

As if spirited from the sky, Humphrey and Reggie appeared, dressed as Holmes and Watson, bellowing our names across the crowd. I caught Sloane's eye, smiled, then reached down for her hand and entwined our fingers.

"Valiant! Enchanting! Dashing!" Humphrey said, crushing us to his barrel chest. "Reginald, have you ever seen two people more fit to be our dates this evening?"

Reggie tipped his hat to us, looking tiny next to his giant, red-haired husband. "I don't mean to diminish his compliment, but Humphrey *does* say that about most of our dinner guests."

Sloane laughed. "We're in fine company."

"Truly a night to be remembered," Humphrey said. "Can you imagine, glimpsing Doyle's words, written in his own hand, unveiling secrets we can only dream about."

Society members were filling in, calling to Humphrey. From the corner of my eye, I caught Sam and Freya in their disguises appear at the edge of the crowd. They both gave me a quick nod. It had been a long time since I'd had the privilege of being in the field with my agents.

"Can you imagine if Bernard could be here?" Sloane said, slipping her hands through Humphrey's extended arm.

Humphrey winced. "I tried again, sent him message after message. Eudora assured me he was made aware and that he couldn't possibly return given how far away he is right now."

"Where on earth is he?" I asked, keeping my tone teasing.

"It's beyond my understanding," he said. "We'll simply have to remember every single detail so we can relay to him upon his victorious return."

We stepped inside the auction house and into a room with a magnificently domed ceiling and classic paintings on the walls. In the very center, beside heavy security and beneath glass, were the secret pages of Arthur Conan Doyle. Even I felt compelled to see them, and until now they'd been nothing more than a convenient clue, leading us closer to catching Bernard. The sincere awe on the faces of those surrounding the table kick-started my interest.

I glanced at Humphrey and Reggie—two boys on Christmas morning, spying a puppy with a red ribbon beneath the tree. They were already moving forward. Sloane and I followed, diligent. These two were our shield from Eudora's wrath tonight.

A sharply dressed white man, with a yellow bowtie and a gray mustache, greeted Humphrey and Reggie warmly. Sloane squeezed my fingers, and I assumed she also recognized him to be James Patrick. *JP is a yes.*

"And Daniel and Devon, of course," Humphrey was saying. "My esteemed American guests. Fans so devoted they flew all the way here to spend time with the Society."

A split-second of anger flickered across James's face before he concealed it. I caught it, and I guessed Sloane did as well. "Eudora's told me so much about you," he said. His handshake was much too tight, jaw much too clenched. Sloane sized him up like a sparring partner she couldn't wait to defeat.

"Has she?" Sloane asked. "What an absolute treasure. Daniel and I have been delighted by the warm reception she's given to us, especially since we know how busy she is."

Security guards appeared at the far edges of the room—a solid flank of stoic muscle. They wore uniforms identifying them as Kensley security, not Dresden, but I felt confident they were for Sloane and me.

"A treasure she is," James said. "Humphrey, do you have a moment?"

"I do not!" Humphrey said, clapping James on the arm across the table. "I only have eyes for this at the moment, as do my esteemed guests."

Sloane cast a sideways glance my way. Thank *fucking* god for Humphrey Hatcher. Of all the people I thought might be inadvertently helping me catch Bernard Allerton, I'd never anticipated it being his best friend. Another guest grabbed James's attention, but I didn't miss the scathing look he cast my way.

The table we stepped up to displayed the contents of Arthur Conan Doyle's undiscovered private effects, which Humphrey was viewing with the devotional posture of a penitent.

"This," he said, tapping the glass. "This is the man's wallet. His *wallet*. Have you ever seen such a thing?"

Sloane bent over, looking sincerely captivated. I stared at her beautiful profile, backlit by the golden light, similarly captivated. When she placed her hand on Humphrey's arm, there was such vulnerability in the gesture. I hoped, more than anything, that Humphrey Hatcher was an innocent man. Maybe it was his affectionately paternal nature that drew both Sloane and me in, that grabbed our trust and held on tight. While I at least had two mothers and Codex in my life, Sloane had not a single soul—not a funny cousin or a kind uncle or a grandparent she could call.

"It makes him human," she said, smiling when Humphrey's face brightened. "Brings him closer to us."

"Enchantress, you read my soul," he said. "To think of a genius using something as pedestrian as a wallet. I mean, it boggles even the most serene of minds. And this, see this right here? A letter to his brother, Kingsley, before he passed away after the war. These are drawings... *Reggie, look at the drawings.*"

Sloane was laughing, following along with Humphrey's antics, asking questions about every single item beneath that glass. She was one hell of an undercover agent, but the woman in front of me was honestly connecting with these two scholars. It was no cover, no lie, no con.

I bent down and kissed the ball of her shoulder.

Also not part of our cover.

Every item, Humphrey exclaimed over. "We'd heard he kept letters from Teddy Roosevelt, but to see them in *bloody person*. Daniel, look the man's signature. So bold!"

I bent down and eyeballed a small piece of history—a letter exchanged between two famous men who respected each other. This letter, preserving it, protecting it, that was what Codex *was*. I saw Sam and Freya speaking to a group of people, felt Sloane's hand in mine, knew Delilah was patrolling the parking lot while Henry was searching for missing clues. Every single one of us was vital to protect the history right in front of us.

"Extraordinary," I said. "A once-in-a-lifetime experience. I'm saddened to think of these items disappearing into a private collector's hands tomorrow, if I can be brutally honest."

"We all are," Reggie said sadly. "These belong with the Society."

"I won't be able to bear the auction tomorrow," Humphrey said. "Not now that I'm seeing them here like this."

I scanned the crowd and found James speaking with Eudora, caught the guards at various hallways leading away from this main room. We'd studied a map online today back at the hotel and knew there to be three exits, this front entrance, and a giant basement of storage we were positive was heavily secured. And where were the—

"Oh, I *love* being betrayed by my closest colleagues," Eudora said in a voice that *sounded* sweet but dripped poison. All four of us turned from the table. She beamed a nasty smile our way, flanked by two security guards.

"Humphrey, didn't I ask the Society not to associate with these two liars?" she asked.

"Oh, Eudora," he thundered. "Didn't I once ask you not to speak to me like I was your damned *child*?"

Nostrils flaring, she ducked her head. "Keep your voice down, you fool. The *media* could be here."

"Then you'll love not making a scene," he replied, cheerful. "Daniel and Devon are my guests, and you will now shut the hell up."

In another world, Humphrey would have made a great addition to the Codex team. Sam and Freya hovered in the periphery. I held my palm out below my waist, flat as in *stay*. With a curt nod, Sam turned slightly and pretended to point something out to Freya.

"Never mind," Eudora said, eyeing Sloane and me like a particularly tasty lunch. "You're not the fool, Humphrey. These two are, since apparently they care not at all about their own personal safety."

"Sorry for dumping that martini on you last night," Sloane said. "Bill me if you can't get the stain out."

I hid a smile behind my hand. Watched Eudora turn flame red before spinning on her heel and leaving. The guards followed, but in no way did I think we were safe to move about.

"Is that what this is all about?" Humphrey asked. "You stained her dress?"

"I have no idea," Sloane said. "Does she usually physically threaten people?"

He stroked his beard in thought. "Yes, she does."

"What a leader," I said. "No wonder you all miss Bernard."

"Now *that's* a leader," Humphrey said. "*Oh,* is that a diary I see?"

Humphrey and Reggie rushed back to the glass while Sloane and I had a moment alone. With a conspiratorial look, she shifted back into the crowd, dragging me with her. As casually as we could, we pushed the boundaries of what was available to us, peered into hallways and calculated guards-per-exits. Watched James and Eudora conferring, watched the Sherlock Society members stare at the glass table. All of it went into a mental catalog for later discussion, but I felt frustrated that we still couldn't figure out how this plan to steal these papers might go down—or if there was even a plan at all.

I had one eye trained on Freya and Sam throughout our wandering. Eventually the four of us converged, in front of Doyle's diary and close enough to Humphrey to feel his protection. I nodded again at my team—concealed a smile at their disguises.

"Evening," I said to Sam.

"Hello," he replied. Directly behind us stood a group of people speaking in excited tones and whispers, pressing against our backs to view the antiques. I knew all four of us were listening, could *feel* our focused energy. There was rapid discussion of what was found, the legacy of the family, the auction house, the potential bidders, tomorrow's event.

And then—new people must have arrived. We could hear names and greetings. More pressing against us to see the items. Something rooted me to the spot, a name I'd caught that set my teeth on edge.

"So sorry," a voice said. "I didn't quite catch your names?"

There was a pause. My pulse spiked. I strained to hear again what the man had said.

"Julian," was the reply. "Julian King. And this is my business partner Birdie Barnes."

## 39

### ABE

*O*nly years of rigorous training kept Sam, Freya, and me from outwardly reacting to the names *Julian and Birdie*. My first thought was an unprofessional "what the fuck" followed by a roar of noise in my ears. I exhaled as slowly as I could, slid my eyes to my left to find Sam's jaw set hard.

"You know," I said to Sloane. "I'd love to get some air. How about you?"

One look at me was all it took. "Absolutely," she said quickly.

Two people forced their way between my shoulders and Sam's. The man tapped the glass, turned to his female companion. "Birdie, it's just darling. Have you ever seen such magnificence?"

Sam caught my eye over Julian's hunched back. We'd had no indication of Julian and Birdie's whereabouts since Sam and Freya had assumed their identities to infiltrate The Empty House. We didn't even know if they were real people.

Would they recognize the two people standing next to

them, even in disguise? The two private detectives who had used their names to help arrest their circle of friends?

Slowly, as if walking away from a bomb, the four of us backed away, careful not to draw any attention to our movements. Humphrey was nearby, but we couldn't risk drawing his bellow our way. I gripped Sloane's hand as we kept moving, heart bruising my ribcage, breath short. Our measured steps seemed to take an eternity, and once we reached the center of the room, all four of us turned and rushed quickly through the heavy front doors.

"Let's call a cab," I said, beneath my breath. "Calmly."

Nodding, Sam raised his hand as we reached the curb. Glancing back to make sure we hadn't been followed, I called Delilah. As soon as she picked up, I said, "Get back to the hotel."

"Done," she said.

A cab stopped in front of us, and we climbed inside. After slamming the door and giving the driver instructions, we stared at each other.

"Is someone going to tell me what the hell is going on?" Sloane asked. Her phone rang. "Shit, it's Humphrey."

"Don't answer," I said. "You can call him tomorrow and invent an excuse." I ducked past Sloane to find Freya and Sam open-mouthed and shell-shocked. "Tell me you heard what I heard."

Freya and Sam exchanged a look. "I believe I heard that couple introduce themselves as Julian King and Birdie Barnes," she said. Each word seemed heavy with the deeper implications of what this meant. I rubbed a hand across my mouth, momentarily distracted by the persistent alarm bells ringing and ringing in my head. The federal agent in me knew that *all* of these people coming together was no fucking coincidence.

I nodded at Sloane. "Tell her."

Freya let out a long, shaky breath. "When Byrne and I went undercover to infiltrate that secret society, we assumed the identities of a real couple I'd been following online. We later learned they were highly skilled con artists."

Sloane's eyes shot up to mine at the word *con artists*.

"They owned a bookstore in San Francisco, and their names were Julian King and Birdie Barnes."

"What the *fuck*?" Sloane said.

At the time, Freya knew Julian and Birdie to be new members of The Empty House and were beloved in the antiquity's community. The couple bailed on attending the Antiquarian Festival—an act that ultimately allowed Sam and Freya to assume their identities.

They were never seen or heard from again.

No pictures of them existed online; no patron had ever actually met Julian *or* Birdie in person. At first, we assumed they were involved with Bernard. But after the case, and their disappearance, Freya's best conclusion was they were probably con artists operating in the rare book world— buying books illegally, selling them illegally, burning bridges left and right while pretending to be on everyone's side.

In the chaos of the arrests, Julian King and Birdie Barnes's real names and personas had fallen to the wayside, and to my knowledge no legal actions had been taken against them.

My mental alarm bell became an air raid siren. Glimmers of what I knew I should do next bubbled up in my mind, twisting my stomach and tightening my throat.

"So what in the fresh hell are they doing here?" Freya added. "And *why* in the fresh hell are they using those names?"

"I haven't a goddamn clue," I said. "Sam?"

"Sir," he said.

"You know what we need to do, right?"

Cowboy mission or not, if the Codex team had encountered real criminals, wanted by the FBI, we needed to actually call the FBI. I was too overloaded on adrenaline to feel much about it, although I knew I'd be disappointed later. To get so close only to bring in the big guns would potentially wound my pride forever.

"We'll call the Deputy Director as soon as we return."

"Wait, Sam's dad, you mean?" Sloane asked.

"The word *dad* gives him a lot more credit than he deserves," Freya said.

Sam chuckled softly. "You're not wrong. He'll know the nature of the FBI's involvement with them and what we need to do."

The cab stopped in front of the hotel. We jumped out and raced to the room, expressions a mixture of grim determination and wild excitement. I opened the hotel door to find Henry and Delilah, pacing about.

"I just made it back," Delilah said. "What happened?"

"Julian King and Birdie Barnes were at the event tonight," Freya said, tossing her bag onto the bed.

"*Holy shit*," Henry and Delilah said in unison.

"Our thoughts exactly," I said.

Freya dropped her head into her hands. "I cannot fucking believe it. When I heard their names, I swear to god my heart actually stopped beating."

"I hate to say it, but it could be random," Sam said. "We always thought they were an intermediary between illegal buyers and illegal sellers. Maybe word has gotten around in the rare book community that a major haul is being auctioned tomorrow, and it attracted the vultures."

"Maybe," I said. "None of this feels random, though."

"Abe, we have to call this in," Delilah said.

"I know." I looked at Sloane, who was already seated behind Freya's laptops with a focused expression. "Sloane."

We made eye contact over the top of the screen. "What is it?"

"If we call the Deputy Director, and they have to take action here, and it leads to catching Bernard, I mean we'd all *hope* it would, but your contract, I'm not sure what Louisa..."

Sloane shook her head immediately. "My deliverable is finding Bernard and giving him to the proper authorities. So whatever road leads to Bernard's capture is the one I want to be on. And con artists like Julian and Birdie deserve to be behind bars. Call him."

I swallowed hard. "It could still work out well for you, career-wise."

She waved her hand. "Let me worry about my contract. You do what we're supposed to do."

I held her midnight gaze for a second longer than was professional—because I understood what she was potentially letting go. I had watched this case become more and more personal to Sloane and less and less about the money or prestige. Still, it was her career potentially on the line, not mine.

"Thank you," I said. She winked at me—flirtatious—and I busied myself with shedding my jacket before I did something stupid like kiss her in front of my agents.

"Sam, how quickly can you get your dad on the phone?"

"If its urgent, he'll step out of a meeting to speak with me," Sam said. "Give me a second."

Deputy Director Andrew Byrne and I had always had a contentious relationship. At the Bureau, we'd butted heads often, and when I'd left to start Codex, he'd made his disdain apparent and very public. The man's lack of respect for private investigators was well-documented, and having to involve him in The Empty House case had been a pissing contest I hadn't enjoyed. The man despised when I was right, and I'd *never* admit the few times he'd been. Stealing his son from the Bureau to work for Codex had been the final nail in the coffin for our working relationship.

Sam stood, on the phone, shaking his head and speaking quietly. Freya was perched on the table where Sloane sat—they were both watching Sam carefully. Delilah paced along with me, while Henry sat in the chair with his arms crossed, thoughtful.

"Hey," I said to Henry. "Anything at the bookstore?"

"Nope," he said. "It was dark, the sign indicated they were closed for the night. Nothing sparked a memory, unfortunately."

"Okay," I said, clapping him on the shoulder. "Good work though. We'll keep Peter on the back burner."

Sam's voice on the phone grew louder, drawing my attention. "Yes, sir," Sam was saying—and handing the phone to me.

I put the phone on speaker again so the whole team could listen in. "Hello, Andrew," I said.

"Abraham," came the curt response.

Nostrils flaring, I caught Freya's dramatic eye roll. "My team and I are working a case in London right now, and we believe may have stumbled upon two persons of interest in The Empty House case."

"Who?" Icy but professional.

"Julian King and Birdie Barnes," I said.

There was another long pause—sounds of a door closing. "And what are American private investigators doing in London?"

I looked at Sam, who nodded at me. "Looking for Bernard Allerton."

The name hung heavily in the tense air—I had five people watching me while attempting to discern what the hell we did next.

"To be clear, you and your entire team are in London searching for one of the FBI's most wanted men?" Andrew repeated.

"Yes," I said.

The seconds ticked by—slow, dramatic. And then the Deputy Director of the FBI cleared his throat. "So you must have received my email?"

## 40

# SLOANE

"I'm sorry, what did you say?" Abe asked, looking truly astonished. Sam was on his feet, striding toward the sound of his father's voice on the phone.

"The confidential email," Andrew Byrne said. "The one with the reports. You must have gotten it?"

Sam snatched the phone up. "Dad."

I saw Freya's face soften. So did Abe's.

"Yes, Sam?"

"What did you do?"

"I merely sent an anonymous email to your supervisor letting him know my thoughts on where Bernard Allerton might be," he said. "We are all familiar with the various *shortcomings*, shall we say, of the Bureau. *At times*."

Abe and Sam stared at each other. "And what would you like us to do with this information?"

"I believe you know," the Deputy Director said. "Or I wouldn't have sent it."

Tension radiated from Sam's posture. Every person in the room looked suspended mid-action—breathing fast, bodies bent forward. "And you sent it to Abe and not to me?"

The room filled with sounds of rustling paper and Andrew clearing his throat. "My decision had no bearing on your abilities, Samuel. It's less suspicious for an email to end up in a former colleague's inbox than in my own son's. And I assumed Abe would take swift action with the information and involve you immediately."

Sam shot a wry smile at his supervisor. "He did involve us. Although not *immediately*."

Abe held out his palms in apology, his own smile tugging at his lips. "I'll be apologizing for the next decade."

Sam re-focused on the phone call. "Then do *you* know why Julian King and Birdie Barnes might be in London, flashing their names around at a private auction?"

"Julian and Birdie weren't ever a focus on any investigation," Andrew said. "I was in a meeting last week, reviewing the testimony of the members we arrested. Because you and Freya assumed their identity, The Empty House members all believe they were part of a wide-scale federal sting operation. Julian and Birdie, in their minds, never actually existed as real booksellers. The Empty House members believe Julian and Birdie were two undercover FBI agents, working them over for a case the whole time, even online."

Sam turned to stare at Freya, who was chewing on her lip. "I guess..." she started. "Shit, I guess that makes sense, though."

"From a Bureau perspective," Andrew continued, "We don't have any records of Julian and Birdie's existence—not the store, not any sales, nothing."

Abe paced, hand on the back of his neck. "Is that why they're comfortable using those names out here, in London?"

"Well, the only people who think they *might* be criminals are the eleven members of The Empty House, and they're all about to start their prison sentences," Freya said. "To people in London, would they have any idea who they were?"

I'd never actually interacted with Julian and Birdie, but if they were anything like my parents, they lived their lives with a strong sense of self-preservation and an even stronger sense of confidence. A confidence that could absolutely put them at risk of being caught.

"If they're real con artists," I said. "And they feel like their con is still intact, they'll keep it intact for as long as they can. Sounds like they were on the run well before Freya and Sam co-opted their identities. I read through the media reports on the case. Codex was mentioned but not the names Sam and Freya used while undercover." I crossed my arms across my chest, trying to keep my voice light. "Your typical con artist is part psychopath, part narcissist. They have no conscience. And it means they have a grandiose sense of self. Both of these traits make it likely that Julian and Birdie see no fault in being here in London. If they're here to con their way into owning the Doyle papers, they believe to their core they have every right to be here."

A few seconds of silence followed.

"I think you're fucking right," Freya said. We exchanged a tiny smile. Providing even the smallest insight to this team felt important in a way I couldn't name yet.

"I think you're right too," Henry said. "And I think the world of book thieves is too small, and Bernard's role too powerful, for the appearance of Julian and Birdie to be random. Because Bernard is the biggest narcissist of them all. He snaps his fingers, and every single thief comes running."

"Abraham." The Deputy Director's voice cut through our conversation like a medieval gong.

"Yes?" Abe asked, weary. He was distracted. I could see his brain working to pull together the final threads.

"Are you close?"

We all knew what he meant.

"The closest we've been," Abe said. "There's an auction tomorrow. We think Bernard's making a move. If we don't grab him, we'll be grabbing another thief the authorities will be able to use to get to him."

"And that's why I sent the email to you," Andrew said.

"What are you going to tell the Bureau?" Sam asked.

"I don't believe I have anything to report given that this call went to voicemail and we never actually spoke," he said. "Correct?"

Abe released a sarcastic-sounding breath. And he grinned slowly. "Correct."

"And Sam?" Andrew asked.

"Yes, sir?"

"Just give me a call when you get him."

## 41

## SLOANE

*I* woke to sun slanting across my pillow. I caught the time—just past 6:00 am—and swung my hand out to the space next to me. Which was empty.

Rubbing my hand across my face, I sat up, blinked again. The door to the balcony was open, the smell of fresh coffee wafting in, and it didn't take much to guess that Abe Royal was probably sitting out there, admiring the view, and thinking about today.

The day.

The day we were officially going after Bernard. And with the unofficial approval of the Deputy Director of the FBI.

There was a murmuring to my left—Delilah, talking in her sleep. She and Henry had fallen asleep on the bed next to ours while Freya and Sam had crashed out on the trundle bed and couch. The room had the appearance of the morning after a college party; people sprawled out, snoring, having only gone to bed a few hours earlier. Jacked up on adrenaline and slightly nervous after being chased by guards, the entire Codex team had crashed in our room after discussing plans and strategies for tonight's big event.

331

Running a hand through my snarled hair, I looked around at these four detectives who were already sneaking their way into my heart.

On the deck, Abe sat in a chair with a cup of coffee, staring at the view with a distracted, nervous look. The newly duplicitous organ in my chest slammed against my rib cage at the sight of him with sleep-tousled hair and a hint of stubble. After the rest of the team had fallen asleep, he had dragged me against his chest and cradled me there all night—nose against the crown of my head, arms wrapped tight. I had dropped immediately into a sweet, dreamless sleep.

I padded barefoot across the deck and gave him a silly smile. "Good morning, man-on-vacation."

Abe swung me onto his lap and buried his face in my hair. "Good morning, Ms. Argento."

His voice was scratchy with sleep, and exhaustion was etched around his eyes. "Let me guess," I said. "You stayed awake and watched over everyone last night."

"Leaders protect their team," he said, nonchalant. There was nothing nonchalant about this man guarding the people he was afraid to fully love. "And you're awake early."

"Who can sleep on such a big day?" I said, brushing a strand of hair from his forehead.

He rested his chin on my shoulder and stared past me. We sat in silence for a minute, gently rocking back and forth. The chaos of our instant attraction was as multi-dimensional as a diamond, dazzling and sharp, electric and erotic. But then soft and muted, comfortable and safe. Abe held me tighter, and I nuzzled my lips against his temple.

"What's wrong?" I asked quietly.

"What if I made a mistake?" he asked. "My whole team flies here. We get all excited that we're going to capture this mastermind who has evaded prosecution for years. The Deputy Director of the goddamn *FBI* puts his complete faith in me. And everything, all of it, could be for nothing." Another pause, another gentle rock. "What kind of person does that? Keeps hunting a white whale that won't be found?"

For a while, we watched pedestrians on their way to work, buses and cars, the opening of shops. All the normal things that occur on the morning before a busy Friday.

"I used to steal from my parents," I said, gulping around my usual resistance to share. His body went taut, face turning toward mine. "There was a summer where we worked amusement parks for fast cash. There's no real skill to that con, just taking advantage of people who are sun-drunk and happy and usually have lots of cash in their pockets."

That summer I remembered watching those close-knit families, out for the day to simply have fun together, and not understanding how they existed. The more I saw them—the laughter, the teasing, chasing each other with ice cream cones—the more my brain went into freak-out mode. *Something's not right.* Not about them. About *me*.

"My parents were running this photography scheme," I said. "They took photos while copying people's credit card and personal information to use for stealing identities. Later, they'd unleash me on people waiting in those long rollercoaster lines and watch me like a hawk as I pickpocketed loose cash. Working like that, working fast, you're not grabbing a certain amount of cash, you're grabbing whatever bill you can pinch between your fingers. So I'd slip out hundreds of dollars without the person knowing." I paused, remembering how powerful I felt to finally control even the tiniest amount of my destiny. "I couldn't give it all back. I needed my parents to believe I was earning my keep. But in the intervening seconds between the mark's pockets, my fingers, and my parents' hands, I'd steal what I could from the pile and return it."

Abe's brow furrowed, and I couldn't read the look in his eye. "That sounds very dangerous given what your parents' reaction could have been."

I smiled, a little sad. "I didn't have anything else to do as a kid besides practice. And it made me feel good. It was small change, literally, what I could return to them. But in our quest to balance the scales of justice, every act shifts the weight."

His hand idly stroked up and down my spine. "If we don't catch him tonight, we tip the scales the wrong way."

"If we don't catch him tonight," I countered. "It's only because we've caught someone else in his chain of criminals. Maybe it's a smaller shift. It's still a *shift*." I leaned in, kissed the tip of his nose. "And given the extraordinary circumstances that have put you and I on this path, together, twelve hours away from going after what we want the most..." I shook my head. "I'm not a person who believes in fate. But something *big* is going to happen tonight. Can't you feel it?"

His gray eyes searched mine. "I feel it," he murmured. He leaned in to steal a kiss, fingers sliding through my hair to hold me still. My lips parted, my tongue met his, I inhaled the scent of his skin and the roughness of his rare stubble. "I feel it," he repeated, this time with lips caressing mine.

"Well, good *fucking* morning," Delilah said from the doorway, startling us both. I jumped and laughed when Freya appeared next to her, both of them clapping.

"Good thing you got that shared hotel room for you and

Sloane, boss," Freya smirked. "You know, for safety purposes or whatever."

"Am I to be accosted by my agents on my own vacation?" Abe asked.

Delilah snorted. "A hundred pots of coffee are on their way to our room. And breakfast."

Freya tapped her chin with a scowl. "And I don't mean to be the *Abe* of the group, but my colleagues are out here necking when we only have the biggest case of our lives to solve."

Abe's valiant effort not to laugh dissolved—and his husky morning laughter curled my toes.

I stood, dragging Abe with me. "Come now, Mr. Royal. It's a beautiful day to right the scales of justice."

## 42

### ABE

7:01 p.m., and I was out of the shower, slicking my hair back and studying the face of a man whose criminal obsession was finally—*maybe*—coming true tonight.

The auction began at 8:00, and the six of us were set to leave for our various positions in twenty-nine minutes. Henry, in disguise, would stake out Mycroft's Pub, which allowed him to watch Adler's. Sloane and I were playing a fancy couple out on the town, strolling past 221B Baker Street. Delilah was attending the auction tonight—at this point, she was the only Codex member who didn't have the potential to be recognized.

Freya and Sam would be hiding out in the parking lot at the Kensley Auction House, waiting to grab people or call the cops or chase down suspects. It wasn't a perfect plan by any means, but the six of us would be covering as many hot spots as we could to cast the biggest net we were able.

I knew now that Sloane and I would have never pulled this off on our own. The team was necessary. Always.

As usual, Codex had sprung into quick action after we'd gorged ourselves on breakfast and coffee. The relaxed laughter and conversation as we ate was a necessary balm to my spiky nerves. As was seeing Sloane open for them the way she had for me. I behaved and kept my hands off of her all day. I still took enormous pleasure and strength from the smiles she'd flash me like bolts of heat lightning. The euphoric rush was the same.

*Call me when you get him.*

I scrubbed my face down the towel, accepting I was going to be a nervous goddamn wreck the entire night. Heart hammering, chest tight, I tied the towel around my waist and walked out of the bathroom—only to be killed dead on the spot by the goddess.

"You'll certainly stand out in that," I managed.

Sloane turned slowly, lipstick raised, and smiled like a pin-up model. "You told me to dress nicely. This is nice."

"You and I must have varying definitions of *nice*."

She stood completely naked in front of the dresser mirror in nothing but silver stiletto heels, bent close to apply a scarlet color to her lips. Her body was a display of shadow and light, full curves and strong muscle, mysteries and secrets. All that raven hair was secured in a bun, revealing her profile, baring her neck. I had no choice but to drink in her astonishing beauty, to fall prey, yet again, to her captivating spirit.

"How much time do we have before we need to leave?" she asked.

"Twenty-seven minutes."

Her lingering perusal of my mostly naked body made it obvious why she was asking. Tonight was no night for distraction. She and I both knew that in our bones.

"Pity," she said. Her widening smile was less flirtatious and much, much more emotional.

*Can't you feel it?*

I let my towel drop, enjoyed her hungry perusal as I pulled on black briefs over my extremely obvious erection. Sloane reached for a long chain necklace and moved to drop it over her head.

"Wait," I said. I walked until I stood directly behind her, our eyes meeting and holding in the mirror. "Allow me."

With precision, I dropped the chain between her naked breasts, dragged it along her skin before finally clasping it at the nape of her neck. My fingers gripped the back of her neck possessively, squeezing once.

"Thank you," she said, voice extra smoky.

I curled my fingers in the lacy fabric of her underwear. Holding them up, I said, "May I?"

"Please," she replied, turning around to face me. I was back on my knees again for Sloane, staring at her in complete and total adoration. She stepped carefully into the fabric, and I slowly slid it past her ankles, along her calves, past her knees. My fingers lingered, stroked as they moved higher. Higher still. If I gave into temptation and pressed my face to her cunt, we'd never leave this room. But I did press a fairly filthy kiss to the inside of her thigh as I finally positioned her underwear where they were supposed to be. I exhaled, feathered my breath across her stomach, dragging my mouth along her hip bones. Her fingers roamed my hair, sifting the still-wet strands.

"Now you," she said, nodding at my pants. With a wolfish grin, I stood and slipped them on. Sloane hooked her fingers in the belt loops and yanked me over, zipping my pants with her own feline smirk.

"Are suits the only thing you wear, Mr. Royal?" she asked. Her fingers traced down my chest, danced along my ribcage.

"One of the many things past girlfriends have been

annoyed by," I said. I selected a bracelet from the dresser, grabbed her wrist. "I believe the actual charges against me were *'never has fun.'*" I draped the silver over her skin, clasped it. Raised her wrist to my mouth to kiss it. "Letting go is hard for me. The only way I survived what happened with my mother was by exacting a precise control. Fun will exist once I'm done fixing all the wrong in this world."

Sloane held out my crisp white shirt. The hotel had gone above and beyond laundering and drying our soaked clothing. As I slid my arms into the sleeves, she pulled the material up my shoulders. Smoothed her hand down the strip of chest and stomach still bare.

"Control feels safer," she said. "I get it."

I knew she did.

She closed each button with deliberate movements, midnight eyes glued to mine. "How often do you indulge in sex with strangers?"

I caressed the side of her face with my fingers. "When needed. How about you?"

"When needed," she repeated. Smiled. Shirt closed, I tucked it in, handed her my belt. The confident way she handled the leather gave me too many erotic fantasies.

"Tie," she said, palm outstretched. I placed the silk material between her fingers, allowed a mostly naked Sloane to knot my tie. Again.

"Do you dress the men you sleep with?" I asked—a bite of rare jealousy in my words.

"That would imply I was there long enough to do anything except get what I came for and then leave," she said. Tie fixed, she stepped back to examine its precision. I looped my arm around her waist and yanked her back into me.

"Why do it for me?" I asked, mouth lingering near hers.

Her lips curved seductively—the color of a poisoned apple, delicious and sinful in equal measure. "Because it's *you*."

The fortress around my heart wouldn't be able to take such a skilled dismantling much longer.

She handed me the hanger from which a long red dress hung. I dropped to my knees again, and her hands landed on my shoulders as she stepped inside the pool of scarlet fabric. Her expression was stripped bare of anything but raw honesty. "I find it interesting that the two of us crave control. But whatever is happening between us is pure fucking chaos. *And* fun."

I laughed softly, nuzzled my cheek against her leg. "You're having fun with me?"

"The most fun I've ever had," she said. "Aren't you?"

I analyzed the teasing lightness I had in my chest whenever Sloane was around, the desire to show her things, tell her things, whisk her away to wild and exotic vacations. "Very much so," I said—voice rough at the edges. I slipped her dress up her thighs, over the swell of her ass, along her ribcage, rising rapidly with breath. At her bare breasts, I moved the fabric softly over her hard nipples, tying the straps behind her neck.

She looked down at herself. "How do I look?"

"You are the most enchanting creature I have ever seen," I said. I bent down, kissed her cheek. "Chaos personified." Hands on her shoulders, I turned her toward the mirror so she could see herself.

"What I can't figure out," I continued. "Is why I'm craving this type of chaos for the first time in my life. My life was strict order before you came along. I can't get enough of you."

I smoothed my arms around her waist and kissed her throat.

"Racing headlong into passion is something I've never done before," she whispered. Sloane and I weren't the kind of people who eagerly shared their feelings. I recognized this as a verbal sidestep to '*I like you a lot.*'

"I'm happy we're racing together," I said, knowing she'd understand my own sidestep.

"I think whatever *this* is," she said. "Is different. It's why it feels so important." She swallowed, paused. "So... life-changing."

Talk about a gift I never wanted to *stop* opening— Sloane's shy vulnerability was enough to repeatedly bring me to my knees.

"Tonight," she continued. "Whatever happens, we do it together. Like we said." She held my hands tightly.

"Together," I promised. "And I'm still here, chaos and all."

"And I'm not going anywhere," she whispered.

## 43

## SLOANE

*A*t 8:01, the Codex team were in their positions. Abe and I strolled casually down Baker Street on a fake date. Henry played the role of lonely academic at the pub across from Adler's. Delilah was an American auction fanatic, excited to meet bidders at Kensley's. And Sam and Freya were literally hiding in the shadows of the parking lot.

The night had a liquid dream-like quality to it. A brief respite from the rain had the clouds overhead dispersing, revealing the moon. It seemed like everyone in London was out, enjoying the nice weather, as Abe and I kept tabs on the Sherlock Holmes museum. Which was dark, empty, and closed.

"Don't forget to breathe," I said to the exquisitely handsome man next to me.

"Hard to do when you're around, Ms. Argento," he murmured.

I touched my hot cheeks. "Oh my god, was that a *line*?"

He made a show of turning casually toward the museum, checking things out. "See? I'm fun."

We shared a quick smile before getting back to the business at hand. Abe Royal slowly dressing me like I was a priceless artifact was an experience I would never be able to forget. My body had never felt so achingly alive, so seen and revered. It had propelled me to speak the truth, to step out on the tight rope of my emotions regardless of whether or not he followed.

He had. *I'm still here, chaos and all.*

What happened after tonight was a conversation we'd yet to have, but all I needed in that moment was confirmation that this intensity was gripping us both equally. Over seven days, I'd gone from concealing my name from this man to sharing secrets that had never seen the light of day. I hadn't burst into flames either or gone running back into the shadows.

*I wasn't them.*

My parents wouldn't have partnered with Abe in the first place, let alone risk cold hard cash to do the right thing and call the authorities. If *Argento Enterprises* was going to continue to flourish the way I wanted, then recognizing I was truly on the right path was as vital as scoring big clients.

Our phones buzzed at the same time with a text from Sam: *Julian and Birdie just arrived. Delilah, I'll text you a physical description and what they're wearing.*

Abe gave me a short nod. We walked around to the back of the Sherlock Holmes museum, noticed nothing out of the ordinary.

"Maybe this wasn't the right place for us to watch," he muttered.

I wasn't so sure either. We were trying to stake out all the suspicious places where Bernard could be hiding, but the museum seemed absolutely uninhabited—at least from the outside.

Another text at 8:10 came through, this time from

Delilah: *I see Julian and Birdie. I also see Humphrey and Eudora. Auction starting soon.*

A minute later, Henry's message indicated that Adler's was also closed. No other suspicious activity. Abe's entire body was tight and practically shaking with nerves. We kept walking, looping back around, until I directed us to a nearby bench.

*Auction starting*, Delilah said. *Julian is coming in hot with the bids.*

"Dammit," Abe said. "They're the key, right?"

"Except they're legitimately purchasing these papers," I pointed out. "They're not the thieves. Although maybe Bernard is paying them to do this, then we catch them in the hand-off *to* Bernard."

"Or they're the distraction," he said softly.

I crossed my legs, draping the fabric around my heels. "Did we ever settle on what the final piece of that paper meant? *Irene says it's a go.* Who is Irene?"

"A member of the Society that we never suspected, perhaps?" he suggested.

"I checked," I said. "The whole list of all the members. It feels like a symbol or a secret message or—"

Abe looked at the museum before turning to me quickly. "The Sherlock Holmes story *A Scandal in Bohemia* has a character named Irene Adler. *The* woman. Not a romantic love interest, but the woman that bested Sherlock and captivated him with her wit and cunning."

A thousand lightbulbs exploded over my head. "Shit, that's right. I remember this story. The Society members have a significant love/hate relationship with Irene Adler."

"I'm going to guess Bernard loved her," he replied.

I clapped him on the arm. "*Adler's* Bookshop. *Irene says it's a go.* Something is going to happen there."

Abe leaned forward, elbows on his knees, and gave one last look at the museum. "Okay," he finally said. "I think you're right. Let's move."

We both stood as our phones rang out with another update from Delilah. *Bidding went fast. Julian and Birdie are the winning bidders at $6 million. They're being swarmed by a lot of people, including the media. They don't look very happy about the number of news cameras here.*

A beat later, from Freya: *We'll stay outside, grab them when they finally head to the parking lot.*

"But what are they—" Abe started, until his phone rang with a call from Henry. He placed it on speakerphone immediately, pulling me in close.

"What is it?" Abe said, tense.

"The second Delilah told us they'd won, every single light in that bookstore came on," Henry said, voice barely above a whisper. "The person flicking on the lights was Peter Markham. And, Abe, listen, this sounds bizarre, but I think I know why we recognized him."

Abe and I bent close, breath frozen.

"I think that man is *Jim Dahl*."

Abe's fingers tightened on the phone. "The fake intern who stole the George Sand letters?"

"We all studied his picture the day Sam and Freya went to tail him," Henry said. "And it was bothering me, why I couldn't place him. I pulled up our old emails from Francisco, with Jim's employee photo and compared it to pictures of Peter Markham online. Same height, same face shape, same eye-color. He's dyed his hair and added a beard."

"That's *why*," Abe said swiftly. "I knew we knew him. We're coming. I'll call Freya and send Delilah your way. For god's sake, don't let him out of your sight."

Abe grabbed my wrist as we started sprinting toward the street where the cabs were.

"Dahl the forger, right?" I said, thinking back to that day in Bernard's office when Abe had explained the many characters of The Empty House case.

Abe hailed a cab, face lit up with every emotion under the sun. "I assumed Bernard used Dahl as one of his many thieves. Maybe he's his *forger*."

"An expert forger is exactly what Bernard would need to ensure he was never caught," I said. "The letters of authentication, for one thing. And Henry's signature on those documents, right?"

He looked at me like I'd just presented him with a rare first edition of his favorite book. "Right," he said, in awe. "You're absolutely right."

We jumped in the first cab and Abe had the driver speed toward Adler's. While I sent Delilah a text ordering her to meet us, Abe called Freya.

"What's up?" she whispered. "Sam and I are literally hiding behind a Dumpster."

"Henry saw Peter Markham in person, and he thinks he's Jim Dahl in disguise."

"*Fuck a duck*," Freya swore. Muffled, she repeated the same thing to Sam, who had a similarly crude reaction.

"Do you see the resemblance too?" Abe asked.

More muffled speaking before Freya got back on the line. "We're accessing a picture of Peter Markham from his website. Let me look at it again."

We could only stare at each other and wait. My heart was in my throat with every second.

"Abe, we think it's him," Freya said grimly. "I can't *believe* this. Sam and I got pretty close the day we tailed him to the book festival. He was never apprehended, same as Julian and Birdie."

"Have Sam call his dad and get him to send help your way to the parking lot. I'm sure the authorities will want Julian and Birdie arrested once we tie them in with Dahl and Bernard," Abe said, face pressed to the window.

"Got it." Freya hung up, and Abe reached for my hand in the darkness. We sat, hands entwined, for five jittery minutes until the cab braked to a fast stop in front of Mycroft's Pub.

Abe and I snuck inside as soon as we could, giving us a perfect view of the bookstore windows—hopefully without Peter noticing the two private detectives dashing down the street. Henry motioned us to his small table in the corner.

"He's in the bookstore, no other signs of movement," he said.

Delilah strode in a second later—looking glamorous in a floor-length gown—reaching for her fiancé's hand.

"Are you okay?" she asked.

Henry pointed at the store. "We need to get in there."

"Did those papers really go for six million dollars?" I whispered to Delilah.

"Yes, and Eudora seemed edgy—she jumped a mile in her seat when the auctioneer hit the gavel. James Patrick seemed about ready to puke."

"And Humphrey?" I asked. I'd seen the very dregs of human nature, knew the universe wasn't always a pattern of just *good people* and *bad people*. But I desperately wanted Humphrey and Reggie to be plain old good people.

"They were sad. They were..." Delilah bit her lip. "They appeared devastated to see it bid on like that. Reggie kept patting Humphrey on the back and telling him he was going to be okay."

Sudden movement in the bookstore had all of us ducking to the side, peering out cautiously. There was Peter, cleaning up a few books, writing on a sheet of paper. Everything appeared innocent as hell, but all four of us knew how easily that façade could be built.

"Sam slipped me this," Delilah said, exposing a tool I recognized.

"To pick locks?" I asked, surprised.

Abe pocketed it immediately. "I have a little experience with this. Sloane, do you think you can get Peter to the door while the three of us find the closest side door?"

I smoothed my palms down my dress. Nodded through a long breath. "How long would you need?"

"A minute," Delilah said. "Maybe two. Also, because Freya's not here, I would be remiss if I didn't point out that our extremely ethical boss, Abe Royal, is about to break into a bookstore without cause *or* a warrant."

"Oh, how the mighty have fallen," Henry mused.

Abe lifted a shoulder, cast a sly grin at my questioning look. "Told you I could be fun."

## 44

# SLOANE

*I* wouldn't have much time to grab Peter's attention and get him to trust me. The last time Peter Markham had seen me, I'd been throwing a drink in Eudora's face after being accused of being a private detective. I didn't need much time, though. I only needed him to doubt his perception of me for a minute while distracting him from Abe breaking into his bookstore.

I strode as confidently as I could across the street while Abe, Henry, and Delilah snuck around the back. Peter was shoving a book back onto a shelf when I knocked on the window. It startled the shit out of him, which was good. Fear weakened our defenses.

The second he turned, confused, I waved and flashed him my most charming smile. I tracked the few seconds it took for him to recognize who I was—but when he did, the panic that overtook his body felt like taking a jumper cable straight to the heart. Because as much as I'd hoped we were on the right path, there were enough *what if*s about tonight to rattle my certainty. Yet his raw reaction at the sight of me felt like a blazing, neon sign that declared '*trouble is afoot.*'

Peter took a step back, already turning, when I pressed my face to the glass and said, "Didn't we once meet at Reichenbach Falls?"

He froze. Spun back around, face a mixture of intrigue and anxiety. He was still silent, still frozen in place.

"Peter, I'm not who Eudora says I am," I called through the glass. "I'm here in London because I've come into possession of something. A *big* something." I paused, noted the slight drop in his shoulders. "A big something that could use your special and unique skillset."

"Leave or I'm calling the police," he said, slowly backing away. His head whipped around, toward the back, so I tapped on the glass again.

"But I can *pay*," I said. "Whatever amount you received for your last job, double it, and that's where I'd start."

Peter was a thief, after all. And so, like many con artists before him, he took a reluctant step forward toward the person offering him money. Which was when I saw Abe, Delilah, and Henry slipping out from behind the cash register.

Peter jumped hard, back into the bookshelf, and whatever Abe was saying with that cool, impassive face of his had Peter paling dramatically. Henry walked over quickly, let me in as he checked to make sure we hadn't been noticed. He flicked the switch next to the door, blanketing the store in near darkness. A backroom light cast an eerie glow through the space.

Behind Henry, I caught the flying, graceful movements of Delilah, who put my own hand-to-hand skills to an instant shame. Within a minute, Peter was trussed up and immobilized. Although he was *furious*.

She slapped a piece of duct tape over his mouth. Shrugged.

"Well done," Abe said, pulling a chair in front of Peter. He sat with a kind of elegance, crossing his legs like we had all the time in the world. Henry and Delilah were fanning out, searching. I wasn't convinced a whole team of Dresden security guards weren't about to stream—

"Oh, *goddammit*," I said as our three best Dresden friends came in through the same back entrance and launched themselves at us with frightening speed. Peter was yelling behind his duct tape as Delilah and Henry tag-teamed the first guard, taking him to the ground with ease.

With that same elegance, Abe stood, picked up his chair, and walloped the second guard across the back. Delilah threw tape across the room, and Abe bit a piece off to restrain his wrists.

The third guard was my old pal Linebacker. The moment he threw himself at me, I pepper-sprayed him —*again*. Then picked up the closest hardcover book and smacked him across the face with it. Delilah kicked his knees out, sending him to the ground before subduing him.

"Nice moves," I said. She was breathing hard, hair a bit mussed, but other than that still looked gorgeous in her gown.

"Not so bad yourself." She winked.

"She's always had a Xena Warrior Princess vibe going on," Henry told me.

"So three guards," Delilah panted. "And no emergency button, as far as I could see. Which means Peter has this place watched. They must have seen us enter and followed behind."

Peter was still staring at us with wide eyes as the guards wiggled like giant fish nearby. Abe kicked the chair out of the way and crouched in front of the man.

"I don't know what your actual name is, Peter. I do know

that two months ago, in Philadelphia, you masqueraded as an intern at The Franklin Museum where you stole the George Sand letters. And helped to steal a rare first edition of *Don Quixote* from Dr. Bradley Ward. And I'm going to guess that you know where the hell *Bernard Allerton* is."

Peter's entire body shook until he composed himself, lifting his chin and glaring defiantly.

"*Abe.*"

Delilah's voice was thick with emotion. She stood in front of a giant bookshelf with the words *The Great Game* scrawled in elegant cursive over the top. All three of us were there in an instant. Delilah was breathing quickly, fingers shaking as she reached for the books.

"It's an entire Arthur Conan Doyle collection," she said. "And this row right here is just copies of *The Hound of the Baskervilles.*"

Henry and Delilah exchanged a shocked look.

"What?" Abe said sharply.

"The last time Henry and I encountered a copy of *The Hound of the Baskervilles*," she said. "A secret passageway appeared behind a bookshelf."

## 45

## ABE

*I* crouched down next to Delilah, tracing the row of thirteen red spines.

"Where?" I asked. "At Victoria's?"

Henry blew out a breath. "The way that Delilah and I accessed Victoria's secret passageways was by pulling a book from her bookshelf. It unlocked the door and sprang it open. *The Hound of the Baskervilles* is Bernard's favorite. He..." Henry cleared his throat. "He would always talk about Victoria whenever he was handling that book. We had a rare first edition at the McMaster's Library he was unbearably proud of."

I turned from my prone position and stared at Sloane. Her eyes dazzled with pure excitement. "Any guess why there are thirteen of them?"

"Thirteen members of The Empty House," Henry said. "Bernard loves his symbols."

Sloane dropped next to me, cupped my face with her palm. "Together."

I struggled to swallow past this rising emotion—that even if searching for Bernard turned up fruitless, meeting this woman, trusting this woman, *falling* for this woman was actually bigger, bolder and much more beautiful.

"Together," I repeated.

I pulled the first book. Nothing.

"It's only because I'm nervous," Henry said. "But I feel compelled to share with everyone the relevance of the name of this bookstore."

"Irene Adler, *the* woman, right?" I said to Henry.

Sloane pulled the second and third book. The fourth book. The fifth book.

Nothing. Her lips pressed into a grim line.

I pulled the sixth book and the seventh.

"Exactly," Henry said. "And she only ever appeared to Sherlock Holmes in disguise. Hiding in plain sight. He never saw her as she truly was."

*Hiding in plain sight.* I looked over at Sloane.

The eleventh book. The twelfth book.

Nothing.

Delilah squeezed Henry's hand.

Sloane hooked her finger into the thirteenth copy of *The Hound of the Baskervilles* and pulled it. Waited—every single one of us holding our breath.

The entire bookshelf creaked open.

"Oh my god," Sloane whispered.

An intense calm settled through my body in that vital moment, a total clearing of my nerves and my racing thoughts. I remembered ten years ago, a file landing on my desk with the research I'd requested on a famous librarian in England that didn't seem quite right. Four years ago, starting Codex and wondering if I'd ever have the chance to go after him for real. One year ago, sitting in front of a guilt-stricken Henry as he nervously shared his remarkable story.

And one week ago, meeting Sloane at the lecture, both

of us leaning forward in our seats at the name *Bernard Allerton*.

I grabbed Sloane's hand and stood slowly. Peter and the guards were making loud, wild sounds behind their tape. Behind the secret door was a narrow, shadowy hallway.

I held out my palm to Henry and Delilah, who were primed for immediate action. I mouthed *wait*.

Sloane and I slipped between the gap and into the hallway. It was wall-papered, and on the wall hung old black-and-white photos I couldn't make out. We reached a warm light, an open door, a large living room.

There was a fireplace. An expensive-looking sofa. Built-in shelves filled with novels. An open bottle of expensive whiskey.

And sitting in a high-backed chair, book open on his knee, was Bernard.

I blinked, sure it was a mirage. But Bernard remained in focus, staring at Sloane and me like we were minor annoyances.

He was that fucking confident.

Sloane and I stood, silent and shocked.

"Well, don't just stand there," he said, in his dignified British accent. "Sit, *sit*. I can't have the great Abraham Royal in my home away from home and not offer him the finest whiskey on the market."

If Henry and Delilah had called the police, we'd need only a few minutes to keep him in place. So Sloane and I sat down for whiskey. With a famous con man.

"And you are, my dear?" he asked. His back was ramrod straight, no cane.

"Sloane Argento," she said. "Private detective."

"*Two* private detectives in my midst?" Bernard smiled. "How charming. I've got a soft spot for detectives, given my devotion to Holmes. Although my guess is you specialize in cheating spouses? Naughty college students?"

"Book theft, actually," Sloane said coolly. Bernard's nostrils flared, but he remained calm.

"I'm sure you've already heard that Julian King and Birdie Barnes successfully won their bid tonight at the Kensley auction," I said.

He cocked his head. "I'm afraid I'm clueless as to what you're talking about, Mr. Royal."

I crossed my ankles. "I don't think you've ever been clueless a day in your life, Bernard. I think being publicly humiliated over the loss of Doyle's private papers was hook enough to cause you to make a greedy mistake."

"Oh, do go on," Bernard said. "I love a good story."

I wanted to smash that whiskey glass in his fucking face.

"It's probably easy, holed up in this fancy safehouse, to keep pulling the strings on your criminal empire," I said. "But you shouldn't have orchestrated a deal so close to home. What was James Patrick going to do for you anyway? If Julian and Birdie didn't win, would he have feigned ignorance of the theft? Did he make it so that they *could* win?"

"*JP is a yes*," Sloane drawled. A violent shiver worked through Bernard's body. "It's amazing all the people who will be implicated when you're arrested. How quickly this flimsy house of cards is going to fall. All because of Arthur Conan Doyle."

Bernard's laugh was extravagant. "If you think I've worked my entire life to build something with the fragility of a house of cards, Ms. Argento, you're a damned fool."

A protectiveness surged in me, causing my hands to form into fists. At this point, I should have known better. Sloane could protect herself.

"If you think you're going to escape the law again," she

said slowly, as if speaking to a child. "Then you're fucking irrational. Humphrey misses you, by the way."

The first sign of emotion—however distant—flashed across his face. "Humphrey is the human version of a bloody golden retriever. He misses everyone when out of sight for more than two minutes."

"Funny that you never told him," she said. "Never told him who you really are."

Bernard took a long sip of whiskey but kept his eyes trained on us. "A man can't have one friend who sees the best in him?"

"Ah," I said. "It makes more sense now. I'm sorry to discover your friendship with Humphrey was always about placating your delicate ego, Bernard."

He laughed again, but it was bitter and violent sounding.

"Victoria misses you too," I added. "She narrowly avoided prison time because of you."

I was swinging for the fences, trying every vulnerability we knew about the man. The look on his face told me he'd kept tabs on his lady love.

"Victoria is not a woman who can be caged."

"You don't even care that she protected you?" I said.

His jaw tightened. He swirled the liquid in his glass. "Sacrifices, Mr. Royal. We all make them in this life. Besides, I've heard Victoria is doing fine for herself now. A little house arrest won't keep her down."

"Is this your house arrest?" I said, an edge to my voice.

"If you think I'm giving away any actual secrets to *you*," he said. "You're an even bigger fool than she is."

I chuckled softly, brow raised. "My contacts at the FBI have assured me the members of The Empty House are feeling less loyal towards their leader since you left them to rot in jail. So keep your secrets, Bernard. They should be coming to light any day now."

Tension stretched between us. I wasn't sure how much longer the man was going to play along.

"I've been on sabbatical for eleven months." Bernard shrugged, lazy. "You can ask Eudora. You can ask Louisa, my boss at the McMaster's Library."

"Oh, Louisa," Sloane said. "She hired me."

The glass paused at Bernard's lips. "What an intriguing development. This space I'm living in has always been made available for members of the Sherlock Society. We've had many covert meetings here. I'm not doing anything wrong or illegal by living here."

I glanced furtively around the room. It was a small space but stylish—it was shaped like a one or two-bedroom apartment. Except no windows, and the only entrance appeared to be through the secret bookshelf.

"Sound-proofed?" I guessed.

"For privacy," he said, smiling like a shark.

I gave him the same dangerous-looking smile. "The man formerly known as Jim Dahl is also tied up out there," I said. "In case you were wondering where he was."

*There.* That shocked him—or whatever Bernard's version of *shock* was. His face blazed with true anger, only momentarily. He hadn't liked that. His shark-smile deepened, grew sharper at the edges.

"Thank you for the information," he said. "I had been wondering. Which, if that's the case, means I'd love to bring the two of you into my, what did you call it, *flimsy house of cards*? I offered something similar to my former colleague," Bernard said. He looked right at me. "You know him, don't you?"

I gave him a curt nod.

"And he didn't take the bait?" Sloane asked.

"Oh, it wasn't bait, Ms. Argento," Bernard said. "It was five million dollars. My colleague, Henry, is one of those silly men that believe scruples, morals, ethics are real. When they are only figments of our collective imagination. The only real thing is money."

"How much would you deal us in for?" she asked. And there was a hardness in her tone that sped my pulse. The charming former con artist had come out to play.

"For you two? Ten million dollars." The man said this with such *outrageous confidence* I saw how easily he had managed this criminal empire and remained hidden. For most people, money did outweigh morals.

"That's a *lot* of fucking money," she said, chuckling softly. "Can you believe it, Abe?" She kept her expression neutral when she peered my way. But flicked her eyes once to the left—her tell. Her tell on *purpose*. We just needed to keep Bernard talking and distracted for a few minutes more.

"I cannot believe it. And what would this ten million do for you?" I asked, playing into Sloane's game. Whatever it was. Trusting she was right.

"Keep this secret," Bernard said sharply. "Give me time to... move to an even more secluded location for my sabbatical. Gather my things, gather my guards. It shouldn't be too arduous of a task for the two of you. Besides, don't you get profit from my alleged misdeeds?"

*This son of a bitch.*

"We do actually," I said. "Doesn't Holmes need an adversary? Isn't Moriarty just as vital?"

"Yes, Mr. Royal. Life is boring without a villain," he said. "Although money makes villains of all of us. Once embrace that human weakness, you can turn it into strength."

Sloane's fingers tightened on her glass almost impercep-tibly. I knew she understood that weakness intimately.

"Besides, if it's only the three of us," he said. "This secret could stay safe for years and years to come. Who else would possibly know?"

The sweetest sound in the world hit my ears. Sirens. With my own confident smile, I raised my hand and beck-oned behind me. "Henry?"

I would never, ever forget watching Henry step into this room with Delilah close behind.

"Good evening, Bernard," he said.

The glass of whiskey shattered on the floor.

Bernard was effectively speechless; anger turning his face red, then purple. He made a move to rise from the chair, but Henry held up a finger.

"I wouldn't," Henry said. "This time I *did* call the authorities."

There was a loud banging on the door as police sirens invaded the small space.

Henry slid his hands into his pockets. "Ah," he said. "That would be them just now."

## 46

## ABE

*W*e had two minutes, maybe less. Bernard stood, hands shooting out for something— probably a weapon—and Delilah snapped, "*Don't.*"

Bernard paused, eyes scanning the room.

I leaned forward in my chair—made sure I captured Bernard's frantic gaze. "I'm sorry to be the bearer of bad news," I said. "But the four people standing in front of you are *not* villains. And I intend to personally guarantee that you spend the rest of your life in prison."

He visibly paled, shaking. Henry strode right up to him, confidently. Still calm. "Thank you for making me complicit in your crimes, Bernard. If you hadn't done that, I wouldn't have met Abe. Wouldn't have become a private detective. Wouldn't have met my fiancée." Henry lowered his tone. "And if you hadn't made me complicit, I wouldn't have fucking *found* you. What did you say to me that night? *It's only a crime if you get caught?*"

Police officers shoved their way in—all of us stepped back, hands in the air. Except for Bernard, who suddenly looked as small and cowardly as he truly was.

"Looks like you got caught," Henry said.

"That man is Bernard Allerton," I said loudly to the first police officers storming in. "He is a known international suspect for theft and forgery, among many other things." Bernard's hands were wrenched behind his back as he was cuffed. His confidence had been drained away, replaced by a sputtering, nonsensical babble. He was afraid—possibly for the first time ever.

The four of us were shoved backward by officers, through that narrow hallway and out into the book-store. The scene had transformed into pure pandemo-nium; sirens wailed, and London police filled the room, with paramedics tending to Peter and the guards. Like sleepwalkers with concrete around our ankles, we slipped out the door and onto a street rapidly filling with people.

"Henry," I started, turning toward him, seeing his deter-mined expression as he watched authorities fill the store. When he finally gave me a wide, joyous smile, I could only grip his shoulder and hope he understood how deeply I felt in that moment.

"I'm glad you were there," I finally said.

"I'm glad we were *all* there," he replied. The squealing of car tires had us spinning around—a slightly disheveled Freya and Sam stumbled from a taxicab just as Bernard was walked out of Adler's Bookshop in handcuffs, surrounded by police officers. The look on his face as he saw us was cold, righteous fury.

"Oh... my... *god*," Freya said.

"Sir?" Sam said, staring.

"Please meet Bernard Allerton," I said wryly.

"I can't believe this is happening," Freya wheezed.

Next to me, Sloane entwined our fingers, squeezed

tightly. Peter and the guards were next, also in handcuffs. "I'm guessing you called your father?" I asked.

"He got in touch with Interpol when I told him about Julian and Birdie and whatever might be happening here," Sam said, still staring in wonder. "He knows we think that man is Jim Dahl."

"I can't believe this is happening," Freya repeated. Delilah hugged her from behind, the two of them watching the scene with wide-eyed wonder.

"Are you going to make the next call?" I asked.

"Do you want to?" Sam asked, taking out his phone.

I shook my head, looped my arm around Sloane, and pulled her hard into my body. "I'm good, actually."

The five of us watched as former Special Agent Samuel Byrne dialed the Deputy Director. The second the man answered, Sam said, "We got him, sir."

I couldn't read the expression on Sam's face once he hung up. "Well?"

Sam grinned, crookedly. "He said he was extremely pleased at the outcome."

"Which is basically your father's version of awarding you a medal of honor," Freya said. On tiptoe, she grabbed Sam's face and gave him a smacking kiss on the cheek.

"We all have a role to play in ensuring justice is being served," I said. "It just so happens that Codex is better at that than most." The answering smiles of my team collided against my chest, melted the remaining ice around my heart.

"And Julian and Birdie were taken into custody with the help of whoever Sam's dad called," Freya said. "Once we give our statements, we can name James Patrick and Eudora as well."

"Word is traveling fast," Henry murmured. As Bernard stood, hands cuffed, amidst the red-and-blue lights, a large crowd of people were gathering, which was a form of punishment for Bernard in and of itself.

"It's Society members," Sloane said. "Someone must have alerted them. And is *that*—"

But Sloane didn't finish, too busy striding off toward a sweet-looking older lady wearing a conservative sweater set.

Eudora Green.

Although the look on her face as she took in the tableau in front of her was one for the record books—shock, terror, confusion. The second she saw Sloane, she turned and tried to run.

Sloane caught her immediately, dragging her by the arm to the police officer standing in front of us.

"Eudora, how lovely to see you again," I said, giving a small bow.

"*You*?" she snarled.

"It's important to cultivate true friends in this world," Sloane told her. "Just don't make friends with two private detectives sent here to put people like you in prison." She turned to the police officer. "This woman was protecting and hiding the wanted criminal right over there."

Eudora shrieked as the officers took her away for further questioning.

Sloane winked at me as she rejoined us. I pressed my lips to her temple. "Daniel and Devon's final act of rebellion," I said against her skin.

I clapped my hands together. "We need to go give statements. Call who we need to call. And then I'll be buying the most expensive bottle of champagne I can buy for the team of detectives that caught Bernard Allerton."

In the sea of swarming officers and yelling criminals and flashing lights, I watched my team's final reactions in slow, beautiful motion. Freya turned to Sam, jumped into his arms. He spun her around as she laughed.

Delilah held her palm to Henry's face; he stared at her with deep, unending devotion, holding her close. Every single one of them had played a role in getting us here—from the day I'd met Henry until now.

Fingers curled against my own. Sloane's. Her beautiful face was a shimmering mix of peaceful and ecstatic—her smile was sensational, body vibrating with happiness. I dipped my mouth to hers and kissed her. My mind spun, erupted with brightness. I pulled back but kept our lips close.

"Nice work back there," I said.

"Thanks for trusting me," she replied. "We did it, together. And while you were on vacation at that."

My mouth curved into a smile. "I wouldn't have had it any other way, believe me." I tucked a strand of hair behind her ear. "Maybe this chaos between us isn't reckless at all. Because if it's not coincidence, I'm fairly certain we could call this *fate*."

The look that came over her face stopped my heart with its all-encompassing hope, trust—and a deeper emotion I wasn't sure was possible so soon.

Love.

I was pretty damn sure Sloane Argento was staring at me with *love*. Codex had a world of work still ahead of us and a long list of questions. Capturing these five people tonight didn't mean everything was automatically closed up and tied off. I sure as hell didn't know what would happen next between Sloane and me when we returned home to our respective cities, hours apart. But when she kissed me breathless, all of the unanswered questions vanished.

A familiar bellow roared through the busy scene.

Instead of its usual cheer, this time the voice was filled with despair.

"Humphrey," Sloane gasped, stepping back. We turned toward the source of the pain. There was giant Humphrey, in his Sherlock Holmes best, standing at the edge of the crowd with his equally distraught husband.

"*Bernie?*" he asked, arms outstretched toward his best friend in handcuffs. The police officers placed him in the back of the car. Bernard didn't acknowledge him once. Startled, Humphrey turned, spotted us.

"Devon? Daniel? Wait... is that *Henry?*" Humphrey's hands flew to his head. "What in the bloody hell is going on?"

Resolute, Sloane stepped forward and touched his arm with a look of pure compassion. "Come sit with me for a second, Humphrey. I need to tell you a story."

## 47

# SLOANE

*W*hile the Codex team slipped into the pub for a celebratory bottle of champagne, Humphrey, Reggie, and I sat on the sidewalk directly outside. We could see them in there, framed by the window, laughing together as they celebrated their hard-fought victory.

Next to me, Humphrey was in total shock. Reggie less so. I got the impression he'd always suspected Bernard was *off*. But this wild tale of book theft and manipulation still surprised the quiet academic.

It had taken an hour, but I'd finally finished the long tale of Bernard Allerton—and who we all were. Per the usual, Humphrey had reacted with dramatic gasps and outbursts at every secret and true identity revealed. Now he sat morosely next to me, Reggie's arm around his shoulders. This sad mountain of a man was even harder for me to accept than his surprise and outrage. I'd never wanted to actually hug a stranger before. Now that's *all* I wanted.

"Sixty years of lies," he said, accent thicker the sadder he became. "You were right, Reggie. You noticed it. Did everyone? Was I a joke?"

I shook my head fiercely, thought about Henry and his bright light of sincerity. Humphrey was the exact same—with an uncomplicated zest for life that was easily mocked and manipulated by con artists like Bernard. What Bernard had said back there about this man—*he's a golden retriever*—betrayed Bernard's total lack of empathy or understanding of being a human. Humphrey Hatcher was the most alive person I'd ever met.

"You were never a joke," I said fiercely. "Bernard chose you to manipulate *because* you are so good. Caring and sincere, would do anything for the people in your life. That makes you the kind of person this world should be filled with. That makes you the kind of person people want to keep in their lives."

I stopped, a rush of emotion pricking my eyes, even though the last time I'd cried in front of another person was Debra. But this, all of this, was now over—and would I ever see Humphrey and Reggie again?

"Why on earth would a person do such a thing?" he said.

I exhaled, toeing the sidewalk with the tip of my shoe. "Some people view others as tools, chess pieces to move around, walking wallets to steal." I touched his arm. "Some people view others as the friends and family we need in this world to keep going. View those relationships like a garden to be tended. Treasured and cared for. *You're* that kind of people."

"I am an unstoppable force of valiant passion," Humphrey said—this time with a small smile. I laughed, relieved.

"You are," I said, patting his arm again. "You truly are, Humphrey."

He nodded inside, at the pub. "That's your family."

"Them?" I asked, turning to watch the five detectives, glowing in the cozy light. Abe must have felt me staring because he turned. Gave me a smile that curled my toes and set my pulse racing.

"Yes, them," he said. "You, your Mr. Royal, these detectives. They are quite clearly *yours*."

"Mine," I repeated, rolling the word around on my tongue. Recognizing it for the truth that it was. "I don't have a biological family."

"You don't need one," he said, waving a hand through the air. "Friends are better."

"Trust me," Reggie said. "Once Humphrey meets you, you're instant family."

I gave them a long look, feeling shy. "If you both," I said, voice nervous. "If... if you both wanted to come visit me, back in America, I'd like that."

"A visit to see the enchantress across the pond?" Humphrey exclaimed. "Why, we'd board the next flight! Isn't that right, Reg?"

"That *is* right," Reggie said kindly.

I breathed out again, happy to see a bit of Humphrey's lightness return. It was going to be a long journey for Humphrey to accept the real role Bernard Allerton played in his life and the significant loss of a friendship he'd held dear for six decades. It wouldn't come easy.

Maybe the tiniest amount of good could come out of this. Shifting the scales of justice, making the world better—bit by bit, person by person.

Abe, Delilah and Henry, Freya and Sam. Humphrey and Reggie. Over one week's time, the circle of people I could trust had expanded to include all of these names.

"You two would make a fine pair of uncles," I said,

nudging his arm. Humphrey guffawed, clapping his hands in the air. He was going to be okay in the end. I could tell.

"And Reggie and I have often longed for a niece," he exclaimed. Reggie nodded, laughed.

I smiled, chin in my hands, feeling less and less like the daughter of two con artists and more and more like the woman with a future she'd never seen coming.

"Now go get in there and be with your family," Humphrey said. "Reggie and I will need to make some arrangements for the Society, start to unravel this shit mess Bernard and Eudora have landed us in."

I stood and brushed dirt from my dress. "For what it's worth, my money is on *you* being the next president, Humphrey."

He clutched his chest. "Slayed! Again!"

Laughing, I gave him a final wave, then ducked close to the door to make one final call as I eyed the jubilant Codex team through the window. Louisa's voice, when she answered, was strung tight with nerves.

"It's a very, very long story," I began. "But I just watched Bernard Allerton be placed in handcuffs."

I could hear her sharp intake of breath. "Where was he?"

"London," I said, smiling up at the starry sky. "In Adler's Bookshop living in a secret apartment built behind a bookshelf."

"My god," she said.

"I'll be in tomorrow," I said. "I'm sure you'll be receiving a call from the authorities soon. And I'll tell you everything. But my contract has been completed."

*Nothing* about this case had gone as I'd envisioned it. Yet everything missing in my life had suddenly appeared and made my success possible.

"Thank you, Sloane," Louisa said. "You did an amazing thing tonight."

I hung up. Smiled again to myself. And finally opened the door and entered the pub.

"There she is," Freya cheered, waving a bottle of champagne. "Our sixth team member." They gave me a silly round of applause, and I paused to bow, catching Abe's flirtatious grin.

"How are Humphrey and Reggie doing?" Henry asked.

I took the glass of champagne Delilah handed to me. "Heartbroken yet strong. I have a feeling Humphrey and Reggie will be in our lives for years to come."

"I'd welcome that," Abe said. "There's a lot that we don't know about tonight. Bernard's ultimate plan, who he was using, the key players. The fates of James Patrick, of Eudora, of Peter. It might take a while, but I look forward to doing that work with all of you."

Henry raised his glass of champagne and faced all of us. Delilah was wrapped around his side, gazing at him with pure devotion. "I'd like to give a toast to Bernard."

"Uh, what?" Freya said.

Henry smiled. "That man did his best to destroy everything he touched, let money and greed take priority over our shared culture and history. And instead of believing in the power of books, he used them. Used people, too. The night I first met Abe was the worst night of my entire life. But—" Henry paused to kiss the top of Delilah's head. "He's the reason we're all here, together. He is the reason I'm going to marry Delilah in three months. He's the reason Sam and Freya reunited. And he's the reason Abe Royal is spending time, romantically, with Sloane. He's the reason Codex exists."

Abe smiled, looked down at his glass—cast a raised brow at me. "You told them we were romantically involved?"

"Oh, she didn't have to tell us Abe," Freya said. "It was obvious the second we saw the two of you together. We never knew you were such a reverse *cougar*. Damn."

I held up a finger. "I believe I'm the reverse cougar in this situation."

"I stand corrected." Freya beamed.

Abe kissed my hand to the cheering laughter of his team. I winked, chugged my champagne to another roar of applause.

"To Bernard," Abe said. "And to all of you." He squeezed my hand tight as he set his glass down. "Contrary to popular opinion, I am a man able to love. And I might not be *the best* at showing it, or saying it, but I do love all of you. Very much."

For once, Abe's team didn't tease or joke. They came around the table to wrap him in a messy and clumsy group hug.

"Aw, we love you too, boss," Freya said.

And over the tops of their heads, Abe stared at me with the full force of his emotions, vulnerability and all.

*I'm still here*, I mouthed.

Outside this pub, Sherlock Society members were clamoring, gossiping, standing around in a daze. Cop cars took up the street, police officers patrolled and questioned people, and Bernard Allerton was on his way into custody.

And inside this pub, clutching a glass of champagne and smiling at Abe, I finally found my family.

## 48

## SLOANE

*J*t was past dawn the morning after we'd caught Bernard Allerton. Abe looked relaxed and handsome in his sleep. There was no white whale to chase; he was no longer Ahab on an endless hunt. He was merely the brilliant man in my bed.

The brilliant, *naked* man in my bed. And I knew just the way he deserved to be woken up.

I crawled onto his naked body. His skin was hot from sleep. His eyes, still sleepy, fluttered awake. I kissed his chest. His smile turned dirty. His breathing hitched.

"Aren't you a beautiful sight to wake to," he said, voice gravelly. Rough.

I bit his nipple.

He hissed with pleasure. He wound his fingers in my hair and dragged me up. Our lips met in a kiss that was both harsh and tender, bruising and sweet. He looped my hair around his wrist, holding me in place. I could tell by the look on his face what he wanted to do. With a sly grin, I shook my head, kissed his jaw. Kissed down his strong throat—his chest, my fingers threading through the silver hair. Tugging. Another sharp breath from him, followed by a sigh. Sexy man. *Strong* man. Last night was the highlight of my professional career. And stepping through that hallway and into a room that held Bernard *fucking* Allerton was only made more perfect because Abe was by my side.

And last night, surrounded by Freya and Sam, Delilah and Henry, getting tipsy on champagne and laughing at their stories—I could feel the complicated knots of my heart unravel. Fall away. It was so much more terrifying to be vulnerable in this world. And so much more possible with a man like Abe, gently encouraging me to *open*.

"Sloane," he whispered. A plea. His fingers were still in my hair, but my mouth was trailing open kisses down his stomach. So fucking gratifying to mess with this man's control, to be the one to bring this level of unfettered pleasure onto his face. "What are you doing?"

"You know what I'm doing," I said. I licked my tongue across his skin, tasting him. He groaned, fingers tightening. His cock was hard, like steel, pressed to my body the farther down I explored. The second I reached his cock I sat back on my knees to admire it—the delicious, veined length of him. All that primal, raw strength. It didn't matter how many bespoke suits Abraham Royal had, how many college degrees or years of FBI agent promotions.

Beneath all of that was a hard, hungry man who was twisting my hair in his fingers and yanking my head to the right.

I ran my tongue along my teeth. "Do you have something to say?"

A snarl threatened to overtake his mouth. "I won't last. Not with you. Not like this."

I held his gaze. Lowered my mouth to his cock. "I believe in you."

It was a privilege to take that man into my mouth, to take him as deep as I could. To taste him, tongue him, indulge in the simplicity of his moans, my sighs. His fingers, my hair. His cock, my mouth—the heady, rich taste of him was immediately addicting. And so was watching him come fully undone, give in to his urges when he had nothing to do except receive sexual pleasure. The harder he pulled my hair, the hotter I got, the deeper I took him, the more intense he became. Our eyes remained locked until he couldn't stand it anymore—head falling back, hands dragging me off his cock and up his body. There wasn't even a question. Abe shoved me back, kissed me breathless, and slid his cock slowly, *slowly* inside.

I dug my nails into his ass, pulled him harder against me. He groaned against my mouth. Gave me a hard, brutal stroke that made me cry his name.

"Sloane," he said, setting a rhythm I loved, needed, craved.

"Ye-yes, *yes?*" I panted.

"When we get home, our real home," he said, voice on edge. "I want to come to where you are. Or you can come to Philadelphia. I don't care as long as we're together." His cock between my legs was a steady, driving thrust, and it felt so goddamn good I couldn't handle it. I kissed him, clung to him, chanted his name.

"Abe, *Abe, yes.*"

"Yes, as in '*don't stop?*' Or *yes* to what I said?" He held my palms down, entwined our fingers. Rocked into me over and over and over. He was going to make me come before I could tell him '*yes, please, I'll go anywhere.*' Which I managed to pant out through a sloppy, fevered kiss.

"Can I come to you?"

"To Philadelphia?" he asked, smile starting to form.

Sweat beaded on his brow. My toes were curling, back arching, nipples hard, sensitive.

"Please, I want..." God, this man. Only Abe knew I wouldn't be able to ask for this, that I needed it to be *fucked* right out of me. "I want you. I want to be with you. Home isn't... my home isn't..."

His thumb swiped away a tear. He didn't slow his movements but drove his cock into me harder, deeper, more intently. "It's okay, you can tell me."

Abe held my face tenderly. Which allowed me to say, "My home isn't a home."

"Mine either," he whispered. He brought our mouths together. "You would make it one, though."

I couldn't speak coherently after that—I was so overcome with euphoria. We orgasmed together in a panting, sweating, nail-scratching mess. He swiped another tear, then another. But it just wasn't possible for me to leave this man.

His chaos was too beautiful.

Our destinies were too fated.

## 49

# SLOANE

*T*hree hours later and I was back in front of Louisa Davies, in her office at the library where Bernard Allerton would *officially* not be working at any longer. Especially once his trial started.

Louisa, to her credit, couldn't contain her surprise or excitement as I unveiled the entire story to her. "He was living in a *bookstore* in *London*?"

I grinned, crossed my legs. "Adler's. Behind a secret bookshelf. We'll learn more soon, but it appears as though the Sherlock Society used that space all of the time for secret meetings or to store things like stolen books."

She closed her eyes. "All this bloody time."

"Hiding in plain sight," I said. "Although, it wasn't a bad spot. With the exception of Peter, who would ever know he was there? A *lot* more information will shake out in the coming days and weeks, and I'll keep you informed of all of it." I swallowed, lifted a shoulder. "Louisa, I need to be totally honest with you. I can't claim sole responsibility for this contract." I nodded at the sheet of paper. Nodded again, grimly, at the sizable check she'd had cut for me already.

Money I'd earned and needed. It just didn't sit right with me not to admit that I'd actually worked with a team.

"About a week ago, I partnered with Abe Royal and Codex, who flew out here to search for Bernard on their own. At that point, my leads were drying up and our deadline was looming. We helped each other. We were together when we captured Bernard," I said.

She looked utterly surprised. "I... I don't know what to say."

There was a knock at the door. And then Abe and Henry stepped inside. Both looking extra dashing in their suits, both looking extra relaxed, given the one thing they'd wanted had finally been achieved.

"*Henry*," Louisa said. She stood up, clutched at her neck. "I so hope Abraham conveyed to you how thankful I was at the recovery of the *Tamerlane*."

"He did," Henry said. "Honestly, we were happy to do it. And Abe, Sloane, and I are just happy to see Bernard in the hands of the proper authorities. You know it's been a long and emotional journey for us all."

My heart did a strange, fluttery thing when Henry had included me. Abe caught my eye. Winked.

Louisa pressed a hand to her forehead. "I owe you an extraordinary apology. If I had believed you that night, we wouldn't be in this atrocious mess. I can't say I'm sorry enough, honestly."

Henry touched her arm, which was a nice gesture. Because Henry Finch was a genuinely nice person. "I appreciate it. But he had us all fooled."

"Still," she said. "It's the principal of the thing."

She looked at Abe. "And I feel like I should have kept Codex instead of letting the authorities slow everything down for the past year."

Abe gave a polite nod. "If you hadn't waited and hired Sloane, we never would have met." His smile grew. "It was fate."

I had to look away to stop the heat that threatened to overtake my body. This fucking *man*.

"Abe and I were going to wander the campus for a bit," Henry said to me. "Unless there's anything else? We promise we'll provide all the pertinent details regarding Bernard's case and whatever happens next."

Louisa was contrite. "You wouldn't reconsider becoming a librarian again, would you?"

"No," he said—immediately. "I'm a private detective for life now. Thank you for the offer. And one never ceases to be a librarian. I'm just more on the justice end of things."

Louisa watched them leave, still clutching her neck, looking distraught. I tapped my finger on the payment, thought about those photos of Bernard and Henry at various awards ceremonies. "Didn't Bernard have a foundation here? A scholarship program, for new librarians?"

"He did," she said. "I'm not sure what we'll do with it now."

I tapped my check again. "If I gave half of this to the foundation, would you let me give it a new name?"

*I*t had been almost one year—exactly—since I'd found Henry standing at the back of this library, staring out at the beautiful gardens of Oxford University.

He'd had his entire world turned upside down just forty-eight hours earlier. And I'd gone ahead and trusted my gut instinct that, deep down, he'd make one hell of a private detective. And he had.

I slipped my hands into my pockets, surveyed the students strolling across the green. "How do you feel now?" I asked.

"Relieved," he said, an echo of our former conversation. "I'm not lying this time. I am relieved. I know why you were obsessed with finding him for so long. Bernard represents the worst attributes of humanity. The longer he stayed hidden, the more he would have stolen from the world. All of us finding him, together, is exactly what needed to happen."

"I agree," I said, letting out a long sigh. "I'm anxious to know more. Anxious to know how he stayed hidden this past year. But that restlessness is gone. I feel much more settled."

"Does Sloane have something to do with that?"

I hid a smile. "Yes, she does."

"Good," he said. "I speak for all of Codex when I say *thank god*."

"Thank god, what?"

Sloane walked up, smile on her face. She was so much more open around people now. Her sultry edges were still there yet softened for those she trusted. And she was trusting a lot more.

"Thank god we met," I explained, looping an arm around her shoulders.

"Ah," she said. "Makes sense. I am truly magnificent."

I kissed the top of her head.

She turned toward Henry and touched his elbow. "I gave half of my payment to Louisa to re-fund the scholarship program Bernard used to run. With a new name, of course." She handed him a slip of paper. "It's now called the Dr. Henry Finch Fellowship."

Henry took it, read it. Looked back at her like he couldn't quite believe it. "Sloane, you... you absolutely *did not* have to do this."

"I wanted to. I was more than happy to." She shifted on her feet. "Henry, until I was seventeen years old, I was raised by two parents who were con artists. They forced me to do it too." She didn't look to me for courage—she didn't need to. "My parents earned their living by taking advantage of people. Corrupting their trust, manipulating them. The reason why people like my parents, people like Bernard, are so successful at it is because humans want to trust. To connect. To love." She touched his arm. "I wanted you to know that none of this was your fault. And I'm so happy to see that your ability to love and trust and connect wasn't stolen from you by Bernard. That gives me hope."

Henry hugged her. I could see her face, and the look she was giving me was pure excitement.

"Thank you," he said. "And I hope you come work for Codex. Actually, one year ago Abe approached me here, gave me his business card. Told me I'd make one hell of a private detective."

"Is that so?" she said.

"It is," he said. "He changed my life forever. But you already know that about Abe." Henry nodded behind him. "I'm going to take one more walk around. Meet you at the front?"

The minute Henry left us, I knew what I needed to do. "You are magnificent, truly."

Sloane was giving me that captivating smile while her hair blew softly in the breeze. I felt in my jacket pocket for a business card, the memories of doing this for Henry were so strong and emotional. I hadn't anticipated how much one man could change in twelve months.

Her smile turned sly. She held a business card that said Codex between two fingers. "Do you think I'd make one hell of a private detective or what?"

I kissed her—hot, hungry, urgent. "If Henry and Delilah work together, and Sam and Freya work together, there's not one fucking reason why I can't work with my gorgeous, charming, *sticky-fingered* girlfriend."

She tapped the card against her chin. "So, to be clear, you're offering me a job?" She examined it closely, then studied me. "And I'm your... girlfriend?"

"Yes, god, yes, I'm offering you a job," I said. "And also *please* be my girlfriend."

"This morning, what we talked about, being with each other after all of this," she said. "You meant it."

It wasn't a question. It never had been.

"I meant it," I said. "I will break the speed limit driving to see you in New York. Do not doubt it. We can split the time between each city. I will figure out how to make it work if you don't want to move to Philadelphia. Or even if you *do* want to move but *don't* want to work with me and my taco-obsessed team of detectives. Anything for you. I will do *anything*—"

This time it was Sloane who kissed me, a kiss full of possibility, of fate. A kiss full of our future.

"I meant what I said too," she whispered. "My house isn't a home. You would make my life feel like home. We've only known each other a week, I *know* this is chaos, but I refuse to sidestep my feelings for you, Abe. *I like you.* More than I've ever liked anyone." Her hand found a spot directly over my heart, palm pressed down. "Trust is hard for me. I promise not to give up. I'm still here."

I interlaced our fingers over my heart. "And I'm not going anywhere."

Her teasing smile reappeared. "And we're two worka-holics who have promised each other to have more sponta-neous *fun*. We can't do that if I'm living two hours away from you, now can we?"

"How many cooking classes do you want to take? I'll sign up for every damn one on the flight home."

Her laughter was unfiltered joy. "Not cooking. I'd like to see you on a dance floor, Abraham. Tango lessons."

"I'm a man of many secret talents, as you know," I said, kissing right below her ear.

Sloane held up the business card again. "My business is

important to me, Abe. I built it on my own but I... I *liked* working with a team."

"Perhaps you could consider a merger?" I asked.

She hummed beneath her breath. "Less my boss, more my business partner."

"Equal footing," I said. "I like that even better."

Her eyes searched mine. "So do I, actually. My only suggestion being Freya told me you had a strict PDA policy for the office. And I've never known you to keep your hands to yourself, Mr. Royal."

I didn't even try and hide my happiness. "I'll begin revising our personnel policies immediately."

## 51

## SLOANE

*Three months later*

*Philadelphia, PA*

*J* was wearing a pink crown and a sash that said *Birthday Girl*—although it wasn't even close to my birthday. But, according to Freya, we needed a formal coronation—her words—celebrating my official start as a private detective working at Codex.

All six of us were sitting around in Abe's office. I was perched on the end of his desk; he was giving me too lascivious of a look for the workplace, even if he'd just revised his personnel policies.

Freya, Sam, Delilah, and Henry were all clapping for me.

"Thank you, thank you," I said, standing and taking a bow. It had been three months since we'd all left London, and while I was still in the process of moving my life from Brooklyn to Philadelphia, Abe had already invited me to live with him in his fancy condo near City Hall.

I'd said yes, of course, both of us dedicated to making our house a real home.

Working with Louisa had been my last official case as *Argento Enterprises*. I was now merging my old cases and former clients with Codex's and settling into a new routine as the sixth member and Abe's business partner. Equal footing, as promised. Those five years working on my own had been vital to my own self-discovery, but it was time now to be part of a team.

In the intervening moments, I spent every second I could with Abe or with Codex. They were friends—*we* were friends. Delilah and Freya had permanently adopted me into their girl gang, and I'd never, ever, ever, been happier. Our taco Tuesdays had become legendary, and most Friday nights Delilah and Freya dragged me to their favorite bars and restaurants in the city—for drinking or dancing or talking the night away.

"Although I'd like to point out that Henry and I didn't receive a sash or a crown or any kind of formal welcome," Sam said, bemused.

"Sloane's a girl," Freya said. "So it's more exciting all around. *And* she's Abe's girlfriend, and her existence means Abe will be a lot nicer to us."

"No guarantees will be made," Abe said, eying us with affection.

To me, he said, "I can't imagine Codex without you. You were the final missing piece, Sloane."

I reached forward, squeezed his fingers. "And you were mine."

After the nonstop adrenaline of that week in London,

Abe and I were simply *together*. The adjustment for two (former) lone wolves was not without its challenges, but our trust, our intimacy, and our growth deepened every single day.

We were also having the most frivolous, silly fun of our lives. Dance classes, cooking lessons, picnics on our living room floor, weekend road trips, and lazy brunches in bed. After my first video chat with Abe's moms, they'd told him, definitely, that I was *the one*.

After we'd hung up, I crawled into his lap and kissed his cheek. "The one, huh?"

He'd scooped the hair off my shoulder before kissing me back. "If I'd called them the night we met, I could have told them the same thing."

We didn't get out of bed that night *or* the next day.

Our nights together couldn't accurately be put into words, except that I woke each morning with wild sex hair, bite marks on my throat, and a smile of smug satisfaction. We had also broken our fair share of tables in Abe's home.

There was another reason why today was so exciting. Sam's father had sent us all the information he had on Bernard and the criminal organization that Codex had helped bring tumbling down. Abe, sensing my shift in thoughts, rapped his knuckles once on the desk.

"Now that Codex is officially a team of six," he said. "Shall we dive into it?"

There was a chorus of "please—for the love of god—*fuck* Bernard for *real*" to which Abe smiled discreetly. "We have the Deputy Director to thank for this, by the way. Though I did appreciate your father thanking Codex in his press conference about Bernard last week."

"Sam may have had something to do with that," Freya

said. "Andrew Byrne might be... kind of... almost becoming a... half-way decent human being."

"Finally," Sam remarked dryly. "He was curious to hear our thoughts after we see all of these updates."

Codex had still received its fair share of smaller cases. Bernard had fallen, but low-level book thieves were still using a stray *Reichenbach Falls* code word every so often. For the most part, they appeared opportunistic in nature, not orchestrated on a grand scale. Codex was grateful for a *bit* of peace and quiet.

Freya projected her laptop screen onto the large white wall and opened all the files Sam's dad had sent. "Now our glorious leader has read through all of this, right?"

"I have," Abe said. "If you pull up those first few pictures, I'll walk us through."

Bernard Allerton's mug shot appeared on the screen. He bore a regal pose, academic, but there was true fear in those eyes. Henry let out a long, relieved sigh.

Delilah kissed his cheek. "You did it."

"We did," he said.

"We sure fucking did," Abe said. More pictures appeared on the screen, more mugshots.

"The night that Henry confronted Bernard, he fled to London to hide away in the secret apartment at Adler's Bookshop, owned by Peter Markham aka Jim Dahl. The Sherlock Society of Civilized Scholars had been using that apartment for years to host all manner of secret meetings or to store stolen books," Abe said. "Bernard often used that space after he'd come into stolen inventory—it was an ideal place to hide things before being sold off to a private owner."

"So that was always Bernard's plan?" Henry asked.

"It seems like," Abe said. "He knew that, as a wanted

suspect, his ability to travel would be limited. He still went around London from time to time to meet with Eudora or interested buyers. That's why Interpol agents were able to get a few pictures of him. But he was fast, and smart, so always evaded them in the end."

Henry was shaking his head. "All this time, and he was thirty minutes from Oxford."

"Those credit card charges in Prague and Germany?" Sam asked. "A red herring, like you thought?"

"Someone in his network did that for him, but we're not sure who yet," Abe said. He tapped on a picture of Peter Markham. "This man, Nicholas's grandson, is an expert criminal forger. He's been Bernard's partner for years. Also known as Jim Dahl, he forged the George Sand letters. He forged Henry's signature on those letters."

"Jesus," Henry said, fingers to his mouth. "An expert forger would have made Bernard's thefts even easier to pull off."

"And it did," Abe said. "Peter's job this past year has been to protect Bernard. Dresden guards were on sight at all hours at the bookstore. During the six months he was here in Philadelphia, pretending to be an intern at The Franklin Museum, the shop was closed down and protected by guards at all times. There was nothing to suspect, certainly not that a man was living in there behind a bookcase."

Delilah's brow furrowed. "Jim would have been an intern at The Franklin Museum while we were working to recover the stolen Copernicus."

"Yes, he would have," Abe said.

"We might even have met him," Henry sighed. "And would have had no idea all the things he was planning on doing. *Or* that he was helping to hide Bernard all along."

Abe leaned forward, brought up the mugshots of James Patrick, Julian and Birdie, and Eudora Green.

"James Patrick has confessed that he and Bernard had a decades-long partnership that involved the buying and selling of stolen books and antiques using the Kensley Auction House as a cover. Julian and Birdie—*not* their legal names—are good friends of Bernard's. Like we suspected, they are con artists who provided the perfect fencing operation for a thief like Bernard to pass his stolen books through. They have been traveling the world for years, pretending to set up bookstores, only to con the hell out of both the buyers *and* the sellers."

"And my favorite lady, Eudora?" I asked.

"Your favorite lady is currently in big trouble for concealing a wanted criminal's whereabouts as well as for her part in buying and selling stolen books. Also for being in charge of the threats against Sloane and me."

"Even in her mugshot, she looks like she'll bake you a pie with venom in it," I said.

"So what was the plot?" Delilah asked. "Did he actually want those papers?"

Abe crossed his arms, looking absurdly pleased to tell us this. "Bernard was informed by James Patrick that these new private papers were going to be auctioned off in a week. Bernard brought James into a scheme to gain ownership of those papers himself. Julian and Birdie were brought in to bid—legally—to provide a safe smokescreen between their purchase and Bernard receiving them into his private collection. As compensation, Julian, Birdie, and James would receive payment from Bernard as well as a few select materials *from* the collection."

Freya leaned forward, adjusting her glasses. "And if Julian and Birdie's bid hadn't been the winning one?"

Abe knocked his knuckles against the wall of mugshots. "*Then* James would have worked with Peter Markham to steal the papers that night. Plan A, Plan B. Unfortunately for Eudora, she was used as cover for all of it."

"Wait," I said, smiling. "You mean Eudora didn't really know a thing?"

Abe tilted his head. "Not exactly. It looks like Bernard used her to protect him. The plan she thought she was helping to execute was a fake one."

"Well, no shit," I said, astounded. "What did Eudora think was going to happen?"

"She thought Bernard was orchestrating a theft and that the Sherlock Society would ultimately get the stolen papers. She thought *she* would be getting them that entire time. When Bernard told her he was concerned for his safety—because you and I were following him—he sent Eudora after us."

"In the form of guards and muggings and fires, I'm guessing," I said.

Abe nodded. "Exactly. A guard took that picture of us, and Peter wrote a threatening note on it. The guards tried to mug us and attacked us outside the cocktail bar. They followed us; they lit our rooms on fire. Eudora did it without question because it's *Bernard*. And because she wanted those papers just as badly. It's why she told anyone within earshot that the Society would *absolutely not* be bidding on them. When they eventually ended up stolen, she didn't want the Society to look suspicious."

Delilah stared at Eudora's picture. "How did Bernard know you were in London in the first place? That's what I can't figure out. If you approached Eudora as *Daniel Fitzpatrick*, why would she have reason to suspect you?"

Abe swiped his thumb across his lip—looking even

more pleased. "The day after I met Sloane, I visited Eudora at 221B Baker Street. I gave her the code."

"Reichenbach Falls?" Freya said.

"Yep," he said. "Gave her the code and asked her to get a message to Bernard. That I might have special access to those papers if he was interested. Eudora, in her confession, told agents that when she reported this conversation to Bernard, he asked to review the security camera footage from her office."

"Oh my god," Freya said. "So he saw you on *camera*?"

"He saw Henry Finch's private detective boss in Eudora's office, using a fake name but a real code word," Sam said. "He was right to be alarmed."

Bernard's picture remained on the wall.

"What are you thinking, Henry?" Abe asked.

Henry sighed. "Greed has always been Bernard's vulnerability. And Arthur Conan Doyle his obsession. The combination of the two caused him to finally make a real, human mistake. Bernard's fatal flaw will always be that he doesn't believe he's done anything wrong."

Abe stared at the picture for a minute. "The best news is that based on the strength of the evidence against him, Bernard will spend the rest of his life in prison. And many, *many* of these other criminals will be joining him. Including several from the Sherlock Society."

"What about Humphrey?" Delilah asked. "Any word on Bernard's whimsical best friend?"

"Humphrey and Reggie are innocent of Bernard's crimes," I said. "And visiting Abe and me in Philly in a few months."

Freya slammed her hands down on the table. "We are going out. *All* of us. And getting absolutely drunk."

Four of us said, "*In*."

Abe, with a friendly eye roll, finally said, "I'm sure I'll make an appearance."

"And the extra good news is that Humphrey is the new president of the Sherlock Society of Civilized Scholars," I added. He'd called us afterward, thanked Abe and me again for opening his eyes to Bernard's deceit. And promised that he remained an unstoppable force of valiant passion, even as he was still mending his broken heart.

"One last bit of news," Sam said. "My father heard this from an Interpol source. Bernard has been engaged in serious letter writing with the one person who's been contacting him regularly. Victoria Whitney."

Delilah shook her head with a smirk on her face. "Unbelievable. You've got to hand it to Victoria. She's never stopped being herself."

"And she's never stopped loving Bernard," Henry said.

There was a long pause—everyone taking in the abundance of good news, sifting through it. A sense of peace settled over me. Happiness. Completeness.

"Welcome to the team, Sloane," Freya said. "We got the worst guy yet. All the rest should be gravy."

Abe chuckled. Straightened his tie. "I always told this team that Bernard wasn't our purview. That our purview were the books, and books alone. And they are our main priority at the end of the day. Our main priority and the best one." He paused, studied us. "But I'm so proud we caught him. And so proud to call you my family."

Abe looked at me and I nodded, understanding him completely. Recognizing the strength it took him to reach out, be accepted, to expose himself to be a man with a big, open heart after all.

"Gone soft," Freya teased. "Told ya."

"It's true," he said.

"We can choose our own families," I said. Held Abe's gaze. "For me, that's all of you."

"Those Hawaiian shirts did help after all." Freya sighed dreamily. "Because we got you, Sloane."

I squeezed her hand, too overcome to say anything else.

"Every single one of us came to this place surviving a kind of betrayal," Delilah said. "We were all searching for a place that would become a home."

*Home.* I understood that word now. My parents had ripped it from me at an early age. And now another con artist—Bernard Allerton—had helped deliver me to Abe, this family, this new life. I stared at his mug shot one last time. Bernard was just a man who believed the world needed villains.

Codex was a team dedicated to the opposite.

Abe's phone rang, which generally signaled a new case. Sam and Freya leaned forward in excitement. Delilah flipped open her notebook. Henry straightened his glasses with a knowing grin.

"What happens next?" I asked Abe.

His smile was full of promises. "We get the damn book back."

# EPILOGUE

## ABE

*M*y new priority in life was making my three-month-old daughter squeal with laughter.

Ruby and I had spent the better part of an hour on the rug, playing peek-a-boo, a game she never seemed to tire of. Every time I held my finger toward her, she gripped it, held tight, while staring at me with the same luminous eyes her mother had.

My heart had seen its last fortress. If Sloane had dismantled those bricks with her vulnerable beauty and endless charm, then Ruby was ensuring I was stripped bare for the world to see, every day. *Soft* didn't even come close.

I scooped up my still-laughing daughter—whose curly hair was just like Sloane's—and stretched out on the couch with her to nap. Ruby still fit perfectly on my chest, and as I rubbed circles into her small back, her steady, sleepy breathing calmed me.

As did the raven-haired goddess, strolling into our living room with a happy smile on her lovely face. She bent down, gave me a sweet, lingering kiss, and then curled up next to me. I tucked a strand of hair behind her ear.

"What's the source of this smile?" I asked.

"Your mother. And Jeanette," she said. "We were planning their next trip up here to stay and help with Ruby. Your mother shared some very cute stories of you as a very serious little boy, Mr. Royal."

"There's work to be done, always," I said.

She snorted because she knew that to be a lie. Sloane and I both worked incredibly hard at Codex—the whole team did—but the two of us had cheerfully handed in our workaholic membership cards to become a family. A real family. And that meant nights at home and weekends at the park and enjoying every single moment we had.

Our relationship had moved at warp speed, which aptly fit the unrestrained chaos of our love. Six months after meeting, I married Sloane on the beach in Miami. My mother was the proud officiant. Jeanette, Henry, and Sam stood next to me. Delilah and Freya stood with Debra, the incredible woman who had helped my wife secure her freedom.

Humphrey and Reggie walked Sloane down the aisle, of course.

My wedding ring was engraved with the words: *I'm still here.*

Sloane's ring held the words: *I'm not going anywhere.*

One year later, we welcomed our daughter Ruby to the world. There had been not one moment of doubt or regret.

"It was a very nice phone call," Sloane said, brow lifted. "In fact, she's compiling additional adorable stories as we speak. Might even have Freya turn it into a video we can share at our next team meeting."

"I'll have to call in sick perhaps," I mused.

She leaned down and pressed her face to Ruby's back. "How is my favorite princess?"

"Still the world's best princess," I said, stroking Sloane's hair. Holding these two precious beings to my chest gave me an unbelievable sense of tranquility. As had watching Sloane open her arms—slowly, but surely—to the love and trust available to her now. It had involved a lot of painful work, of shedding past fears and working through our vulnerabilities. We were doing it, every single day.

Thanks, in large part, to Ruby.

"Oh, Freya sent the pictures she framed for all of us," Sloane said, reaching across the table for a package. "I want to hang them over the fireplace."

I handed her the dozing Ruby, and she cuddled the baby sweetly against her chest while watching me flip through the pictures.

The first photo had been taken at Henry and Delilah's wedding at the Long Room at the Trinity Library in Ireland. Delilah looks exquisite in her white gown, and she's laughing as Henry hugs her close, flanked by the rest of us. We are grinning like fools, a little drunk, and a lot happy.

Only the six of us knew the significance of that location. It had been the venue where The Thornhills had gotten fake married. The wedding had taken place four months after Bernard's final capture. Henry and Delilah had gone for their honeymoon after that, and I'd shut all of Codex down for two weeks. With strict orders for *everyone* to go on vacation.

A real one this time.

And with Sloane's charming encouragement, the two of

us had ended up in Belize for two weeks, where we'd done nothing but have passionate sex and lie on the hot sand.

I chuckled at the next picture. Freya and Sam had a newborn daughter named Zelda, and the frame held their birth announcement. Somehow, Freya had convinced Sam to dress up as Agents Mulder and Scully from *The X-Files* while Zelda was a tiny, baby alien. The card read: *Freya and Sam are pleased to welcome the birth of their daughter. Please send tacos.*

I continued to enjoy the pleasant, nostalgic sounds of Sam and Freya bickering in the office—although their verbal sparring was more good-natured than when they'd been my students. They still pushed each other, though. And continued to flagrantly disregard my PDA policies.

"Look, Ruby, it's your cousin," Sloane said, tapping the glass. Ruby waved her hands excitedly. "If she's anything like her mom, she'll be a fighter just like you."

The next picture was of Henry and Delilah, smiling with all the love in the world on the day their adoption paperwork was finalized. They'd worked with the same adoption agency where Delilah had been adopted by her fathers. Henry and Delilah are hugging a beaming, three-year old boy named Milo. On lighter days at Codex, Milo sits at my desk and pretends to "work" with me—an image that always sends the rest of my team into glorious laughter.

"The last picture is my favorite," Sloane said, rocking the baby.

I looked down at it. Looked up at my wife, the siren who *still* had me under her spell. Although she and I knew what it truly was.

"I love you so much, Sloane," I said, voice rough as I stared into her eyes. Ruby gurgled against her chest, and

Sloane smiled, patting her back. Stared at me with the warm sunshine at her back, lighting her like a true goddess.

"I love you, Abe," she said. Leaned in for a flirtatious kiss. "Let's hang this, shall we?"

And I did, placing the picture right above our mantelpiece. Because at the end of the day, Codex was about books. And justice. Righting wrongs and saving pieces of history.

But it was also about what was in this picture: Sloane and me in her hospital bed, holding Ruby, who had been born six hours earlier. Before that, I'd been at Codex, leading a meeting when Sloane had called. In her calm, smooth voice, she had said, "I believe I'm going into labor?"

Freya, Delilah, Sam, and Henry drove me to the hospital and watched me lose my fucking mind out of worry. All four had stayed in the waiting room for hours while I watched Sloane become a mother. And the moment my daughter was placed in my arms, and I became a father, was the moment my heart became *permanently* open.

In the picture, Sloane, Ruby, and I are surrounded by my team. Freya's smile is incandescent. Sam is holding her tight, cheek pressed to the top of her head. Henry is clutching a grinning Delilah to his chest. They are both laughing. The six of us—seven, including baby Ruby—are frozen perfectly in time. More than a team of private detectives. Even more than a group of friends. We are a family.

Which is what Sloane and I had been searching for all along.

# EXTENDED EPILOGUE

## ABE

Humphrey and Reggie were going to kill the entire Codex team using liquor.

Only Sloane and I had been able to stay merely *tipsy*, and that was because we knew these two Sherlock Holmes-loving academics from London could drink an entire rugby team under the table.

The trick was to do one shot for every three they demanded. A trick that Sloane had warned everyone about hours before we'd arrived at this British pub near our Philadelphia office.

From the looks of things, Freya, Sam, Henry, and Delilah had cheerfully ignored the warning. I was extremely pleased to have such a rich collection of memories to potentially blackmail my team with.

Sloane's lips brushed my ear as she leaned in to whisper, "Fucking amateurs."

I grinned and planted a kiss—with teeth—on the side of

her neck. "If we keep our wits about us, I can more expertly provide you multiple orgasms when we arrive home."

She responded by shoving all of her shot glasses to the middle of the table. I laughed, and she winked at me. "You've got yourself a deal."

"Now what are *these magnificent lovebirds* whispering about over there?" Humphrey bellowed. His voice had grown more robust as the night wore on, and the Codex team was so obviously obsessed with him that they'd started yelling joyously in response.

Reggie, as usual, watched his husband with a quiet devotion as he elegantly sipped his whiskey. Sam's hair was mussed, and his tie was crooked. Henry and Humphrey kept laughing hysterically over old, shared memories. Delilah was wearing Freya's glasses, and Freya was one shot away from dancing on the table.

"Guys, guys, *guys*," Freya slurred. "Can we fucking *give it up* for Sloane fucking Argento over here? Thanks to her, Abe has been in a good goddamn mood every goddamn day of the week."

My team—and even Humphrey and Reggie—gave the two of us a hearty round of applause. Sloane shrugged casually. "It's all the sex."

"Oh, we can tell," Delilah said. "Abe's *whole vibe* the past few months has been *I'm having a lot of sex.*"

"Without saying it, of course," Sam said.

"A man never reveals the secrets of his intimate affairs," I replied while dropping my hand high on Sloane's bare leg beneath the table. I curled my fingers into her skin, stroking and scratching. The sexy, feline look she tossed me over her shoulder just about killed me dead. I gave us twenty minutes, max, before we made a polite but hasty retreat.

Humphrey and Reggie had been the most delightful

visitors to Philadelphia this entire week. I'd watched Sloane's heart expand and expand and expand with every hour she spent with her adopted uncles. We'd been to the opera and seen plays and taken them to the best restaurants in the city. My face actually hurt from smiling—a new occurrence—but it was impossible not to when Humphrey Hatcher was in the room.

But between our London visitors and our usual Codex workload, Sloane and I hadn't had sex in a week. Our longest and most painful dry spell ever.

"Smart lad," Humphrey said, swinging his pint around. "Sex makes a man hale and strong!"

I arched a brow at Reggie, who gave a secretive smile. "We do alright for our age, actually."

"How did your proposal go?" Freya asked. "Who proposed to who? Or did you propose to each other?"

Reggie's smile widened. "Oh, Humphrey wanted to propose to me. That kind of romantic gesture is in his blood."

"Picture this," Humphrey said, setting down his glass so hard liquid sloshed over the rim. "I'd suggested we take a sunset walk through the park, and Reggie didn't suspect a thing. We'd spent the day at several Sherlock Holmes lectures, so you know we were in a romantic and amorous mood."

I caught Sloane's eye. She was grinning from ear to ear.

"Halfway across the park, I pretended to spot an orchestra set up for an evening performance. We walked over, and all the members turned as one to play 'When I'm 64' by The Beatles."

"Oh my god, it's too cute, I *cannot*," Freya said, tears running down her cheeks. Sam chuckled, tugged her into his chest, and kissed the top of her head.

"And as they played the song, Humphrey got down on one knee and said—"

"Let's grow old together and wear matching tweed suits for the rest of our lives." Humphrey sighed. "I even put his ring in a deerstalker hat, since I'm assuming Mr. Holmes would have approved of our romantic union."

"Oh, absolutely," I nodded.

"And I said *yes*, of course." Reggie laid his head against Humphrey's massive shoulder.

"Valiant passion," Sloane murmured. She reached under the table and held my hand.

"Indeed," Humphrey boomed. "And now, *more shots*."

We didn't even make it twenty minutes.

We made it ten, and due to the sheer drunkenness of the table, our visitors and my team let us go without *too much* good-natured ribbing. Sloane and I enjoyed a quiet—but sexually tense—cab ride home.

And the second she reached the front door of our condo, I had her up against it. She arched her ass right against my cock as I kissed my way through her hair and up her throat.

"Mr. Royal, you'll scandalize the neighbors," she cooed.

"Then open the damn door," I growled.

She complied with a sexy laugh, dragging me by the tie behind her and slamming the door shut. I reached down and hooked my hands beneath her knees, tugging her legs high around my waist as I walked us into the living room. Fucking on a couch seemed too clumsy and amateur for the gorgeous goddess in my arms, but it was the first soft surface we came to.

I threw her onto it and fell to my knees. Yanked her into

me as her long legs wrapped around me tightly. Our mouths connected in a kiss as hungry as our first one—every kiss between us retained that same frenzied, urgent yearning. My hands tangled in her hair, and her fingers worked open my fly.

"Not so fast," I whispered, then bit her bottom lip.

"Seven days, Abraham," she moaned. "I thought about fucking you in your office so much I should be used as a warning example in our HR policies."

I pulled down the straps of her dress and cupped her full breasts in my palms. "Next time it's just you and me in that fucking office, I'm taking you on that desk."

"Yes, *please*," she said. My mouth left wet, bruising kisses across her collarbone, her breasts, my thumbs working across her nipples until Sloane was boneless and panting. I reached beneath her dress and worked her underwear down her legs before tossing them across the room.

Her thighs pressed hard to my face as I feasted on her pussy. I abandoned any sense of teasing or foreplay and licked her clit with rapid, intentional strokes. In minutes, my beautiful, alluring, sticky-fingered girlfriend was grinding against my face and calling, "*Now, now, now, fuck me now.*"

I had her flat on her back, legs spread, not a second later. My pants came down just far enough for me to free my cock. I took in the scene around me—both of us still mostly clothed, Sloane's hair snarled and my lips wet from her pussy. Would we ever be sated?

I hoped not.

I thrust my cock into her and was shocked by the instant pleasure. Her fingernails dug into my ass as I plunged into her without mercy. Each drive of my cock brought both of us to the dazzling edge of ecstasy. Our lips never left each other, and our quick breaths became one, her sighs spurring me on. When we climaxed together, only minutes later, I shuddered with the intensity, face pressed to her hair as she stroked her fingers along my spine.

"Let's never..." she panted "...go seven days...without fucking...again."

I kissed Sloane for a long, long time. Seconds became long, lingering minutes as our kiss became sultry, then sweet, then love. When we finally parted, tears were in her eyes.

"I have an even better idea," I said. "Let's never be apart. Ever."

"We should grow old together and wear matching tweed suits," she said with a smile that caressed my heart. She and I both knew the future we wanted together. And a real proposal would be coming soon—there was no point in waiting when you found your soul mate in London while tracking the same book thief. But still. I wanted it to be as romantic and beautiful and unique as the woman in front of me.

"I'll start planning the orchestra now," I said, kissing her cheek.

"I'd like that very, very much," Sloane said. "Now let's go fuck on the dining room table."

# A NOTE FROM THE AUTHOR

Dear reader,

We got the damn book back.

These characters have been with me for more than two years now. Their voices, their thoughts, their donut preferences – all six members of the Codex team have taken up permanent residence in my heart and I hope they never budge. This series pushed me in the best way possible and I experienced tremendous growth as a writer while crafting each Codex book.

When I walk around Old City, in Philadelphia, it's easy for me to picture Henry and Delilah, strolling hand-in-hand down a cobblestone street while talking about their dreams. Or Sam and Freya on a bench outside of Federal Donuts, laughing through one of their many endless competitions.

It's extremely easy to picture Abe and Sloane, in glamorous attire, on their way to the opera – the dramatic skyline behind them as they both shine beneath the city lights.

I can see the six of them at used bookstores, at breweries and taco stands, in historic buildings and on front stoops. I feel their commitment to justice, their love of literature, and their devotion to each other. This series is as much a love letter to my hometown as it is to the magic of old books. Because all of us can attest to that feeling in your heart when you step inside a bookstore. There's isn't anything else like it in the world.

Before Codex was a series, it was a short story I'd written for KU Korner on Facebook – a short story that wouldn't quit my imagination. A story that demanded to be told. When I look back at those old notebooks and scribbles, it's overwhelming to understand that those scribbles became three novels, six characters and an entire world filled with secrets and code words, heroes and villains. Just a reminder that if a story is demanding to be told, don't be afraid to tell it, to follow that voice on a creativity journey. Whatever comes of it could be magnificent and magical. And I promise you: the journey is always worth it.

In the course of writing this book, I had a lot of fun with Sherlock Holmes and London geography! Those from London will immediately recognize that I seriously shrunk the distances between some of the real locations: The Langham Hotel, The Sherlock Holmes Museum at 221B Baker Street, the Royal Opera House and Midnight Apothecary (which is a very real and very cute cocktail bar!) This was merely to make it faster for Abe and Sloane to get around.

The McMaster's Library is not real, unfortunately, although Oxford University very much is! Mycroft's Pub is based on the Sherlock Holmes Pub, also in London. Adler's Bookshop and the Kensley Auction House are also creations from my imagination.

The fictionalized story of Sir Arthur Conan Doyle's private papers being auctioned off was inspired by an article in The New Yorker called 'Mysterious Circumstances' – a long read but I highly recommend it. His children and relatives have been fictionalized for this story as well.

The Sherlock Society of Civilized Scholars was my invention – however, Sherlock Holmes societies are abundant and well-respected throughout the world. Many Doyle scholars do identify themselves as Doyleans or Sherlockians and the Baker Street Irregulars is a real international literary society.

My final send-off for Codex fans is a wish for your days to be filled with code words and clandestine tunnels, coincidences that are really clues, and an underground auction or two. May your bookshelves reveal mysterious passageways and your perfume bottles contain absinthe. I sincerely hope Victoria Whitney sends you a love letter and the Alexanders invite you to a secret dinner party (but don't forget your mask). And if Humphrey Hatcher invites you to the pub, take him up on his offer.

As always, I hope to meet all of you at Reichenbach Falls one day.

Love,
  Kathryn

# ACKNOWLEDGMENTS

All of my gratitude for the following people who helped shape Abe and Sloane's love story:

Thank you always to my best friend (and genius developmental editor) Faith. You are a true gift in my life and these books wouldn't be the same without your wise and thoughtful edits. I'm so happy we were able to go on this Codex journey together. Thank you for shepherding me through my first romantic suspense novels.

A big thank you to Jessica Snyder for her developmental edits and line edits and for catching all of those pesky plot holes. You are a story wizard!

To Bronwyn, Jules and Jodi: you are epic beta readers. Your work on the Codex series has helped me level up in every way and working with the three of you is a privilege. Thank you for holding my hand through the process and being my cheerleaders when I needed the love.

A huge thank you to the lovely Alicia McKilligan for providing her wonderful expertise on the city of London and caught all of my dialogue mistakes from my British characters. I'm so grateful to you!

All of my love forever goes out to The Hippie Chicks. I know how long you've been waiting to worship Abe Royal and his stern heart. I hope this story did him justice. Thank you for your Codex love and for believing in this intrepid band of book-loving private detectives. I'd send Federal Donuts to you all if I could – you certainly deserve it!

All the tacos and hugs go to Joyce, Tammy, Lucy, Rick and Tim for being Team Kathryn and also awesome all the damn time. I'm so lucky to work with you beautiful geniuses!

For my Mom and Dad: thank you for believing in me! These books wouldn't be here without your love and support!

For Walter: Are you a good boy? You are a good boy! The best boy.

To Rob: I'm currently typing this at a picnic table in our backyard in Vermont – just one adventure of many we have planned together. Your strength and kindness never cease to amaze me and I'm always, always lucky to call you my husband and partner and road-trip companion. I will love you forever.

# HANG OUT WITH KATHRYN!

Sign up for my newsletter and receive exclusive content,
bonus scenes and more!
I've got a reader group on Facebook called **Kathryn Nolan's
Hippie Chicks.** We're all about motivation, girl power, sexy
short stories and empowerment! Come join us.

Let's be friends on
Website: authorkathrynnolan.com
Instagram at: kathrynnolanromance
Facebook at: KatNolanRomance
Follow me on BookBub
Follow me on Amazon

# ABOUT KATHRYN

I'm an adventurous hippie chick that loves to write steamy romance. My specialty is slow-burn sexual tension with plenty of witty dialogue and tons of heart.

I started my writing career in elementary school, writing about *Star Wars* and *Harry Potter* and inventing love stories in my journals. And I blame my obsession with slow-burn on my similar obsession for The *X-Files*.

I'm a born-and-raised Philly girl, but left for Northern California right after college, where I met my adorably-bearded husband. After living there for eight years, we decided to embark on an epic, six-month road trip, traveling across the country with our little van, Van Morrison. Eighteen states and 17,000 miles later, we're back in my hometown of Philadelphia for a bit... but I know the next adventure is just around the corner.

When I'm not spending the (early) mornings writing steamy love scenes with a strong cup of coffee, you can find me outdoors -- hiking, camping, traveling, yoga-ing.

## BOOKS BY KATHRYN

BOHEMIAN

LANDSLIDE

RIPTIDE

STRICTLY PROFESSIONAL

SEXY SHORTS

BEHIND THE VEIL

UNDER THE ROSE

IN THE CLEAR

WILD OPEN HEARTS

Made in the USA
Las Vegas, NV
06 February 2021

17334131R00246